The Burgla
the Five O

"This is the home of Mr. and Mrs. Lawrence Kilo-witz. According to police, an armed man, described by the victims as white, male, about thirty years old, broke into the house in the early morning hours. While the entire family slept, he stole an estimated hundred thousand dollars' worth of the wife's jewelry.

"Did you get a good look at the man? Would you know him if you saw him agian?" the reporter asked.

"Certainly," said Kilowitz, who never got a look at the intruder's face at all. *"I'll know him when I see him again, except that this time he ain't going to get away in one piece, and you can believe it."*

The burglar turned off the set. His eggs were cold. Everything had gone wrong. Except he wasn't caught. . . .

Mell Lazarus

The
Neighborhood
Watch

PUBLISHED BY POCKET BOOKS NEW YORK

Horty, this is for you,
in your sweet memory

The 65th Precinct, NYPD, and the 37th Congressional District of New York do not, at this writing, exist. Nor, in fact, does Kingsborough Beach, Brooklyn.

"Swinging on a Star" by Johnny Burke and Jimmy Van Heusen. © 1944 by Burke and Van Heusen, Inc. Copyright Renewed and Assigned to Bourne Co. and Dorsey Bros. Music Inc. All Rights Reserved. Used by Permission.

POCKET BOOKS, a division of Simon & Schuster, Inc.
1230 Avenue of the Americas, New York, N.Y. 10020

Copyright © 1986 by The Marsucat Corporation
Cover photograph copyright © 1987 Mort Engel Studio

Published by arrangement with Doubleday and Company, Inc.
Library of Congress Catalog Card Number: 85-16203

ISBN: 0-671-63388-0

First Pocket Books printing June 1987

10 9 8 7 6 5 4 3 2 1

POCKET and colophon are registered trademarks
of Simon & Schuster, Inc.

Printed in the U.S.A.

Acknowledgments ⸻

The author acknowledges, with gratitude, the generous assistance of several people with certain aspects of this novel. Among them are Hal Bloomberg, of the Police Department of the City of New York; Dick Gross, the electronics security specialist; Jay Daniel Silverstein, the New York attorney; Sally E. Mitchell, the California attorney; Abby Goell, the art appraiser; and Kathleen Hale, of the Los Angeles *Times*.

He also wishes to thank Susan Schwartz, his editor at Doubleday, and Kathy Robbins, his agent, for bringing their respective skills to this project.

Sunday Night, June 17 _____

With a last glance at the Kilowitzes, I left their room.

It had been easy.

I wondered if there was time to check the daughter's room. It was only 1:22.

I pushed open her door, slowly. A babysmell, pablum and fresh diapers, sweet and nostalgic, filled my nostrils. Ahead of me was the bed, on which the daughter was visible as a dark form on white sheets. To the right of the bed was the crib. To my left, a dressing table. I went to it. It held more stuff than Harriet's shelf had, but the only things of any value were a wristwatch and a string of pearls. I hesitated, decided not to take them.

As I turned to leave the room, I looked down at the young woman. She lay on her side, uncovered, wearing only panties, her hip high in a stylistic curve. I averted my eyes for a second, then looked again.

She began to move, turning onto her back, her breasts shifting.

Suddenly the whites of her eyes gleamed.

"Who the hell are you?"

She sat up; a scream was beginning.

I put my hand over her mouth.

—from *Hot Prowl:
The Diary of an Unlikely Burglar*
by Loring Neiman

Tuesday, May 15 _____

ON A MORNING four weeks prior to that episode, Loring Neiman awoke from a rather sweet dream (of peace, as provided by power and riches), got out of bed and padded downstairs to the kitchen. He switched on Mr. Coffee, then went to the front door and opened it just wide enough to see if the New York *Times* was close enough to reach, in his jockey shorts. It was, more or less, and as he fished it into the house he divined the weather: balmy, beautiful, one of those special May mornings. He went back upstairs, scanning the front page and calling as he went, "Let's move it, girls! It's after seven!"

From their bathroom, an anguished: "Daddy, I just got *in* here! She didn't let me in for ten—no, I mean *twenty* minutes!" From their bedroom, another, more pithy, response: "Bulldoody."

"Bulldoody . . . ?" Loring echoed, wonderingly, under his breath.

He dropped the newspaper on the floor in the open doorway of his small study, the room in which he worked, went down the hallway into his bedroom and closed the door behind him. He took off his shorts, dropped them into the hamper in the closet, went into the bathroom and got under the shower.

Afterward he massaged his scalp vigorously with his fingers for a full minute and combed his hair, which was mostly black (maybe 10 percent early gray) and longish and certainly ample for his age. But he examined the comb anyway. For the

3

past few years he had even been checking his pillow every morning for hairs that might have decamped during the night, as though he could order them back. His late wife, Arlene, had once said that Loring Neiman's fight to save his hair was one of the great conservation projects of the twentieth century.

Back in the bedroom, at the full-length mirror, he made his usual comparison of his midsection profile to that in the photograph of himself taken in the Army, seventeen years earlier; the comparison still seemed good. His musculature was almost what it had been as a twenty-five-year-old soldier. Seventeen years of handball at Brighton Beach Baths.

All in all, he felt he looked fairly decent. Not handsome, never handsome, but friendly-looking.

Loring then dressed quickly in what his daughter Katie referred to as his "working costume": a pair of old corduroy pants, a sweat shirt (this one proclaiming The College of the City of New York, although he had actually gone to Syracuse University) and a venerable pair of loafers (the world's oldest living Weejuns, Arlene had dubbed them).

Working costume, yes, but today was not a working day. It was a waiting day, the last of thirteen waiting days; before it was half over he would get the official response to the best thing he'd ever written.

As he straightened up his bed, it occurred to him that the bedroom, with its floral comforter and flounced curtains and yellows and lavenders on its walls, looked, after almost three years, as though he still shared it with a woman.

Downstairs, he put some Crave in the cat's dish and took the girls' eggs and muffins from a refrigerator festooned with artwork and compositions. Then he poured himself a cup of coffee and sipped at it while the eggs boiled.

Katie came into the kitchen dressed for school in the Jordache jeans she'd requested on her last birthday, her twelfth. She was braiding her auburn hair. "Morning, Daddy." He leaned down so she could kiss him. "Could I *not* have a muffin today? Maybe just like a Wheat Thin?"

"For breakfast? Wheat Thins are for cocktails. You'd have to have a martini with it."

"I'm getting fat," she said, setting the table.

"Like a regular hippo. Who told you that?"

"I can see."

Little Briana ran in, shouting, "Eddie Kilowitziz said she was fat!" She sat down at the table and began swinging her chubby little legs to the beat that seemed to measure her entire waking day.

Katie shot her six-year-old sister a murderous look. "He did *not!* Nobody said it, I said it!" She gave Briana an elbow as she passed her to sit down.

"If he said it, then Eddie Kilowitziz is a jerk," Loring offered.

"Daddy, it's not Kilo*witziz,*" Katie said. "It's Kilo*witz.*"

From inside her glass of milk, Briana said, "It's her boyfriend!"

"He—*is*—NOT!" Katie screamed.

Since they were born, Loring had been in awe of his daughters. He adored them; they were a pair of personified miracles. And since their mother's death, he felt vaguely responsible—threatened, actually—whenever the two of them fought. He wished they would grow closer together, never be rotten to each other, even though he understood their occasional conflict as a normal part of their passage.

"Briana," he said, "it isn't nice to tell your sister's secrets. Someday she might have some really good stuff to share, and you wouldn't want her to hold out on you, would you?" He nodded wisely for emphasis. To Katie, he said, "So. You and Eddie Kilowitz. Should I call the rabbi tonight?"

Katie, her mouth full of Wheat Thins, responded with, "You didn't shave again, Daddy."

Just like her mother, a major American subject-changer.

"So what?" he said. "Only men who go to offices or otherwise earn their livings away from home have to shave every morning. Why else do you think men like me become writers?"

5

"But don't you have to go to a big business meeting in the city today?"

The pleasant surge of excitement again. He certainly did have a big meeting today, which fact had probably engendered last night's wonderful dream.

"I do, I do. With my editor, about my new book. But not until lunch."

"Just make sure you shave before you go, Daddy," Katie said.

It was a quarter to eight, time to go to school. Loring got up from the table with his dish and cup and put them on the sink counter. "Okay, kids. Leave the stuff on the table and let's get this show on the road."

"What does that mean, Daddy?" Katie asked as she cleared the table anyway. "My gym teacher always says that. What does it mean?"

"It means when, say, a show, or better yet a circus, is about to move to the next town, the guy in charge always says, 'Let's get the show on the road.' Get it?"

A wide smile of understanding from Katie. "Oh, right!" The smile held while she wiped the table, and Loring figured she was mentally rehearsing the explanation to offer at her next gym class. Maybe even to Eddie Kilowitziz.

When Loring backed his car out of the driveway they were surprised by a marvelous splash of pink on the lawn; their small dogwood had blossomed during the night. And so, also, had its cousins, on lawns up and down Averly Street.

"Oohh, Daddy," Briana squealed, nearly crushing the red folder that held a week's collection of her handmade first grade treasures. "Can I walk? To smell the trees?"

"No, baby. You can open the window."

"Why do you always have to drive us?"

"*You*, not *us*," Katie put in, quickly. "I walk to school a lot. Daddy has to drive *you* because real little kids can't take care of themselves."

"I'm sure both of my daughters can take care of themselves," Loring said. "After all, they are intelligent little persons."

"We're *persons?*" Briana asked, astonished.

"Yes. You're regular persons. So to speak." He waved to Lynn Isaacs as she picked up the newspaper from her lawn. "Mainly, I drive you because I happen to like driving you."

And he did. He had worked at home ever since he sold his first book and joyously quit his high school teaching job, nine years earlier; driving the girls to school gave him a sense of helping to start the universal workday.

But more to the point, he enjoyed the short, slow trip up Dale Avenue, past Barnsworth, Oulden, Heather and Usley streets to the school, which was on Gerrold. A pleasant route, lined with great old oaks, elms and sycamores, the branches of which formed gazebos over most of the streets.

Kingsborough Beach. A beautiful neighborhood, unique in urban Brooklyn not only because of its special, semiprivate atmosphere, but because of its geography, as well. Until ninety years ago it was the easterly tip of the very sandbar that supports Coney Island, Brighton Beach and Manhattan Beach, but was separated from them at that time by a man-made channel, given the unlovely name of Dredge Channel, after the machine with which it was dug. Shortly after the channel came to be, a short and slender isthmus— the Brighton Street Causeway—was created, connecting it to the mainland. Since then, with Sheepshead Bay on its west, the Atlantic Ocean to its southwest, Gerritsen Inlet to its north and Rockaway Inlet to the south and east, Kingsborough Beach had been a peninsula.

In Loring's imagination, it was a miniature Land's End— only three blocks wide and twelve long—so narrow and near to sea level that high tides during the 1960 hurricane had caused the ocean and the bay to meet, a foot deep, in mid-neighborhood.

The homes were mostly very good single-family ones, large and smaller, individually designed and custom-built at various times and under every influence one could name: Tudor, Norman, colonial, Cape Cod, contemporary. Spanish, even, with red tile roofs. Many stately, with impeccable lawns and landscaping. And here and there the gemstones, the original mansions, baroque, some of them, in the manner of the 1910s and '20s. These mansions had existed on the peninsula in exclusivity for many years until gradually, around them, the community created itself, of Brooklyn's new elite: nine hundred families, mostly upward-bound, many wealthy and influential—businessmen, merchants, doctors, dentists, lawyers, a sitting judge, a retired judge, a New York State assemblyman, the U.S. congressman from the district, the 37th, and at least one quietly aging ex-gangster.

Loring and Arlene had both grown up in Flatbush, where they met and fell in love. After their marriage they moved into a small apartment on Avenue J, but spent weekend after weekend wandering respectfully through Kingsborough Beach, visualizing a future life there.

Eventually the Neimans found a house in The Beach they could almost afford, bought it and moved in. They soon realized that Kingsborough Beachers regarded the channel and the inlets as moats between them and Greater Brooklyn —the squalor and turmoil of Brighton Beach, the anger and filth of Coney Island, Bed-Stuy, Brownsville. To them, Kingsborough Beach was a special enclave, exempted from the dynamics of the rest of the city. The area was, if not Fort Apache, their Fort *Mishpuchah*, offering the wraparound sense of comfort that came with knowing the names of practically everyone they saw on the streets.

Both Katie and Briana were born there, in the comparatively small brick-and-fieldstone house in which they still lived.

And in which he wanted very much to stay.

Loring turned onto Gerrold Street and guided his four-year-old 320I slowly through the glut of cars in front of the two-story colonial building that was the Kingsborough Beach Elementary School. It was small-townish and pleasant-looking, unlike his own P.S. 206, thirty blocks away, which was large and square and had iron mesh on its windows and, like most grade schools in the New York City system, resembled a maximum-security institution.

The girls kissed him good-bye, got out of the car and

wound their way through the mob of kids into the school yard. He stared after them, watching little Katie carefully shepherd her littler sister through the crowd, craning his neck until they were out of sight.

Judith Lieb's silver Jaguar stopped alongside of Loring's car, its passenger window open.

"Hi gorgeous don't forget tonight!"

The Neighborhood Watch. He *had* almost forgotten it. Loring's house had been broken into, the week before, the fourth local burglary in as many months. Judith and Sidney Lieb immediately decided it was time to form such a group and volunteered their home for the organizational meeting. They had never been burglarized, but they shared his shock.

He waved and nodded. "I'll be there, I'll be there."

Judith blew him a kiss and moved on. He liked her, accepted her personal flamboyance, and he liked Sidney. They had always been extremely kind to Loring and his young family, and more so since Arlene's death.

He lit a cigarette—he had cut down to ten per day—and was about to pull away when he spotted Elizabeth Blaug, talking to her little boy. She was wearing a pair of beige slacks and a sweater and seemed especially intriguing that morning; she had the air of a woman who had just gotten up and hurried out still smelling warmly of sleep and bed. Loring thought about trying to get her attention and chatting for a moment or two. Or maybe even inviting her to have some coffee. But there were too many cars and parents and kids around and she was already getting into her own car; there was no way to do it without getting out of his car and running over to hers. And that would have been altogether too awkward, too much trouble for him to have gone to just to say a casual hello to a married neighbor with whom he'd never really exchanged more than a dozen words.

Besides, he hadn't shaved.

As Elizabeth Blaug drove away, Loring wondered if she might possibly show up at the meeting at the Liebs' that evening.

Loring realized his car was hemmed in by a Cadillac, which

was empty and rather cavalierly double-parked. He knew it belonged to Elias Shapp, one of whose pleasures was to drive his granddaughter to school every morning and then, in his own good time, drive the eight blocks back to his large Baldwin Street home to resume whatever it was he did in his comfortable retirement.

As he crossed in front of Loring's car to get to his own, Shapp recognized him; they had seen each other at a hundred dinner parties. He thrust his large silver head at Loring and growled, "How you doin', kid? Long time no see."

"I'm fine, Elias."

"Good. See you around."

"See you around."

Shapp got into his car and slowly pulled away.

His was the only presence in Kingsborough Beach Arlene had been afraid of. It made Loring uncomfortable, too. Elias "Voncie" Shapp was reputed, in his time, to have killed ten men on behalf of Murder, Inc. It amazed Loring to think that when a gangster "retired," many otherwise sensible people no longer felt threatened by his proximity. They sought his company, in fact. He thought of Dylan Thomas: "The conceit of outlaws is a wonderful thing; they think they can join the ranks of regularly conducted society whenever they like."

Why not? Loring thought. *It invites them to dinner.*

Loring drove home innocent of the fact that in six days he, too, would be an outlaw.

Loring got to the Four Seasons at twelve-fifteen. The hostess told him that a secretary had called to say that Mr. Gelfmann would be a few minutes late. She showed him to a table, from which he ordered a Gibson on the rocks. He never minded getting anywhere a couple of minutes before whomever. To him, as a person who worked at home, any appointment that required getting dressed and leaving the house to travel somewhere usually had small anxieties connected with it; getting there first gave him a chance to settle them and make himself at home.

Sipping his drink, he wondered how much ground this

meeting with Jamie would cover. Would he ask for cuts? *Quarantine* was the best thing Loring had ever written, tight and lean, and there was little in it that could come out without damage to the whole. Would his book, which he had turned in late, be on the fall list for November, or would it now be January? Would Jamie have some ideas (or maybe even sketches!) for the jacket design? He wished he'd brought along that photograph of Arlene he once took in Stockbridge, which he thought could be worked into the layout, as part of a montage.

He also wondered whether Jamie could just possibly (please God) have had the check drawn for the balance of his advance, the forty-five thousand that was due on acceptance of the final manuscript, just so he could bring it along (and Jamie liked to do such things) and hand it to him today.

Loring looked up at the famous rods, suspended high over the bar: hundreds of long, slim, brass-colored rods, pointing downward, which never failed to draw the eye. As often as he had seen them he was never able to figure out how they related to the decor of the restaurant. At that moment, however, he thought they might possibly be symbolic of the rain required by the house trees, which are redecorated four times a year in accordance with the season. This being spring, the trees had had green leaves and little blossoms affixed to their branches.

Suddenly Jamie appeared, carrying a fat manila envelope. "I am sorry to be late, Loring."

"That's okay," said Loring, meaning it. They shook hands warmly. Jamie put his things on an empty chair and sat down.

The waiter was there instantly. "And how are you today, Mr. Gelfmann?"

"Fine, thank you. I think I will have a dry Manhattan, please."

Although not quite thirty-five, Jamie Gelfmann had the mien of a much older man. He was overweight and so felt that he couldn't wear the casual rough clothing worn by many of the young book people in New York. Instead, he stuck to expertly tailored suits from the Savile Row wardrobe that was an annual gift from his employers, in which outfits Jamie looked nonetheless rumpled and nondescript. Arlene Neiman used to describe him as "the laundry pile that walks like a man." Loring always (even in the fifteen-year-old tweed sports coat he was wearing at the moment) felt dapper in the company of Jamie. Moreover, he respected him as the editor who had lent his gifts for analytical reading and syntactical prosthetics to Loring's three previous books. The two men, during their nine-year relationship, had become comfortably attuned to each other.

So Loring felt he knew when something unpleasant was on Jamie's mind.

Like right then.

He had the feeling his editor might be about to tell him that Marlow & Roth would have to put off publishing *Quarantine* until next spring. Or something like that.

Or was what he was feeling natural to any author facing the editor who was about to report for the first time on the completed manuscript of his first novel?

He watched Jamie take a long sip of his drink and then set the envelope down on the table between them. Loring guessed it contained his manuscript, but inferred nothing negative from the move.

And then Jamie said, "I'm afraid I do not have very good news for you, Loring."

Loring felt his cheeks and temples flush. "What's wrong, Jamie?"

"We have problems, Loring."

"Well, what's, uh, what sort of problems?"

"Your novel just does not work."

"It 'does not work.'" Loring swallowed hard. "Jamie, I . . . you know what? I've never really understood that . . . all-purpose editorial phrase. . . ."

"Loring, you have never heard that phrase before. You are an excellent writer—of nonfiction. This"—he tapped the package—"is not your métier."

Loring stared at his editor. "Jamie," he said, his voice pitched a little high, "it was my métier two years ago, when you loved the outline, wasn't it? I could certainly do some more work on it, if you think it needs it, which you obviously do. . . ."

"Well," Jamie replied, carefully, "perhaps. But it needs a lot more work than I think you should do. It does not come off."

"Specifics, please. . . ."

"There are no specifics. *Quarantine,* in my opinion, was a good idea for a novel, the story of a widower trying to cope with the loss of his wife. It seemed rich and poignant when you proposed it, but the way you've handled it, it never takes off. It is heavy, and more than a little pretentious. There is no *luft.* His problems are maddeningly mundane. Besides, the lack of a meaningful new relationship would lose us the women who buy this kind of fiction." With disappointment in his voice, he added, "I wish you had come to me chapter by chapter, Loring. I really do."

"I don't work that way."

"I know. And I left you alone. But I should not have. What you have done here, apparently, is loosely chronicle your own experience, a love affair—and forgive me for saying this— with the memory of your wife."

Loring looked stricken. Jamie touched his arm and said, quietly, "Put it aside, Loring. Start something new. What you do best, a good, solid piece of nonfiction."

"Jamie, are you out of your mind? It's not that simple! I've given two years of my life to this thing . . . haven't accepted any other assignments! Two goddamn years, Jamie! It's eaten all the savings Arlene and I had."

He suddenly felt he was becoming abusive of an old and good friend. He cleared his throat. "Look, I'm sorry, Jamie. Crying in my booze is not my style, but it's just that this is more than just some driving yen to write great fiction. I mean, screw the National Book Awards, you know? I've been counting on the rest of my advance. . . ."

Now Jamie looked everywhere but at Loring. "If this were a couple of years ago," he said, "I might have been able to work something out on that, given the position you're in. But now, in these times, it's not possible. M&R is no longer a family-owned house. We are a subsidiary of ICC, and . . ."

The waiter handed them each a menu. Loring looked at his, blankly, then put it down. He took another sip of his drink, but it had gone sweet. After a long moment he said, mercifully, "Jamie, I'm going to pass on lunch, okay?"

Jamie nodded.

"I'm saving my appetite for dinner tonight, the girls and I are having our weekly spaghetti festival." He picked up his manuscript. "With the special sauce we invented. Contains every exciting flavor known to man, including a teaspoon of Fox's U-Bet."

"That sounds very delicious," Jamie said with a little smile. "How are the girls? Okay?" Loring nodded. "And you? Are you seeing anyone special?"

Loring shook his head and got up. "Forgive me, Jamie. I'll talk to you soon."

As Loring walked across the room he once again was aware of the brass rods, but this time with the feeling that they really looked rather lethal hanging there, in dense pack, suggesting some futuristic version of the primitive weapon trap familiar to watchers of old Tarzan movies.

Driving south on the FDR toward the Battery Tunnel, he gloomily wondered, at first, if whatever poet was in him would survive this.

But then, a shock wave: the long-quelled realization that he now also faced full-blown financial disaster.

The second mortgage Loring had taken out two years earlier—to help carry him and his two young daughters through the writing of *Quarantine*—was in default. Aggravated default. He had not been able to make a payment in the last ten months. The entire amount, thirty-five thousand dollars, had therefore come due. With his house, of course, as collateral. Ted Krause, his lawyer, had been stalling the bank's attorneys for five months now, through the whole, bizarre, slow-motion Ping-Pong game: the bank's Summons and Complaint, his General Denial, the bank's Summary Judgment. As of a few days ago, however, the referee issued his so-called Report and Computation, and it was now the Newgate Trust Company's turn again. All it needed was a confirmation from the court. Which it would get.

While writing the novel, Loring had paid only passing attention to the process. He had blithely counted on the second half of his advance to save his house.

As he drove past Bay Ridge, Fort Hamilton, the Verrazano Bridge, he cataloged his other, smaller but growing debts: utility and phone bills unpaid since March; his word processor, only four months old but already an addiction, on which he had yet to make a single payment; orthodontia for Katie; the car he was driving; and so on and so on.

Loring had no contingency plan against the possibility that *Quarantine* would not be accepted, because he had expected no such situation. In his adult life he had always considered himself to be pragmatic in dealing with most problems, but with finances he was bad. Childish. Arlene had handled them. She had been good at those things. But even she never had to deal with a money problem of this magnitude.

He certainly could not deal with it.

At home, he went up to his study. It had been filled with characters and incident and dialogue for two years, but at that moment, as he walked in, it seemed empty. The fat manila envelope he'd brought back with him felt meaningless in his hands; he put it into the back of the closet. Then he sat down. Tentatively. As in a dentist's waiting room.

His study would have been, for a normal family, the small third bedroom. He had given Arlene carte blanche to decorate it for him when they bought the house, and her choices of dark green carpeting and pale green walls and the parsons tables and bookcases she'd bought unfinished so she could white-enamel them herself still obtained. The photos and memorabilia she had framed for him still hung, stood or leaned about the room.

He got up and straightened one picture, moved another. Puttered. There were snapshots of them and the kids. There was the wedding picture. A large color photograph of Gener-

15

al Westmoreland, autographed and presented to Loring when he had exited 'Nam, which Arlene had put into an old frame that said "My Soldier Sweetheart" on it. A snapshot of Loring, Arlene and Joe Heller, taken in Truro. Photostat of his first check as a writer. Formal invitation to one of the swearings-in of Congressman Norman Berger, on which the Government Printing Office had actually spelled it "Congresman." Loring's parents, both dead. Arlene's parents, alive and well, but in Fort Lauderdale, may they rest in peace. Libretti of two operas through which Loring had slept while Arlene wept. Menu from the restaurant on *le deuxième étage* of the Eiffel Tower, where they had celebrated their first anniversary. Cheap production prints in various sizes of paintings by the Jewish impressionists: Lesser Ury's *Winter Day in Berlin,* self-portraits by Leonid Pasternak and Max Liebmann, Moise Kisling's *Man with a Pipe,* Isaac Israels' *Serafino da Tivoli.* Two identical prints of Isaac Levitan's fabulous, brooding Russian landscape. *When I love a painting, I love a painting.*

On the shelves, Bartlett's, Roget's, Webster's, Cassell's, Peter's, Rosten's. Neat stacks of *Geographics, New Yorkers* and *Smithsonians.* Roth's *History of Jewish Art,* an Abrams edition of Pissarro. Bulletins from the Guggenheim, through which they had coaxed young Katie a few times in the hope of inculcating her with something beyond the Smurfs.

A three-drawer file, jammed with clippings. His "morgue."

The only things new in the room since Arlene died were his beloved computer/word processor and the special desk he had bought to hold it.

Puttering. He had nothing to do. He missed the characters in his novel.

Loring sat down at the telephone, thought about calling Elliot Silverbach, his agent. Instead, he pulled the Rolodex over to him and, in succession, phoned *Playboy* magazine in Chicago (where an old friend of his was an associate editor), ...rd *Times* in Detroit (where he knew no one, but felt they .....w of him) and the New York *Times Magazine* (for which he'd written a piece, five years earlier, on the Port Authority of New York). He queried them all for possible assignments.

His *Playboy* friend was no longer there. The new man told him that they were overstocked on nonfiction, but if something fell out he'd contact Loring and they'd talk. *Ford Times,* where they really didn't know of him after all, said they had no unassigned projects, but if he had any ideas they'd be glad to consider them. An associate editor of the New York *Times Magazine* said what he was looking for just then was someone to go to Ethiopia for a few months.

Loring rocked back and forth in his squeaky swivel chair. Arlene had had a friend who edited a small Westchester-Fairfield magazine called *Gold Coast.* She was a sort of bleacher-seat fan of his.

He called her, not sure whether he did so to get his ego refurbished or to sniff for work or just to kill time. And she was thrilled to hear from him. They chatted for a few minutes and brought each other more or less up to date. When he happened to mention his burglary, she immediately asked him if he would consider writing a couple of thousand words on the subject, from the victim's point of view.

"How it felt, you know, Loring, to have your house broken into? I could sure use it if you think it'd be worth your time." And then, "I can only pay four hundred dollars. But we pay on acceptance, and I'll put your name on the cover and I swear to God you won't have to rewrite a single word!"

Without enthusiasm, he said, "Okay."

He hadn't worked since completing the final draft of *Quarantine,* two weeks before. The way to go, he decided, was to start right then and knock the piece out quickly.

He faced his word processor (a shade guiltily; it was a fugitive from repossession) and turned it on. The master program was already in drive 1. As the main menu appeared, the screen bathed him in its familiar green glow, wrapping him in the special environment it always seemed to create. He stuck a floppy disk in drive 2 and typed

4

for the Edit-RAM version. While waiting for it to load (it took almost half a minute, an eternity, in computer terms) he wiped and put on the half glasses he wore for working. When the drive stopped whirring, a message on the VDT screen asked the name of the file he would be working on. He typed

BURGLAR

and hit the return key. The drive searched the disk, found no such file, and asked him if it was okay for the computer to create it. He typed

Y

for Yes. The computer went along.

The cursor presented itself in the upper left-hand corner, blinking at the ready. The screen was like a clean sheet of paper. The first thing was to dirty it up. He typed

BURGLAR PIECE—LORING NEIMAN

and leaned back in his chair. He didn't have the batch of notes he usually had at such times, previously researched stuff, to prime him, because this article was to be drawn from his recent experience and developed, as *Gold Coast*'s editor had instructed, into a think-type piece, conveying feelings and philosophy rather than fact. Maybe it was going to be harder than he had thought.

As he tried to think his eyes roamed the room, fell on the shoe box filled with bills, mostly unopened, that sat on the floor by the wall near his desk. Phone bills, gas bills, department store bills. Arlene's incredible hospital bills, dating back three years. In this blessed, wonderful country of ours a seven-month catastrophic illness will financially destroy the average family.

He got up and removed the box from his field of vision, sat

down again. He could no longer see the bills, but he knew they were there. They had a life of their own.

And to snuff it out would take a hell of a lot more than this shitting article would bring.

He typed

> Person or persons unknown broke into my house one recent spring afternoon. They did so by removing some panes from a louvred (check spell) dinette window. Once inside, they first opened a better exit for themselves—the side door—and then went from room to room, selecting what they intended to steal. Their choices added up to about $4000 worth of things, including my late wife's jewelry, a camera and a couple of fairly expensive sweaters.
>
> All of that was accomplished neatly, within twenty minutes, according to my next-door neighbor's report of his dog's behavior (it had barked the burglar in and barked him out, without arousing its owners' suspicions).
>
> In spite of the (something) of the burglary, I was (jolted) by it. (find better word) Unless you've been burglarized, you cannot appreciate the feeling. Our space had been intruded upon, our clothes closets and drawers had been opened, their contents handled.
>
> Our privacy, the sanctity of our home, had been violated.

Loring stopped, out of gas. He pressed Control/I to bring the cursor into the command mode, then typed S for Save. It was almost six o'clock, time to get dinner going. A question: Was it eight and a half minutes or nine and a half minutes that had finally achieved, last week, spaghetti of a consistency exactly between Katie's chewy and Briana's nice and soft? And there was the Neighborhood Watch meeting that evening. He didn't want to go, but felt he should; the burglary he was writing about had inspired it. It might even spark the piece for him.

"No more *Delia?!*" Katie was shocked.

"No more Delia. From now on we keep the house clean by ourselves."

Katie and Briana, in their pajamas, were both on Katie's bed. Briana was snuggled among the pillows, eyes heavy with sleep, but Katie was closely concerned with the situation. "But what about poor Delia? This is her job!"

"It's only one of her jobs. She works for lots of people. Don't worry about her. She'll land on her feet."

"'Land on her feet,'" Katie repeated. She liked that one.

Earlier, during dinner, Loring had told the girls that his publisher had run out of money and it would be a long time before they could pay him for his book. That news didn't faze Briana at all, but it had seemed to strike Katie as a bit odd. Since then he had been gently preparing them for some changes. For one thing, their three weeks at Kinderland Day Camp this summer were not to be. Beyond this, he explained that there would have to be a general tightening up, in terms of things like new clothes, eating out and the use of the phone and utilities. A new bike for Katie was impossible. He would fix and repaint the old one for her. Briana's interest in piano lessons, not to mention the piano they might lead to, would be put in abeyance for a while.

He didn't like his little money chat with them. Verbalizing, even in little-girl talk, the business of having to cut back had deepened his uneasiness.

Briana opened her blue eyes. "Daddy, are we poor?"

He picked her up and put her into her own bed. "Not poor, baby. Financially embarrassed."

"What's 'fidashully embassted'?"

"Briana, butt out!" said her older sister, getting under the covers. "This talk isn't for little kids. Daddy and me'll worry about it." To Loring, "Can I read?"

"Yes."

"You said we have to save lights."

"We do, but a half hour of the Snoopy lamp won't break us."

Downstairs, in the kitchen, Loring called his lawyer, Ted Krause, who lived a couple of blocks away. He asked Ted when they could get together to talk about Loring's options with Newgate Trust.

"I could drop over tomorrow night. How's that?"

"If that's the soonest."

"It is, I'm sorry," Ted said. "And I'll tell you something very frankly, unless you've got the thirty-five thousand, it's going to be a short conversation."

That's right, asshole, joke.

Loring called Lester McGinty, a friend from his teaching days, who supervised the English Department for the Board of Ed. He asked Lester what the chances of a job would be if—just if—he should want to get back into the system. Lester's response was hollow. He told Loring they weren't hiring for English just then, and if they were, he'd have to get on a very long line. Besides, he guessed that Loring's license had probably expired.

A job, in point of fact, wouldn't do it, Loring knew. On a salary it would be years before he caught up with his debts. He needed lump dollars, immediately.

Besides, he thought, he was not a working stiff. He was a writer of books.

Marcia the baby-sitter arrived at eight. Loring gave her the Liebs' number, then went upstairs to tuck the girls in.

Katie asked, "Daddy, why do we have to have a sitter if we have to save money?"

"Good question. It so happens I pay Marcia the money I save on shaving cream."

"Where are you going?"

"Marcia knows where I'll be. Just at the Liebs'."

"A party?"

"No. It's what you call a Neighborhood Watch meeting."

"What's that?"

"It's something to keep away burglars."

"Good," said Briana, her mouth full of thumb. "I hate buglars."

Judith Lieb, her sienna hair curled into tight little balls, looking, as Arlene always said, "her usual yenta-chic," sat on the window seat near the piano, talking with her husband, Sidney, and a uniformed policeman. She noticed Loring when he came in, waved to him.

He was surprised by the size of the meeting. Three dozen

households were represented, close to seventy people, most of who were already seated on folding chairs in the living room of the Liebs' comfortable Dutch colonial house. Others milled noisily near the dessert service that was being set up on the massive oaken dining table. Loring joined them.

Hattie, the Liebs' housekeeper, handed him a cup of coffee. She looked in his eyes. "You lookin' bad, Mr. Lorin'. Do you want some snapps inside of that coffee?"

Loring smiled, shook his head. He wondered if Elizabeth Blaug was there.

Burt Klastorin asked him if they had caught his burglars yet.

"No," Loring replied, "and I doubt they ever will."

"Believe it," Klastorin agreed. "Police work in this city is strictly do-it-yourself. In my business when we get hit at least we've got federal laws and federal cops." He owned a large interstate trucking company. "We don't depend on any county mounties."

Fred and Lynn Isaacs spotted Loring. Fred grinned as his cute wife waved her hands in the air and cried, "Author! Author!" She never failed to do this whenever she saw Loring, and it made him feel as idiotic as it made her look. They weren't the only local people who behaved awkwardly around Loring. Rosalyn Martinson, for another, always seemed to make a painful effort to use better English when speaking to him. "Do you see what you started, Loring?" the builder's wife said to him, indicating the size of the crowd. "This entire meeting is due specifically and entirely to yourself!" Most Kingsborough Beachers regarded the work life of a published writer as exotic, and Loring as somewhat of a celebrity. They were proud of him, and he got a lot more attention from them than he craved.

Celebrity, shit. There wasn't a person in that room who couldn't buy and sell Loring Neiman. And that evening, to him, they all seemed to radiate an even more solid, trouble-free affluence than usual.

Sidney Lieb, an athletically built man with a shaven head, began tapping loudly on his coffee cup with a spoon. When he had everyone's attention, his wife, Judith, stood up to introduce the police officer.

"Captain Costello is the man in charge of our local precinct and he is here tonight to help us start our Neighborhood Watch and tell us a bit about how we can protect our lives and property, so let us welcome him warmly and girls try to forget how good-looking he is and pay attention to every word he has to say, Captain Costello."

She led the applause as Captain Costello rose to his feet. He exuded an automatic charm, endorsed by a motion-picture moustache and brilliant teeth. At forty-five, Costello had reached the stage in his career at which he was more politician than policeman.

Nodding to Judith, he said in a rich voice, "Thank you, Mrs. Lieb. I *do* like that red hair."

The crowd giggled.

From the way Captain Costello's impeccably tailored tropical worsted uniform fit, it was obvious he wasn't wearing all the usual equipment under his blouse. In fact, whenever he went before important civilian groups it was his habit to lock his equipment belt—with its swivel-holstered Colt Mark III service revolver, cartridge case and handcuffs—in the trunk of his private car, against regulations. Costello was not unarmed, however, because he carried a small off-duty firearm, a 9 mm automatic, in an ankle holster that didn't spoil his slender silhouette.

"Ladies and gentlemen, as Mrs. Lieb told you, I'm Captain Costello. My first name is Carroll." He smiled. "And that's why I became a cop."

They laughed.

"I've been commanding officer of your precinct, the Six-Five, for three years now. Normally, my community relations officer, or someone from my Neighborhood Police Team, does this sort of thing on my behalf. However, I have so many good and dear friends here in Kingsborough Beach—Sidney Lieb, Leo Goldstein, Fred Isaacs, to mention just a few—that I decided to come over personally tonight to address your concerns."

He paused, assumed a serious expression. "In this city, ladies and gentlemen, a home is burglarized every twelve seconds. A shocking statistic. But even more shocking is the fact that, in over half of them, the perpetrator gets in through an unlocked door or window. An *unlocked* door or window," he repeated. "Now, I am here to ask you, first of all, to please lock those darn doors and windows—"

They tittered.

"—and then to tell you some other ways in which you can help us, your police, to discourage the vermin who want to take what you work so hard to get."

From where Loring stood he could see everyone in the room. Elizabeth Blaug was definitely not there.

The captain went on. "Housebreaking is an old, old crime. Ever since the first caveman moved into the first cave, some other caveman has wanted to get inside of it and steal something. And it has evolved into a game of wits, ladies and gentlemen: yours against theirs. Your burglar, even the amateur, is an intelligent and gutsy fellow. The best thing would be if you could make your house impregnable, but that's impossible to do. So the next best thing is to make it difficult and risky enough so that he'll pick somebody else's house instead.

"Your basic antiburglar defense is simple: stay at home." He paused. "Failing that, make it look as though you're at home. You can do that with lights and sound. When you leave the house, it's very easy to connect up your lights and radio to an automatic timer, so your house appears occupied." He seemed determined to look into everyone's eyes at least once during the evening. "And if you're away for a few days, or weeks, either stop your mail and newspaper delivery or have a neighbor pick them up for you every day, so they won't pile up and send out a signal that you're on vacation."

Costello pointed out that these measures might deter the casual, cruising burglar; the dedicated one, however, could determine, by calling the house or even knocking on the front door with a cover story, whether anyone is actually at home or not. "Therefore," he said, "it is fundamentally important to make certain there are no simple, easy ways for strangers to get into your home."

Referring to notes on a pad, the captain described the difference between ordinary spring-latch door locks and the more secure single-cylinder dead-bolt types with long, two-inch throws. He also touched on the various electronic security systems that were currently on the market.

"You should do the most you can afford," he said. "Whatever you invest is cheaper than paying for more police."

Someone in the back remarked, louder than he had intended, "The cops are overpaid, anyway!"

He instantly drew remonstrative shouts from several people in the room, especially little Irving Pincus, an eighty-five-year-old of birdlike frailty, who said, "Hey, who's that, Murray Levine? You shmuck! There ain't a police officer in the New York's Finest who don't earn his salt, so shut up!"

Murray Levine was mortified. Captain Costello, not knowing whether this Murray Levine was important or not, diplomatically allowed as how, in some cases, he agreed with him. "But, in all fairness, I've got to tell you that most of the men and women in my command earn their salaries."

There was spirited applause at that. Irving Pincus nudged Loring and said, in his raspy whisper, "Bullshit."

"But regardless of how professional he is," Costello went on, "your average police officer does not have the time to keep an eye on every single house in his sector, every shift. That's the plain fact, because the priority has got to be your more violent crimes—mugging, armed robbery, assault, rape. . . ." His eyes traveled the room, trying to gauge their response to this. "And I'm sure you wouldn't want it to be any other way. Unless, of course"—with his best smile—"you just happen to have been burglarized!"

More laughter.

He suddenly clapped his hands together, startling everyone. "All right! Tell me: Who here has been burglarized, lately?"

Three hands went up. Pincus nudged Loring again. "You got, raise your hand."

Loring didn't feel like becoming part of Costello's act, so Pincus raised his own hand and pointed to Loring.

"Here, Captain, this man just got robbed last week. Loring Neiman, from 2906 Averly Street, the famous writer." Then he added, even more extraneously, "The house right behind mine, I live on Levon Street."

"Four of you," Costello said. "May I ask you all a question? How did the perpetrators enter your homes?"

He pointed to one victim, Ed Hart, who responded with, "They walked right in through my front door while my wife was out shopping. They got her rings. To the tune of fifty grand."

"Your door was unlocked, sir?"

"Yes."

"How come, may I ask, sir?"

Hart shrugged. "It's warped, sir, from the ocean air."

Costello looked at Hart with mock disapproval. "And you never fixed it?"

There were giggles as Hart grinned sheepishly and said, "It's still not fixed!"

The captain shook his head and pointed to another victim, Edna Backus. "And you, madam?"

"They broke a window and crept in."

"During the day?"

"Yes. While I was at the beauty parlor."

The third, Gertrude Solky, told Captain Costello, "They jimmied the lock on my side door and cleaned me out, but so thoroughly, you could *die.*"

The room laughed again. This was better than "Queen for a Day."

"Night or day?" the captain asked.

"It was daytime, Captain," Mrs. Solky replied. "I was at a matinee."

This brought snickers from a few men.

Costello now looked at Loring, in the back of the room. "Mr. Neiburg? Can we hear your tale of woe?"

"Nei-*man,*" Pincus corrected.

Everyone turned in their seat to see Loring. He felt

annoyed. "My dinette had louvered windows. They broke in by removing them, last Tuesday afternoon, while I was out with my kids."

"All right, then. I see all four burglaries were in the daylight hours. There were no hot prowls among you." He explained that "hot prowl" was a police term referring to a burglary that is committed while the family is at home, usually asleep. "Some professional burglars like it because they know where everyone is. They feel safer. It eliminates the chance of being surprised by someone suddenly coming home. And—and this is interesting—a department psychologist once told me that, besides an element of voyeurism, it makes the lowly crime of burglary seem more exciting and romantic. In other words," Costello added, "you might say it turns them on."

"For your victim, then, the hot prowl is the most harrowing type of burglary to contemplate." The room buzzed in agreement. "But if it makes you feel any better, there hasn't been a hot prowl around here in many years."

Costello went on to point out that there was no apparent pattern to the four burglaries, which suggested that the perpetrators were various, probably juveniles, "who sometimes work in teams, family affairs, sending a skinny little ten-year-old in through a small window or a doggie door, who then opens up a door for the others.

"Your nice, well-to-do area, like Kingsborough Beach, is going to attract more and more thieves, random or otherwise, and it's going to be up to you to help your police as much as you can."

Larry Kilowitz raised his hand. "If a guy shoots a burglar, is it murder?"

The room hung on Costello's answer.

"Sir, I would hate to think that anyone in this lovely neighborhood keeps a firearm."

"I got news for you, Captain," Kilowitz said, "there's more guns around here than El Salvador."

Captain Costello put his hands over his ears. "I didn't hear that." Then, seriously, "Let me answer your question this way: during the commission of a felony, if *I* shoot him, no, it's not murder. If *you* shoot him, well, you'd better do it inside your house, or drag his body into the house afterward. Also"—he waggled a finger at Kilowitz—"you should be prepared to show the homicide detectives your pistol permit."

While Captain Costello was talking about solid-core doors that could withstand kicking assaults, Elizabeth and Andrew Blaug came in. There were no empty seats, so they walked through to the dining room archway and stood next to Loring. Neither of them seemed to recognize him. Loring caught a funny look from Judith, at the other end of the room. She raised her eyebrows and nodded in Elizabeth Blaug's direction. He had no idea what she meant.

When the police captain's lecture was over, he gave Judith and Sidney some printed material for the Neighborhood Watch organization, including a batch of *Take a Bite Out of Crime* pamphlets and household information forms to be filled in by member families. Then, after shaking hands with as many individuals as he could, he left.

Judith Lieb was acclaimed director of the Neighborhood Watch. She immediately appointed a committee to procure signs for lampposts, lawns and windows and then handed out the pamphlets and information forms.

The living room people drifted toward the dining room buffet and the meeting became a party. Gallons of good-smelling coffee were poured, round after round of hazelnut tortes, strawberries in white chocolate and peach soufflé came out of the kitchen.

"How are you, boychick?" Leo Goldstein's pudgy, crease-lined face always lit up in a special way whenever he saw Loring. Leo was having coffee with the Koppels, the Paiges and Miriam Pincus. He beckoned Loring over to them, gave him a bear hug.

"Good, Leo. How are you?"

"Always terrific, you know that! I just took delivery today on my new 633csi. You should see it, you'd cream."

"Yeh," Wally Koppel said. "If only it wasn't such a Nazi car!"

"Nazi-shmatzi," Leo said, *"Af beir gezundt."*

Leo owned a small brokerage, as well as a seat on the New York Stock Exchange. He was about ten years older than Loring, lived with his wife in a large house on the corner of Loring's street and Dale Avenue. Their son was at Princeton. When the Neimans came to the neighborhood, Leo and Sandy Goldstein had immediately been drawn to the attractive younger family. At one time, years earlier, Loring and Arlene decided to brick over their small backyard and made a home improvement loan from a local bank. When Leo learned of it, he had appeared upset, insisting they should have come to him because he could arrange things like that, at little or no interest.

"You want to know what I think about burglars?" Leo asked, his eyes twinkling. "Lemme quote Shakespeare. Morris Shakespeare, my cousin's tailor. He said: 'Who steals my purse steals shit!'"

As Leo roared, Loring wondered how much of his shit Leo would be willing to lend him right now. If any. If he had the courage to ask.

". . . in a safe," Herb Paige was asking, incredulously, of Miriam Pincus, "with a broken lock?"

"Yeh, well, I think it's broken," replied the old woman. "In my dead son's room, *alavah sholom.* I never wear them anymore, so I haven't looked in God knows how many years. Irving would know."

Paige scratched his head. "I'm having trouble believing that of you, Miriam."

Wally Koppel, who lived next door to Miriam and Irving Pincus, said, "Believe it." He kissed the top of Miriam's gray head. "This girl, God bless her, is from another era, you know what I'm saying, Herby? She even keeps these two-hundred-year-old candlesticks, solid silver, antiques—are you ready for this?—standing out in the open in the dining room, where every shmuck and his brother can put his hands on them." He looked at his tiny neighbor, who was smiling up at him. "Am I lying, Miriam? What are they worth, twenty thousand? More?"

Miriam shrugged. She was enjoying the attention.

Herb Paige laughed. "Who counts, right, Miriam? I guess when you get beauty you don't get brains, too." He noticed Loring, talking with Leo. "Hey, Loring, how are you? How's the book coming?"

Loring said, "Slowly, Herb."

Judith Lieb stepped over to them, looking very official, with her clipboard. She wanted to talk to Loring, privately. Before she took him away, Leo said, "Monday night, boy-chick. You're free?"

"I think so, Leo."

"Good. We're making a dinner party. I want you to come. Sandy'll call you."

Judith asked Loring if he would like to be captain of the western half of Kingsborough Beach.

"No, Judith. I eschew rank. Especially when there's paper work connected."

"Well you're pencilled in gorgeous so think it over." She took a closer look at him. "You look like you had a heavy day."

"Fairly."

Judith glanced around the room, located Elizabeth Blaug, nodded in her direction. "Maybe it'll lighten up yet."

"What is all this, Judith? What are you trying to say?"

In the less than two years since the decent interval elapsed, Judith Lieb had gone out of her way to try to fix Loring up. She'd introduced him to three or four unattached women, fruitlessly. He figured that it probably went more to her own needs, vicariously met, than to his.

"Don't play games with me," she said. "I saw you at the Habib party last month and you never once took your eyes off that one."

Loring didn't know it had been that obvious. "And you don't disapprove?"

"How could I disapprove of anyone getting laid and from

what I know it'd be a novelty for both of you." She took his hand. "Come on and let me try to make a *shiddoch.*"

The Blaugs were sitting with their coffee in front of the brick fireplace, more or less alone. Andrew Blaug was just about to suggest to his wife that they go home when Judith came over.

Andy rose. "Good evening, Mrs. Lieb. Interesting talk he gave, what we heard of it. Very useful." Loring came into view just behind Judith. Blaug extended a hand. "Andy Blaug. This is my wife, Liz."

"Yes. I'm Loring Neiman. We all met briefly at the Habibs' one night."

"I recall," said Andy, who didn't.

Elizabeth invited them to sit down. Loring took a chair opposite her. She looked extraordinary. Her dark hair, always shoulder-length whenever he'd seen her before, was now tied tightly back with a ribbon. She wore navy slacks and a red silk blouse under a white cardigan. And he was struck anew by her eyes, a pale Pacific blue.

She said to Judith, "You really go all out, don't you? I was just telling Andy that he and I have been to bar mitzvahs back in Belmont that had less lavish buffets."

Her voice was clean, crisp.

Judith dismissed the compliment. "My brother works for the caterer at the temple," she said, "so I just press a button in my kitchen and a red light goes on in their kitchen and ten minutes later, *voilà!*"

Loring tried to reconcile the Blaugs. They didn't look as though they belonged together. At that close range, the man had a pleasant enough face, but an ancient, burnt-out expression. "Liz," on the other hand, had the kind of uncommon good looks—not what Loring would call pornographic beauty, but uncommon good looks—that put his senses on edge. He wondered if she and her husband got along.

He became aware that Andy was now staring at him, maybe because he had been staring at Elizabeth.

"You bought the old Cohen house on Ramsgate, didn't you, Andy?" Loring asked, an excuse to return the stare.

Before Blaug could answer him, a beeper on his belt went off. He looked at Judith, who said, "Use the phone in the den, it's quieter, I'll show you." She led him away.

Liz said to Loring, "Yes, do you know it?"

"Know what?" He had forgotten his question.

"The Cohen house. You asked if we bought it. We did."

"Oh. Yes, I know the house. It's a beauty."

"Especially the upstairs," Liz said. "They evidently liked their personal comfort."

Do you? he wondered. "Cohen manufactured bathroom appliances," he said. "Toilet seats and . . ."

Andy and Judith returned.

"I've got a woman in labor," Andy said to Liz. "I'll drop you home first."

Loring's heart sank. Would "toilet seats" be the last thing she'd hear him say that evening?

Liz put her cup on the coffee table and started to get up—a shade slowly, Loring felt—but Judith stopped her. "We'll finagle you a ride home Liz stay awhile."

Liz looked inquiringly at her husband. "Maybe I will, for a little while. . . ."

Loring examined his fingernails.

Andy nodded, kissed Liz on the cheek, said hasty good nights to Judith and Loring and left.

"As a matter of fact, Liz, Loring could drop you," Judith said. "Couldn't you gorgeous?" She squeezed his shoulder as she walked away.

A fine piece of parlor engineering.

"Sure. Of course." Loring fumbled for his cigarettes in his jacket pocket. "Just let me know anytime you're ready, Liz."

She refused a cigarette; Loring lit his. He told her that he understood Boston had been her home, and she explained that she had just begun working as a speech pathologist at Mass General when she met Andy, who was doing his residency there.

"We got married, had a baby boy, wholesale, and moved here about a year ago so Andy could take over his father's practice."

Loring tried to appear casual as they chatted, his body language suggesting no more than polite attention. Actually, her proximity excited him.

"How old are you?" He realized the question surprised her, so he added, "At my age, I can ask that of very young women without offense."

Liz laughed. "Regardless of your age, questions about *my* age don't offend me. But they will, starting in August, when I turn thirty." She noticed he had gentle eyes, with a faintly superior smile behind them. She was about to ask him what he did for a living when Manny Gold occurred at Loring's side, with a glowering Larry Kilowitz in tow.

"Loring, hey, Loring, you gotta hear this. Larry says burglars should be put to death because burglary is like rape! Arnie and I think he's nuts," Manny Gold said. "What do you think?"

"About killing burglars, or Larry's being nuts?"

"No, no joke, Loring," Gold persisted. "Do you believe burglary can be compared to rape? I mean . . ."

"I've never thought about it in those terms," Loring replied. He looked at Liz.

"Compared to rape? Ridiculous," she said. "I've never heard of a robbery victim rendered incapable of relating even to her own husband for five whole years after her . . . her underwear drawer was rifled."

Larry Kilowitz glared at her and said, "Look, miss. When a guy breaks into your house, he violates your life. He's a sick goddamn animal who should be put to death. Tortured to death." He punched his thigh with a fist. "I would *kill* anybody I found in my house. Anybody!"

Liz looked at Loring. "Remind me never to go there for coffee."

"You think that's funny, miss?" Kilowitz asked. "If a guy is crazy enough to sneak into your private house, he's crazy enough to do anything, like violating your wife and daughter and murdering the whole goddamn family in their fucking beds!" His lips quivered. "And excuse my language, but that's my personal opinion."

Liz looked at her watch. To Loring, she said, "I have to go. If you're not ready, I really don't mind walking. . . ."

They pulled up in front of her house and Loring cut his engine. Ramsgate Boulevard was the seawardmost street in Kingsborough Beach. The ocean could be heard sucking the shoreline, a hundred yards away. The air was fresh and salted.

"Would you like to come in for some coffee?" Liz asked.

"No, thanks." He looked at his watch. It was 10:25. "But if you have a few minutes I wouldn't mind just talking, out here?"

"Fine. I haven't sat in a parked car since my senior year at high school. Do we neck?"

Loring felt a rush. "Not on a school night."

They were parked under an enormous Dutch elm which, in another month, would be fat with big leaves, but which even now rustled respectably in the light Atlantic breeze. And it shaded them from the streetlamp. Loring felt more relaxed with her now. Nobody was watching them. He could smell her. There was a long moment of quiet as he wondered just how foolish he was prepared to get.

"You never shut up, do you?" Liz finally said.

Loring laughed. "I'm sorry. I guess a man of forty-two has a responsibility to be interesting. Okay, let's see . . . what can we talk about that would interest a woman not yet thirty?"

That was foolish, right there.

"Try real life, for openers," she said. "You're a widower?"

"Yes."

"What was she like?"

"Nice. I loved her a lot." He smiled at Liz. "But then, have you ever heard a widower admit he didn't love his late wife?"

"No, but you I believe. You look like a man who's missing somebody."

"Or something?"

"Somebody." She waited, then said, "Talk."

He usually had trouble unfolding in this manner. But not

34

so, now. He told Liz about the pain of watching Arlene die. "The worst is, I no longer have the grief to keep me company. Or the activity. Jesus, the activity! She fought like hell, we fought for her, I tried to get everyone else to fight for her. I tore Sloan-Kettering apart, insulted and embarrassed every oncologist in the city of New York."

Liz said, "And then it was over."

"And then it was over. And all I felt was this profound, full-bodied relief."

"Except," she said, "that when relief comes, it means all hope is gone."

He nodded. There was a quiet beat. Then he asked her about her and her husband.

"A very good man, respectably imperfect."

"You mean he forgets anniversaries, leaves the toothpaste uncapped?"

"I mean I'm second to his work and the people he works on."

Loring shrugged. "He is a doctor."

"To the tenth power. He's already gotten official word that he's the Messiah. Which is all right with me, except he keeps waiting for me to get the Word, too."

Loring was impressed that she'd said that with no apparent rancor. He asked her how come.

Liz smiled, her teeth chalk-white against her shadowed skin. "I love him."

That saddened him.

She glanced at her house. "I'd better go in. This whole burglary business, I never gave it a thought before. But now it scares me." She looked at her house again. "I love the house, but it looks like a great big pushover, all of a sudden. There isn't a lock that works on any of the windows down there." She pointed up the driveway. "Andy keeps all kinds of things around, methadone, morphine, God knows what else. We need some lighting around the outside. I could be getting burgled? . . . burglarized? . . . even as we sit here."

"Four burglaries in four months isn't exactly an epidemic. Besides, he said there were no hot prowls."

"I must have missed something. Hot what?"

"Hot prowls. That's when the family is home. Like right now, your son and . . . who, a housekeeper?"

"Yes. You know, I almost agree with that terrible little man, that Larry . . ."

"Kilowitz."

"Kilowitz. Burglars must be strange people. I really can't imagine anyone capable of creeping into someone else's house. He'd either have to be crazy or terminally brave."

"Neither. I've done it."

"What? You've done it? How do you mean?"

"In Saigon, in '66. I was in the Army, the CID—that's Criminal Investigation Division—and I had to break into houses and flats three or four times a week."

"To catch Communists?"

"To catch Democrats and Republicans! Americans, grunts who had gone AWOL, mostly, deserters, black marketeers. And just plain criminals."

She pondered that. "Well, at least you were a lawman."

"Of sorts. I don't recall ever getting a warrant of any kind. And in 'Nam at the time nobody ever knew from habeas corpus. We just went and did whatever had to be done."

She felt that when he spoke, earnestly, she could see the little wheels turning inside of him. She liked it.

"You don't seem a military type."

"I am not now, nor have I ever been, a military type. I was recruited on campus, at Syracuse, graduated into my commission. It seemed more interesting than teaching, and since I really wanted to be a writer, I thought a touch of war would give me something to write about."

"Did it?"

"Sure. A lot of letters, to Washington, explaining that my father was sick and needed me at home."

Loring did not tell Liz that while he was in Saigon he had volunteered, largely out of boredom, for a mission he had felt was more outrageous than audacious: the kidnapping of a wealthy local Frenchman who was suspected of supplying stolen American matériel to the VC guerrillas in the area. He was too powerful and well placed to be accused in the normal way, so the Thieu police asked the Military Assistance Command to help out with a sub rosa operation. The mission involved Second Lieutenant Loring Neiman, A.U.S., and an ARVN, in a quiet invasion of the Frenchman's house. It ended successfully. They spirited the man out without a shot being fired. Loring never knew that subsequently the Frenchman was turned over to the same local police who had been loath to arrest him in the first place, tortured into a confession. He spent the remaining month of his life in a tiger cage.

When it all blew over, the U.S. Army, in its retroactive wisdom, chose to launder the operation and go public with it by presenting Lieutenant Neiman's act as one of exceptional importance and courage. They awarded him the Bronze Star for meritorious service in a ceremony at MACV headquarters. Loring secretly felt they had simply liked the idea of a New York Jewish liberal "hero" to help counteract the growing antiwar movement back home. He accepted the medal but had refused to help publicize it.

"I should go in. Andy will be home soon, I'm sure." Liz was getting edgy.

"Don't worry. Messiahs are above jealousy."

"Jealousy?" She looked at him. "About *what?*"

He wished he hadn't said that. It was presumptuous. He smiled and shook his head. Foolish thing No. 2.

"Anyway," she added, "good night, Loring Neiman, and thank you for the ride home."

In profile, he noticed, her mouth had a little upturn at the corner. She unlatched the car door, extended her hand. He took it, drew her to him and kissed her, full on the lips. She stiffened. He let go of her as the car door swung open and the interior light went on; she looked like a rabbit caught in the glare of headlights.

Just before she got out, she said, without smiling, "You want to hear my thinking on that? It was way out of character for you. You're the shy type."

She slammed the door behind her. To the steering wheel he said, "I thought so, too." Foolish thing No. 3.

Marcia, the baby-sitter, was dozing on the living room sofa, her mouth open adenoidally, her school books scattered on the carpet. He woke her, and she told him everything had gone well.

"There were only two calls. Your cousin Esther and a Mr."—she checked her note—"Carlin, from the Newgate Trust Company. He said you should call him the first thing tomorrow."

"Oh. I see. Okay."

He paid her and watched from his front door until she got safely inside of her own house across the street. Then he went upstairs and peered into the girls' room. All was quiet. He went into his bedroom.

"First thing tomorrow."

He pushed "Mr. Carlin" from his mind, preferring to dwell upon his current feeling, which was new and exciting, explore it for a while. When he was driving away from Liz's, he had regretted his idiotic pass. Now, though, he was beginning to feel better about having made it. It was a given that he would like, for whatever reason, to get close to her; his impulsiveness in the car, then, would either make the situation or break it. Being drawn to a married woman was stupid enough. Panting around her for the next few months, courting her desultorily, by innuendo, watching and waiting for signals, would be even more stupid.

This would clear the air. One way or another.

One of Loring's last thoughts before falling asleep was another brand-new one: to call Jamie Gelfmann in the morning and tell him he'd now like to submit a rough idea for a new nonfiction book. A pop history of Brooklyn. And (and this was the *real* point) get a big advance on it from Marlow & Roth.

Wednesday, May 16 _____

WHEN LORING GOT back from dropping the girls off at school he went into the kitchen, poured himself a cup of lukewarm coffee and lit a cigarette.

He spent a few minutes thinking about the manner in which he should present the Brooklyn idea to Jamie Gelfmann. Mainly, he felt, it was important that he not propound it as a hot new idea, but rather as one he'd wanted to do for many years, but never had the time.

Stop feeling like such a fucking beggar.

He lit another cigarette, forgetting that there was one burning in a saucer, and dialed Jamie's Larchmont number. Lorraine answered, and after some amenities she told Loring that Jamie had left for the city earlier than usual and would probably be at the office by now.

He dialed Jamie's office.

"He's in a meeting, Mr. Neiman. Can I have him call you when he's clear?"

"Please. It's important. Thanks."

Upstairs in his study, he booted up the word processor and loaded the Burglar file.

Yesterday's last paragraph read

Our privacy, the sanctity of our home, had been violated.

Loring scrolled through the piece from the beginning. It was terrible. He couldn't even remember where he was going with it. Privacy? Sanctity?

39

He typed

> Had we been there, my or my daughters' lives might have been threatened. We might, in fact, have been killed.
> When we got home and realized we'd been burglarized, I searched the house and grounds, barehanded, for whomever.
> At first, I was angry enough to hope I'd find someone, but by the time I'd looked under the last bed I was grateful that I hadn't.

He leaned back in his chair and gazed absently out of the window. It was another gorgeous day. The yard looked nice, the azaleas along the back of his property starting to bud. Would the house be his long enough to see them flower? The hydrangeas on the other side of the fence, belonging to the Pincuses, were in the same state. Beyond them, the Pincuses' house was flocked with bright young ivy leaves. The lovely building itself seemed to look especially secure and permanent. And why not? Pincus was retired from a large paint business, a chain of stores in Brooklyn and Queens. Serious money for five decades. It should be secure and permanent. Loring wondered if that house had ever been broken into, as his smaller, more vulnerable one had. Had Pincus's sanctity ever been violated?

The phone rang.

Thank God. Jamie.

"Hello!" he almost shouted.

"Hello, Mr. Loring Neiman, please." A prissy voice.

"Speaking."

"Mr. Neiman, this is Mr. Carlin, of Biolos & Biolos, foreclosure attorneys to the Newgate Trust Company. I'm calling in reference to the equity source account on your property at—"

"Right, I know. I, ah, could I call you back in an—"

"It won't be necessary, sir. I'm calling to inform you that we now have an order from the court confirming the referee's report. Your attorney, Mr. Krause, asked me to call you and tell you this. I suppose he doesn't like delivering bad news."

"He doesn't . . . uh huh. And so . . . what's the next step?"

"The next step is a notice in the newspaper that your home is up for sale."

"Sale?"

"Yes, Mr. Neiman. It's an auction."

Auction. His brief, disconnected talks with Ted Krause had never taken him that far. "Auction, as in auction on the courthouse steps?"

"Literally, yes, on the courthouse steps, sir." He paused. "Unless you're in a position to pay the entire accelerated debt. Thirty-five thousand eight hundred dollars and sixty-three cents, which sum includes the bank's legal costs, to date."

"I'm paying it, of course. I just wonder if I can ask you to hang in there for, oh, a day or so, until I can get to it?"

"Get to it?"

"Yes. It's been a long time, getting to the papers and things. I'll also have to talk to Mr. Krause. It's really a mess down here."

"When, exactly, would that be, Mr. Neiman?"

"A couple of days, tops."

"In a couple of days, sir, you'll be able to bid on your house, and possibly buy it back. At today's price, of course, but you would certainly be eligible to do that."

"I don't want to do that, Mr. Carlin. Let me call you tomorrow, please."

"I left my phone number and extension last evening. Do you have them? It's—"

"Yes, yes, I have all that. No problem. Talk to you then."

Loring hung up. There was a ball of fear in his chest.

He looked at the blank VDT screen. The cursor was blinking, blinking patiently.

Loring wondered, if an auction sale would bring more money, why were they still calling about his debt?

He had to get his mind back to work.
He began typing again.

> I called the police. While waiting for them to show up, I washed all
> the toilet seats and then phoned everybody in the world—specifically
> my cousin and two or three friends—mainly to hear some civilized
> voices and reconnect to life as it had been earlier that after-
> noon.
>
> Three hours elapsed before a lone police officer finally got to my
> door. Although he wore a uniform and badge, I made him show me his
> I.D. card before I would let him into the house.
>
> His "investigation" was cursory. At the scene of a crime,
> uniformed patrolmen do not play detective, contrary to what we see on
> television.
>
> (Etc etc etc)
>
> When I asked him what the chances of catching the burglars were,
> he said they were practically nil. "They're kids. Burglary is a piss-ant
> crime," he added. "We're too

Loring pressed Control/B, and the text scrolled back to the beginning. Using Control/K, he deleted

BURGLAR PIECE—LORING NEIMAN

and typed, in its stead

THE PISS-ANT CRIME by LORING NEIMAN

and then scrolled forward to where he'd left off. He continued typing

> busy with the serious ones." We
> were interrupted by a couple of squawks on the cop's walkie-talkie.
> They were unintelligible to me, but whatever they said, he had to leave
> in a hurry.
>
> As he did, he handed me a card with a phone number on it and

said, "Call them, Mr. Neiman, they'll send you a copy of my report for your insurance company,

Loring stopped and reread what he had written thus far. It was still flat, but it was a start.

Jamie still hasn't called back.

He looked out at his yard again. He'd never gotten around to putting roses in alongside of the garage. Or buying the swing set for the girls.

Elizabeth Blaug, a reasonably contented married woman.

He wanted very much to see her again.

His gaze rose to the Pincus house. A third again larger than his, it was built of brick below and stucco above, a style of the 1930s. Fifty years of ivy clung to it, wiring it into the environment.

And on closer look, not really well maintained. Especially considering how much money they had. Besides, Irving had been in the paint business, yet the wood trim needed painting. Not altogether surprising, though, given the fact that Irving never spent a dime, not even on himself. In a community of people who practiced conspicuous charity, he was a total anomaly.

He typed

so your burglary isn't a total loss."

And so really how secure, in terms of burglary? Even from that distance, about eighty feet, Loring could see what looked like at least two possible points of illicit entry: a basement window, slightly askew in its frame, and a kitchen window which was, as far back as he could remember, always open six inches from the top. It still was, at that moment.

He made a mental note to call it to their attention.

Ted Krause, who lived two blocks away, on Oulden Street, came over about eight that evening. The girls cleared the

Junior Scrabble from the table, kissed Loring and "Uncle Ted" good night and went up to bed.

Carrying a cold beer for Ted and a White Label on the rocks for himself, Loring ushered his lawyer out onto the small stone terrace to talk. Loring loved sitting on the front terrace, which was ringed with boxwood and offered a view of the little dogwood on the lawn. It was a tree he wanted to see as much as possible while it was still in bloom. And while he still owned it.

Ted, an energetic, good-looking thirty-eight-year-old, came across like a hotshot, but really wasn't. Since the Neiman family had moved to The Beach, he had handled certain matters for them—their purchase of the house, their wills—their domestic boilerplate. But Loring had never asked him to involve himself in the sale of his three books because he didn't feel that Ted had the experience or imagination to deal on that level. Book contracts were complicated. Besides, to Loring, Ted Krause tended to obfuscate things even more than most lawyers. And Ted, although not burdened with sensitivity, had long ago guessed this to be Loring's attitude, and so always carried a vague air of resentment whenever they were together. Their meetings, therefore, were never rich. But he was a neighbor.

"Again with the Chapter Thirteen, Loring? We already did that, four months ago, remember? Which I told you at the time wouldn't work, but it at least bought you a couple of extra weeks."

"A lot of people seem to do it, Ted. How come it didn't work for me?"

"You don't have enough income."

"I don't have enough income to go bankrupt, is that what you're saying?"

Ted sighed. "You want to talk in ironics, then talk in ironics." He sipped some beer. "But hear the bottom line: there are no more legal options."

"There have to be," said Loring. Wishing would make it so.

Ted wondered if all creative types were that naïve. "I've

exhausted them all, Lor. Now you need cash on the barrelhead. When will the rewrites on *Quagmire* be done?"

Quagmire. "You mean *Quarantine.*" Loring had lied to him about the novel, told him the publishers wanted extensive rewrites and the money was not yet his. "Not for months. Months," he said, dismissively. He lit his eleventh cigarette of the day. "How much time do I really have, Ted?"

"Like Carlin told you, days, at most."

"Are you sure? Carlin sounded as though they were a little reluctant to go ahead and foreclose, were still waiting for my money. Why would that be?"

"I don't think it *would* be," Ted replied. "The real estate market is down a little, yes, but this"—he indicated the house—"happens to be Kingsborough Beach, not some piece of shit in Borough Park." He adjusted the sunglasses that were still parked on the top of his head after his golf day at Belle Harbor Country Club. "Hear the bottom line: they'll sell it out from under you in a couple of days. Then comes the city marshal."

Loring flicked his cigarette out onto the lawn. He regarded Ted, looking relaxed as hell in his white slacks, feet up on the brick railing. *The sadistic son of a bitch is enjoying this.*

"Ted, you are my fucking lawyer. Get me the money!"

Ted was startled by Loring's tone. "I'm your lawyer, not your magician. I fended the bank off for almost eight months for you."

"Not with any brilliant lawyering you didn't!" Loring snapped. "You exercised the automatic options provided by the state of New York, in its sublime fucking benevolence."

Ted now looked insulted. "Well, if you happen to think that's how easy it was, well, so be it."

"Yes. Now get me the money."

"Loring, knock it off! Where the hell am I going to get you the money?"

"Lend it to me."

Ted forced an incredulous smile. It spoiled his good looks. "Loring, I haven't got that kind of money! For christ's sake! You think I'm a millionaire?"

"Then borrow it for me."

"From who?"

"A bank. One of your other clients. Your father-in-law. Anybody."

"Clients and father-in-law are out of the question, Loring. As to a bank, they wouldn't make you a loan. Why don't you ask Marlow & Roth? Wouldn't they give it to you even before the rewrites are done?"

Loring didn't answer.

"Ask them," Ted said. "It's always no until you ask. You're an important guy, come on like one. Let them see it come through."

From an asshole who's had two lousy marriages and a kid out of control on dope I need lessons in Effectiveness?

"Go home, Ted."

"Good, Loring. We'll talk again. Meanwhile, hit up Marlow & Roth. It happens to be your only shot."

Thursday, May 17 _____

THE NEXT DAY Loring, wearing his best blue suit and a tie, collected Katie and Briana at school and brought them home to wash up. He was going to apply for a loan at a local bank and somehow had the notion that if he showed up with his two little kids, he'd look more responsible. Or pathetic.

"Daddy! The cat threw up!" It was Briana, calling from the girls' bathroom.

"Where?"

"Here."

"So clean it up and let's go."

"Don't you want to see it first? Mommy always wanted to see ours before we—"

"It's not necessary," Loring replied. "We have to go."

"Please, Daddy!"

Katie shouted, from their bedroom, "Bri, Daddy doesn't *want* to see it. Fathers have weak stomachs!"

In the car, en route to the bank, Briana asked Loring if it was true that fathers have weak stomachs.

"Yes, it is true. When you girls were little and I was alone with you I couldn't even change your diapers."

"You left us *dirty?*"

"No. I called the paramedics."

Katie giggled. Briana wondered who the "pair of medics" were.

While Briana and Katie played games with deposit and withdrawal slips, Loring told the floor loan officer, a very

47

young woman, that he would like to borrow thirty-six thousand dollars and would secure the loan with his house.

"A second mortgage," she said.

"Uh, yes." Then: "I plan to pay off an existing one with this money, you understand."

She nodded knowingly and asked him to fill out a credit/net worth statement. Loring looked it over. It seemed surprisingly short and benign to him.

When he had done so, she read it over without question or comment. Consulting her watch, she told him he was very lucky because the branch board would be meeting in about an hour, right after closing. If they approved him, he would hear in the morning and they would probably send their appraiser to look at the house in the afternoon, if it was convenient for him. He could pick up his check right after that.

Loring was amazed. "That's all there is to it?"

"That's all!" she said. "This is a modern bank!"

"Wow! The wonderful world of usury!" Then: "Could I possibly hear tonight?"

She wrinkled her brow.

"I mean," he said, "just whether the board approves me. The rest of it can wait until tomorrow."

"I'll tell you what. I'll call you myself when I get home." She wrote his number on one of her cards and put it in her purse. Then, impishly, she added, "I hope this is all right to do. I'm new at this."

"It's not just all right, it's wonderful," he said. "Thanks so much, Mrs. Luggera. What's your first name? Rita? Cute name." He signaled to the girls. "Hear from you later, then. I love you, Rita."

They were home fifteen minutes later. While changing out of his money-borrowing suit, the phone rang, just one ring, because his answering machine, which was still turned on, intercepted. Loring recognized the voice and listened without picking up.

"This is Mr. Carlin. I had expected to hear from you today, Mr. Neiman, but did not. I'll wait until tomorrow. 555-2100, extension 8. Thank you." Click.

"Fuck you, Carlin," Loring said.

He went down the stairs two at a time and bounded out into the yard to light the barbecue. As he began the pleasant ritual by squirting lighter fluid on the briquettes, he thought of how hideous it would have been to lose this beautiful, comfortable house that sheltered everything and everyone he loved in the world. Where would he and Katie and Briana have gone? Moved in with his cousins in Bensonhurst? Or would he have had to leave Katie and Briana with them, or someone else, and go live at the Y?

Fuck you, Carlin!

Katie, sensing his great mood, put their favorite 78 record on, Bing Crosby's "Swinging on a Star." She switched the sound to the yard speakers. ". . . and all the *monk*-eys aren't in the zoo, ev-ry day you meet quite a few. . . ." Outside, she took her father's hand and they danced their special version of the lindy, to which she always brought a special gracefulness. ". . . he can't *read* his name or *write* a book. . . ." "You *can* write a book, Daddy!" "Yes, but I *can't* read my name!" "His back is braw-ny and his brain is weak. . . ."

They had barely finished their chicken when Rita Luggera called.

"Mr. Neiman, the bank has denied your loan application."

"What?" Her words didn't register.

"Your loan. The bank cannot make it." She paused, but Loring said nothing. "Do you want to know why?"

"Sure," he replied. "There's nothing like a little bad news to garnish big bad news."

"Well, there are a lot of reasons. For one thing, you prorated your income of the last six years. You earned hardly anything for the last two. Also, your TRW isn't very good. It shows a slow repayment history."

"Correct."

"And maybe you don't know this, but it also shows you have five lawsuits pending against you. American Express, Macy's, Abraham and—"

"But no judgments, Mrs. Luggera. Aren't I innocent until

proven guilty? Besides, Mrs. Luggera, your bank would have my very house as collateral."

She sighed. "That's the main thing, Mr. Neiman, and you never told me this: your house is in *foreclosure*." She actually sounded hurt by his omission.

"Which," he said quietly, "is why I need the goddamn money."

"Mr. Neiman—" Her voice broke. "I got screamed at for bringing this in. *Screamed* at! The board said no legitimate lender would give you a dime."

Friday, May 18 _____

P OP HISTORY OF Brooklyn? How much have you done on it?"

"Nothing yet, Jamie. Just some notes."

Jamie Gelfmann had finally returned Loring's call, forty-eight hours after Loring had called him. But with apologies.

"I don't understand. When you say 'pop history,' do you mean a Jewish-oriented thing? Bagels and lox and lockers at Brighton? Or a more comprehensive history of the borough?"

"Well," Loring replied, "I thought a folk history, rather than a serious one, Jamie. Something that would appeal to Brooklynites and ex-Brooklynites, wherever they are now. The definitive walk through the culture peculiar to this place." *Is that ambiguous enough?*

"The hundredth anniversary of the Brooklyn Bridge was a while ago, Loring, and that might have been something to peg a coffee table book to. Right now, I don't know . . . Of course," Jamie added, "if you are writing a chapter or two with a good strong outline, I would certainly like to see it."

Loring didn't respond.

"In any event, Loring, I feel that I should say this: you understand that a new advance on it would be out of the question, and that M&R would insist upon applying the amount they already advanced you on *Quarantine*."

No, I do not fucking understand that!

"Of course I understand that, Jamie."

Loring went under the shower, held a towel over his face and raged.

Afterward he phoned Elliot Silverbach, his agent. They hadn't been in touch since the day Loring finished *Quarantine,* the day he told Elliot he would never write another line of hard-assed nonfiction crap again, because he was now a novelist.

When Elliot came on the line, Loring told him about the conversation he'd just had with Jamie.

"I'm glad you're thinking straight again, Lor, about nonfiction," Elliot said. Then he added, in a manner that suggested he'd been waiting for the opportunity, "I never felt *Quarantine* worked, Lor, I made that clear to you. When I read it I told you you weren't being a novelist, you were being an autobiographer. Remember?"

"No," Loring replied.

"Yes you do. And if you're now going to ask me to find another publisher for it—which I hope not—I want to go on record as saying that its publication—which I doubt—would not redound to your credit as a writer."

Loring sighed. "Elliot, for postmortems I call Thomas Noguchi. I called you to ask you if what Jamie said about the money is the way it works."

"Yes. Marlow & Roth is perfectly within their rights. The money they paid you when you first signed the contract for *Quarantine* can be perceived by them any way they see fit. They're not publishing the book, so the money's a total loss, unless they apply it to some new project." He laughed. "I'm glad, at least, I made it nonrecoupable!"

"I share your delight. Now tell me what you think of this Brooklyn idea, Elliot. Is it something you can pitch to another publisher?"

"Pitch? Or show?" Silverbach pointed out that inasmuch as Loring's three published books were not superhits, any publisher would want to read a couple of chapters and an outline before talking contract. "Besides, is anyone really interested in Brooklyn? I think even the bridge already had its, uh . . ."

"Centennial. I know, Elliot, I know." Loring's voice dropped. "Look, Elliot, forget it."

"Don't you have any other ideas, Lor? After three books, you're ripe for a blockbuster, something that turns you on and would turn them on to where they'd beg us to accept a hundred thousand advance. . . ."

Us. "Yes. A blockbuster. Queen Victoria's kleptomania, nine hundred pages on how she filched toothbrushes from drugstore counters. Good-bye, Elliot. Regards to the family."

He hung up.

This was to have been his spring and summer of content, having fun with his kids, looking forward to his novel being published in the fall to great reviews, an ABC Movie of the Week. . . .

Drag a new, major work of nonfiction out of his insides right now? He didn't have, as his father used to say, the *coyach.*

In the earlier years there were always plans, his precious evenings filled with work, on good, viable projects. Arlene, stomach out to here, would read in bed while he clacked away at his typewriter in the kitchen of their tiny Avenue J apartment, writing his first book, *Hi, Mayor!*, about small-town municipal governments. At about eleven or so she would join him in the kitchen to read his new pages. Good, bad or otherwise, she always told him they were wonderful. She was a lousy editor but she made good cocoa, and while drinking it they'd make plans. Katie was almost ready to be born and Loring was planning to quit his hated teaching job. Together, they made good plans.

Where is Arlene, and our plans?

Gelfmann, Krause, Silverbach—whom she always called my German High Command—why aren't they saving me?

Loring plopped into his chair and turned on the word processor. Fecklessly, he booted up the Burglar file, and typed

Let's get back to what the cop said about the "piss-ant crime."
I can remember when I was growing up in urban Brooklyn,

burglaries, regardless of the dollar amount, made the newspapers. They were read about with horror and indignation.

Nowadays, they barely make the police blotter.

"Burglary" is the legal term for what happened to me but lately, through overuse, the word has begun to sound trivial. (Offer better words, stealing, grand larceny, etc.)

Since when is grand larceny a "piss-ant crime"?

More importantly, when did the forceful invasion of a person's home by anti-social people with felonious intentions become a "PISS-ANT CRIME"?

And why is the system geared more effectively toward recovering the dollar value of the loss than it is to the prevention of the crime or the apprehension of the criminal? Is the price of what was stolen all we are really concerned about? Doesn't the crime register as a human insult in and of itself?

And what of the psyches of burglary victims, their loss of trust in their environment?

Imagine. They're going to take away my house.

He looked over at the Pincus place. Irving and Miriam's environment for fifty years. Fifty years in the same house. Their family had grown in it. Now the Pincuses, heading down the homestretch, were shrinking in it. They lived there alone. Miriam had never even employed a live-in housekeeper. Just the two of them.

Notwithstanding the peeling paint, it was beautiful.

Downstairs there was a kitchen, with a door out to a flagstone patio. To the left of that, curving out of the building, was the graceful bay window of a large dinette. Above it, on the second floor, was a room with a set of double windows and a door that opened onto a small, railed balcony, the floor of which was the roof of the dinette. To the right, the master bedroom. Above everything, a walkable attic.

And just what would a burglar find in that house, Loring wondered? They certainly owned a TV set or two, possibly even a VCR. The obligatory hardware crap, attractive to high school–age burglars from Brighton or Sheepshead or Canarsie. If the Pincuses had any major treasures, he didn't know what they were. Flatware, he would guess.

Granted, my experience wasn't as atrocious as it would have been if I or one of my daughters had been (hurt) by the burglar.

Silver. Miriam had silver. Of what kind and value, he didn't know. Except that he had the impression it was significant.

Candlestick holders. Antique candlestick holders. Displayed, in Wally Koppel's words, "where every shmuck and his brother could put his hands on them."

Twenty-thousand-dollar candlesticks, he had called them.

Loring tried to imagine what kind of candlestick holders could be worth that much.

Then it seemed to him that Miriam Pincus herself had said, that same evening, that she keeps jewelry in a safe with a broken lock.

Where?

In the dead son's room.

Loring's back was beginning to bother him. He saved his text, turned off the word processor and stood up to stretch and move. He walked to the supplies closet and, from the top shelf, took down Arlene's old opera glasses. With them he brought the Pincuses' basement window six times closer. He could see that it had long since lost its battle with the sea air. It was definitely out of whack, one hinge completely separated from the fifty-year-old wood. The window was not out of its frame, but it would interest a prowler.

Incredible community, he thought. People placing their trust in little more than an equable history and a friendly, suburbanlike atmosphere. And the people they live among, only because they've known them for years. Never mind that they know some of them to be unintelligent, careless or even malevolent.

And just what would twenty-thousand-dollar candlestick holders (if they existed) translate into, in post-burglary terms? Half? Was it possible that someone with the inclination and the balls could enter that building, maybe through a basement window, lift a pair of candlestick holders from a table or wherever they stood and realize ten thousand tax-free dollars? For, perhaps, only twenty minutes of tension?

He put the opera glasses back on the closet shelf. It was close to three. Time to go for the girls.

On the way to the school he thought that by now the Pincuses must surely have digested what they learned at the meeting the other night, read the pamphlets, been given pause by it all and locked their things safely away.

Let's hope so, he thought.

Eddie Kilowitz was with the girls. Katie had invited him to come home with her so they could do some heavy homework together. He was a tall, clunky-looking kid, reminding Loring of an emerging hillbilly. And he spoke with what Liz Blaug and her speech pathologist buddies would call a lallation.

"Heggo, Mr. Neiman. I gike your car."

"Daddy," Briana began before she was even in the car, her voice heavy with pent-up grief, "Katie wants to give him Mallomars and milk!"

"Well, why not?" Loring asked her.

"Because there's only two left, and she says I have to give him *mine!*"

"Oh, keep quiet," Katie said. She leaned over into the front seat. "No, Daddy, look: I told her *I'm* the one having the company, and that I want for me and him to sit in the backyard and have Mallomars and milk together. Why can't she *understand* that you can't make company sit around like a stupid idiot without feeding him something?"

Eddie Kilowitz sat there seemingly oblivious to all of this. He had his father's sensitivity.

"Briana, tell you what," Loring said. "Why don't you donate your Mallomar to your sister's cause and you and I will go to Emmons Avenue and get some orange Italian ices?"

In the rearview mirror he saw her tearstained face explode into a big smile.

Eddie looked at Katie and said, "My mother don't get me eat Maggomars, but she never said Itagian ices."

The four of them wandered Emmons Avenue, slurping their ices, listening to the screaming sea gulls, watching the fishing boats come home. *Anna B, Explorer II, White Cloud, Chief, Ranger, Cynthia W.* Every day the boats left before it was light, returned at four or so in the afternoon, reeking of their catch, their people tired and salty and brick red.

And the private cruisers, moored to white buoys, just offshore. *Angel Eyes, Last Cent, Baby Bloo, Homeaway, Sundowner.* About forty feet out rode the beautiful twenty-eight-foot *Lady-O-Day.* It belonged to Jerry and Merle Sutton, who lived on Heather Street. Merle happened to be on board at the moment, sitting on deck, apparently sewing little curtains for the portholes. She peered toward shore, recognized Loring and the girls and waved to them.

"Hi, love!" she shouted. They all waved back.

How much money must a guy have, Loring wondered, to own, without strain, a boat like that, worth eighty or ninety thousand?

Hi, love.

He also wondered how much love there actually was in that greeting and, if there were love sufficient, how much of their money Jerry and Merle Sutton would cheerfully lend him, if he asked. How much and for how long?

As he and the three kids strolled slowly across the Brigham Street Causeway, heading home, Loring mentally ran down a list of names, people who had avowed affection and concern for him and his little family during the past nine years.

There were quite a few, quite a few, but no matter how he tumbled them, one name kept bobbing to the top: Sidney Lieb.

Best bet. Very best bet.

The moment he got back into the house, Loring went upstairs and called Sidney at his office.

"Loring! Is everything all right?" Sidney was unused to hearing from him at the office.

"Oh sure, Sid, everything's fine. I just have a quick question."

"Ask away, my friend."

"Can I see you tonight, about something rather important?"

"Tonight I'm going to Boston. In fact . . . in exactly twenty-five minutes I'm going to LaGuardia. The thing of it is, I got a bundle on the Celtics, I want to see they handle it wisely! You want to call me there late tonight? The Ritz-Carlton?"

"Uh, let's see . . . when are you coming back?"

"Late tomorrow night."

"Then this can wait, Sid. Can I see you sometime Sunday morning?"

"Anytime Sunday morning, Loring, for sure."

"Great. Thanks."

"Sunday morning, I'm all yours. Body and soul."

"Thanks, Sid, see you then. Have a nice flight."

"Zein gezundt!"

Loring hung up. He was perspiring, although it wasn't that warm, and he felt a great relief. An intelligent move, finally. He'd overridden his ego.

On the kitchen windowsill, tucked away among old telephone messages and supermarket tapes, Loring found Marcia's note with Carlin's number written on it.

He took a deep breath and dialed it.

Carlin, who had been a banks' foreclosure attorney for six years and felt he had a good sense of an adversary litigant's inclinations, was truly surprised to hear from Loring. He had been, in fact, just about to call him.

"Mr. Carlin, I just wanted to tell you you'll be getting your check," said Loring, trying to project more dignity than he had on Wednesday, "by the beginning of next week."

"Really? Do you mean, Mr. Neiman, Monday, the twenty-first?"

"Yes. I . . . no, wait. . . ." Sid would draw the check on Monday, probably on a Manhattan bank, which meant that

Loring would then have to get it certified and sent off to Carlin's Brooklyn office. "I mean Tuesday."

"Tuesday, the twenty-second?"

"Yes, I think so."

"You think, Mr. Neiman?"

"If I live, Mr. Carlin."

"I beg your pardon?"

Loring sighed. "Tuesday, the twenty-second, for certain."

"Very good. Will you be mailing it, Mr. Neiman, or bringing it in?"

"Mailing it."

"On Tuesday, the twenty-second?"

"Yes."

"That's no good, Mr. Neiman. I have to have it in *hand* by Tuesday, the twenty-second."

"I'll deliver the . . . thing, okay? You'll have it Tuesday, the twenty-second."

"The full amount, sir?"

"The full amount, sir."

"A cashier's check for . . . thirty-five thousand eight hundred and sixty-three dollars and seventy-seven cents?"

"In United States currency."

"I will count on that, Mr. Neiman. Can I count on that?"

"Carlin, have I ever lied to you before?"

Loring got into bed about nine that night and tried to watch some television. He rarely watched TV, and when he did it was very late at night, old movies, preferably about the British, preferably World War II. He'd seen *Rommel* fifteen times. Prime-time TV watching always seemed indolent to him, because during his teaching years the best time he'd had for writing was those good, precious middle-evening hours.

With the remote control, he flipped from channel to channel, finally turned the set off.

Arlene and their plans. Maybe they were right here, now. After all, it was she who had brought Judith and the avuncular Sidney into their lives. Left to his own social devices, he'd have never gotten this close.

How much, exactly, should he ask Sidney for? More than the thirty-five thousand and change? Forty thousand? It would be wonderful just to get the big one off his head; then he could start writing again and maybe the little ones would all get taken care of.

He'd have to open up, totally, to Sidney, tell him everything, with complete candor. Painful candor.

Was there any chance Sidney would resent him for putting him on the spot? How could he? Sidney was a major manufacturer, factories all over the Far East, his sportswear labels were famous. More to the point, the Lieb philanthropy, even in this community, was a legend; he was among the heaviest donors to many Jewish and other charities. Always on the side of the angels.

And he loved Loring and the girls.

Loring got out of bed and went into his study. In the darkness he felt for and found some cigarettes on the desk. As he lit one he glanced over at the Pincus house in time to see their master bedroom light go out. Early to bed.

Loring sat down at the desk, switched on his Tensor lamp and referred to a five-by-seven card. Taking a deep drag on the cigarette, he picked up the telephone receiver and dialed a number.

It rang twice. Liz answered. "Hello?"

"Liz?" Loring spoke in a low voice.

"Yes?" she replied.

"This is Loring. If you can't talk, just listen. If you can't even listen, say I got the wrong number—"

"Who? No, I . . . you must have the wrong number. Sorry." She hung up.

Loring wondered why he had done that. He felt asinine, coming on like a creep. He had never in his life responded to a woman in quite this way. Besides, what encouragement had he gotten from her?

He went back to bed, thinking that a thing like this, with this woman in particular, would take a lot of energy. Still, there was this powerful new feeling that he had to get close to her, a stranger from Boston, married to another stranger.

How foolish, how foolish. One was never too old to make a jackass of oneself. . . .

Loring had been dozing for about five minutes when his bedside phone rang.

It was she.

"I'm in the candy store on Brigham," Liz said, wearily. "I'm sorry if I sounded uptight. It was nice to hear your voice, but the Messiah was sitting right there."

"I figured."

"Loring, please don't do that to me anymore, okay?"

"Okay. My word. But I really want to see you again. Is that possible?"

She exhaled. "Give me a chance to think about it. What exactly are you . . . looking for?"

"Beats the hell out of me."

"Um huh. Let me think about this, Loring. By the way, where did you get that name?"

Loring laughed. "An invention of my mother's. She never knew one in her whole life."

"A woman after my own heart. Look, call me. Tomorrow morning, after nine. We'll talk."

"Good. Thanks."

Just before she hung up, she said, "Loring?"

"Yes?"

"Where were you seven years ago, you bastard?"

Saturday, May 19 _____

LORING DROVE THE girls to Kinderland Day Camp for its annual open-house orientation festivities. Although they knew they wouldn't be enrolling this summer, Katie and Briana wanted to spend the day there; most of their friends were doing it, and it was free.

He had no reason to expect Liz Blaug to be there, but he looked for her. She wasn't.

Loring left the girls there and went home. There he sat and watched the kitchen clock as it closed on nine. Tomorrow he'd be seeing Sidney Lieb; today seemed to stretch endlessly in front of him. He wondered if Liz would help him pass it.

At one minute after nine, he called her. "Would you like to come over here?"

"No. For a couple of reasons. First of all, I don't want to be seen going in and out of your house, Loring. God, what an elitist name! Second, I've got an appointment. I'm going into the city, shopping—"

"Alone?"

"No, with Lydia Kramer."

"Oh. Could you alter your plans just a little, the Lydia Kramer part, and go into the city, but with me? We could have lunch."

There was a long pause on her end. Finally, "I hate doing that to Lydia. She's been very nice to me since we moved in."

"Meet her after lunch."

"After lunch," she repeated. "You make good, devious sense. . . ."

"You'll do it?" He was elated.

"Yes."

"Oh, jesus, that's great! I'll pick you up at your corner—"

"No," she said. "We'll go separately and come separately. Just tell me when and where in the city."

"Okay. Café Lautrec. It's on East Forty-ninth Street, between First and Second. High noon."

While shaving, Loring remembered that the Kinderland thing would be over at three; if he were to be back home in time to pick up Katie and Briana, he would have to leave the city by 2:15. This would give him only about two and a quarter hours to spend with Liz. Which fact gave rise to a better idea.

Half-shaved, he phoned Lew Stuart, an old friend. Lew was an art director who lived in Westport but worked in New York and kept a small apartment there. Loring arranged for Lew to call the superintendent of his building and tell him to admit Loring.

Then he called Liz back.

"Cold feet, right?" she said, when she recognized his voice.

"Liz, listen: instead of meeting me at the Lautrec, please meet me in front of 128½ East 36th Street."

"What place is that?"

"It's the apartment of a friend."

She didn't respond. Loring closed his eyes and added, very quickly, "I thought we might make love instead of lunch."

He held his breath.

"I'll be one hungry girl," she said.

After he parked his car, he walked up to Thirty-sixth Street. From the corner, he could see Liz already standing in front of Lew Stuart's brownstone building. Her hair was down, shoulder-length, and she was wearing a dress, the first dress he'd ever seen her in, a knee-length one of light blue silky material, translucent in the noonday sun. At the distance she looked marvelous.

Up close she looked even better. They shook hands. She

seemed more nervous than she had sounded on the phone. He wondered if he did, too.

"Sorry," he said. "I tried to get here before you did."

"I wanted to get out of the house fast," she said. "I told Lydia Kramer a hideous lie about not feeling right and wanting to see my doctor." They entered the building. "I was afraid she'd call back for more details."

In the tiny vestibule, Loring rang the bell marked "super." As they waited, her closeness excited him.

The inside door was opened by an older man.

"Yes?"

"Hi, I'm Loring Neiman? Mr. Stuart said he'd call you about, ah, letting me into his apartment?"

"What? Mr. Stuart didn't call me."

"Your wife, maybe?"

"Got no wife. Mr. Stuart didn't call me about nothing."

Loring glanced at Liz. He felt embarrassed, clumsy. He asked the super if they could use his phone to call Mr. Stuart in Connecticut; he would charge it to his own phone.

Grudgingly, the man agreed, led them up to his third-floor apartment.

There was no answer at Lew Stuart's house.

Loring thanked the super and he and Liz started down the stairs, silently. As they passed the door to Lew's second-floor apartment, Loring stared at it, wistfully.

"I guess I get fed, after all, huh?" she said, cheerfully. "Come on, Loring, it's not that bad."

"It's that bad," Loring responded. "That irresponsible son of a bitch." He stopped them in mid-flight. "Wait a second."

She wondered why as he quietly led her back up the stairs to Lew's door. He examined the lock closely, then reached for his wallet. There was only one lock on the door, and it was one of the standard Yale spring-latch type.

Loring took a Visa card from his wallet and inserted it into the narrow space between the tongue of the lock and the doorframe. It was difficult, at first, to get the card moving, but once it started, it took only slight pressure and a little jiggling to make it turn the corner and, invisibly, slide along the curved side of the latch bolt. It pushed it out of the strike and back into its lock.

The door swung open.

Liz was impressed. "Where did you learn that little number?"

"The Army. As I told you—"

"Ah yes! The Saigon Capers."

"Right." As they entered the apartment, Loring ruefully remarked, "My credit card, like my credit, is now bent out of shape."

"And so will your friend be."

"No. I'll leave him a thank-you note. He'll forget he forgot to call the super."

The studio apartment was inexpensively furnished, mostly secondhand things and castoffs from Lew's Westport home. But it did have a nice mantelpiece and, facing it, a new-looking convertible sofa bed.

Loring fixed two martinis at the tiny wall-kitchen-cum-bar. He handed Liz one, and they sat down, trying to feel at home.

They each contemplated the sofa bed as they sipped their drinks in self-conscious silence.

Finally Liz stood up and began unbuttoning her dress. "Is the maid coming in to open the bed?"

Laughing, Loring pulled open the sofa bed, found two sheets and two uncased pillows in the closet. As he put it all together, more or less, she stepped out of her dress. She had on panty hose and a white bra.

Loring watched her, entranced, as she removed the bra and rolled off the hose. Naked, she struck a pose.

"So . . . here I am," she said, "completely and totally embarrassed."

He started getting undressed. "You have really good legs."

"So do you," she responded.

He asked her how tall she was.

"Five four."

"Good." It had been Arlene's height. "I'm used to handling that size."

In spite of her act, he could see that she was tense; her smile was bright, but the corners of her mouth twitched slightly. He went to her and hugged her, very tightly, for a long moment. Then they kissed and got into bed.

They lay there and talked for a while, new-friend talk. He told her about the girls, how Katie treated him like a teenaged son. She told him about her aborted career as a speech pathologist, how much she would have loved the work. He told her about his mother-in-law, how she spoke with the clearest diction and the worst grammar in the world. "She would say things like, 'I—do—not—know—no—body —what—does—things—like—that.'"

They laughed. He wondered if he should tell her what was going on in his life at the moment, but decided not to.

"I miss working," she said. "It's lousy, at twenty-nine, waiting for the main event to start."

"You're a wife, a mother. What's more main-eventful?"

She groaned. "You, too? That's what my husband says. He thinks it would be dumb, going entry-level at my age."

"So tell him to go to hell."

"No. I don't want him to go to hell. He's a good man."

He remembered her saying just that, the other night. "Good man." *A euphemism for "If you look deep enough he's not the louse he behaves like."*

She went on. "I'm determined to bring the best out of Andy Blaug, but it's not easy. He's too strong for me." She sat up, looked at Loring with a sudden expression of pleasure. "But you, I think, are probably the Mudpie of Gibraltar." She kissed his nose.

Her breasts, very pretty ones, dangled fetchingly just above his face. He touched them. "Do you know the difference between Jewish breasts and shiksa breasts?"

"Is this a joke?"

"No," he replied. "It's Neiman's Boob Law. *God, I'm reverting to my sophomore year!* Jewesses tend to have rounder breasts, gentiles more pointed ones. You, clearly, are a shiksa."

She peered down at her chest. "So I am. I never heard that before."

"We only just met. What's your ethnic composition?"

"Got an hour?" she said. "Let's see . . . at last count I was English, Danish, Hungarian, German and one thirty-second Cherokee—my try for affirmative action."

"Did it work?"

"No. Thank God I was born a woman or I'd have nothing to complain about. The—"

Loring pulled her down to him and kissed her, his tongue in her mouth, tasting her, really tasting her, for the very first time. He went to her breasts, sucked her nipples out and hard. And as he did, his hand went exploring on its own, slowly, moving down to her belly, her mound, slipping inside, gently plying her clit with its fingers. She began to move in a rhythm, her knees up, her legs getting slack, going wide. All the while he watched her face, saw her eyes close, her lips part, her tongue moisten them, her white teeth just visible, her head roll from side to side. She came, groping for him as she came, ". . . ohgodohgodohgodohgod . . ." and found him flaccid.

She opened her eyes and looked at him. "Was it something I said?"

With an apologetic smile, he replied, "Needs work, I guess."

Liz sat up, all business. "Think Ravel's *Bolero*."

Very intently, she began to roll his penis between her palms, wide circles, base and top simultaneously. He continued to stare at her face, fascinated. "You are so damn beautiful."

"Close your eyes," she ordered. She took him in her mouth.

It's been years.

He got hard, first moaning, then almost gasping with ecstasy, harder, harder, very hard

bring the best out of Andy Blaug

until he began to go soft again.

There are three of us in this bed.

She stopped. Looking at his penis with mock seriousness, she said, "We seem to have a net tumescence here of about twenty percent."

He shrugged.

She kissed him on the mouth. "That's what I like about you. No alibis."

"I'm trying frantically to think of one."

Liz put her head in the hollow of his shoulder. With their arms around each other they lay there quietly, and rather happily, for a long while.

After much fervent good-bye kissing in the vestibule of the building, Liz went to Bonwit's and Loring went home.

Sunday, May 20 _____

THE PHONE WOKE him. It was Liz.

"Did I wake you?"

"Yes," he said, heavy-voiced.

"If you have a hard-on, I'll kill you."

"What time is it?" He looked at the clock radio. "Nine-thirty." Whenever he got up later than seven, he felt like Rip Van Winkle. "Jesus. I must still be on California time."

"When were you in California?" she asked.

He yawned. "Fourteen years ago. Where are you calling from?"

"Home. He's playing golf, with three other OBs."

"The Messiah Open, huh. . . ." A wave washed over Loring; he remembered. "Hey! I'm seeing Sidney Lieb this morning!"

"Sidney Lieb?"

"Yes. I'll tell about what, later. Can I . . . can you call me later?"

"Yes, darling."

Darling.

Sidney Lieb looked forward to seeing Loring. It had been weeks since they'd spent any time together, and Loring was one of the few people in The Beach by whose attention he was flattered. Sidney, a self-made man who would forever be a little rough around the edges, was proud to be regarded as a friend by someone of Loring's intelligence. Not to mention cultural status, for he understood Loring to be a "famous writer." Whenever he had occasion to introduce Loring to

71

anyone, he always threw in something like, "Loring wrote three books, you know. We have them all." Indeed, all three of Loring's books were prominently ensconced on a shelf in the Liebs' den. But like many married people, Sidney felt that if his spouse listened to WQXR or attended lectures on Goethe at Brooklyn College, there was no real need for him to do so; inasmuch as Judith had actually read Loring's books, Sid was satisfied that he had absorbed their contents by conjugal osmosis.

"Tell Hattie to lay out something, with coffee, some bagels, cream cheese, some smoked cod, slice up some onions, bring it in here."

"Tell me yourself, Mr. Lieb. I'm standin' right here," said Hattie, irritably. To Judith, she said, "How come he never sees me, when I'm standin' right upside of him?"

"Because his alleged mind is in Madison Square Garden."

"Bullshit. It's because I'm always trying to figure out how I'm going to earn the money to pay her salary," Sidney retorted, indicating Hattie.

"Hee! Thatta be th' day! You got more bread than Jesus and Moses put together!"

When Hattie left the den, Judith said, "Whatever Loring wants, give it to him, I have a feeling something's wrong."

"Give it to him?" Sidney echoed. "What makes you think he needs something? Probably just advice, on something."

"Nobody spends a beautiful Sunday morning like this with the likes of you unless they need something terribly."

Judith and their son, Spencer, left the house.

Loring showed up a half hour later, with the girls, who were delighted when Sidney invited them to play in Spencer's magnificent custom-built tree house.

Loring had always felt comfortable in the Liebs' lovely Dutch colonial. It was warm and unpretentious, like its occupants. He and Sidney sat in the den, Hattie's generous brunch spread before them on the coffee table. Sidney was pleased to see him. He fussed with the table setting, got up for a moment to draw the blinds against the bright morning sun. Until Loring's eyes accustomed themselves to the dimness, the wallful of custom-framed awards, citations and other calligraphed, hand-illuminated expressions of thanks to Sidney Lieb were nearly illegible.

When Sidney sat down again, his shaven head reflected, with a glint, the tiny bit of light left in the room.

"So. How are you, Loring?"

"Fine, Sid, fine. Yourself?"

"Well, the thing of it is, my rotten Celtics lost Friday night. So what can I tell you? You're not a sports fan, are you?"

Loring tried to seem sympathetic. "No, but I understand. It's the way the basketball bounces."

"What? Oh, yeh. The basketball bounces, all right." He cream-cheesed a salted bagel, put it on Loring's plate. "Here. This is the best one." Leaning back, he said, "So. What can I do for you, my friend?"

Loring took a sip of his coffee. He felt nervous, but it was the nervousness of coming home. "Sid, you know the book I've been writing, the novel about Arlene?"

"Sure. May she rest in peace. Sure I know."

"After almost two years of work, my publisher has rejected it."

Sid looked surprised. "Can they do that?"

"Yes, they can. And did."

"Boy, that's . . . what they can do, huh?"

"Yes. My point is, this turn of events has put me in a very . . . bad position, finan—"

"Why did they do that?"

"They just don't like it. For many reasons, Sid, none of which can be dealt with. But it's a total loss, in terms of the time I've spent on it. And it's caused a big problem for me."

"But you're such a good writer, a first-class writer," Sidney said. "Aren't you?"

Loring smiled, weakly. He felt as though he were taking down his pants. "I like to think so, Sid. But fiction, as it turns out, is not my métier."

"Your what?"

"My thing."

"Oh. To me, writing is writing."

Loring picked little pieces from his bagel. "Now, in order to live," he continued, "during the two years I was writing it, I took out a second mortgage on my house—"

"I thought only my business was aggravating. Yours is, too, eh?"

"Well, it's become so, Sid. Anyway, I'm in default, and frankly, I don't have the money to pay it."

"Get a lawyer. Stall. You can stall those things for months."

"I have stalled. And stalled. I'm finished, Sid. They're putting my house up for auction."

"Oh, my God!" Sidney said. He was truly aghast. "It went that far, huh?" He shook his head and sighed. "I guess you'll just have to cash in something."

"Cash in something?"

"Cash in something, anything. It's an emergency, don't you understand? Cash in some municipals."

"Municipals? Sidney, I don't have any municipals. . . ."

Sidney stared at him. "Didn't you buy four, five years ago, when I told you to?"

"No, I didn't. I had no—"

"Boy, when Sidney Lieb talks, nobody listens." Sidney rubbed his hand across his pate and looked away. "You've got to have something, Loring. Everybody's got something."

"I don't."

"How old are you?"

"Forty-two."

"Forty-two. You mean a big, successful forty-two-year-old writer with two small children doesn't have anything?"

Loring shifted in his seat. "Sid, first of all, I have never had any of what are called 'bestsellers.' I've made a living from writing, a good one, for almost ten years now, but jesus knows, it hasn't been tons of money. . . ."

"Yeh. Yeh." Sidney now seemed agitated. "Most men of your age have a quarter, a half a million in net worth. These days, especially, with interest rates so high. I'm surprised, really surprised, at what I hear you saying to me."

"It's the nature of the work I do, Sid. It's not like a

business, where things are going for you after they're organized in a certain way. This is a . . . craft."

"A craft. You've been weaving little baskets. Well, so. You've got aggravation. I agree with you."

"Yes."

"I know the feeling well. You think your business is aggravating? You should be in the rag business, like me!" He laughed, hollowly. "That's aggravating!" There was a pause. "So. What can I do for you?"

Loring's heart skipped. "I need to borrow some money from you. Forty thousand dollars, to be exact."

Sidney gaped. "Forty thousand dollars?"

"Yes. It would bail me out, let me keep my house." He wished he could see Sid's eyes more distinctly. "Then I would do some free-lancing for a while. That would keep the girls and me going, until I get another big project going—"

"Loring, I don't exactly keep forty thousand dollars laying around here in a cookie jar."

"I didn't imagine you—"

"But the thing of it is, even if I did, it wouldn't apply here." Sidney was kneading his forehead. "Loring, let me tell you a little story. My brother, Aaron—you've met him here, right? —was in your position, ten years ago. He came to me, needing money. Not as much as you, but money. I says to him, 'Look, Aaron, if I lend you the money, you are going to be in debt to me. Our relationship will suffer. You won't be able to pay me back, it's so much money. You'll avoid me. We'll end up never seeing each other, because a brother never sues a brother. Here's what I'll do, instead,' I says to him. 'I will give you a job, four hundred a week, in my place,' I says. 'You will run a department. You will run the Interplant Expediting Department.'

"I made the department up for him. I says, 'That way, you'll be working, you won't owe anybody anything, we'll still be brothers who talk to each other.'

"He took the job, Loring. Today he's the happiest man alive."

Loring's teeth were so tightly clenched, his jaw ached.

Sidney went on. "So. What I'm saying to you is that I would not give you a shit job like Aaron's, but something where all your full talents are put to use. . . ." He rose, paced the den. "A real job, Loring. You would be my . . . my special assistant! You would work directly with me, handling special things, connecting up with the ad agency, dreaming up ideas, seeing our labels are handled properly, all like that.

"Same money as my brother. Four hundred a week." He stood still, faced Loring. "I like it! You like it, too?"

Loring got to his feet. Quietly he said, "Sid, soon, maybe in a few days, I'm going to lose my home. My daughters and I will be put out on the street, by marshals, along with our furniture. This—"

"No problem!" said Sidney. "You will never sleep in the street, and that I promise you! As long as Judith and I are alive, you and your family will never sleep in the street. We've even got room here, if push comes to shove. Don't worry."

"Thanks, Sidney. I appreciate your . . . little scenario. But it's not possible."

Loring walked out of the room, down the hall toward the rear door.

Sidney followed him. "Why not possible?" he shouted. "Are you crazy? Your house is now a liability! Trade it in on a clean start! You got two kids to think about!"

At the rear door, Loring called out to Katie and Briana. "We're going, girls."

The girls liked it back there. "Can we stay longer, Daddy?"

"No. You wanted to go to the movies."

They looked at each other; of course they wanted to go to the movies. They clambered down out of the tree house. Loring turned and saw Sidney scowling at him.

"Don't look at me like that, Sid. I need forty grand, not a job in your factory. Forty grand."

Sidney Lieb's expression softened. He put a hand on Loring's shoulder and said, "You're that determined, you'll find it somewhere."

* * *

Outside, in the dazzling sunlight, Loring picked Briana up in his arms and walked rapidly, blindly, down Horning Street, Katie half running after them. When they turned onto Dale Avenue, a greeting from Wally Koppel, driving by, went unnoticed. Loring was seared by humiliation, fighting to keep down a fulminant anger.

As he was passing Leo Goldstein's house, he thought of just walking in and asking Leo for his help, begging him for money. He stopped at the foot of the walkway and, for a wild moment, considered doing it. But no. That was not the way to go. He would be seeing Leo the very next night, Monday. He would make himself stronger by then, come on man to man, with none of the obsequious shit he had just displayed in front of Sidney Lieb.

Later, he put the girls into the Oceana Theatre for a three-hour kiddie matinee. Then, parked on Brighton Beach Avenue, he just sat in his car for a while. His father had once told him, "When you're down on the balls of your ass, be a man and cry."

So he did.

After which he drove, of all places, to the Blaug house. Andy's car was not there. Their housekeeper answered the doorbell.

"Mrs. Blaug? Is she home?"

"*Sí.* Wait."

A moment later Liz came to the door, a surprised smile on her face. She wore white shorts and a halter. Loring's heart lightened.

In a loud voice he said, "Mrs. Blaug, I'm here on Neighborhood Watch business."

"Oh. How may I help you?" Her little son had trailed after her.

"I hope you remembered about joining me and some others, going to the 65th Precinct for that meeting with the captain, and so forth?"

"Yes, Mr. Neiman, I do," she replied. "I know how important and-so-forths can be in these dangerous times. Do I have to change into something more burglar-proof, or am I dressed all right for the meeting?" To her son, she said, "Justin, I have to go with a bunch of people to a meeting. Stay in the backyard, or watch television." She turned and called toward the kitchen, *"María! Yo vuelvo en una hora! El niño está aquí!"*

They got into Loring's car and drove out of The Beach. At Knapp and Emmons they got onto the Belt Parkway, eastbound. Neither of them said a word until he had turned off at the Canarsie Beach Park exit, pulled up in the end of the parking lot closest to the pier and stopped.

They rolled down their windows. It was sunny, but cool.

She regarded his drawn face. Then, very quietly, she asked, "Is this from your meeting with Sidney Lieb?"

Loring nodded, lit a cigarette. He drew on it and exhaled a lot of smoke. People, a small cluster of them, were fishing off the end of the concrete pier about a hundred yards away. There were some season-rushing sailboats out on Jamaica Bay. A loose squadron of gulls wheeled above.

Loring asked, "Who was it, Scott Fitzgerald, who said that the first thing you learn after forty is that your friends won't save you?"

"What's happening, Loring?"

For some reason, he had been afraid that if he ever told her about his novel, his house, the miracle he needed, it would reveal some weakness, drive her away. But he took the chance anyway, at that moment; he told her everything, up to and including his morning with Sidney. Afterward he watched her, half expecting her to start distancing.

Her response was shock, but at Sidney Lieb's insensitivity.

"Unless," she said, "he doesn't really have the money, after all, and was too embarrassed to admit it. Lots of people live like that."

Loring shook his head. "I've seen him write checks for sixty, seventy thousand dollars' worth of Israel Bonds, at rallies. Just so he could outdo Walter Krupp or Leo Goldstein. . . ."

"He might see that as personal survival, of sorts. You, well, he tried to help you, in what he felt was a good way." She thought for a moment. "Is there anyone else you could ask?"

He shrugged. "Maybe Leo. Leo Goldstein."

"That's good. I understand he carries more money than you need in his pants pocket."

"I have a feeling he'd respond like Sid did."

"You never know. Loring, you've got a lot of friends around here. They seem to adore you, compete for your attention, to the point of nausea. And they're good people. But maybe you're asking for too big an amount. Maybe you could get smaller amounts, from various people?"

"I'll take up a collection. Dress the girls in rags, send them door to door, with a hat." He glanced at her. Her expression made him realize she now felt foolish. He dropped his cigarette out of the window, took her face in his hands. "I'm sorry, Liz."

"Andy is still paying off his equipment, Loring. Otherwise, I hope you know I'd—"

"Jesus, Liz, I don't want your money. You're helping me just by sitting here listening to my . . . keening about this shit." Her eyes, reflecting the sky and water just then, looked more gray than blue. He studied them for a moment, starting to believe that what he saw was real concern for him.

She said, "Yesterday I put on two different earrings. I got mascara on my collar. I forgot my key and locked myself out of the house. I made sandwiches for Justin and handed him an empty lunch box." She kissed him. "You've been walking around in my head."

"I have?"

"Yes. All last night and all day today. You're an irresistible combination of opposites: strong and vulnerable. Brilliant and naïve. Funny and serious."

He smiled in spite of himself. "Don't forget father and mother, successful and poor. Horny and impotent."

Abruptly she opened her door, stepped out and pulled the handle that made the seat back recline. Then she motioned to him to get over onto the passenger seat, which he did. She got back into the car. Her knees on the floor, she opened the belt and fly of his chinos and pulled them down. Her mouth closed around his penis and she began a long, sucking motion, grazing her bottom teeth gently along its underside as she did.

He lay back, his eyes closed, getting hard, as she wriggled out of her shorts and panties and straddled him, weighing down, bringing him very deep inside of her, loving his face and head with warm hands and sweet mouth, filling spaces in him as he filled spaces in her. . . .

Later, in front of her house, Loring said, "Neighborhood Watch meetings like this scare the pants off burglars."

Leaning into his car window, she whispered, "We'll talk. Right now you're running down my leg."

Monday, May 21 _____

HELLO, THIS IS Loring Neiman. I can't come to the phone right now, but if you leave your name, number, the time you called and a brief message, I'll get back to you. Wait'll you hear the beep."

"Mr. Neiman, this is Mr. Carlin. It's five-thirty, Monday. I'm calling to remind you that tomorrow is Tuesday, the twenty-second. I'll be in my office all day, expecting your certified check. Thank you." Click.

Loring took the telephone answering machine from the table and placed it on the floor. Then he kicked it to pieces.

From her room, Katie's voice. "Daddy? What happened?"

"Nothing, sweetheart. I dropped something."

Later, getting dressed, Loring took a shirt from his dresser. As he closed the drawer, he noticed that he was doing so with the back of his hand. Thinking back a moment, he realized that he had opened it with the sides of his fingers. He had been doing that sort of thing, unconsciously, for a day or so.

"Here, boychick. I know what you like."

Leo Goldstein handed Loring a scotch on the rocks. One of Leo's prides was that he always knew what his guests wanted to drink.

"Thanks," said Loring. As they moved into the living room, he asked, "Who's here?"

"The usual bullshitters," Leo replied.

Loring knew the Blaugs wouldn't be, because they weren't important enough.

"What can I tell you," Leo continued. "When my wife makes a party, she thinks it has to be a stockholders' meeting."

By that he meant that all of the people were not only friends and neighbors, but, with the exception of Loring, clients of Leo's brokerage.

His small but successful brokerage, plus the seat he owned on the New York Stock Exchange, had earned for Leo one of the most desirable houses in Kingsborough Beach. It was situated on the corner of Loring's block, at Averly Street and Dale Avenue. Seen from the street, the massive stone house was not the most beautiful; it had too much of a midwestern stockiness about it. Besides, like many of the area's larger homes, it was too big for its lot, most of the original property having been sold away, piece by piece, during the seventy years since it was built.

But inside there was a baronial living room with a cross-beamed ceiling that was visually supported by deep, turn-of-the-century crown moldings. On the other side of the wide center hall was an oval-shaped dining room and a large, quiet library, all in the original cherry oak. Toward the back of the house, past the family eating room and the butler's pantry, was a service-only kitchen with a walk-in freezer larger than the master bathrooms in lesser houses.

Loring had been in the house many times, and never without marveling, even at the taste reflected in the decor, a taste that belied the Goldsteins' lower-middle-class background and attitudes. This evening, in particular, the burnished rosewoods seemed to glow, the oak parquet floors shone like ice.

The first guests he became conscious of were the Liebs, and their presence made him uncomfortable. Judith was as friendly and effusive as ever, but Sidney seemed to have an embarrassed reserve about him when he and Loring shook hands.

Besides them, there were seventeen other guests, including, as always, some of Kingsborough Beach's prime movers. Judge Robert Mushkin, the aging bachelor of the Kings

County Supreme Court, was talking about the new baseball season with Walter Krupp, owner of six large automobile dealerships, while Marla Krupp, his wife, exchanged recipes with Naomi Berger, whose husband, Norman Berger, the congressman from the district, discussed Governor Solarz with Assemblyman Dan Pringle and his wife, Debbie, as Judge Matthew Beilenson, retired from the court of appeals, commiserated with trucking magnate Burt Klastorin and retired businessman (and former associate of Buchalter and Reles) Elias "Voncie" Shapp about the crime rate, at the same moment that wealthy widow Freda Woods, builder Arnie Martinson, his wife, Rosalyn, and chain shoe store owner Fred Isaacs were listening to Harriet Kilowitz, wife of paper box manufacturer Larry Kilowitz, tell them that she and her husband had just installed a security system and, for its control number, had decided upon the last four digits of their telephone number.

Watching Leo move among his guests, playing butler while their actual "man" supervised the meal preparations in the kitchen, Loring wondered when would be the best time to have a private word with him. Sid Lieb's presence was inhibiting. If Sid were to notice him and Leo absent themselves from the party for even a few minutes, he might guess (scornfully?) what they were talking about. But then again, so what? Tomorrow night would be too late, and Leo's office tomorrow morning was too iffy; he had never seen Leo's business persona, and, for all he knew, it could be a difficult one.

No, it had to be this evening, and reasonably early, at that, because later on, Leo would be too drunk and sleepy to be coherent.

Loring gravitated, as he often did, to the small black-and-white pencil drawing that unobtrusively hung on a wall near the entrance hall. It was of a tree and was signed "Adolfo Belimbau." Leo had had it for years, dismissed it as "a crappy little thing, no colors, I bought from this farmer outside of Naples for twenty bucks." Loring liked the naïve, tentative pencil strokes, the soft finger shading on the trunk of the tree.

As he sipped his drink and studied the drawing, Congressman Berger came over and said hello to him. Berger was an affable, clean-cut man of about thirty-nine, with a blow-dried look. Born upstate, near Rochester, he had carpetbagged himself into Kingsborough Beach.

"Great to see you again, Loring," he said, shaking Loring's hand. "Where have you been hiding?"

Loring had written speeches for Norman Berger during both of his election campaigns, for nothing. The congressman's gratitude each time had been profound enough to have his office send the Neiman family printed invitations to the swearing-in following each election. And, in between elections, all of Berger's regular political mailings. But, except for the occasional dinner party like this one, there wasn't much personal contact.

Loring said, "Where have I been hiding? Here, among your constituency."

Judith Lieb interrupted them, with her usual lack of ceremony. She told Loring he had been drafted; he was now co-captain of the Neighborhood Watch.

"*Co*-captain?" he asked.

"Yes with Elizabeth Blaug." She grinned lasciviously. When Congressman Berger had drifted away, Judith said, "I want you to know how sorry I am about yesterday, I finally twisted it out of Sid and Loring he's just that way period, a very peculiar man with ethics all his own, thinks lending people money corrupts them."

"Don't worry about it, Judith, it's—"

"Please try to understand and don't hate him he feels very bad about it, he loves you, we both love you."

During dinner, Loring was seated next to Naomi Berger. While her husband was busy with his partner on the left, Naomi—a doll-like, strikingly pretty woman—told Loring that the congressman was interested in having his biography written.

"We want you to write it, Loring."

"I'm flattered, Naomi. For how much?"

She looked surprised. "For a percentage of the sale of the book, I suppose. Isn't that the way it works?"

"Sometimes," he replied, "when the book is about a major public figure."

"Well?" Now she was astonished. "Norman is a *great* congressman! He's on two important committees now, and has been to Israel four times and even told off Arafat, on French TV, one time. Didn't you know all that?"

"I don't even watch American TV, Naomi. With all due respect, no writer who needs to make a living can afford to spend two years writing a biography about a young second-term congressman. Unless, maybe," he added jokingly, "he murders his wife."

Naomi Berger abruptly turned away. Loring finished his dinner.

An hour later, at the bar, he found himself face to face with Leo.

"Leo, can I speak to you for a second? I need a favor. That is, I've got a problem. . . ."

Leo smiled. Hard. "You got a problem, boychick? Well, *I* got a problem, too."

Loring looked at him quizzically.

"My problem is, one of my guests was insulted here tonight. And guess who did it?" Still smiling. "You."

Loring flushed. "You're not talking about Naomi Berger . . . ?"

"I'm talking Naomi Berger, whose husband is United States Congressman Norman Henry Berger. A very important man, to me, at least. You know why? Because next year he goes on the House Banking Committee, and in my racket, I need friends on committees like that. Why do you think he's here, because his wife has good tits? Wrong."

"Leo, I . . . I'm sorry. I might have been a little caustic, but I didn't think I was insulting. Her approach to me was just so . . . idiotic, you know. . . ."

"She's a wife." Leo pinched Loring's cheek, hard. "Now

85

have a drink." He started away, then turned and said, without the smile, "Don't make me lose trust in you."

Loring went to the guest lavatory. Sandy saw him about to try the door, and told him it was taken. She suggested he use one of the upstairs bathrooms.

He thanked her and went upstairs.

While splashing cold water on his face, he realized that Leo's lecture had been a restrained one and he was much angrier than he had appeared to be. Under normal circumstances, Loring's only dignified move would have been to leave, go home. But this night, even though there wasn't a chance in hell that he could reraise the subject of his problem, he did not want to end the evening on that note. Nor did he intend to attempt an apology to Naomi.

Loring stepped out of the bathroom and headed for the stairway. Just as he was about to descend it, he paused. Farther up the hall the door to the master bedroom stood open.

Not knowing why, he walked to it, slowly, his hands in his pockets. He peered in. Leo's huge bureau was then in view.

A magnificent dark-wood bureau, with a fiddleback grain on its double doors, fluted posts on the sides and a hand-carved capital piece along the top.

A stupendous bureau.

The Chase Manhattan Bank of bureaus.

There was no one else on the bedroom floor at the moment.

A feeling, one he would best remember as an angry, childish recklessness, took him.

He moved quickly to the bureau. Holding the pewter knobs by their very edges, he opened its doors. Inside, a center section was comprised of three small personal drawers. Using the side of one finger he slid open the topmost one. It held Leo's checkbooks and passports and many rings of many keys. He closed it and opened the second drawer. A collection of silk ascots. A four-inch-thick sheaf of hundred-dollar bills.

With no perceptible hesitation, he cut part of the sheaf and stuffed it into his pants pocket.

The third drawer. A tray holding a million cuff links and shirt studs and collar pins and tie tacks. Alongside of it a tangle of wristwatches, a dozen at least, mostly gold.

He grabbed two watches at random and slipped them into an inside jacket pocket.

Then he closed the drawer, shut the double doors and walked out of the room.

Carefully, slowly, holding on to the banister because he was made dizzy by the blood pounding through his neck, he went downstairs to rejoin the party.

Leo was ceremoniously warming the brandy he had discovered on his last trip to Europe, singing its praises as he did. Loring hated brandy but accepted the snifter that Leo offered him.

His hand fluttering like a hummingbird, he drank it. Belted it. It went quickly to his head, but did little to mitigate his nervousness. He wanted to leave—the bulges in two of his pockets felt like brand-new warts on his nose—but instinct told him he needed to spend at least a few more minutes there. A few apparently relaxed minutes. He plunked himself down on a sofa, the picture of comfort and satiety, among Assemblyman Pringle, Burt Klastorin and Elias Shapp. They seemed pleased that Loring had joined them, tried to include him in the conversation. Loring pretended to listen. He toyed with an ear of the family's cocker spaniel as the dog lay alongside of the sofa.

At one point, Loring saw Leo dash upstairs. His heart all but quit for the whole time Leo was gone. In three or four minutes, though, Leo came down, still smiling, looking nothing at all like a robbery victim.

Finally, although it was only twenty minutes later, Arnie and Rosalyn Martinson announced that since tomorrow was a labor day, they had to go home. Silently thanking God, Loring now felt able to leave. He looked around, caught Leo's eye and signaled to him that he, too, had to go.

"You, too, boychick? Since when do *you* work?" Leo said, laughing.

Loring said good night to everyone, and Leo saw him to the door.

"Call me sometime, boychick. I'll take you to my gym. Knockout broads there. Forty-year-olds with bodies like twenties. No shit."

"Thanks, Leo. I will."

Not a word about my problem. Fuck him.

Loring left.

Escaped.

By the light of his bed lamp he counted the cash. There were thirty-seven one-hundred-dollar bills. That amazing clump in the drawer must have held about twenty thousand dollars!

Then he looked at the watches. Real Leo Goldstein watches: one was a Concord Mariner, solid gold, with a gold link band. The face was square and outlined with about forty one-point, full-cut diamonds. The other watch was a Piaget, fourteen-karat gold with a round black face, probably onyx. There were diamonds instead of numbers.

Superwatches.

He put it all in the drawer of his nightstand, then lay awake for a while, thinking and winding down. He felt drained by tension, much the way he felt after a couple of hours of writing anything.

But for the first time since the first chapter of *Quarantine*, he had the sense of having really succeeded at something. *Would guilt come in the morning?*

Probably.

As he sank slowly into sleep, he recalled a time when he walked three blocks back to a store because he realized the guy had given him fifteen cents too much change. . . .

Tuesday, May 22 _____

"DADDY! WAKE UP! We're gonna be late!"

Katie and Briana's tiny voices, tiny knocking outside of his door. Ted Brown on the clock radio. It was twenty minutes to eight. He dragged himself out of bed, into the bathroom, splashed cold water on his face.

The night before suddenly shifted into focus, and with it a wave of disbelief.

He wondered at what he had done. Or marveled at it.

Loring tried to test his feelings. It was morning, the vulnerable time, the armor still leaning over there against the wall.

Exactly how do I feel? Afraid? Guilty? Remorseful?

More questions, tumbling through his head as he hurried into his clothes:

Did Leo, or anyone, think I behaved peculiarly last night? Or that I left too early? Was there any way Leo could connect our aborted conversation, my words about a "problem," with the loss, if he's discovered it? If he ever discovers it? Did I mention the word "money"? No. Should I keep the cash, but somehow get the watches back into his house?

Well? Do I feel afraid?

Guilty?

Remorseful?

None of the above.

He felt safer than he had all week. A few thousand dollars safer.

When he got back from the school the phone was ringing. It was Carlin.

"Mr. Neiman, today is Tuesday, the twenty-second. I'll be here until four o'clock. What time can I ex—"

"Mr. Carlin, would part of it help?"

"Part payment? No, sir. A cashier's check for the full amount."

"I don't have it."

"You don't?"

"No."

"I see. Then—"

"Enjoy my house."

"I'm afraid there's nothing more to be said, Mr. Neiman."

"Yes there is, Carlin. Namely, that you are a piss-ant cocksucking fucking professional leech bastard. And I would appreciate your calling back after three so you can tell my two little girls they're going to have dinner in the gutter in front of their house next week."

Carlin was silent.

"Will you do that for me, Carlin? You miserable shit-eater?"

Carlin sighed. "I've been called names worse than that, Mr. Neiman. I even had my collarbone broken once, right outside of a courtroom, by a foreclosee." He added, "I hope you feel better."

"I don't."

"I'm sorry, then," Carlin said. There was a pause, and when Carlin spoke again, his voice was lower. "Would some more time really help you, Mr. Neiman, or are you just—"

"Stalling? Jerking off? Another day won't help, but a few weeks might. Why?"

Carlin answered slowly and softly. "We have over four hundred cases in this office. Sometimes papers get lost."

Loring played that back. He felt a sudden rush of hope, wondered if he really knew where Carlin was going with this. "I . . . I'm sure they do, Mr. Carlin, big office like that. Things sort of . . . slip through cracks."

"Exactly," Carlin said. "They slip through cracks. For just a little while, then they turn up again."

"Uh, what . . . causes them to get lost?"

Carlin's voice got even lower. "Two."

"Two? Two what?" Loring was whispering now, also.

"K."

"K." A little shock. "I see. For . . . how much time?"

"Three, four weeks."

"Four weeks is better."

"Friday, June twenty-second."

"Okay," said Loring. "Now . . . how, when, where?"

"Noon today. Corner of Montague and Court. Front of the Stanhope Grill. I'll be holding a *Wall Street Journal* and *Newsweek.*"

"Okay."

"You can definitely do this?"

"Yes."

They hung up.

That's why he kept pushing for the money, giving me time: to set this up for himself?

The guy's good at it! Must add ten grand a year to his salary! Two thousand bucks.

He realized, with a thrill, that for the first time in years he could afford something.

Loring parked in a lot around the corner from the Stanhope Grill at three minutes after noon.

He was surprised when he saw the man who was holding a folded copy of *The Wall Street Journal* with *Newsweek* superimposed in front of it. He had expected Carlin, by the sound of his voice, to be older and thinner. Instead, he was only about thirty or so, and rather chubby.

Feeling that Carlin would want the briefest possible contact, Loring readied the envelope that held twenty of Leo Goldstein's hundred-dollar bills.

"Mr. Carlin, I presume?"

The younger man looked at Loring, smiled faintly. "Mr. Neiman."

Loring held out the envelope. "Don't spend it all in one place."

Carlin took it and walked away.

Loring bought himself a bloody Mary at the bar of the Stanhope Grill, which was cool and dark and beginning to fill with lunch patrons. He rarely drank anything before five o'clock, but felt this was a special sort of occasion. The pressure was off him, at least the heaviest pressure, for a month. Of course, the month would pass quickly, but it offered some time to think, to make better plans. Maybe to organize another book idea. A good one, a blockbuster, as Elliot Silverbach had said, that Marlow & Roth would want so desperately to publish that they'd agree to forgive the advance on *Quarantine* and start a whole new ball game with Loring.

He felt the familiar, pleasant, bowel-deep thrill he always felt when a plan of action was beginning to form, a good idea was close at hand. He sipped at his drink and tried to identify that idea in his brain and isolate it so it could begin developing.

Within fifteen minutes, he realized that either it was being coy with him, or there was no such idea at all.

On the way home, Loring stopped at his bank on Ocean Avenue and deposited the remaining seventeen hundred dollars into his checking account so he could take some of the bills out of the shoe box that night and pay them.

He also decided not to return the watches.

Wednesday, May 23 _____

THE MORNING SKY was colored a gunmetal gray, promising rain. Loring had ordained foul-weather gear for the girls, and Briana already wore her yellow slicker, which she loved. Katie, however, had refused to wear hers, preferring, instead, to roll it up and carry it.

As they all got into the car, Katie noticed that Loring was also carrying an article of clothing, an old gray plaid soft hat he'd bought years earlier at Abercrombie.

"Why do you have a hat, Daddy?" she asked. "You never wear a hat."

"It's going to rain, and I'll be out part of the day," he told her. "Got to take care of what hair I've got left, you know."

"Rain is bad for hair?" Briana asked.

"According to many experts."

"That's weird, Daddy," Katie opined, with a pitying look at him. *"Mucho* weird."

Loring wondered how mucho *more* weird she'd think he was if she knew he had slipped a pair of sunglasses into one of the inside pockets of his corduroy blazer.

Not to mention the two wristwatches in the other.

After dropping the girls at school, he continued on up Gerrold Street and turned left onto Bay Boulevard. The view toward the Channel was obscure and runny in the wet air. With their ceiling very near to zero, the sea gulls were doing their maneuvering low over the surface of the water, making only short dives for garbage and the occasional fish.

Loring was going to look for a jewelry store, preferably a large and busy one, but he had no idea which neighborhood to try. It wasn't until he reached Coney Island Avenue that he decided to take the Belt Parkway into the city, to the midtown diamond center.

The way to start was to find out exactly how much the watches were worth.

Wearing the hat and sunglasses, he wandered the block on West Forty-seventh Street between Fifth and Sixth avenues, trying to select one of the hundreds of jewelry stores and marts and booths-with-marts and counters-within-booths, and approach someone for an appraisal. And he wanted that someone to be friendly and benign in appearance.

The man was young, wore a skullcap. "Yes, these are real, all right. We retail them for about five thousand, each."

Loring was pleased. He didn't know they were worth quite that much.

"I see," he said. "Very good. Well, how much do I owe you?"

"For what? The appraisal?" The young man smiled. "Nothing."

"Well, thank you very much," Loring said. Then, "Do . . . you buy watches? Would you be interested in buying these?"

The jeweler cocked his head. "I'll tell you something. I wouldn't buy these watches from you if . . . *afilo az mein eigenah momma volt dir arein beim handt*. You know Yiddish?"

"Not much."

"What I said was 'Not even if my own mother brought you in here by the hand.'"

The rain had begun to fall. Loring hunkered his shoulders against the wet chill and began walking a couple of blocks farther west. It seemed to him that Eighth Avenue was the last place he could recall seeing a pawnshop.

There were no other customers in the shop. Behind a barred window sat the pawnbroker, a thin, Dickensianlooking man with a pepper-and-salt beard. Loring felt the man looked like Carlin had sounded. The broker put down his newspaper and nodded at Loring.

"Hi," Loring said. "I have a couple of wristwatches I would like to pawn." He fished them out of his pocket. "These." He laid them on the slate counter.

The pawnbroker lowered the loupe that was attached to his eyeglasses and examined the watches. Loring looked around, feigning nonchalance. The walls were hung with things, pawned articles, he guessed, that were now being offered for sale by default. A lot of musical instruments, he noted—guitars, saxophones, bass fiddles. But then, these were the environs of Broadway.

The broker looked up. "I used to be a jeweler. It still amazes me that intrinsically—the diamonds, the gold—these things are worth maybe a few hundred dollars. But as a watch, to keep time, to adorn the wrist and proclaim the status of the wearer . . . well, the craftsmanship is what you pay for." He bent to the watches again. "I still enjoy beautiful things."

Who gives a shit? Loring did not like this man, even if he did fancy himself a poet. And his breath would defoliate Central Park.

Finally the pawnbroker said, "I can lend you fifteen hundred dollars on each."

Loring said, "Eighteen hundred."

"Fifteen hundred."

Loring nodded. He tried not to show his delight.

The broker drew a ledger over to him and picked up a pen. "Driver's license, please."

Loring was taken by surprise. "Driver's license? You need a driver's license?"

The man squinted at him. "You expect me to lend you money without knowing who I'm lending it to?" He slid the watches back to Loring. "Especially as you are wearing sunglasses at an inappropriate time."

They stared at each other.

The bastard thinks I'm a thief. Loring was mortified. He picked up the watches and headed for the door.

"Wait." It was not a command to stop. It was softer, oilier. Loring looked back at the pawnbroker. "I've got a friend," the man said, "who you might take them to. He buys merchandise like that."

"Watches?" Loring asked, dully.

The pawnbroker shrugged. "Anything of value. In distress circumstances." He leaned on the counter, chin in hand. "From people who like to protect their privacy."

Loring said, "Oh. Ah . . . where is your friend?"

"Do you know Brooklyn?"

"Sure," Loring responded. "Fairly well."

"All right. Bay Ridge. Farraday Street." He gave Loring a piece of paper and a pencil. "Write it down: 1443 Farraday." Loring did. "It's a big secondhand store. Just ask for Cody. I'm Lewis."

He sat in his car and regarded the place called *Farraday New & Used—Estates Bought & Sold,* wondered if the door under that sign could actually be a gateway to the underworld.

Jesus. What the hell am I doing here? Why can't I just sell books, like other authors?

The rain was coming down heavily now. Gusts of wind rocked neon signs and sent a garbage can rattling down the street. Under ordinary circumstances he would have waited for it to abate somewhat, but extremely bad weather puts a special cast of characters on the streets: those on desperate business.

He made a run for the store entrance. Soaking wet, he opened it. A little bell tinkled.

Nice touch.

You're a writer. It'll be an interesting experience.

Inside, he wiped the water from his sunglasses, put them back on. The large, poorly lighted place was jammed to the ceiling with old furniture and exhausted appliances. It smelled dank, like a cigar factory his father had once taken him to. A young Puerto Rican leaned against a table, emptying some cartons of metal fittings.

Loring asked him, "Is Cody here?"

"Hey, Cody, guy iss here!"

A man stepped from the gloom at the back of the store and came toward Loring.

"What can I do for ya?"

"Ah, Lewis sent me. . . ."

Cody reversed direction, beckoning Loring to follow. "Yeh. He called me. Hat an' sunglasses. Come in the back."

Loring followed him to a small, cluttered rolltop desk. Cody was a bulky man, muscle gone to fat. He had short dirty-blond hair. As they drew into the light of the desk lamp, Loring saw that he was about his own age. And he had hard eyes.

"Rainin' enough for ya?"

"Quite," Loring replied, trying to control his voice. All of his adult life he'd had the habit of falling into the speech pattern of whomever he was talking to, semiconsciously, a way of getting closer. This time, however, he wanted to keep a distance; he spoke carefully, neatly. "Lewis told me you might be interested in purchasing my watches."

"Maybe. Lemme see." As Loring handed him the watches, Cody asked, "Got a name?"

"Mike."

"Got a last name?"

"No."

Cody snorted. "Okay." He looked the watches over, turning them in his hands, peering at God knew what as he angled them into the light. "Makin' sure these are the same watches Lewis seen. He's the appraiser, I ain't."

"Oh, they are," Loring assured him.

Cody winked. "I know. Like Lewis said, this one got some dirt on the case right here, see, an' this one got a little scar on the fifth link down. Yeh, I'll take 'em." He looked at Loring. "A grand each."

Loring protested, weakly. "These are five-thousand-dollar watches."

"Not for me. For me they're twenty-five-hundred-dollar watches. I need a hundred and fifty percent markup." He indicated the room. "Big overhead."

"Thanks," Loring said, "but no thanks." He started to rise. "I want to sell them, not give them away."

Cody grabbed Loring's forearm in a surprisingly powerful grip. Without seeming to strain, he slowly pulled Loring back down into his chair.

"Take it easy, Mike. You wanna deal, so let's deal! How much you lookin' for?"

Loring thought for a moment. The unexpected demonstration of Cody's strength had made him feel even queasier than before. Frightened him, in fact. "Fifteen hundred each," he finally said. His mouth was dry.

Without response, Cody opened the long top drawer of his desk. In it, bolted to the drawer, was a green metal lockbox, which he opened with a key from the ring attached to his belt. Like Leo's drawer, it was stuffed with money. He counted out three thousand dollars in tens and twenties, and handed it to Loring. "I'm easy."

"Thank you," Loring said. He shoved it into his pants pocket without recounting it.

Cody put the watches into the box, locked it and closed the desk drawer. "Spic steals." Then he looked at Loring and smiled again. His eyes were really like marbles. "It's a business doin' pleasure with ya, Mike." He offered his ham of a hand. Reluctantly, Loring shook it.

"Is that it?" Loring asked.

"Sure. What do ya want, a 1099 form?" Cody asked, with another, bigger, snort.

Loring got to his feet, this time Cody allowing him to, and they walked to the front door.

"Got anythin' else? I c'n always use stuff like this."

"No," Loring replied. "That's it."

"If ya ever do, bring it to me. I'm easy, right? If it's watches, rings, jewelry, silver, anythin' like that, ya gotta show it to Lewis first."

"I understand," Loring said. Just before he left, he could not resist asking, "How do you know I'm not a cop?"

"Cop!" Cody responded. "I don't give a shit if you're the fuckin' commissioner. You see me break any laws?" As he opened the door for Loring, he added, "Anyway, half my suppliers are cops."

The sun was coming through, and the Belt Parkway was beginning to dry. He realized he was still wearing his sunglasses and hat, and the hat had begun to smell of wetness. He took them off and put them into the glove compartment.

Nearing home, he was feeling better, cooling out.

All cash. No taxes. Between Leo's money and Leo's watches, Loring had realized sixty-seven hundred dollars. Like earning, maybe, ten thousand. And all, counting stealing time and fencing time, in just a few hours. Three thousand of it he would put aside toward the second mortgage.

He wondered if Cody could have seen his license plate as he drove away. *No.*

Tonight he would take the girls to Zellen's, on Brighton Beach Avenue. They loved the baby lamb chops, the carrots and peas.

Robin Hood. I steal from the rich and give to the poor. Except I'm the poor.

God, is half the world crooked?

He stopped at his grocery, the little Italian grocery at which he'd been shopping for the past few months because they gave him credit. The store had dunned him once or twice, but they never cut him off.

He settled his bill with them, four hundred and fifty-three dollars, with cash. Mario was so grateful he presented Loring with a huge Genoa salami. Loring bought some things, mostly staples, but also a few luxuries: Portuguese sardines, Danish cheese, marinated artichoke hearts, a jar of Mario's wife's homemade pasta sauce.

As he drove up Knapp Street, Kingsborough Beach appeared, across the bay, as a long, low sleeve of greenery capped by gables of red and gray and white, looking very lush and private, mist-polished in the new sun. It was still his home.

That night, after dinner, he took Katie and Briana to see the Kingsborough Beach Community Players' performance of *Fiddler on the Roof* at the Jewish Center. He'd seen the play several times before. Sitting there, in the darkness, his daughters on either side of him, listening to the familiar music, feeling relaxed, he tried once again to coax some sort of idea—a method—out of his brain.

On the other side of the auditorium, Andrew Blaug whispered heavily to his wife, "Who is 'Briana Neiman's father'?"

"What?" she said. She had been absorbed in the play. "Who? Oh, that's Loring Neiman. You've met him. Twice, I think."

"You went to a meeting with him on Sunday?"

"A meeting? Oh. Yes, I did." Fear rising, she pointed to the stage. "Andy, watch the show—"

"What happened at the police station?"

"Shhh. Nothing. The captain wasn't there, something got screwed up. I came home."

There was a shush from behind them.

"No you did not. You were gone from noon until after two. More than two hours, Liz, according to the programs Justin told me he watched on television while you were gone."

Another shush. They stopped talking.

Later, in their car, Andy asked, "What did you and he do for all that time?"

"Andy, I doubt we were . . . I was gone all that long, at all. What are you driving at?" Then, in a burst of inspiration: "Child neglect? Maria was there, and believe me, Justin was fine!"

"I'm not accusing you of child neglect, Elizabeth."

"Then what are you accusing me of?" Her voice broke.

He stared ahead through the windshield, his face wearing a painfully confused expression. "I'm just wondering how in hell you saw fit to go to a meeting at the police station in shorts and a halter that are only fit for your own backyard—not have the meeting and yet disappear with this . . . Loring Neiman for two solid hours." He looked at her. "Two solid hours with him, half-naked, with your nipples and buttocks showing?"

Loring got into bed with an anchovy and onion sandwich and thirty-odd Neighborhood Watch forms. Each member family had filled out one of the forms, and, as co-captain, he was supposed to copy and distribute them so that everyone had a complete set.

Entered on them was specific information about each family, nothing confidential, but, read in a certain context, illuminating: the names and ages of full-time and part-time members of the household, the hours of their usual coming and going, descriptions and license plate numbers of their vehicles and those of frequent visitors, the names and working hours of domestic help and gardeners, the nature and name of any special security services they might use, telephone numbers to be called in the event of an emergency, and so forth.

He had resented the responsibility when Judith thrust it upon him, considered the package of poop sheets as so much crap. But that night they seemed interesting.

Thursday, May 24 ⎯⎯⎯⎯

S HE CALLED THE moment Andy left for work.

"Loring, he's suspicious about Sunday."

"Really. What did he say?"

She told him. "My story was that you and I went to the police station but the captain had forgotten our meeting, so we just went someplace and had some coffee."

"Just you and I?"

"Yes. I didn't think it was a good idea to involve anyone else. He might check."

"Right." She had good instincts.

"He went berserk about the shorts and halter I wore."

Loring smiled at that. "You should have told him I did, too, and got them off you as fast as I could."

She asked him if there was anything new on the money front.

"It's taken a little turn for the better."

"What happened?"

"I'll tell you about it."

"The house?"

"I'll tell you about it, Liz. Not now, though."

Upstairs, at his word processor, Loring booted the Burglar file. *Gold Coast*'s four hundred dollars was still four hundred dollars.

If he could write a lot faster, get five shit assignments like this a week, he'd . . . no, *ten* pieces a week . . . he'd make four thousand bucks. That way, in ten weeks he'd have the forty grand he needed. Except he needed the forty grand in four weeks.

Twenty shit pieces a week, he'd have to write.

The file came up on the VDT screen. He read the last paragraph he'd written.

Granted, my experience wasn't as atrocious as it would have been if I or one of my daughters had been (hurt) by the burglar.

He typed

But maybe we weren't only because we weren't around when he was. Nevertheless, my family's living style

His family's living style. One kid's teeth looked like they were all in business for themselves, the other kid played piano on the kitchen table. And the father is a professional beggar.

He typed

has changed in that I am in love with Elizabeth Blaug, a reasonably contented married woman and I want her I want her more than anything but let's stick to the fucking point here:
burglars
beggars
for a minute I thought they had the same number of letters. Burglars never have to beg for anything. They just go and get it, in the American way. (Make statement here re celebration of american criminal. Thieves as celebrities etc)

Loring picked up the phone, dialed Ted Krause and asked him what the statute of limitations was on burglary.

"Let's see, I think . . . let me ask my partner. Can you hold?"

"I have nothing but time, Theodore."

Ted was gone for almost a minute.

He didn't even ask me about the foreclosure.

Back on the phone, Ted said, "Kalish says it's five years."

"Five years. Thanks." Loring paused. "While we're at it, could you ask Kalish another quickie?"

Ted sighed. "A quickie, okay."

"A burglar is caught on the premises but he doesn't have the loot in his hands. Is it still a felony?"

"I can answer that. It's a misdemeanor because they can't establish that he's a burglar. The charge would be Breaking and Entering." He added, "If they even prosecute him."

Boinie the Attoiney.

"Unless he just walked in through an open door," Loring said, "when it would simply be Trespassing, right?"

"I believe that's right, yes. Why do you want to know all this?"

None of your business, asshole. "Research, something I'm writing."

"What are you writing?"

He didn't even ask about the foreclosure.

"Thanks, Ted. Talk to you soon."

Getting dressed for the rabbi's retirement dinner that evening, Loring wondered what kind of sentences burglars were getting lately. If they catch them. And if they prosecute them.

He was seated at a table with the Liebs. Judith's seat, next to Loring's, was empty during the early part of the evening while she fluttered around the ballroom. Sidney, who seemed very friendly again, was seated on the other side of the table.

Loring was grateful for Judith's space and Sidney's distance; he didn't feel like talking.

The Goldsteins' table was right next to the Liebs'. Loring hadn't seen them since Monday night. When Leo and Sandy spotted him, they waved and smiled, the same cordial wave and smile they normally gave him. He smiled back.

Business was as usual, all around.

Liz and her husband were at a table across the room, too

far, even, for Loring and her to exchange glances, although he had seen them come in and she looked positively edible.

And where do they serve their sentences? If they catch them. And if they prosecute them. Is Sing Sing still open for business? I don't know. But Attica certainly is. But Attica is not for white, middle-class, sensitive Jewish intellectuals. There must be other places, the kind with tennis lessons.

Judith finally took her seat, next to him. She gave him a kiss on the cheek, then leaned back and surveyed him.

"Look at you gorgeous in your blue suit and red foulard tie, you look adorable, now tell me what you've been doing and who you've been doing it to, as if I can't guess?"

Gently he said, "Judith, can I disabuse you of all that, once and for all? I am not involved with her. Or any woman, for that matter."

She sucked in her cheeks.

"Honestly," he went on, lightening up a bit. "I'm waiting for you. The minute you get safely through menopause, let me know."

"You're probably lying in your teeth," she said. "I wanted to put their table next to ours but she wouldn't let me, which is a good sign, so I'm expecting some major excitement from you two, the neighborhood has been too straight lately."

The ballroom quieted. Rabbi Rabin blessed the bread, then began welcoming everyone, Shonkoff, Isaacs, Martinson, Kilowitz, missing not a name. When he got to Loring, he said, "Mr. Loring Neiman, the celebrated writer, respected, honored and exalted by his profession, and yet one of us, a neighbor, a friend, a congregant"—like all good clerics, the rabbi said everything three times—"who has, on so many occasions, readily, willingly and ably given of his time, his prodigious talents and his knowledge on behalf of our members." He referred to Loring's lectures to the Temple Sisterhood on his work as a writer.

Loring wondered if Liz was smiling at all this.

As the rabbi droned on through dozens of other names, Loring, bemused, stared at the back of Sidney Lieb's shaven head. He thought, *Say it's the middle of the night. I am awakened by a sound. I get up, find Sidney, along with Leo Goldstein—the two men I now dislike the most in Kingsborough Beach—rifling my desk drawers. Accomplices, come to rob me. I grapple with them, subdue them both, tie them up.*

Now, I would be angry. I would question their character, their judgment, even their mental health. Then I would remember their families, their children, their standing in the community. Their Jewishness, their landsleit.

Embarrassment hideous. Indignation profound. But do I, could I, call the police and have them arrested, prosecute them, send them to prison? Even a tennis one?

Of course not.

Out in the lobby, when the evening was over, Fred Isaacs caught Loring's eye and beckoned to him. Fred was with a couple, a tall, moustached man in a bad dinner jacket who looked familiar, and a very short woman with a sweet face and teased hair, who didn't.

"Loring, you remember Captain Costello, commander of the 65th Precinct?"

Loring's scalp tingled.

As an afterthought, Isaacs added, "and his lovely wife, Lucy." To Costello, he said, "Carroll, this is Loring Neiman, the writer."

They shook hands.

Costello said, "I heard Rabbi Rabin speaking of you tonight, Mr. Neiman. And this doesn't reflect on your reputation, but rather on my provincialism—but what kind of things do you write?"

"Books, Captain. About anything I think will sell. I'm a thoroughgoing commercial artist."

"I don't blame you!" said Costello.

"Oh, you're so lucky!" chirped Mrs. Costello, Lucy. "I write, sometimes, too! Maybe you'd look at some of my stories sometime, Mr. Neiman?"

"I'd be happy to, Mrs. Costello."

She beamed at him, Fred Isaacs beamed at everyone and there was nothing more to say. Loring was about to excuse himself when he saw the Blaugs approaching, led by Andy, who did not look sociable. Liz's face was tightly set.

"Pardon me," Andy said, "but aren't you Captain Costello?"

An alarming thought struck Loring: Blaug was about to bring up last Sunday's non-meeting. Liz's expression confirmed it.

Costello replied, "Yes, I am. And you, sir, are . . . ?"

"Dr. Blaug. This is my wife, Elizabeth. I understand you were supposed to meet with her and Mr. Neiman last Sunday. And that you simply forgot about it."

Costello's smile faded. He had no idea what the fuck this guy was talking about, but was embarrassed to say so. Besides, he had no desire to explore it, within earshot of Fred Isaacs and other high-rolling Kingsborough Beachers.

So he shrugged. "I'm sorry, and I apologize to all concerned, Dr. . . . " He was lousy with names. "But sometimes, in a big, busy precinct . . ."

Blaug turned to Loring. With a simulated smile, he asked, "Do you think the captain seems contrite enough about it?"

"Contrite enough for me, Andy."

Andy pressed. "More importantly, does he seem even remotely knowledgeable about it?"

Oh, shit. He's out for blood. Loring said, "It's a big, busy precinct, Andy."

Liz had been exerting a gentle but steady pull on Andy's arm. He looked at Liz, then at Costello again, seeming to smell collusion. "I know," Andy finally said, "it's a very busy precinct."

There was a beat. *Is this as far as he's taking it?* Loring turned to the police officer. "Which reminds me, Captain Cos—oh, first of all, is it the Italian Cost*ello* or the Irish *Cos*tello?"

"Neither," the captain replied. "It's the Spanish Cos-*tayo*. But Costello will do."

"Ah. Okay. Could I ask you something? I'm co-captain of our Neighborhood Watch," Loring said, with a smile, "and I wonder if you could sit down with me for a minute or two while you're here and very briefly sketch me in on your patrol system here in The Beach?"

The commander of the 65th Precinct was relieved. He led Loring to a settee and they sat down for a few cordial minutes. Fred Isaacs, also relieved, slowly ushered the Blaugs to the front door.

At eleven-thirty Loring started walking home from the Jewish Center. At the corner of Levon and Dale, Radio Motor Patrol car number 1165 came slowly toward him, its spotlight running across lawns, poking around on porches, probing up driveways. It seemed he wasn't finished with cops for the evening.

As the RMP drew closer to Loring, the spotlight suddenly turned and bore straight into his face. His heart leaped. He stopped in his tracks, shielding his eyes with a hand.

The RMP rolled to a stop. Both doors opened and two young, hatless police officers popped out.

"Stand right there, please!" One of them stayed by the car while the other walked slowly toward Loring, a hand resting heavily on the checkered grip of his holstered .38.

"Live around here?" he asked.

Loring replied, "Yes, of course."

The cop believed him. Loring looked right. Still, "Got some I.D.?"

"Sure," Loring said. He turned his body so they could watch his hand as he fished his wallet out of his back pocket. "Did I do something wrong, Officer?" He handed over his driver's license.

The cop didn't answer.

"Is that a tough question?" Loring asked.

The young policeman glanced reprovingly at Loring, then examined the license in the glare of the spotlight. He read Loring's name and address aloud (it crossed Loring's mind that cops always read I.D. out loud), then compared the description on the license with Loring's appearance.

Loring wondered if anyone on the block was watching all this from a bedroom window. He forced a smile.

"Come on, fellows, what's up? I'm a writer. Let's make a story out of this. It's the most interesting thing that's happened to me since an hour ago, when I had dinner with Captain Cos-*tayo*."

"Who?"

"Costello. Carroll Costello, your commanding officer."

The cop handed Loring's license back to him. To his partner, he said, "He knows the captain." He was bored again.

The other one averted the beam of light to the ground, said to Loring (with a tinge of respect), "You're a writer? Of what? Stories? Newspapers?"

"Stories, right," Loring said. "All about cops and robbers."

"Yeh?" The first cop laughed and pointed to his partner. "Put this guy in one. Call him John, the Hot Dog!"

John, with a self-conscious grin, pointed back. "This guy's the character, not me! I could tell you stuff about him'd curl your hair!" They got back in their car. "Sorry we bothered you. Have a nice night."

He got under a hot shower.

Hey you, hands up!

Me, Officer? What is this, Nazi Germany, a man can't stroll his own neighborhood?

Bullshit, mister.

Bullshit, is it? I had dinner with Captain Cos-tayo. He's going to love hearing "Bullshit"!

Captain Costello? Gee, I'm sorry, sir. Hey, you're Loring Neiman, the writer, ain't you? Excuse me, sir. Have a nice night.

He sat at his desk, in the dark. He felt good, rather good.

From his window he looked at the Pincus house. Then he closed his eyes, let his mind roam the neighborhood: Kilowitz. Isaacs. Mushkin. He looked at the Pincus house again. There were interiors he was more familiar with, but the proximity was ideal, the entry was obvious.

The daylight hours would be out of the question; I'd need the dark, the very dark.

Irving Pincus had volunteered much more information on his Neighborhood Watch poop sheet than it had requested, including the fact that he and his wife went to sleep especially early on Tuesday nights, because on Wednesday mornings they always got up at six to do their gardening.

He looked at his wall calendar. It was Thursday, May twenty-fourth. The following Tuesday was the night before a new moon. Which meant almost no moon at all.

Presently he got up, went into his room and got into bed.
Could I do it.

How. Would I need tools. What tools. Am I in physical shape. What would I wear. What are burglars wearing this season. My jogging suit. No, it's yellow, too bright . . . I'd stand out like a great big fucking firefly. Something dark. I'd need dark. . . .

Friday, May 25 _____

THWACK THE YOUNG guy returned Loring's angle shot with one of his *thwack* own and then pulled a slick, dancy little block to the bargain. The black ball ran off the court, out of range. Loring was sucking in the morning air like a jet engine. He hadn't played in months.

Reach for the sky! What are you doing here at this hour?

Shhh! I thought I saw an intruder, someone, heading into the Pincuses' driveway!

Good story, asshole! Get 'em up!

Let's ring the Pincuses' bell, wake them up, see which one of us is the asshole.

Thwack on the young guy's next serve the ball spun like a gyro; Loring almost tore his back in half getting to it, managed a bad drop shot, but the young guy, smiling all the while, picked it up *thwack* with a smashing killer shot. Loring went for it but missed, flattening himself against the wall at thirty miles an hour.

Hands up!

Hands up? Look, asshole, I'm Loring Neiman, the writer. The New York Times Magazine? *I can make more fucking trouble for you, have your badge by noon tomorrow. While you're standing there with your head up your ass, my neighbors could be getting robbed!*

You're right, sir. Which way did they go?

That way. I'll help you. . . .

The young guy took all three games, 7-1, 7-1, 6-0. Loring

wet his towel at the water fountain and, putting it over his face, sprawled full-length on a bench.

After a while he got up from the bench, peeled off his handball glove and pulled his sweat pants on over his shorts.

That afternoon, still on an oxygen high, Loring went to five different stores in four different neighborhoods: Flatbush, Bensonhurst, Canarsie and Coney Island.

He purchased five items, one in each of the stores. They were a small wood chisel, a short-handled ball peen hammer, a roll of black electrical tape, a tiny penlight and a chamois cloth.

Then he went to a camera shop for a pair of film editor's gloves. They came only in white cotton, so he went to a supermarket for an envelope of black cotton dye.

At a men's-and-boys' store on Avenue U he bought a cheap pair of dark blue canvas deck shoes and a black nylon sports bag, the soft kind.

Finally, at a do-it-yourself plastics center on Cropsey Avenue, he purchased a square-yard sheet (the minimum size they would sell him) of .015-gauge styrene, clear.

A crook's tour of Brooklyn. Everything but the last item could have been procured within blocks of his house. If there were such a thing, and they ever heard about it, he'd be the laughingstock of the Burglars' Association. But covering all that geography made him feel safer. And the stop-and-start nature of the afternoon forced him to roll everything over and over in his mind, to test his plan, as well as his resolve to go through with it; there were moments during the afternoon when it made eminent good sense, others when it seemed idiotic.

He wrapped many layers of the electrical tape on the face, then the ball, of the hammer. He did the same to the top of the chisel handle. Then he cut a two-by-three-inch piece of the styrene and stashed the large remaining piece in the top of his supplies closet.

After carefully washing his fingerprints from the hammer, chisel, penlight and piece of styrene, he put on the cotton gloves and rolled all the items up in the chamois cloth. Then he tucked the whole thing into the sports bag.

He hefted it once or twice.

The Pincus Kit.

There was still room in it for a pair of large Pincus candlestick holders.

He took off the gloves and immersed them in a bucket containing the black dye solution, and put it on the floor of the closet.

Later, on his way to pick Katie and Briana up from school, it struck him that maybe he should wear a ski mask.

Should he? To be seen *in flagrante delicto* would be tantamount to being caught; his face was known. But to be caught while wearing a mask would leave absolutely no ambiguity to the situation; there could be no denying what he was about.

No mask.

No, Raddit, no!

He smiled. That was what Briana had once said, at age twenty-three months, when she saw Bugs Bunny about to put on a fright mask that she knew would scare the hell out of sweet Elmer Fudd.

Tuesday, May 29 _____

A<small>T ABOUT THREE-THIRTY</small>, while Katie was talking home-work on the phone with Eddie Kilowitz, Loring asked Briana if she would like to take a walk with him. She would go anywhere, anytime.

"Where, Daddy?"

We're going to case the joint. "Oh, just around the block."

At the corner they turned left onto Bay Boulevard, then left again onto Levon Street, the Pincuses' street.

He slowed their pace. She began skipping ahead of him, but as they drew closer to the Pincus house, he called her back and took her hand. He wanted to be seen, unmistakably, as walking with her.

Loring was disappointed that the Pincuses were not outside. He spotted an old shopping newspaper, brown from the sun, lying folded on their front lawn.

Quietly he suggested, "Baby, would you like to bring Mr. and Mrs. Pincuses' paper in to them?"

Briana ran to it, picked it up and marched to the front door.

He hung back, at the sidewalk.

"Ring the bell," he said. She did.

When Miriam Pincus came to the door, she was surprised and delighted to see them.

"Ketzalah!"

Briana, twisting the little newspaper in her hands, smiled bashfully.

Miriam bent and kissed her. She wanted to pick Briana up and hug her, but she wasn't that much taller than the six-year-old. "You came to visit us?"

Loring sauntered up the walk. "Not exactly, Miriam. We were just taking a walk and noticed the paper. Briana wanted to bring it to you."

Briana was peering beyond Miriam into the house.

"What a sweet ketzalah! The paper I don't need, but just for that"—she looked at Loring—"can I give her a nice homemade brownie and a glass of milk? Do you have time?"

Loring looked down at Briana, who was beaming hopefully up at him. Smiling, he said, "I think you made a sale, Miriam."

Inside, Miriam yelled upstairs for her husband. "Irving, come down, we have company!" To Briana and Loring, she said, "Come in the kitchen."

The house had a familiar old-Jewish smell, like the homes of Loring's grandparents. He imagined hardly a thing had been changed or replaced since the couple first set up life there. Everything looked brown. Not the "earth colors" of their younger neighbors, but the sepia of age and wear.

Miriam led them toward the kitchen by way of the dining room.

And there they are, dead ahead.

As advertised.

The twenty-thousand-dollar candlestick holders, standing side by side, taller than I had envisaged them.

He paid them no apparent attention, but as he ushered Briana past the buffet table on which they reposed, he was intensely aware of their eighteenth-century silver magnificence, accented with wide bands of hand enameling in what he took to be the Russian style. They thrilled him.

Irving Pincus, in house slippers, carrying his newspaper, joined them in the kitchen. Loring felt that the couple looked older in their natural habitat than they did when they were out. And with that observation came a prick of shame.

Irving, unconcerned with what circumstance had brought the Neimans into his house for the first time in three years, immediately launched into a conversational monologue, directed at anyone, about the Secretary of Defense, and how rotten he was to Israel.

Briana was installed at the kitchen table, a brownie and a glass of milk set before her. Loring knew it would take her only a minute or two to scarf it up, after which they should quickly leave.

While Irving regaled the room about U.S. foreign policy, Loring, nodding assent all the while, noted that the kitchen door, which was open, had a new-looking dead-bolt lock as well as the old spring-latch one. But there was no evidence of any electronic alarm device.

Finished with her brownie and milk, Briana was as anxious to go as Loring was.

"Don't be strangers!" Miriam called from the front door.

"We won't," Loring said.

Walking home, he was totally convinced of the efficacy of his plan for the evening.

Okay, mister, reach!

Stop, Officer, I've got to talk to this man! Loring, darling, what is this all about?

Miriam, there's nothing I can say. I came here to steal from you, and I've been caught, red-handed. It's as simple as that. But I want you to know I've been under terrible financial pressure. What I tried to do here tonight was for . . . my children.

Oh, my God! Your ketzalahs! Your two little ketzalahs!

Yes. I'm afraid their father is a thief. I . . . I'm so ashamed. . . .

Well, Mrs. Pincus, should I put the cuffs on him? You ready to press charges?

What are you, crazy, Officer? Go. Just go. This brokenhearted man is one of us, our neighbor, our own, our friend. Go! Here, Loring, have a brownie and milk.

A little after eight that evening Marcia, the baby-sitter, arrived. Loring told her the girls could stay up as late as nine, if they wanted to.

119

"I'm walking just over to Emmons Avenue, meeting some friends for dinner. I could be home a little on the late side, so don't worry, okay?"

"Did you leave a number?"

"I can't, Marcia, because I'm not sure which restaurant we're going to wind up in. We might even drive out somewhere, I don't know. Anyway," he added, "my car will be here in the driveway, so . . ."

"So it'll look like you're home," she said, smiling. "I don't worry about burglars, Mr. Neiman."

He laughed a little. "I do."

It was 8:30. He planned to enter after midnight; there were almost four hours to kill. He began by walking over to Sheepshead Bay and having some littlenecks and beer at a small Irish bar. Not too much of either.

In his underwear, huge boxer shorts with a French seat, Irving Pincus said, "Sleep in the other room. I told you a hundred times, sleep in the other room. When I can't sleep, I gotta read the paper. If I gotta read, I gotta put on the light, true?"

Miriam Pincus replied, "So read. Since when do I have to sleep? In—what is it?—fifty-seven years I'm married to you I never slept one single minute. Another night wouldn't kill me."

Ten minutes later, at 8:40, they were in bed, Irving reading the New York *Post*, Miriam snoring evenly at his side. If he were ever asked to describe the one abiding theme sound of their marriage, Irving would unhesitatingly say it was his wife's snoring.

After about twenty minutes, Irving put aside the newspaper and turned off the light.

At 12:50 Loring got home from the Kingsway Theatre, but did not go into his house. Instead, he went quietly up his driveway to the garage. He could see the Pincus house and noted that all its lights were out.

In the garage he took off his slacks, shirt and sports jacket and tucked them under last summer's Do-Boy pool. From a shelf he took a pair of his pajama pants, dark brown, and a long-sleeved navy blue sweat shirt, and put them on. Then he changed from his loafers into the dark blue deck shoes. They seemed a little tighter than they did when he bought them. He fished the sports bag—the Pincus Kit—out from behind a carton, removed the cotton gloves from it and slipped them on. They felt good on his damp hands. Then he picked up Briana's Raggedy Ann doll.

Loring walked across his backyard and dropped the loaded sports bag over the fence, onto the Pincuses' side. From that viewpoint the Pincus house seemed somehow larger, stronger, less vulnerable.

He threw the doll into the Pincuses' yard. It landed, softly, in a small azalea bush near the kitchen door.

Then, his heart in his throat, he clambered over the fence.

On the other side he dropped to a crouch, stock still, and listened. Every sound seemed amplified in the night air. Dog barking, a block or two away. Night bird, a large one, possibly the local owl, passing overhead. Grass and tiny twigs crunching under his sneakers, even in his near-motionless attitude. Faint television voice, David Letterman's, from the Koppels' house, to his left of the Pincuses'. *Why aren't the Koppels asleep?* Police siren 'way off somewhere, in Brighton.

The only light was from the tiny sliver of moon low in the sky.

He picked up the sports bag and began to move. Staying close to the fence, he worked along the perimeter of the yard on the side away from the Koppels', the side that had the stand of large hydrangeas, much of which bowed over him, making him invisible from the bedroom floor of either house. About halfway to the building, the grass ended and the flagstone began.

At the exterior wall of the kitchen, he stopped to rest; his legs hurt from the crouch. There was a film of sweat on his forehead. The Pincus yard, long familiar, looked strange to him at that close range, in new detail, like one's own thumb under a magnifying glass.

The Koppels' TV set went off. They would now be either closing their eyes to sleep or stirring around the house. He didn't know their nocturnal habits.

Moving again, he crept past the kitchen door without even trying it; the basement window he wanted was about seven feet away.

With a tiny shock, he saw the face of Raggedy Ann staring out at him from under the azalea bush.

You're kidding, Officer! I came over here to pick up my daughter's doll, she lost it here today. Oh, hey, see? There it is! Well, have a nice night!

A wave of—what? loneliness for Briana?—swept him, and he fought an impulse to glance across the yards to the window of his daughters' room. He had determined earlier to avoid doing that.

To keep his nerve he told himself: So far, you haven't done anything; so far, you haven't committed any crime at all.

He examined the basement window. The brown paint was mostly flaked, revealing the original green and, in spots, the original-original blue. He tested the window. It was hinged at the top, and one of its hinges was free of its screws, but the warping over the years had ensconced the frame more solidly in place than it had appeared to be, through Arlene's opera glasses. In spite of some new doubts, he unzipped the sports bag, took out the chisel, hammer and chamois cloth.

He felt silly in his pajama pants.

With the chamois draped over his hands and the tools, he began tapping the chisel between the frame and the casing. The layers of tape on the tools deadened most of the sound, the chamois absorbed the rest.

Twenty taps along the bottom and sides, timed randomly so as not to set up a discernible sound pattern; occasional levering of the chisel. After five or so minutes, the window seemed to be free. Loring pushed it, carefully, inward. It hung from one hinge.

The window was open.

Feet first, he lowered himself into the basement. When he felt solid cement underfoot, he reached outside and brought in the sports bag, rewrapped the tools and put them back into it. Then he closed the window.

He had broken and entered the home of Mr. and Mrs. Irving Pincus.

By the light of his tiny penlight he found the wooden steps that took him up to the landing that served the side door of the house. He prudently unlocked that door, as his future exit, and continued on up the few more steps to the door that would open into the kitchen.

It was locked, from the other side.

A spring latch. He took the little piece of styrene plastic from the sports bag. Thinner and more flexible than a credit card, it moved easily; the door opened. He was in the kitchen.

Slowly, worried about floor squeaks (he'd noticed some, earlier that day) he walked across the kitchen and into the dining room, to the buffet table. Even in the dark the candlestick holders had a rich but muted luster. He picked them up, one at a time, and placed them carefully in the sports bag, one on each side of the chamois-wrapped tools. They fit, very snugly.

Loring turned and walked back to the side door, finished, ready to go home.

All of this, in spite of an intense, metallic fear, had been accomplished quickly and swimmingly, in less time and with much less trouble than he could possibly have expected.

It was too easy.

Which suddenly made him think he might look to see if there was anything else he could steal.

The rumored jewelry in the allegedly broken safe?

No.

Yes.

Carrying the sports bag, he recrossed the kitchen, went through the dining room and into the living room. There he went down on hands and knees, feeling he would be less obtrusive, safer, moving about the house that way. The rugs, ancient orientals, felt thick and friendly between his fingers, reminding him of hours spent on his parents' rugs, tracing the designs with his tiny toy cars.

You're rejecting the reality of this situation. Keep alert. This is war.

War, shit. I'm having the time of my life.

Pincus could not sleep, after all. He groped for the button on the lamp that was clipped to the headboard, and turned the light on. Then he took his dentures from the nightstand and slipped them into his mouth; he could not read without his teeth. The newspaper was on the bed between him and the snoring Miriam.

On all fours, with the utmost stealth, Loring started up the carpeted staircase to the bedroom floor. It occurred to him that he was committing the most audacious of burglaries, the kind of burglary the police refer to as a "hot prowl."

At the top of the staircase he halted. There was lamplight leaking from somewhere. His eyes at the level of the floor, he looked to the right, toward the master bedroom. Its door, at the end of the hallway, was wide open and there was a low light on inside.

There hadn't been any light visible from the yard, ten or so minutes ago.

He could see almost half, the foot half, of the bed and could tell, even through the comforter, that the two of them were in it. One of them, either Irving or Miriam, was snoring quietly.

Someone broke wind.

People do fart in their sleep.

There was no other sound.

The room in which the unlockable wall safe was said to be was an unused one, the dead son's room. But which one it was he didn't know. Directly across from him was a bathroom and next to that a partially opened linen closet. At the left end of the hall was a closed door. Stretching himself farther out onto the floor, Loring looked to his right again, toward the Pincuses' room. He was then able to see, on his side of the hall, a third bedroom door. He wondered if that had been the boy's room. On its door he discerned a small, dark triangular object. He closed his eyes for a moment, then opened them and looked at the object again; it was a little school pennant.

Besides the low snoring, there was still no other sound from the Pincuses. The old man had probably fallen asleep with the light on.

Or maybe not.

Loring considered backing quietly down the stairs and getting the hell out of the house with the candlestick holders, rather than attempt to traverse the hall, check a rather dubious safe and then try to retrace his steps without being seen or heard.

Instead, he swallowed hard and made a decision he would never fully understand if he lived a hundred years.

Very slowly, staying close to the floor, he moved himself up onto the landing and began crawling, bellying, along the carpet runner toward the dead son's room, the door to which was ajar about one-third. When he was close enough to it he gently pushed the sports bag

why didn't I leave it somewhere downstairs?

into the room ahead of him. Then, shifting onto his side to avoid brushing against the door

because every old door squeaks

he slid himself very carefully through the sixteen-inch opening.

Just as he was almost clear, his knee pushed against the door.

Which squeaked. Very loudly.

The sound cut through him like a knife.

"What's that?" from the master bedroom, Pincus's graveled voice.

Loring's body stiffened. He lifted his head slightly and listened.

"What's what?" Miriam's sleep-slurred voice. "Irving, what's the matter?"

"I heard something." Pincus tried to make his voice louder, more confident. "A door opened, it sounded like."

He got out of bed and went, tentatively, to his bedroom doorway, looked out into the unlighted hallway.

Loring moved, undulated, farther into the blackness of the dead son's room. The bed, the dresser, were covered with sheets. His heart was beating madly and he had just become conscious of having a very full bladder.

Pincus cleared his throat. "Is anybody there?"

"Nobody's there, Irving. Who could be there?"

Loring could now make out the door at the far side of the room. He knew it opened onto the little second-floor balcony. If he could get out onto it, the balcony to the flagstoned backyard was only a twelve-foot drop. *And God knows I've done a lot of twelve-foot drops.*

The balcony door was closed, presumably locked. He thought for a second of slipping under the bed and sweating it out there in the likelihood that the old couple would eventually relax and go back to sleep, at which point he would make a proper exit by way of the downstairs side door. Unless, of course, they stayed up all night, if not forever.

Or called the police.

Or screamed for the neighbors.

Which they could start doing at any moment.

Loring decided, while Pincus was still standing uncertainly in his own bedroom doorway, to go for the balcony.

"Nobody's there, Irving," Mrs. Pincus whispered, also, now, in their bedroom doorway. "Is somebody there?"

"You're telling, or asking? I heard something. From Arnold's room, *alavah sholom.* And what are you whispering? If there's . . . whatever son of a bitch . . . in there, he should know we know he's in there!"

At the balcony door, Loring rose to his feet and, holding his breath, tried the doorknob, slowly. It turned. Gently he pulled the door toward him. It didn't open.

The door was stuck.

Stuck! *Weatherstuck, paintstuck, stuckstuck, like in every goddamn sixty-year-old house around here the fucking door is stuck!*

Pincus stepped bravely into the hallway. "Let's see what's what here."

Loring panicked. He yanked at the door, yanked again. Pincus was now standing in the doorway of the son's room, groping the wall, the wrong wall, for the light switch. Loring could feel Pincus's eyes, Pincus's own fear.

Should I turn and say hello Irving look who's here? Should I wheel and rush at the old man and knock him down knock them both down kick them the hell out of my way before they even see me?

Loring now made a massive pull at the door—and it burst open, imploded, really, almost throwing him off balance, but not quite—and in a second he was out on the little balcony.

Pincus shouted, "Who is that? Stop!" And then, from the hallway, "Downstairs, Miriam, quick!"

Loring threw one leg over the balcony railing and looked down into the yard. He had fully intended to jump, but suddenly the twelve feet seemed terribly high. Then, from down below, he heard the two Pincuses burst out of their side door into the driveway, screaming bloody murder.

"Help! Somebody, help! Wally!"

They began slapping and rapping on the windows of their next-door neighbor's house, fifteen feet across the driveway.

Jumping was now out of the question.

"Irving, is he up there?"

"I'm looking, I'm looking. . . ."

Pincus looked up at the balcony, but Loring had moved very close to the wall of the building, out of the line of sight.

"I don't see nothing." Pincus was reluctant to improve his point of view by moving from where he stood. "He went back into the house, I think!"

"Wherever he went he should drop dead!"

Suddenly Loring heard a second-story window of the neighbor's house slide open, knew it had to be Wally Koppel.

"Irving? What the hell's going on?"

"Call the police, Wally, there's a burglar!"

"Where?"

"Up there!"

"Up there," Wally echoed. "How do you know? Are you sure? How did he get there?"

"He flew there, all right? What's the difference? Call somebody, help us!"

"Wait," Wally said. "I'll see better from the other window."

Wally's wife's voice. "Somebody broke in? I had a feeling something was going to happen tonight! I had a *feeling!* Did you call the police?"

"No."

"Of course not," Clara Koppel said. "That would be too smart. I'll call them!" She disappeared.

Wally's silhouette now appeared at a closer window, from which there was a good side view of the Pincuses' balcony. Loring flattened himself against the stucco wall of the building, his face turned away. He did not want to see Wally Koppel's familiar face peering across at him.

"I don't see anybody, Irving . . ." Wally said.

Actually, he did, but he didn't realize it. It was dark enough to render Loring's black hair and navy sweat shirt almost invisible, with the rest of him, in brown pajama pants, smeared ambiguously by the weak moonlight.

"There's nobody there, Irving. Hold on, Irving, I'm coming down," Wally said.

"Okay, everybody, I called the police," Clara assured them from a downstairs window. "They said they got a car right here in The Beach, so they'll be here in a minute or two, if not next Tuesday."

A moment later, Wally and his two teenaged sons joined the Pincuses in the driveway. Wally carried a flashlight.

"Kevin, Warren, go watch the front of the house. If a guy comes out, back off, you hear? Back off! I'll check the backyard."

Kevin snickered. "Cops 'n' robbers!" He and his brother trotted down to the foot of the driveway.

Wally switched on the flashlight and walked into the backyard. Mrs. Pincus, her voice shivering, warned him to be careful. "Don't be any hero, Wally!"

Wally shined his light around the yard and the bushes. His wife, from the window, said, "For chrissakes, Wally, you don't want to catch him! Give him room to get away! He could have a gun!"

"What kind of gun, they never have guns," Wally said, contemptuously. Then he added, "I want this *schwarzer* bastard."

"Listen to him," Clara shrieked. "He *wants* him! The Jewish Clint Eastwood! Wally, don't be a horse's ass, you hear me?"

Loring stayed in place, against the wall. From time to time the flashlight beam flicked across his body, but the shadows cast by the balcony railing made him impossible to discern. He wondered if his cheek was bleeding from being pressed against the stucco.

RMP car number 848 suddenly pulled up in front of the house. It had run silently, preceded only by its emergency lights.

"Wally!" Pincus shouted. "The cops are here! Thank God!"

"Wally, the police are here," affirmed Clara Koppel.

A window slid open on the other side of the yard. Loring wondered how many of his neighbors were watching this.

From out front he heard the squawk of a two-way radio.

Wally left the yard, went to the driveway, anxious to be the first one to meet the investigating officers; there was a special authority implicit in doing so.

Even from his perch at the back of the house, Loring was aware of the flashing red and white lights bouncing off the houses and treetops around him. It was surreal. The anxiety those stroboscopic lights occasioned even in innocent people became full-blown terror to him then. His loaded bladder was about to burst.

Before Wally could say anything to the police officers, the

Pincuses began blurting out their story, with what Wally felt was altogether too much irrelevant detail.

Loring heard one of the officers ask, incredulously, "You *saw* him?"

"Sure I saw him! What, then, a ghost?"

"And you think he's still inside?" To his partner, "Roy, it's really a 10–31."

"The last place I saw him was when he ran out there," Pincus said, pointing up to the balcony.

"What's it, like a balcony?"

"Yeh, it's a balcony, over the kitchenette," Pincus replied. "I had it built on maybe fifteen, eighteen years ago."

"He ain't there now. Roy, I'm going inside. You call for backup, then circle around the outside, check all the doors, the windows. And listen for me if I call you."

"I got it." Roy had a little boy's voice, excited, nervous. He was no more anxious for a confrontation than the burglar was.

"Whose kids are those?"

"Mine," Wally answered.

"Get them off the street."

Wally called his sons, ordered them back into their house.

The police officer went into the Pincus house through the side door. Wally and Irving Pincus followed him.

"Irving . . ." Miriam Pincus began a protest.

"Leave me alone, all right, Miriam?"

Clara, from her window, said, "Miriam, come inside."

The backyard floodlights suddenly came on, lighting up the yard like the stage of the Roxy. Loring was startled, but then realized that as the lights were all fixed to the building and aimed away from it, they made his balcony even harder to see. He had no idea where the outside cop was. For the moment he felt, somehow, safely effaced where he was. Then he knew the feeling was foolish; it was just a matter of time, minutes or less, before the three of them would be on the bedroom level. He reconsidered jumping, floodlights or no floodlights, making a dash for the fence and getting over it into his own yard.

As he turned his head to survey the route, the outside cop, the one called Roy, suddenly materialized down below. He was checking out the bushes on the perimeter of the yard.

The roof! No place to go but the roof!

Loring had never even been on his own roof. Not since Saigon had he been on any roof. Could he get up there, he wondered. There was a small wrought-iron lantern affixed high on the wall.

He glanced down into the yard just in time to see the cop disappear into the garage. Loring's heart was pounding, demanding more breath than his lungs could provide.

Clutching the sports bag with one hand, he quickly stepped up onto the balcony railing and reached for the eave. He could feel the roofing shingles; they were the asphalt kind, easy to grip.

He put a foot on the wrought-iron lantern, tested it with some pressure. It felt as though it would hold his weight. He plunked the sports bag up onto the roof, then pushed, pulled and hoisted his way up after it.

The roof was peaked at what appeared to be a thirty-degree angle, but once his stomach had gotten a purchase, he felt no danger of sliding off. He worked himself slowly upgrade with his hands and forearms and finally his knees and legs, until he was high enough, safe enough. About halfway up the slope. The asphalt tiles, like sandpaper under his thin pajama pants, hurt his knees.

He was out of sight, then, of any point on the property. Not even from the balcony could he be seen. If he stayed low he would not present an identifiable silhouette against the sky, from any point of view.

Gingerly he rested his head on the roof, relieved for the moment. The coolness of the roofing felt good under his sweating face.

He heard a second police car screech to a halt in front of the house, its doors open and then shut.

Suddenly Pincus, Wally and at least two of the police officers were on the balcony below him.

"If he jumped down from here, Officer," Wally was saying, "he'd still be laying there, don't you think? It's a big jump."

"He's a young guy, in good shape," one of the cops replied impatiently. "Who the hell do you think does these jobs, old farts?"

"Could you do me a favor," Pincus asked him, "and let's please look good in all the closets up here and under the beds?"

Loring thought how obsequious they were with that ill-mannered cop, how Jews, himself included, tend to feel like prisoners in the presence of the policemen, even when they're on the same side.

They went back inside the house, not having given the roof a thought as a possible hiding place for the intruder.

Another window slid open, another house, somewhere behind him; the Kleins'? Sally Libo's? His own?

For the next five or six minutes Loring continued to hear muted sounds of the search within the house—a door being slammed, a shout from Wally: "Officer, did you check this closet?" and once, unbelievably, the younger cop, hysterically yelling, presumably at his own shadow, "Freezeyoucocksucker!"

The thought that the cops might have loaded guns in their hands had not occurred to Loring before. He felt a chill.

The angle of the roof had seemed benign at first, but after a while the weight of Loring's own body seemed to be increasing; his arms and legs began to hurt. They had been working harder at keeping him up there than he realized. He wondered how long he would have to stay there. *When will the police leave and the Pincuses and those fucking Koppels go to sleep?*

Will the sun come up on me?

He could not see Levon Street, but he knew there was a small crowd out there by now. The ache in his bladder had become pain.

Lying on his left cheek, he could see blocks of roofs webbed together by hundreds of treetops. Kingsborough Beach looked rural, countrified, from his unusual angle. If he craned, he could see across Sheepshead Bay to the Moorish tower atop the ghost of Lundy's, itself unlighted, but visible in the ambient glow of Emmons Avenue. In the near ground, a lot of familiar one-family homes filled with people well known to him; just beyond the Portmans' house he could see part of the Fagans', beyond that the Guisewites', the Keesings'.

In the other direction, and a little behind him, he imagined he could see Liz's house.

His watch read 1:43.

He turned his head slightly and looked back at his own house. Not thirty yards away, faintly lit by its tiny Snoopy lamp, was the window of the room in which Briana and Katie lay sleeping.

Like a fog, an estranging loneliness settled over him.

What in God's name am I doing here? When I see my children again, will it be as a free man? Is it all going to end right here on Pincus's roof?

He peed in his pants and began to cry from fear and a loathing of himself he never thought he could feel, never thought, never thought.

The floodlights went out. From the driveway he heard, "So what's a nice Polish boy like you doing in a job like this?" It was Wally.

"That's what my brothers say. They're both firemen." A pause. "Oh, wait a minute, that's not necessary!"

"Take it, take it. I found it. It fell out of your pocket."

"Mr. Pincus, your house is clear. If you find anything missing, call the Six-Five Squad and the detectives'll come out."

"Thank you, boys. Thank the other ones. You're all nice boys."

The officers walked down the driveway. Wally invited Pincus to sleep in his house, and Irving accepted. The two of them walked around the back of the Koppel house to the other side.

The red and white flashes suddenly disappeared from Loring's treetops. He heard first one RMP drive off, then the other, radios squawking as they went. He heard the Koppels' side door slam shut.

Windows all around him slid shut.

Soon it was quiet.

Just crickets.

Fifteen minutes later he began to squinch himself down the slope of the roof, like a caterpillar in reverse. From the balcony he dropped the sports bag into the bushes below, then lowered himself over the side, hung on by his hands for a second, and let go. It was a kidney-rattling drop.

In his own garage, Loring put the sports bag under the Do-Boy pool. The smell of his urine-soaked pants turned his stomach. He took them off, and the sweat shirt, too, wrapped them into a ball and stuck it in a corner.

It was 2:10.

Dressed as he was when he left the house, he let himself in through his side door. Marcia was asleep on the living room sofa. She woke when he entered.

Loring apologized for being so late. She said her mother had been a little mad, earlier, but then got worried that maybe Loring had had an accident. It would be okay.

"You scratched your face, Mr. Neiman. It's bloody, a little."

He watched her cross the street and go inside her own house.

After staring in at his daughters for a long moment, thinking they might get the three weeks at Kinderland they wanted, he went into the bathroom and got under a hot shower. He was bone-tired.

He wondered if he would be arrested in the morning.

I'm scared.

What if the police turn around, come back and are even now searching the neighborhood, including my garage, find the sports bag?

I never saw it before in my life. Must have been stashed there by the fleeing crook.

Did I leave clues, anything, anywhere?

Traces of blood from my cheek on the stucco.

Will they find my blood on the stucco?

No. They don't investigate burglaries that thoroughly.

But this was a big one.

No it wasn't. Ed Hart sustained a fifty-thousand-dollar loss. They never even dusted for fingerprints.

Do they even know anything was stolen?

If they don't, they will tomorrow.

What if someone, some neighbor, some neighbor's kid, in one of those many windows, saw me and recognized me, turns me in?

They didn't. It was pitch-dark. Anyway, they wouldn't have believed their eyes.

He got into bed.

Okay. Is there anything at all to worry about?

Yes. The one thing I am avoiding. The fact that I was foolish enough, stupid enough, to venture upstairs after getting what I had come for.

He lay there, considering that one, trying to separate foolishness from calculated risk and both of those from courage. And trying not to marvel at a courage he thought had been long dead in him.

There had also been anguish and remorse, on the rooftop, but they seemed acceptable. Welcome, almost. He hadn't felt either, that strongly, since the day Arlene died.

Did he feel guilt? Guilt had to be allowed in. He tried to taste some, but couldn't.

Wednesday, May 30 _____

LORING WAS UP at the first light of dawn. He brought the sports bag in from the garage and stored it in his supplies closet.

By noon all of Kingsborough Beach had heard about the burglary. Loring, as a Neighborhood Watch functionary, had gotten four or five calls about the Pincuses' terrible experience. He told everyone he'd write a letter to the 65th Precinct and register their indignation.

He called the Pincuses. Miriam answered the phone.

"Miriam, I can't believe what happened to you people last night. Are you and Irving okay?"

"If you mean are we alive, we're alive. But I wouldn't wish a night like that on Hitler!"

"I can imagine. You actually saw the guy?"

"I didn't. Irving saw. He even grabbed him."

"Who grabbed whom?" asked Loring.

"Irving, grabbed the burglar. Oh wait, darling . . . the detective is leaving. I'll put Irving on. . . ."

The detective!

Irving came on. "Yeh, we had some night here! You didn't hear nothing?"

"No, I—"

"Forty cops, with guns, like a Wild West picture!"

"You have a detective there, Miriam tells me?"

"A detective? Two detectives. One was, you know . . . a fingerprinter."

"What did they say?"

"What are they gonna say? They said there's no finger-prints. It's like nobody was here. Only me and Miriam, our fingerprints they found plenty of."

"That's amazing."

From what Pincus then told him, Loring gathered that a visit from detectives was procedural in cases where the people were at home during the burglary. Even if they had found latent prints, they would be useless unless they had a suspect to compare them with, they told Irving, because the FBI does not routinely run burglary prints through its files.

Loring commiserated with Irving about Washington bu-reaucracy. Then he said, "Irving, I understand you actually grabbed the guy."

"I had him, almost, but he got away, the *momsah.*"

"Wasn't it a little foolish, trying to capture him yourself?"

"He gave me such a shove, my head is still shaking from it, and he jumped down from the balcony in the back and ran like a son of a bitch. He should rot in hell."

"My God, Irving, with due respect, you're too old to be a hero. It's not worth it." Loring lit a cigarette. "But Miriam didn't tell me: did the guy get anything?"

"Sure he got! First of all, he got my great-grandfather's candlesticks, I can't tell you how old they are! He got a couple hundred dollars I had downstairs! He got who knows what else."

No he didn't, you old goniff!

"We're still finding stuff missing."

"Well, I hope you're insured," Loring said.

"Yeh, we're insured, but not for aggravation."

"Well, I'm really sorry about it, Irving. I'll call some of the people on your street—I'm co-captain of the Neighborhood Watch, you know—and try to convey to them how important it is to keep an eye on each other's houses." Loring sighed. "I can't believe nobody saw him coming or going. Did the detectives check on that?"

"Did you check? That's how they checked."

"I guess. Well, as Captain Costello once said, it's a big, busy precinct. Oh, by the way, could you put Miriam back on for a second?"

He did. "Yes, darling?"

"Miriam, getting back to normal life, one of Briana's friends threw her doll over the fence. Did you, by any remote chance, happen to run across it?"

"Yes, it's here, darling. We found it last night, and I figured it had to be your ketzalah's."

Later, Loring put a brand-new floppy disk in his word processor, initialized it and booted it. A blank screen and a blinking cursor appeared. Loring typed

HOT PROWL
The Diary of an Unlikely Burglar

He smiled at that. Then he typed

by Loring Neiman
FOREWORD

I begin this account without pride. However, my recent experience with shame proves that it doesn't kill you.

Nothing in this book should be construed as being, in any sense, an excuse for my acts. However, as a truthful account of why and how a middle-class, college-educated, rather well-known writer and father of two became a burglar, it will naturally produce its own apologia.

When it is completed, I plan to entrust this manuscript to my friend and editor, Jamie Gelfmann (unless it would make him an accomplice-after-the-fact!). And five years from today (the statute of limitations having run out) I will allow it to be published.

If this book finds the market I believe it will, I will consider making reparations to my victims.

At that time, I will explain what I've done, in the best way I can, to my darling daughters and whatever friends I have left, and let public opinion of me be damned.

Loring's phone rang. It was Liz.

"Hi. What are you doing?"

"Doing?" He felt light-headed, the punchiness after concentration. "Working. Working, sweetheart. How are you?"

"He's been beeped away. Would you like me to come over for a while?"

He looked at the screen. "Yes. Can you just give me, say, a half hour?"

"If you can wait that long, so can I. Boy, you must be working on something very, very interesting."

"A blockbuster," he replied.

They hung up.

Loring typed

There is one more thing I should say. The part of me that has moved me in this direction is the same part of me that still believes in my own indestructibility. And I have no illusions about the speciousness of that belief; I am fully aware that we all have our little suicide machines.

CHAPTER ONE

On a Monday morning (five?) springs ago, I awoke from a rather sweet dream (of peace, as provided by power and riches), got out of bed and padded downstairs to the kitchen, where I switched on Mr. Coffee. Then I went to the front door and opened it just wide enough to see if The New York Times was close enough to reach, in my jockey shorts. It was, more or less, and as I fished it into the house I divined the weather: balmy, beautiful, one of those special May mornings . . .

Wednesday, June 13 _____

T WO WEEKS LATER, Loring and Liz sneaked away to East
Hampton, on an early-in-the-season weekday. As discreet and as far from home as they could get, in the
metropolitan area.

It was his idea, an overnight together. He'd been working
on his book for two solid weeks; it had burgeoned, gotten
more demanding in that time, and he wanted a break. Liz told
her husband she would be going to see an old Chicago friend
who had just moved to Manhattan, spend the day helping her
learn the neighborhood, and stay the night. With no phone.
Loring had told Katie and Briana he was going "out of town"
on business. His cousin Esther baby-sat. And so there they
were, out near the end of Long Island, wandering with
unaccustomed freedom in a little anachronism of a place
neither of them had ever seen before. Their "first sleepaway
fuck," Liz called it.

In a tiny store, Loring impulsively bought her a small gold
unicorn. He paid for it with cash—eighty and some odd
dollars—over her protests. He enjoyed making the purchase,
presenting it to her on the spot, kissing away her protests,
watching the sales clerk watch them.

But during dinner at The Mauldin House, the hotel in
which they would spend the night, she put the charm on the
thin chain she was wearing around her neck, and then became
pensive.

"Thank you, darling, it's terrific," she said, sliding her
wineglass in a small damp circle. "But you can't afford it."

141

She was starting to fish again. In the three weeks since he told her that his situation had eased, he'd had to parry her questions about his finances and the new book he was writing. It would have been easy to lie, make up a credible story, but for some reason, he didn't want to do that.

Nor could he tell her the truth.

There had been two more nighttime burglaries in Kingsborough Beach during the two weeks since the Pincuses'. The Isaacs' house was burglarized seven days ago, on a Wednesday night, while Lynn, Fred and their two kids were away in the Virgin Islands. And, just two nights before this one, Judge Mushkin's house was hit, while the judge slept. The Isaacs reported a forty-five-thousand-dollar jewelry loss, and the judge claimed that his prized Queen Anne chocolate pot, circa 1710, had been carried off; he valued it at around thirty thousand. Both claims were accurate. Both times it had been hard for him to overcome his fear and get cranked up, but both times had gone well, easily, quickly, no problems, no cops, no getting trapped on rooftops. Both times the stolen articles were fenced, equitably, by Lewis and Cody.

The only thing wrong with the Isaacs evening was that with no people in the house it had held no climax for Loring; he'd felt no exultation afterward. It was too easy. The Mushkin—the hot prowl—was better for him, more exciting.

After dinner, Loring and Liz went to their room. And there were questions.

"There *is* really a book, yes," he said. "But I haven't shown it to anyone yet."

"Yes?" She waited. "Go on. If no one's seen it, where's your money coming from?"

"I told you, I have a friend who's helped me."

"Helped you?"

"Yes. With a way to put some money together." He smiled, with what he hoped looked like innocent optimism.

"Someone from around the neighborhood?"

"No, a friend."

She didn't like it. "Tell me all about it. Is it a loan? A gift? Work? . . . What?"

He stared at her, suddenly wondering: was he keeping it open, inviting her questions, the probes, because he really wanted her to pull the truth from him? He said, "Please, Liz, I can't. Not yet." His look, now, was serious.

She believed the look, and she was hurt.

"I think I'll go for a walk."

He watched as she pulled on a pair of sweat pants. "If there's anything more interesting than watching you get undressed, it's watching you get dressed again, afterward. Knowing what's going on underneath and watching you hide it from the rest of the world."

"Really," she said, coldly. "You'd go out of your mind in Loehmann's fitting room."

She went to the bathroom mirror. Loring followed, stood close behind her as she brushed her hair. He ran his hands down her hips and across her belly. She felt him getting hard against her, and she squirmed his hands away.

"Don't, Loring. I'm really angry at you. I have been for weeks."

"Then why are you here with me?"

"Because I'm in love with you."

He turned her around to face him. "Really?"

"No," she replied. "I spend part of every day screwing one neighbor or another. I'm easy."

"I'm easy." Who had once said, "I'm easy"?

"Then let me ask you something," he said. "Are you still . . . let me quote you right . . . 'determined to bring the best out of Andy Blaug'?"

"Yes."

No, she didn't really belong to him; he couldn't possibly tell her the truth.

Cody had said, "I'm easy."

"Loring, this secrecy between us, for no reason, I want to go on record as hating it. Remember that."

He put his arms around her and kissed her. She canceled her walk.

They owned each other's bodies.

Guiding himself with his hand, feeling her soft pliant

fleshiness, he entered from the rear. Slowly she sank to the sheets, her hold on him tightening as she did. He could not move; she began rotating her buttocks, and, in seconds, he came.

From the pillow, her muffled voice, with disbelief: "That's it?" She sat up, looked at him. "You're a regular thousand and one Arabian nights, you know?"

Later, in his arms, just before she fell asleep, she asked him, out of the blue, if he thought East Hampton had burglars.

His stomach did a turn. It was odd she should ask that, because his own mind had just drifted back to the same general subject.

"It probably does," he answered.

She murmured, "Um," and became silent. He listened as her breathing became steadier. He had never heard her sleep before, never seen her in complete repose. She looked lovely and even younger. He realized how much he adored her, wondered if he would ever have the peace of mind it would take to muster the strength it would take to organize this remarkable woman out of her husband's life and into his own.

He thought about Katie and Briana, ninety miles away, what it would be like if he and they and Liz were a family.

Friday, June 15 _____

Loring typed

The clock is running on my Second Mortgage. The date I had "bought" from Carlin is approaching fast, but, after taking out for ordinary living expenses, I'm still short of the amount.

My balance sheet looks like this:

Pincus:	Two silver candlesticks.
Value 18,000	NET: 6,000
Isaacs:	Lynn's jewelry.
Value 45,000	NET: 14,000
(Lewis & Cody had to lay this off on someone else.	
Too rich for their blood)	
Mushkin:	Queen Anne Choclte Pot.
Value 30,000	NET: 9,000
	TOTAL: 29,000
Living Expenses:	5,500
Saved:	23,500

Am I the only burglar in North America who keeps records?

Before the twenty-second of the month I need to raise at least another fifteen thousand, net. A monumental figure, in any terms. But for a free lance writer . . .

I tried to get a loan against my life insurance but my broker said it's been paying its own premiums for so long, there's nothing there.

I'll have to do one more job.

But who . . . ?

My choice of Pincus wasn't really a conscious one. I feel that it came to me in a natural way . . . generically, so to speak. And, my decision to hit the Isaacs a fairly obvious one; they were out of town, on vacation, I knew my way around the place, knew where Lynn's jewelry was kept, and felt it would be a piece of cake, which it was.

Choosing Judge Mushkin as a target had been only slightly more difficult. The house was not all that familiar to me, but the item I was after—his silver chocolate pot—was as accessible as the Pincus candlestick holders had been; it stood out and free, downstairs, on the Judge's mantlepiece. There was no upstairs stuff involved.

I had over-reached and panicked on the Pincus job, dangerously. But not so on the Isaacs and Mushkin; I was very prudent. Since those jobs, however, people are becoming alarmed (in both senses of the word). A couple of weeks ago, the Kilowitz family was the only one I knew that had an electronic security system. Now, a lot of them—Goldstein, Berger, Krupp, etc.—seem to be installing burglar alarms. Little blue signs are proliferating on lawns, like mushrooms.

And, speaking of the Bergers, for some reason they popped into my mind yesterday, and I've been mentally walking around their house ever since. But I've heard their new security system described as being very sophisticated, with the loudest alarm in the world. The bells of hell.

Beyond that, the interior of their house isn't all that fresh in my mind, and (since that night at the Goldsteins) there's no casual way I can invite myself over there for a look-around.

No, there'll have to be a better choice than the Bergers.

As you've probably realized by now, it is fear, rather than guilt, that proscribes my activities. The small guilts I do experience aren't even orthodox ones. They come not so much from the fact of my stealing from my neighbors as from my invasions of their privacy, and the things I've accidentally learned about them in the process. Small things. For instance, I was not in any way ever supposed to hear a Pincus fart in the night; Fred Isaacs' insanely personal Polaroid photos of his wife were never intended for my eyes (or at least I don't think so); poor Judge Mushkin's laundry pile still shocks me to laughter when I think of it. It appears that his honor shits in his pants on a regular basis.

Jesus. I really shouldn't know these things.

Around noon today I expect a guy from something called K-M Home Security Services. They seem to be installing most of the burglar alarms in the neighborhood, and he's going to give me a rundown (and estimates) on the various systems available for my house.

I should know a little about how the fucking things work. Not too much, just a little. Why didn't I study electrical engineering instead of English??

For Mr. Kelly's first half hour, he and Loring toured the house, room by room. Then, at the kitchen table, over coffee, Kelly outlined the system he proposed to install. On a rough little sketch plan of the house, he indicated all the doors and windows.

"The whole principle of our system is basically this: When it is 'armed,' as we say, a continuous electrical circuit moves through it. Break that circuit, in any way at all, and the interruption causes the alarm to go off."

"I understand, so far. Just please remember to explain everything to me as though you were talking to a three-year-old. Okay?"

The man looked at him for a second. "All right, Mr. Neiman. I'll try. Let's start at the periphery—the outside—and work in." Kelly pointed to the windows on his drawing. "On each window I put little switches, which are all connected, by wires. When the window is shut, these switches meet, closing the circuit at that point, at least. Follow?"

Loring nodded.

"On each door, also, a switch. The same principle. Ergo . . ."

Ergo?!

". . . when all the doors and windows are shut, tight, the electrical circuit is closed."

Loring nodded again.

Kelly then took a brushed metal plate, about the size of an

electric wall switchplate, out of his case and showed it to Loring. It had twelve push-button numbers, telephone-style, and three little bulbs in a row. "This item is set into your wall. When the circuit is closed, this green bulb lights up. Now, if you're getting ready to leave your house and this green light is not lit, it means there's a door or window somewhere that is not properly closed. So you close it. When the green light comes on, you punch in your four-number code—this second bulb lights up red—and you exit your house." He looked at Loring. "Now, this is important: we put a delay mechanism on the door nearest the control panel, which allows you anywhere from fifteen to thirty seconds of grace—your choice—to get to your door, open it, get outside and shut the door behind you."

Loring nodded. "It works the same way coming, I guess? You unlock your door, open it, step in and you've got fifteen seconds to punch in your code, to disarm. Am I right?"

"Yes, exactly."

"Good. Then I'm still with you. Now, what's this third bulb for?"

"That we call a 'shunt' light. If you would like to have pressure-sensitive traps under your carpeting, for instance, they are related to this bulb, which is colored amber."

"Rug traps? What are they all about?"

Kelly took a small piece of one from his case. It looked somewhat like the padding that goes under carpeting, except that it had a skeleton of electrical wiring.

"They are much bigger than this. When it's laid under your rugs, and wired into the system, it remains dormant, you might say, until someone steps on it. The weight of the person will press"—he demonstrated—"these two layers together, causing the circuit to break. And, of course, the alarm to go off."

"Fiendishly clever," Loring said.

Kelly seemed proud. "Yes, they really are. I recommend them to my clients. I sell total security. For instance, if an intruder circumvents the peripheral system—by, say, cutting a hole in the roof and dropping down into your house—he'd still be in trouble, because these traps, judiciously placed, would soon get him."

"Where are those judicious places?"

"In any room you are concerned about," Kelly replied. "If you have valuables in the living room or the library, you'd want them there."

"Bedroom?"

"No. Even though burglars always go into the master bedroom, I like to place them just outside, under the carpeting in the hall near the bedroom door. That way, you lessen the chance of setting it off yourself one night.

"And, by the way, with a special two-number code you can shunt them into or out of the main system, as you wish."

"Why would I want to shunt them out?"

"Well, you might want to shunt out the carpet traps if, say, you have a sleepwalker in the family, or if you're in the habit of late night trips to the kitchen and you're afraid you might forget and step on the wrong part of the carpet, and so forth. . . ."

"Of course. Sleepwalkers and icebox raiders." Loring thought for a moment. "Let me ask you: What if there's a dog in the house? Won't his weight set off a rug trap?"

"Not unless he jumped on it from a distance. No, it would take more than thirty-odd pounds of pressure to sound the alarm."

"Oh, right. I see."

"Incidentally, these traps also provide a way for you to make sure your system is working. Without arming the system, you shut your doors and windows, then walk over your traps. Every time you step on them, the green light should go out, until you step off."

"That's interesting."

At Loring's request, Kelly made little drawings showing how the switches would be affixed to the windows and doors. He offered two different styles of door switches, each of which consisted of two pieces: the one fixed to the window frame or doorjamb, and the one on the movable part. Ordinarily, especially on windows or sliding doors, they were magnetic, so-called, in that when the two pieces made contact, the electrical circuit was closed. The other style of door switch, however, worked by way of a little spring-loaded protrusion that was set into the doorjamb on the side where the hinges were. The protrusion was held in place by the closed door. When the door was opened, the protrusion, urged along by its spring, followed the door as it swung open, and at a certain point the contact, within the jamb, would break, triggering the alarm. To Loring it looked as though it could be baffled by opening the door very slowly and sliding something between it and the jamb that would keep the protrusion pressed back in its socket. He didn't offer this thought to Kelly, however.

Kelly told Loring about window sensors—bugs—which, cemented to a corner of a pane of glass, would detect any vibration great enough to break the glass. He said that even after scoring with a glass cutter, it was still necessary to use a certain amount of muscle to knock out the scored piece of glass. That shock would break the circuit and set off the alarm signal.

Finally, he explained that the entire system could be connected to a remote monitoring office. When the alarm went off, it would automatically use the telephone lines to signal a computer, which, in turn, called your home. If you did not answer, or answered without using a special code word, the computer called preprogrammed phone numbers of your choice, including any private patrol you'd retained and/or the city police.

Kelly's estimated price for Loring's system was twenty-seven hundred dollars. The monitor service was thirty dollars a month.

"Think it over, Mr. Neiman. My men will be working in the area for the next couple of weeks, so we'd have no trouble scheduling you in."

"I'll think about it, Mr. Kelly. It's a little expensive, but I'll think about it."

After the man left, Loring made some notes, reviewing what he'd learned. The rug trap thing; if a thirty-pound dog would not trigger the alarm, then what would prevent a full-grown man, regardless of his weight, from lying flat out on the floor and distributing his weight over a wider area? He could probably travel across a rug-trapped floor in that manner with total impunity.

Much later that evening, in bed, watching an old movie, Loring suddenly recalled that on the night of the Goldstein party, he had heard Harriet Kilowitz tell someone that the code number that controlled their system was the last four digits of their phone number. This recollection elated him.

He sat up in bed, lit a cigarette.

Could they have changed it since then?

Saturday Afternoon, June 16 _____

T HE SECOND MEETING of the Neighborhood Watch was held at the home of the Kilowitz family. It was so because Loring had suggested it to Judith Lieb who suggested it to Harriet Kilowitz who checked with Larry who said, "Okay, but my house, my rules, and my rule is: No bullshit allowed. *I'll* do the talking."

Their house was one of the newer ones in The Beach, on Horning Street between Dale Avenue and Bay Boulevard. It was a large, well-designed split-level with a handsome redwood exterior.

Loring, Katie and Briana had gotten there about one, early enough for Eddie Kilowitz to invite them to take a look at his own personal computer. It was in his bedroom, on the second level. Facing Eddie's room, at the other end of the hallway, was the master bedroom. In the room nearest the master, Loring noticed as they passed it, the maid was setting up a foldaway baby crib.

After proudly showing them his Commodore 64 and some of its software, Eddie demonstrated something Loring had never known: using a tiny pocket knife, which was attached to his key ring, he cut an extra notch on a floppy disk, explaining that it could thereafter be written to on both sides, rather than just one. Loring seemed to appreciate the revelation.

When he left them to go downstairs, he noticed that the maid was still busy on the bedroom level.

Larry Kilowitz said, "They get along good, the kids. Maybe Eddie'll be your son-in-law someday, hah? How would you like me and Harriet for *mochutanim?*"

"I could do worse," Loring replied. And he actually meant it. To him, drawing in-laws was one of life's crap shoots, a lottery. This owlish, balding little man with outsized hands and feet and a vile temper was no dinner companion, but he seemed to obey a strong familial imperative; if time and fate ever made Katie or Briana a daughter-in-law of the likes of him, Loring could accept it. Prefer it, even, to, say, a gentleman Sidney Lieb, who could guiltlessly break his own brother's emotional legs on some vague social principle.

As to Harriet Kilowitz, he knew her only as a nice, large lady who was reputed to wear jewelry even in the bathtub.

The living-dining area, sleek with chrome and glass built-ins, was beginning to fill with people; there would be more than at the first meeting. Most of the old people and lots of new ones. Assemblyman Dan Pringle, Stanley and Neala Ross, the Foxes, the Alexanders, the Emmets. The stars of the afternoon, though, would be Justice of the Kings County Supreme Court Robert Mushkin and the Isaacs—who'd suffered the most recent burglaries—and, of course, the Pincuses, who were still milking their own experience for all it was worth.

They were the first of the victims to arrive, and Irving told everyone his newest version of their burglary, which featured even more cops, a heavier loss and—his most recent embellishment—an anti-Semitic epithet by the burglar. Loring had seen Miriam and Irving a few times since he broke into their house, so being around them had already resumed its normalcy. But he hadn't been with Judge Mushkin or Lynn and Fred Isaacs since well before their burglaries, and he was apprehensive. He had specifically phoned them earlier in the week to make sure they were coming; he would find himself in their company sooner or later, and he was anxious to get it over with.

The judge, when he finally showed up, immediately became involved with others, so Loring had several minutes to adjust to his presence before he finally had to say hello to him. And at that, Mushkin had his usual shy and preoccupied air—he never seemed to look anyone in the eye—so Loring didn't feel too uncomfortable. But a few minutes later, when he saw Fred and Lynn bounce in, tanned from their vacation, he got a tight, peculiar feeling. They headed directly over to greet him, and as they did, the Polaroid pictures of her flipped through his mind; he felt himself flush.

"Author! Author!" Lynn did her usual act and Fred dutifully applauded. And Loring welcomed it, for a change. They embraced him and told him that they'd had a great time in St. Thomas, but coming home to a burgled house was a bummer that spoiled everything.

"I'm sorry," Loring said.

"Well, we almost died! You know, it's weird," Lynn said, through the smile she always wore regardless of what she was saying, "how you begin to realize you've been robbed, but you can't really believe it!"

"I've had the pleasure," Loring said.

"I'll tell you, Loring, it changes the way you live!" Fred said, earnestly. "We're afraid to go out now, even though we put in a burglar alarm. If we ever leave the house together, all of us, I make Lynn and the boys bend down in the car so if anyone's watching, they won't know we're all leaving! It's craziness, I'll tell you!"

"I know. I know."

Lynn said, "We fired our gardener and our maid. I felt terrible about it, I'm sure they had nothing to do with it, but . . . you know . . . you don't want to take any chances. Now I know how it must feel to be raped, you know? It's . . . awful."

"It is. I'm still a little paranoid myself," Loring commiserated. He felt okay being with them, after all. Being with his own victims, he realized, evoked in him an odd sequence of feelings, which began as nervousness but ended as a kind of superiority. And finally, in only minutes, the natural congeniality of these people toward him had the ultimate effect of—what?—granting him a pardon, of course.

Sidney touched Loring's shoulder. "So. Judith tells me she hears you're doing better, found some work. I'm glad." He gave Loring's arm a little squeeze. "I knew it would work out. It's working out, right?"

"It's working out, Sid."

"Good." Another squeeze.

The meeting began with Judith Lieb's report that she and Sidney had been in touch with Captain Costello to express everyone's concern and officially request more police attention. She said that the captain told them he had already increased the patrol in the area, to the extent that a Radio Motor Patrol unit from Canarsie was now spending half of each nighttime tour in Kingsborough Beach.

Most of the people there felt that this was not good enough. Especially Larry Kilowitz, who said, "Let's send him a buncha roses for being so nice. We're all targets here and I want cops, plenty of cops, on foot, in cars, in helicopters, in Sherman goddamn tanks. Not half a goddamn patrol car from Canarsie."

Leo Goldstein was amused. "Hey, Larry, you got two choices: you can move to the North Pole or the South Pole."

"Aw, shut up, Leo." Larry's face reddened. "Some night you'll get a shiv stuck up your ass by some *schwartzer,* you'll see how funny you think it is."

Leo feigned a sudden pain in the rectum, and laughed.

"Or your wife's," Larry added.

Sandy Goldstein glared at Kilowitz and said, icily, "Kindly leave my . . . anatomy out of this."

"Hey!" Larry shouted. "It's my house, I'll say anything I goddamn wish!"

Loring watched Kilowitz throughout the exchange. The ugly little man was smart enough to have become rich enough in paper boxes to indulge, for example, his wife's well-known fondness for her birthstone, the ruby. The perfect Burmese ruby, at that. He added a pendant, earrings or a bracelet to her collection every month. Smart enough to be able to do that, yet he had the sensibilities of a rhino.

Loring was bored, edgy. He noticed that his heart was

156

racing. By rights, he felt, he should be upstairs, in Harriet's dresser drawers.

Walter Krupp, referring to the Isaacs burglary, suggested that the next time anyone went out of town they should inform their immediate neighbors so their house could be watched. Sam Mendelsohn observed aloud that it was a rather obvious suggestion. Fred Isaacs then said that he and his wife had done that. "We told the Fishbeins and the Warshawers, and Loring, too, as captain. But this is not a criticism of our neighbors," he added. "Nobody's got eyes in back of their heads, and I'm sure they all did their best."

"But it was none too good," Leo put in, with a chuckle.

Judge Mushkin, looking at the floor and shaking his head, said, "The fact that some of us see fit to bicker about this matter is fine, in that it releases some tension. But meetings like this are supposed to raise our consciousness, not our tempers. . . ." His wispy fine white hair seemed to float around his pink head as he spoke.

"You're absolutely right, Judge!" put in Edna Backus. "I personally didn't come here to listen to people insult each other."

"This is a serious problem, and a growing one," the judge continued. "I have seen many thieves during my years on the bench, thieves of every stripe. Most of them are thieves of need, expedience and opportunity. But some"—he looked up for the first time—"are out-and-out sociopaths. And I wouldn't be surprised if that's what we are dealing with here."

There were some whisperings as a few couples conferred. Then Frances Gold bravely asked, "What is a, ah, 'sociopath,' Judge?"

"A sociopath, to put it simply, hates people. In this case, he expresses it by stealing in the most frightful way. Our thief—and I believe the Pincuses and Fred and Lynn and I were victims of the same person—comes at night, while most of us, at least, are at home. That, to me, shows a special contempt of us."

Ellie Habib said, "I don't care if a man breaks in during the day, when nobody's around, but creeping around my house at night . . . that's where I draw the line!"

"Well, well," Larry Kilowitz said, sarcastically, "the dawn finally breaks over Nutley, New Jersey!"

"Shut up, Larry," Harriet said.

"Whoever broke into our homes did some research," Mushkin went on. "He knew about us. He knew about Mr. and Mrs. Pincus, and the Isaacs family. He knew about me. He is good at it. He is becoming more confident with success. And, any confrontation by one of us, some dark night, could prove to be very, very dangerous."

He sat back, on the word "dangerous." Everyone stared at him, soberly.

Assemblyman Pringle, who was an attorney, had sat through many of Judge Robert Mushkin's rambling courtroom speeches. His secret opinion was that Mushkin was well into senility. He broke the silence.

"I don't want to understate the seriousness of the situation, but with all due respects to you, Robert, I don't think we're dealing with any sinister superman here. He's a burglar, period, and like any other burglar, he's going to make a mistake someday. Or night."

"I agree," Loring heard himself say. And then he wondered why he did.

The meeting started to break up at three-thirty. The Blaugs never came. Loring guessed it was because he hadn't wanted to and she was in no mood to push it.

Loring surprised his daughters by inviting Eddie to come back to their house with them. "You and Katie can play with some of our computer games. We have Apple Panic."

"Appge Panic! Oh, wow!" Eddie was thrilled. "I never pgayed that game!" Then his face darkened. "Gee. I better ask my mother."

"What would she care?" Katie asked.

"Because my sister and my nephew are coming from Cagifornia today, gater on."

Katie sighed. "So what? You'll see them *plenty*. Look,

Eddie, my father doesn't let strange kids in his study very much, so you better do it while he's in this kind of a mood."

Loring smiled. "What time is your sister due in?"

"Six o'cgock."

"No sweat. We'll get you back by then. I'll ask your mother, on your behalf."

He walked back toward the kitchen to look for Harriet and found her in the small pantry. After thanking her for hosting the meeting, he asked her about Eddie.

"Why not?" she said. "Larry's going to pick up Joanie and the baby at JFK at four-thirty, they won't be back here till six."

"I've never met Joanie, have I?" Loring asked.

"Not that I can remember," said Harriet. "She and Stuart moved to Los Angeles almost ten years ago, before you moved in. They've only been back here twice."

"Coming back on a family holiday?"

"Just her, for a couple of days. The putz refuses. Says he's got to work." With fingers that had rubied rings on them she absently played with the large ruby that hung from her choker. All were of a dark, rich color. "If you want my opinion, there's trouble in paradise. If you get my meaning."

As he, the girls and Eddie were about to leave the house, Loring saw, for the first time, that the alarm system control panel was on a wall in the front entrance hall. On it the green light glowed unblinkingly, even though there were still thirty or so people milling about the main floor; this strongly suggested that there were no traps under any of the rugs, at least in those rooms.

Just before they exited, he had a wild impulse to punch in 6-3-3-0 to see if the little red light went on. But he didn't.

Katie and Loring took Eddie upstairs to the study. He watched as Eddie booted up the first of the games. When he was satisfied that the kid knew what he was doing, Loring asked, "Eddie, that little pocket knife you used, could I borrow it for a minute or two?"

"My Swiss Army knife? Sure, Mr. Neiman!" He dug into his pocket.

"I have to fix something downstairs," Loring said.

Eddie pulled out the ring that held two keys and the small knife. As he started to detach the knife from it, Loring gently took the whole thing from his hand.

"Don't bother, Eddie. I'll manage with it like this. Have it all back in a few minutes."

He went down to the basement, to the tiny bin that, on the day they moved into the house, he had consecrated as his "workshop." He had then equipped it with about four hundred dollars' worth of Montgomery Ward tools and, for about three months, destroyed toasters, vacuum cleaners and once, even, a Sony television set. Arlene had referred to Loring's workshop as "the place where repair bills are avoided at enormous expense."

From Eddie's key ring he took the two house keys and clamped one of them in a vise, along with a hardware store key blank. Then, with a small steel grinding bit in his electric hand tool, he began carving a duplicate of the original key. It was harder than he thought it would be. It took him almost half an hour. The second key took about the same length of time.

He got back up to his study just as Eddie was loading a disk.

"Hi, Daddy," said Katie, smiling. "Boy, Eddie really knows about this stuff."

From the floppies that were lying around on the desk, Loring quickly gathered that Eddie and Katie had played all the games—Apple Panic, Zork, Clowns. But besides the box of games he'd given them, his little blue plastic box of text disks was also open.

Eddie smiled up at him, modestly, just as the screen presented the catalog of the disk he had just loaded.

HOT PROWL

Loring was stunned: *The little shit has actually booted the word processor program and is about to waltz through my fucking files!*

"Hold it, hold it, Eddie!" Loring stepped to the machine and threw the switch that shut it off. Then he looked at the boy. "Eddie . . . Jesus . . . as a computer person, you're supposed to know that loading someone else's files is like . . . like reading their mail, or their diary. . . ."

Eddie went popeyed and looked at Katie, who said, "It was *my* idea, Daddy. I just wanted to see what was on them. I didn't know they were . . . you know . . . private. . . ." She looked as worried, then, as Eddie did.

Loring touched her face. "That's okay, honey. Nothing came up." He looked at Eddie. "Did it?"

Eddie shook his head. "No, Mr. Neiman. We played every game and I just now stuck that one in the drive to see—"

"Okay. I'm sorry I got so upset. But Katie knows how I am about my work."

"Let's go outside, Eddie," Katie suggested. They got up to leave.

"Oh, hey," Loring said, remembering, "your famous Swiss Army knife." He smiled, handed Eddie the key ring. "Thanks a lot."

When they left, Loring put the Hot Prowl disk back into the little plastic file box and placed it on the top shelf of the closet. He'd have to find a better place to keep it.

Poor Eddie had looked so guilty. Unlike his old man, he had the capacity for shame. Not a bad kid, at all. And his sweet mother has those great rubied things.

Sunday, June 17 ─────────

B Y ELEVEN IN the evening, Larry and Harriet Kilowitz and their daughter had already been home an hour from dinner in the city. Eddie was asleep in his room, the daughter and her baby—the Los Angeles contingent—were asleep in her old room, and Larry, who had just taken his fifth shower of the day, was about to join Harriet in their bed. It was a warm and airless night, after the first uncomfortable day of the season. Not a scorcher, but unusually humid for the date. In the bedroom, he toweled himself dry while standing in front of a small oscillating electric fan. Earlier in the day he had tried to switch on the new central air-conditioning system, but it failed to respond. And so, in fact, had the repair service he'd called. Larry was in a filthy mood.

As he got into a pair of pajama pants, he said, "Shitting thing, you pay seven grand, it sits there one goddamn winter, and bingo, first hot day, it fucks off on you."

Harriet, who was already in bed, reading, shushed him. "You're going to wake up your grandson."

Larry reached behind the nightstand on his side of their bed and brought out the brand-new 12-gauge shotgun that stood on end against the wall. It was of the pump-action type, with a five-round magazine. The magazine was loaded, and on the floor behind the nightstand was a box of twenty-five more shells. Larry had bought it all just a few days before and had yet to fire it.

"Saying good night to your new love?" asked Harriet,

riffling through her magazine. She avoided looking at the firearm. "Why don't you take it to bed with us?"

Larry ignored her. He hefted the shotgun; it had a fine, reassuring feel. The cool steel was good to his touch. He sighted down the barrel of the shotgun once or twice. Then, reluctantly, he put it back behind the nightstand and got into bed.

At 1:02, Loring left his house, dressed in his blue running suit, looking as though he were off on a late night jog along the esplanade.

He was empty-handed. No more "Pincus Kit," not since the Mushkin; the taped-up hammer and chisel had been more tools than he needed. Right then, in one of his deck shoes, were the duplicates of Eddie's keys. In the other was his small piece of styrene, for any locked interior doors. His cotton gloves were tucked in the elastic waistband of his pants. Attached to his wrist by its tiny chain was his penlight.

He jogged the three short blocks along dark streets dappled by moonlight through trees, trying not to think, encountering no one along the way, the neighborhood asleep. As on the nights of the Isaacs and the Mushkin, he had made up his mind to abort if he met anyone, or even felt that he had been seen from a window. And, as with the Isaacs and the Mushkin, neither thing happened. At least, he did not feel that he had been seen from a window, and that was all that really mattered, when one was trying not to think.

Suddenly, almost too soon, he was at the Kilowitz house; he veered sharply into the driveway. There, in the total blackness, he stopped, breathing heavily and perspiring. He leaned against the side of the house to rest.

It was the moment of commitment, the final contemplation of what he was about to do. And, as had become usual at such times, it seemed more preposterous than dangerous. But then, the actual crime had not yet begun.

His eyes became used to the darkness, and he could see that one of the family cars, the Chevy Harriet used for marketing, was parked out in front of the garage, at the head of the long driveway. Just in back of it, within the open garage, he saw a glint of chrome; Larry's Mercedes-Benz was also home.

After a few minutes his body cooled down. He put on the cotton gloves and stepped back down the driveway to the end of the redwood deck that stretched across the front of the house. He hoisted himself up onto it and moved toward the front door, keeping low and behind the deck furniture as much as possible. Along the front of the deck a row of tall juniper bushes stood like silent witnesses.

There were two locks, one in the doorknob and, twelve inches above it, a dead-bolt. He took the keys from his shoe and stood up, black against the white door. His next moves had to be fast ones. He slipped one of the keys into the doorknob, the skin tightening on his scalp, and tried to turn it. It would not.

A wave of relief?

He put the other key in, and that one worked; he heard the lock unlatch. Then he inserted the first key into the upper lock, the dead-bolt, and turned it. It worked; the bolt slid smoothly back.

It's nice doing business with some decent hardware.

The door—unless they'd put a chain or a slide bolt on the inside since yesterday—was unlocked.

Holding the doorknob in a gloved hand, he rehearsed the last four digits of the Kilowitz telephone number: 6-3-3-0-6-3-3-0-6-3-3-0 . . .

Eddie Kilowitz slid the magazine out from under his pillow, rolled it up and headed for the hall bathroom. His sister had interrupted him in there a million times since nine o'clock, either to dump diapers (which stank it up) or take another one of her goddamn cool baths, or whatever. Now maybe he'd have it a couple of minutes to himself. He went in, put on the light and locked the door.

* * *

Loring turned the knob, opened the door and stepped into the entrance hall. The red bulb on the control panel glowed, glowed huge, like a traffic signal.

Fifteen seconds.

Not breathing, he took the two steps to the panel and, praying, praying that they hadn't changed the number, punched, with a finger of a shaking hand, the 6, the 3, the 3 and the whatever.

Oh, god, it's still on, oh god I think I hit the fucking asterisk!

Quickly he did it again, quickly but carefully carefully: the 6, the 3, the 3 and carefully the 0.

And saw the red light go black.

Flat, dead, blessed black.

The baby woke, began to cry softly.

Auto-motherhood: the young woman, in something like sleep, reached out, gave the crib two or three gentle rocks; the baby quieted. She withdrew her arm and tossed her body into a different position, one in which she hoped to find a deeper sleep.

The short staircase to the bedroom level was twenty feet from the entrance hall, but Loring would first open an auxiliary exit. Silently he went through the main floor to the rear of the house, unlocked the kitchen door and came back to the staircase. He knew—everyone knew—there was a safe somewhere in the house, but safes were out of his experiential range. He would try only the master bedroom, and, in fact, only the top drawer of Harriet's dresser. Since time immemorial that's where women had left the jewelry they wore that evening. And Loring knew that earlier on that particular evening the Kilowitzes had taken their daughter out to dinner in the city. If Harriet ever wore her best, it was on such an evening.

But if these assumptions were wrong, he intended to leave empty-handed.

He started slowly up the stairs. The place was hot and

quiet, but a forest-quiet, seemingly still, at first, but then, as one's ear became attuned, alive with natural sounds: faint snores of various pitches, fans whirring in three places, fitful creaking of one bedspring and another. The house was acoustically bad. From halfway up the stairs, he heard the kitchen icemaker dump new cubes into its bin.

The toilet flushed. Loring froze as a door opened with a blast of light that then immediately went out as someone emerged from it. Eddie, little Eddie, crossed Loring's line of sight, went into his bedroom and closed the door behind him.

Loring was dizzied; he sat down on the step and waited, listened.

Three or four minutes later he felt that Eddie had gone back to sleep. Regardless, time was passing. He went on up to the bedroom level.

Eddie's door was closed. The daughter's door was almost completely closed. The master bedroom door was open. He stepped to it, peered in. Larry and Harriet were asleep, uncovered, Harriet in a silk or nylon gown, Larry in a pair of pajama pants. He was sleeping on his left side, facing the windows, she on her right, facing the door.

Built into a mirrored wall was a twin dresser unit. Loring moved to it, slowly. The sound of the electric fan was good, providing a white noise. The dresser had a long mantel-like shelf running its length. On her end of the shelf were dozens of small bottles, boxes and objects. Loring switched on his penlight, leaving it chained to his left wrist, shielding it with his right hand. Its faint glow revealed bottles of toilet water, colognes, odds and ends of makeup, boxes of talcum, tissues, lipsticks, keys, a red leather wallet and jewelry. Maybe enough jewelry to obviate the need to open any drawers.

The most important-looking piece was a large yellow gold brooch, in the shape of a floral spray. It was not beautiful, at least in Loring's terms, but it was set with several faceted rubies, one very large, some small, along with many little diamonds. When he brought the Isaacs stuff to Lewis, the old man had given him a short crash course in fancy jewelry. Among other things, he told him about "light traps," which were tubelike holes that went clear through the metal. When stones were set in them, the piece was considered to be better-crafted. Such was the case with this brooch; each stone was in its own light trap. Lewis would like it.

A sound from the bed. Standing stock-still, Loring watched in the mirror as Larry slowly changed his position, turning completely over onto his right side. Tense, poised to go, Loring watched him for a long minute. But Larry slept. They both slept. Loring thought about how these bombastic people, who took up so much air when they were awake, were so still and helpless then. *No fair; crimes done while the victims are asleep ought to be doubly punished; a necessary human function shouldn't put one at risk.*

Not far from the brooch was a wide platinum bracelet, of what Lewis had described as the "pavé," or paved, type, set with hundreds of tiny rubies. No light traps, but, jesus, an uncountable number of stones. Behind it was a ring that held a high-domed oval ruby, one of the biggest he'd ever seen. Easily three quarters of an inch in diameter.

Loring turned off his penlight. He picked up the three pieces of jewelry and stuffed them down into the crotch of his jockey shorts.

A small white ceramic box, about two by four inches, caught his eye. He wondered why it looked familiar to him, then remembered; it was a thing Larry liked to show his company, an exquisite Meissen snuffbox, circa mid-eighteenth century. The reason Larry showed it off was not its beauty or even its cost, which he had said was exorbitant, but because it was actually a rare example of antique German pornography. The top of the snuffbox was a relief carving that depicted a bucolic scene: a shepherd tending a flock while a demure shepherdess sat under a tree and strummed a lyre. The hinged cover opened to reveal a second cover on which the man and woman were screwing their brains out.

Loring slipped the box into the back pocket of his running pants. Then, despite the haul he'd already made, he slid open the top drawer of Harriet's dresser. In it he could see a lot of lingerie but no boxes or receptacles of any kind. He pressed down here and there but felt nothing underneath.

Time to go.

With a last glance at the Kilowitzes, Loring left their room. It had been easy.

Maybe he should check the dresser top in the daughter's room.

He pushed the door open, gently. A babysmell, pablum and fresh diapers, sweet and nostalgic, filled his nostrils. Ahead of him was the bed, on which the daughter was visible, at first, as a dark form on white sheets. To the right of the bed was the crib. To his left, a dressing table. He went to it. It held more stuff than Harriet's shelf had, but the only things of value were a wristwatch and a string of pearls. He hesitated, decided not to take them.

As he turned to leave the room, he looked over at the young woman he had never met and whose full name he didn't know. She lay on her side, facing away from him, uncovered, wearing only bikini panties, her hip high in a stylistic curve. He averted his eyes for a second, then looked again.

She began to move, turned onto her back, her breasts shifting.

Suddenly the whites of her eyes gleamed.

"Who the hell are *you?*"

She sat bolt upright, a scream beginning. He moved quickly to her, clapped a hand over her mouth.

"I won't hurt you, I swear to God!" he said, in a frantic whisper. "Everything's all right, just let me get out of here!"

He was on the bed, his hand spread tightly over her face, the weight of his body on hers. Her eyes, inches from his, were glazed with terror. Tears began sliding to her temples, into her hair. Her protests were a nasal mewing.

Loring thought, *Can I say "I'm your father's friend, a neighbor . . . this is all a mistake . . . just let me get out of here and you go back to sleep and it never happened"?*

She began to struggle, trying to kick, wrapping one leg

around him. Still holding her mouth, he turned her over onto her stomach and slid his free arm under her, pinning her arms at her sides. Then he slowly stood up, bringing her off the bed and onto her feet.

He whispered again, "I'm not going to hurt you." His voice trembled but it was earnest. "Just come downstairs with me and I'll let you go, I swear it. Don't make it tough for me, please. . . ."

She was small, not very strong, but she kicked the air so violently it threatened his balance. Her thick curly hair was in his eyes and mouth. He hauled and carried her across the room to the bedroom door, where he stopped, listened for a moment to the rest of the house. It was quiet out there. He would take her down to the main floor, then let go of her and run out through the front door. His arms ached. He wondered if the situation were rape of a sort.

They crossed the hall, her legs flailing madly, her heels banging against his knees and lower legs, her body slippery with sweat. As they were about to descend the stairs he lost his balance. Together, they bumped down some of the steps, slid the rest.

At the bottom, he struggled them both to their feet. Then her hand found his crotch and squeezed his testicles between her mother's large floral brooch and pavé bracelet.

Loring bellowed in pain. His legs gave way. He let go of her and sank back to the floor.

She shot up the stairs, screaming through tears, "Help me! There's a guy in the house, there's a fucking *guy* in the house!"

In the master bedroom, her father sat up, wondering about what he had just heard, what he was hearing. Then he leaped out of bed and groped behind his nightstand. Harriet opened her eyes and asked, "Who's going to the movies?"

In his own room, Eddie woke up, slid his hand under his pillow to make sure his magazine was still there and went back to sleep.

Loring struggled to his feet, shafts of pain from his groin to his armpits, a milky way of lights crackling behind his eyes. He staggered to the door.

From the top of the staircase, shotgun in hand, Larry Kilowitz saw his front door standing open; he took the stairs two at a time and was out on the deck in time to see someone run into the Paiges' driveway, directly across the street. Kilowitz leaped over his deck railing and ran out into the middle of the street. There he stopped, took a wide-legged stance and clumsily flexed the shotgun, moving a shell into firing position.

Loring, still hurting, crouched against the side of the Paiges' house in the blackness of their driveway. Then he turned and looked across to the Kilowitz house; with horror, he realized that Larry was standing in the middle of the street with a shotgun,

A shotgun!

pointing it in his general direction.

Loring froze. He knew Larry couldn't see him, but even a near-miss could kill.

Should I shout, run out, surrender? Hey Larry this is all a mistake you know look hey please I'm writing this book see and jesus I'm sorry about this but I didn't hurt anyone I'm broke and up against all kinds of shit you wouldn't believe please let me go I'll explain it all tomorrow here's the stuff I took

A noise behind Loring. He turned his head, saw the side door, twenty feet away, open; Herb Paige leaned out, holding the family cat. Gently he plopped it onto the driveway pavement. The cat stretched itself.

At that moment, for the first time in his life, Kilowitz pulled a trigger.

BOL-LAM!

The Paige family cat was blasted away; it splattered against their garage, forty feet up the driveway.

Paige gasped; with a low "Holy shit!" he disappeared back inside his house. The door stayed open.

A second later, Loring, too, was inside the Paige house.

Kilowitz neither saw nor heard any of that. But, thinking he heard a rustle over to the left,

pump; BOL-*LAM!*

he fired again. The rose trellises along the side of the Deitermans' house took off and collapsed like a pile of sticks against the brick barbecue pit in their yard. Then, seeing something in the Deitermans' front garden,

pump; BOL-*LAM!*

Kilowitz blew their double front door open. A moving shadow on the second floor terrace of the Lesters' house caught his eye

pump; BOL-*LAM!*

and the Lesters' telephone wire whipped loose from their house, the awning on one of their front windows disappeared and their son's CB antenna wavered and fell into the street. The streetlamp went out.

pump; BOL-*LAM!*

The boxwood bushes in the Cummingses' garden disintegrated. Their garden hose twisted through the air like a snake insane.

Eddie, agog, ran out to his father with the box of extra shells. Larry shoved five more rounds into the shotgun's magazine.

Harriet appeared on their front deck, screaming, "Larry, stop it, *stop it!* You're going to kill somebody!"

Larry said, more to himself than to his wife, "That's the goddamn fucking idea. . . ." He saw another movement.

pump; BOL-*LAM!*

A shower of glass, from every window on the first floor of the Cummingses' house. Part of their rain gutter tore away from the eave and snapped straight up in the air.

pump; BOL-*LAM!*

The smooth cedar siding on the Lesters' house turned to pecky cypress. Three of their windows went out. Pictures on the far wall of their living room smashed to bits.

pump; BOL-*LAM!*

A branch fell heavily from the Cummingses' maple tree onto their new Lincoln. The air clouded with pulverized leaves.

172

pump; BOL-*LAM!*
The Paiges' front picture window shattered. A corner section of their roofing peeled off and sailed away.

pump; BOL-*LAM!*
The Cummingses' Lincoln heaved like a boat. The safety glass on the rear window crazed and dumped itself inside the car. Three tires went flat. The vinyl top shredded. The Smolens' house, half a block away on Levon Street, lost its back windows.

Kilowitz's gun was empty again. Eddie offered his father more shells, but Kilowitz was through; he lowered the shotgun and stared, in silent shock, at the four houses he had just raked.

Smoke and the smell of gunpowder hung on the air. It was quiet, like the eleventh hour of the eleventh day of the eleventh month in 1918.

The asthmatic yip-yip-yip of a police siren could be heard in the distance, coming to Horning Street in response to twenty-eight separate calls.

In their kitchen, the Paige family were lying flat on the floor.

Four feet away, Loring stood on the other side of their cellar door. When Herb Paige had run up to the kitchen, Loring had gone down to the basement. He'd been there for almost five minutes, listening.

A young, quavering voice: "Is it over, Dad?"

"I don't know. I think so. I'll see. . . ."

"Herb, don't go to the window!"

"I've got to see, Bonnie! We can't lay here all night!"

A minute later, Loring heard Herb Paige walk back into the kitchen.

"It's over, I think. You know who it is? Larry Kilowitz!"

"Larry! *Why?*"

"I don't know why. He's sitting on his front steps, with some kind of a rifle or a shotgun. Harriet and the kids are out there, too, talking to him. . . ."

Crying: "Why did he do all this? Was he shooting at us?"

"I don't know. He's gone nuts. The cops are coming, we'll

find out what the hell this is all about. I'm going into the living room. You all stay here."

The first police car was out front. Several immediate neighbors were on the street.

Paige came back. "Yeh, it's over. We can all go out."

"Are you sure?"

"Yeh. The cops are here, they're taking Kilowitz inside. Let's go see what the hell the story is. . . ."

Loring heard them leave the kitchen, then heard the front door close. The house was still. He stepped up from the cellar and went to the side door. Peering out, he saw a few people on the sidewalk, in robes and wrappers. They were facing across the street, backs to him. He moved out into the blackness of the driveway.

Presently the street was jammed with police cars, four or more, and people, hundreds of them, who had heard the ten shotgun blasts from as far away as Gerrold and Timberlane streets. Loring walked the few feet down the driveway and joined the fringe of the crowd. Next to him stood Fred Isaacs, Marty Cummings, the Deitermans, the Dreyfusses, the Harts.

"Loring! Can you believe this?" asked Ed Hart.

He wondered how much he would logically know at this point. "I just got here. The noise woke me up; what happened?"

"It seems," offered Deiterman, "that the Kilowitzes had a burglar. Larry chased him out of the house with a shotgun, he has a shotgun, and shot at him, maybe ten, fifteen times. You can't see it from here, but he did a hell of a lot of damage to these houses here." He indicated the adjacent houses. "Especially mine." He seemed proud.

Loring asked, "Was . . . the burglar shot?"

"He's long gone. Nobody knows."

"Was *anyone* hurt?"

"No," replied Isaacs. "I just asked Sergeant Scharlach." He pointed him out. "He's a friend of mine. He says nobody was hurt."

"Is he sure?"

"Nobody was hurt. But it's a miracle."

Loring took a deep breath.

Elias Shapp materialized next to him, wearing a bathrobe. He smiled at Loring. "Hiya, kid. Long time no see."

"Hello, Elias."

Shapp nodded toward the Kilowitz house. "Some piece of work, hah?"

Loring didn't know whether he referred to Larry or the burglary or what. But he agreed.

"People around here are gonna be pickin' shot out of their oatmeal for the next three weeks." He nudged Loring and grinned at him. "Nice quiet neighborhood, hah?"

After a while, perhaps forty-five minutes, the people began to drift away, and, except for a black unmarked sedan parked in front of the Kilowitz house, the police cars had gone. Loring said good night to the thinning group around him and started home. The air still smelled of gunpowder.

Halfway between Levon and Averly streets he knew there was a car without lights following just behind him. It drew abreast. Without breaking his stride, Loring looked over at it.

The police officer in the passenger seat peered at him, then waved. "Hey, how you doing, Mr. Writer?"

The hot-dog cops, John and whoever.

"Hey, fine, fine."

The patrol car came to a stop. Loring walked over to it, leaned easily on the door. John's partner grinned out at Loring from the driver's seat.

Pointing back toward Horning, Loring said, "By the time I got there it was all over. So what exactly was the fireworks about?"

"A burglary. You know Kilowitz? He had a shotgun. The fireworks was the stupid bastard shooting up the neighborhood."

"I don't know what's the good of people having a weapon if they don't know how to use it," said the partner.

Loring asked, "What actually happened?"

John shrugged. "We didn't get in, but the detectives said the guy got a lot of stuff and molested the woman."

"Molested the woman?" Loring was shocked. "Raped her, you mean?"

"According to her, that was his plans."

"My God." He thought of a good question. "And got away?"

"We're still looking." He indicated the empty streets. "Don't you see all the other cops?"

The other one lit a cigarette. "They called in a chopper, but it had magneto trouble." He snickered. "It's still sitting at Floyd Bennett."

John the Hot Dog smacked the dashboard. "That's what I like about this job. Let's roll, Tonto." His partner put the car in drive. "Well, take care. Have a nice night."

In a rear corner of his basement Loring reached gingerly into his underwear and took out the jewelry. When he sat down to examine it he felt and remembered the snuffbox in his back pocket. He took it out. In the light everything—the rubies, the box—was astonishingly beautiful. He put the brooch, the ring, the bracelet and the box into a carton that held some of Arlene's clothing. It was one of several such cartons that had been there, undisturbed, for almost two years. In recent weeks he'd been hiding things in it, until he could take them to Lewis and Cody. It currently held a couple of small pieces of Lynn Isaacs' costume jewelry that Lewis hadn't been interested in; rejects Loring intended to drop into a sewer, but hadn't gotten around to.

Upstairs, he leaned against their doorframe and looked in at the sleeping girls for several minutes. Their dolls, clothes, shoes, game boxes, the sweet smell of their room, had a sharp and poignant familiarity to him, as though he'd been gone a long time.

He'd organized no baby-sitter that night because he hated leaving the house at a reasonable hour and then having to kill hours of time. Besides, since the Pincuses, he had seen no point in having to create a whole evening's worth of alibi for what he expected to be a half hour's absence.

It was almost 3 A.M.

This must never happen again.

What *must never happen again?*

I must never be out for longer than a half hour.

He went into his bedroom and put the telephone receiver back on its cradle. Then he got undressed and looked at his smarting testicles. They were not lacerated.

But there was no sleeping. He went into the study and booted up his Hot Prowl file.

The most disturbing part of the whole nightmare, he realized, was what the cop had said: "Molested the woman." Would it go that way? Could that girl possibly say she'd been molested?

He typed for a while, recapping the episode. Then he added

I have to remember that 90% of it—the sound and fury—was not my doing.

And, of course, thank God in Heaven—nobody was hurt. Or killed.

Mingling with my neighbors in the street afterward, I realize, was a very good thing for me. I know I feel better now than I would have, had I been able to go straight home. Being there seemed to keep me at one with the neighborhood, a feeling I think has been slipping away lately. I almost identified with them, their shock and outrage.

Running into the hot dog cops was good, too. It reaffirmed for me what I hope to be my natural air of innocence.

But jesus—it just occurred to me that if those two cops had been any *other* cops they could very easily have taken me back to the Kilowitzes, resident or no resident, and run me past the daughter! That thought is so scary that my balls have stopped hurting for the first time since 1:30.

If I remember correctly, Harriet told me on Saturday that their daughter would only be around for a few days. Until she goes back to Los Angeles I must stay as far from that household and that street as possible. In fact, school's over for the summer; this would be a good week for me to catch a virus and stay home for a few days.

I'll call Lewis tomorrow and make a date to get the stuff to him; the twenty-second is only five days away.

Incidentally, I think I'll fence just the jewelry; the snuffbox is altogether too distinctive. I don't know why the hell I took it.

My hands are still shaking, but I actually feel quite good. Excited.

As my Arkansan Army buddy used to say, "It's like I been shot at and missed but shit at and hit."

A hot shower, now, and bed.

Monday, June 18 _____

LORING PLAYED SICK. To satisfy his nursing team, Katie and Briana, his nightstand held a small army of bottles: aspirin, ipecac, Pepto-Bismol, milk of magnesia. The property medicines.

From his bedside phone, he called Kilowitz a little after noon. "Hello, may I speak to Mr. Kilowitz, please?"

"Who's calling?"

"A neighbor, Loring Neiman. Who's this?"

"Joanie Heller, his daughter. Hang on."

When Larry got on the phone, his voice had the same tone of burdened celebrity that Loring had heard in Irving Pincus's, after the fact.

He sighed, then, "Hiya, Loring. What can I do for you?"

"I just wanted to touch base, Larry. How are you and the family?"

"How can we be? Fucking mad, that's how I am. I just hope to christ everybody finally got the picture. This is a war: it's us against the cocksuckers. Slimy fucking bastard in here—my private house—steals us blind and beats the shit out of my daughter and tries to rape her! *My daughter!*"

Loring swallowed. "What do you mean, Larry?"

"Did you get the whole story from last night?"

"Only . . . bits and pieces, actually. . . ."

"Well, we're on the five o'clock news! Watch it!"

Larry apparently became engaged, at that point, with someone else. "Shut up!" Loring heard him say. "What am I, a kid? Nobody tells me what to say, now shut up, Harriet, and mind your own goddamn business!" It was his wife.

Loring said, "If this is a bad time, I'll talk to you later. I—"

"Hey. Loring. Do me a favor. Watch the five o'clock news, Channel Four. You'll see what it's all about, last night. The whole story."

The five o'clock news had been on for several minutes. One of the teasers had been about the Kilowitz burglary, a shot of the daughter, holding her baby.

"Here's your eggs, Daddy. Katie spoiled two other ones but she told me not to tell you."

Briana carried Arlene's old bed tray into the room. On it were a plate with two fried eggs, a cup of hot water, a tea bag and a brace of Hostess cupcakes, unwrapped and on a plate of their own. A bud vase held a daisy, freshly wrenched from the backyard.

"Thanks, baby. It looks so beautiful. I'll forget what you just told me about Katie spoiling the other two."

"You don't have to forget, Daddy. Just don't tell her I told you. Oh, she said you should take your temp'ature."

"I will."

When the story came on, it opened with the anchorman.

"Armed burglary in Brooklyn, ten shots fired, a hundred thousand dollars' worth of jewelry stolen, a young woman and her baby threatened with kidnap, perhaps. Susan Henderson has the story."

"Do daddies take theirs from the mouth or from the tushy?" Briana asked.

"What? Oh. Whichever they prefer."

A shot of the front of the house, taken from across the street. Then a cut to across the street, showing some of the damage Kilowitz's shotgun had done.

"Why do kids always take theirs from the tushy and big people always take theirs from the mouths?"

"It's one of the perks of age."

Over the scenes, the reporter was saying, *"More than just another burglary in Brooklyn, but the fourth in a series of daring nighttime break-ins occurred at this home in the exclusive Kingsborough Beach section early this morning. And, before it was over, an attempted sexual assault and a terrifying gunfight between the intruder and the homeowner."*

"What's 'perks'?" Briana asked.

"Privileges. Like not having to answer questions." He glanced at her, pointedly. "When you're trying to watch TV."

"Me and Katie are gonna eat now. Do you want anything else?"

"Just a fork and a spoon would be nice."

"This is the home of Mr. and Mrs. Lawrence Kilowitz. According to police, an armed man, described by the victims as white, male, about thirty years old, broke into the house in the early morning hours. While the entire family slept, he stole an estimated hundred thousand dollars' worth of the wife's jewelry and then attempted to assault their daughter, Mrs. Stuart Heller, who was visiting her parents from her home in Los Angeles. I spoke with Mrs. Heller."

There was the shot of the daughter, holding her baby, in the Kilowitz living room. Behind her stood a glowering Larry Kilowitz. The reporter asked, *"Mrs. Heller, when were you first aware that the house had been invaded?"*

"I just opened my eyes, don't ask me why, it was hot and I had trouble sleeping, and there he was, standing over me, looking down at me."

Kilowitz put in, *"He was going to rape her, right in her father's house!"*

"That's really true," said Joanie Heller. *"The guy was really set to attack me, in my own father's house with my whole family sleeping. Can you believe it?"*

"And your father interrupted this?"

"While the guy was dragging me down the stairs, holding my mouth closed and my arms, you know, like down at my sides, like this. I had nothing on, he tore it off in the bedroom. Then I gave him a kick and, you know, punched him you-know-where and he had to let go. That's when I ran into my parents' room."

181

Larry nodded, impatiently. *"That's when I grabbed my shotgun and went after the—him. I—"*

The reporter asked Joanie, *"Did you get a good look at the man? Would you know him if you saw him again?"*

"I got a very good look at him, for several, many minutes and I would know him in a second."

"Could you describe him for our viewers?"

"Surely. He was white, pretty good-looking, around average height, around my age, I would say."

"Which is what?"

"Twenty-nine, thirty."

"Sir, does your description more or less agree?"

"Certainly," said Kilowitz, who never got a look at the intruder's face at all. *"Except he was bigger than she thinks, and he had a handgun."* He looked directly into the camera. *"I'll know him when I see him again, except that time he ain't going to get away in one piece, and you can believe it."*

The last shot was of the television reporter, standing on the sidewalk in front of the house. *"The fourth, and most shocking, in the series of nighttime burglaries that have been terrorizing this lovely area during the past three weeks. The residents are frightened. A neighborhood under siege. A lovely residential Brooklyn area, becoming the O.K. Corral.*

"This is Susan Henderson, from Kingsborough Beach."

Loring turned off the set. His eggs were cold. Everything had gone wrong. Except he wasn't caught.

The phone rang. It was Judith Lieb.

"Hello gorgeous did you see it just now?"

"Yes, Judith. Kilowitz . . . didn't seem too . . . credible, did he?"

"Well he's a shmuck but he underwent a terrible thing. Listen gorgeous tomorrow at eleven we're all going to Captain Costello's office to read him the riot act."

"Who is?"

"Me, Sidney if he takes the day off Freddy Isaacs Leo Goldstein Walter Krupp Irving Pincus and we hope you."

"I have a virus, Judith. I don't know if I'll be out of bed by tomorrow."

"I'm also going to ask Liz Blaug."

"Yes. Well, give them hell, and call me afterward."

Liz called a few minutes later. Her voice was low and guarded; Andy was home. "Judith said you're sick? What's wrong?"

"Nothing. Just a bug of some kind."

"Good. Same to you, Marion, and give my love to your mother."

Later, Loring thought about calling Lewis, but decided not to just then. He was feeling uneasy. He'd wait another twenty-four hours, see if that police meeting offered up anything else, either in the way of information or a sense of exactly what the authorities thought had taken place.

The authorities.

All of a sudden there are authorities *involved.*

Tuesday, June 19 _____

THE BUILDING ON Avenue W that housed the 65th Precinct had done so for almost sixty years. Local people liked the old three-story red brick station house, preferred it to the modern look of the newer plants in certain favored precincts, such as the 17th in midtown east, which slotted unobtrusively among neighboring buildings and made no statement whatsoever. The 65th stood separate and singular, a little grass in front, two big green glass balls on iron posts flanking a stately entrance, suggesting a courthouse in some rural county seat. Looking at it, one could almost hear some of justice's machinery cranking within.

The Six-Five was commanded by Captain Carroll Costello. Under him there were two uniformed lieutenants, one operational, the other administrative. The operations officer oversaw the neighborhood police team commander, the station house supervisor, who was a sergeant, and the patrol supervisor, who was also a sergeant. The two sergeants, in turn, supervised everyone from the anticrime team to the clerks, matron and switchboard operator. The administrative officer handled the training, planning and clerical agenda.

Besides this basic patrol command, however, the 65th Precinct, like every other police precinct in New York City, housed a Precinct Detective Unit, known informally as a "squad." The squad had its own Homicide Task Force, but specialists of other types were usually called in from borough or citywide units, such as the Arson/Explosives, Sex Crime,

Antiterrorism and Safe, Loft & Truck squads. In times past, burglaries were handled by borough Burglary/Larceny squads, but they no longer existed in the NYPD. Currently, a burglary (unless it qualified for the attention of the citywide Major Case Squad) was handled by members of the Precinct Detective Unit. The day after the Pincus burglary, two detectives from the 65th Squad made a routine appearance at the house because the victims had been at home during the actual commission. The same with the Judge Mushkin job. The Isaacs, though, which was reported an unknown number of days after the fact, was "investigated" only by two uniformed patrolmen. The Isaacs would have gotten a detective or two had they insisted, but they hadn't insisted. The Kilowitz affair not only involved gunfire, but had occurred during the quiet hours; besides four RMPs it drew the four 65th Squad detectives who were working that night, with an Emergency Response Team on standby. Unusual for a burglary.

The 65th Squad of detectives was headed by Lieutenant Frank J. Trezevant, Jr., who worked, technically, under Captain Costello. As in most precincts, however, the squad operated almost as a separate command. How sharp this division of command was in any given precinct often depended on the personalities of the precinct captain and the detective lieutenant.

"Hey, Cal, I hear we're getting a delegation from Kingsborough Beach. I want to sit in."

"It won't be necessary, Frank. I know these people personally, and I know how to give them the assurances they're looking for. It's PR."

"I'm good with PR. And those Jewish princesses like my type."

Costello disliked working with Trezevant, who freely made the distinction between himself as a "working cop" and Costello as a "talking cop." The man had no instinct, in Costello's view, for modern policing; he was a throwback, tactless, with a disturbing tendency to bend the rules. But he'd been an intelligent and resourceful police officer for eighteen years, was a veteran of various Burglary/Larceny squads and, as a matter of fact, considered burglary his personal specialty. So Costello would have to wait until this Kingsborough Beach file either got closed or simply dried up and blew away before talking to his rabbis at Brooklyn South about transferring Trezevant out of the 65th. Until then he would do his best to retain some control over him.

"Don't waste your time, Frank. I'll take care of it."

Twenty minutes into the meeting, Irving Pincus saw fit to direct an observation to the biggest goy in the room, Lieutenant Frank Trezevant. "You know what it was, Sunday night? It was *Kristallnacht!*"

"Say *what?*"

Leo Goldstein laughed. "He said *'Kristallnacht,'* Lieutenant. That's Yiddish, for 'Night of the Broken Glass.'"

"It's German, not Yiddish," Judith corrected.

"Whatever," said Pincus, raising a finger. "It was the night when the Nazis first started in with the Jews, running around in the streets smashing a million windows owned by Jews."

"And that's what Sunday night reminded you of?" asked Trezevant. "You've got a good imagination, mister."

"It's Mr. *Pincus,* Frank," Costello said to his lieutenant of detectives. "Mr. Pincus's relatives were refugees from the Nazis. I'm sure it's easy to understand how he could make that association."

"Excuse my ignorance," Trezevant replied. He was enjoying this group, even though only two of them were women. One a middle-aged redheaded bimbo type, but the other one was good-looking, young, didn't even look particularly Jewish. She wore a blue blouse and a khaki golf kind of skirt, short, well above the knee, and no panty hose. But no eye contact.

Walter Krupp said, "I don't think we came here for a history of the Holocaust. We came to find out when you're going to catch our burglar."

"We will, Mr. Krupp," Costello said. "Either catch him or discourage him. But a lot depends on you people. Is your

Neighborhood Watch functioning? Are you putting everything we told you into practice?"

"Captain, we're not children learning about responsibility," Judith Lieb said. "We're doing our best but we can't live like this."

Fred Isaacs said, "She's got a point there, Cal. We *are* a little like prisoners in our own homes."

Costello leaned forward, his elbows on the table. "I understand what you're all saying, Fred, and I don't fault you on it. But a lot of the concern I've been hearing for the past day or two is based on this Kilowitz episode, a decidedly atypical episode. The Beach residents have got to keep a perspective on this. Sure, it was a bad night, worst we've had in this precinct since I've been here, but I'd hate to see it magnified even more."

"Gunshots in the middle of the night don't need any magnifying," Krupp said. "In itself it's—"

Costello raised his hands. "Ah, but the shots were fired by the *victim*, sir. I can't point that out too strongly. Your perpetrator apparently wasn't armed and no police firepower was involved."

"Kilowitz said the man had a gun," said Krupp.

"No, sir," the captain responded. "He subsequently told us he might have been mistaken about that."

"*Kristallnacht*," mused Pincus. "From that came Dachau."

Costello looked at Pincus, nodded sympathetically. "Yes." Then he went on. "What the public has gotten they've gotten mostly from the Kilowitz family's television interview, and you know what your TV news is all about. Let me give you an example of what we're up against, in terms of potential hysteria. The New York *Post* called me, not an hour ago, trying to get me to call the burglar the 'Big Bad Beach Burglar'! Imagine. 'Big Bad Beach Burglar.' It would be a good headline for them, wouldn't it? You see, folks, your media would want to make this look like World War III. It wasn't. It was just another burglary. And a citizen, with a defensive weapon."

Sidney Lieb, loading his pipe, said, "I'm starting to think

the captain's right, Walter. It was Kilowitz did all the damage."

"He was responding," Krupp said, "to a threat. The problem is: how can we eliminate 'just another burglary'— and another response like Kilowitz's—from our future?"

"We will never eliminate it. We can only minimize it," Captain Costello said.

"It's a miracle," Judith put in, "that nobody was killed standing at their window."

She was lively, more conscious of her body than the younger one, Trezevant thought. He wondered how her tits would look unharnessed. An anxious over-fifty with decent tits can be the most fun. He looked at the younger one again. Or maybe not.

Isaacs said, "People are finding shotgun pellets as far away as Levon and Bay Boulevard." He looked around. "Did anyone know that?"

"They're good for the birds. Helps them digest," Trezevant said.

Costello shot him a glance, then said, "This is a big, busy precinct, folks, but a clean one. A quiet one." He opened a file folder on the desk in front of him. "I've prepared some statistics I'm anxious to show you, in re the number of shooting incidents here as opposed to Brownsville, East New York, Coney Island, and so forth. Would you care to see the figures?" He started to get up so he could pass some Xeroxed sheets around. They were to be the high point of the morning.

Goldstein refused his copy. "Not necessary, Captain. Sit. Rest," Goldstein said. "Personally, I see figures all day long. I'd rather hear what you two guys are planning to do for our protection."

"We'll do what's required," Lieutenant Trezevant said. "Nice Jewish people from Kingsborough Beach shouldn't get involved in police work."

They all looked at him.

Costello started to say something about *all* nice people from anywhere, but he was interrupted by Leo, who, his smile gone, said, "That's an answer? Why don't we just cut the bullshit and get to the bottom line: you get that bastard or we get your fucking jobs." Then he smiled. "Simple? Nice? Do we understand each other?"

Liz fell in love with Leo. Costello glanced apprehensively at Trezevant. Trezevant stared at Goldstein for a long moment. Goldstein, unfazed, stared back. The Insolent Look Contest.

Finally the lieutenant said, quietly, "I'm just going to have to give you more 'bullshit,' mister, and tell you that we're working very hard to do that. And to tell you some more statistics: since this nighttime series started, all daytime and ordinary burglary in Kingsborough Beach has completely ceased."

"That's a thrill," Leo said.

"Yes, some thrill!" Judith shouted at Trezevant, "because it's only that since the Pincuses were robbed everybody's nervous and more careful and they keep their doors and windows locked!"

Liz cleared her throat and spoke, for the first time. "Also, some of us are very concerned about the 'rape' aspect of this episode. Doesn't that put a whole other aspect on 'just another burglary'?" She looked at Captain Costello.

"Oh, I am very glad you raised that, Mrs. Blaug"—and he was—"because it gives me no choice but to tell all here"—he lowered his voice—"in the strictest confidence, that when Mr. Kilowitz's daughter was interviewed by people from our Rape Squad, last evening, she admitted that she was not attacked or molested by the perpetrator in any way, and that he didn't even take the nightclothes off her, as she originally stated; she was sleeping in the nude, practically, in the first place."

Trezevant noticed the glance between Judith and Liz. "You nice ladies look surprised," he said. "Women sometimes throw in 'rape' for a thrill. Professional burglars don't stop to rape anybody."

Liz snapped, "You seem to have more respect for burglars than for their victims."

What great eyes. "Now, I didn't say that at all, did I? I just know how burglars operate. It's my business to." Her glare held. Maybe there was hope.

Costello was wondering what he could say to repair the damage. He had not expected it to go this way. That fuck Trezevant. The only saving grace was the realization that the detective was building a case against himself.

"And since we're speaking of thrills," Liz said to Costello, "I'm not too thrilled with Lieutenant Trezevant's manner and attitude." She rose to her feet, her heart pounding. Costello almost nodded in agreement, until she added, "And I think you are patronizing us, Captain Costello."

Then he looked surprised. "Hardly, Mrs. . . . Blaug! Neither I nor Lieutenant Trezevant—"

"You know something I agree with Liz," said Judith, also getting up, "and I'm very disappointed in Captain Costello for letting his police officers sit around in their shirt sleeves being facetious with frightened citizens." She looked at her embarrassed husband. "Sid, let's go. We'll deal directly with City Hall from now on."

Trezevant thought: They'll get it wholesale. He watched Liz as she walked to the door.

The Beach people went to a diner for an indignant little lunch.

Liz Blaug asked, "Okay: if the police don't respond the way we'd like them to, what are our options? Where can we go from here? Can we really go over those people's heads?"

"You're damn right we can," said Judith. "Have you ever heard the words 'City' and 'Hall'? You thought I was bluffing well that's exactly where the hell we're going. Sidney, you call somebody tomorrow, first thing, we'll show them we're serious."

"It wasn't 'them,'" Isaacs said. "It was that Trezevant. Trust me. Cal Costello is a first-class cop."

Leo Goldstein snickered through his turkey sandwich. "First-class 'cop'? Or 'cock'?"

"What I can't get over is that stupid Joanie Heller," Judith said, "changing her story like that, and now I know why she's suddenly flying back to California tonight, she's embarrassed that she lied on TV."

"So. What can you expect," Sidney Lieb said. "She's a dummy like her father, right?"

"Him and his fucking gun. He is one crazy bastard," Goldstein said.

Liz said, "By the way, Leo, you were wonderful."

Leo pinched his own cheek, then hers. "You weren't too bad yourself, kid."

In the parking lot, as they walked to their cars, it was agreed that Sidney would call the mayor's secretary and Walter Krupp would call a deputy mayor he played poker with. Judith said she'd get Naomi Berger to call Norman in Washington and tell him to fire off a letter to someone.

"Oh, Liz," she added, "would you be able to stop at Loring's house, he's sick in bed, and fill him in? If not I'll call him tonight."

Liz pursed her lips, thought for a second. "I can spare a few minutes, I guess."

Judith was sure she could.

Briana interrupted her piano lesson to shout upstairs: "Daddy, are you too sick to talk to Mrs. Blaug for a minute?"

Loring was pleasantly surprised. "I'll do my best not to expire in her presence, baby. Send her up."

Liz tapped on the bedroom door, entered. She smiled when she saw him. "Men always look funny in bed in pajamas in a sickbed during the day. So deliciously helpless."

"Think of me as a dreadnought in dry dock."

She briefed him on the meeting. "Some lieutenant was there, the detective who's apparently going to take charge of the case."

The "case." "The Kilowitz case?"

"The whole case, all the burglaries."

"I see. What's his name?"

"Trezevant."

"What's he like?"

She wrinkled her nose. "Arrogant. Very cop-like. Slender, sallow, blond, deadpan."

"Did he seem smart?"

She thought about it, then shrugged. "I suppose so."

"But he's not . . . as civilized . . . as Costello?" Loring asked.

"No. Definitely not. Totally different type. Sort of hard-bitten."

"Hard-bitten. You mean aggressive? Determined?"

"I don't know, really. It was hard to tell. He had a very abrasive style. His attitude about Harriet's daughter was damned offensive."

"What was it, his attitude? What did they say about all that?"

She told him what Costello said about the Rape Squad interview. "Then that Trezevant *really* tried to make a liar out of her, implying that women scream 'rape' for thrills."

"Well . . . maybe she did. The guy didn't handle her any differently than he would have if she were fully dressed."

"How do you know?"

"How . . . that's what somebody told me." *Shmuck.*

"It's probably true. She's going back to California tonight, mortified, Judith Lieb told us."

"Really?" *Thank God!* "Too bad. She's the only one who could actually identify the guy. If they catch him."

"'If' is right. They didn't exactly seem galvanized. Mainly sort of defensive."

"Well, you were all sitting there telling them they're not good at their work."

"I suppose we were." She looked at her watch. "I've got to go, darling. Andy's coming home early."

As she kissed him good-bye, he slid his hand under her skirt. She put hers into his pajama pants. He winced; his testicles were still a little tender.

"What's the matter?"

"From the fever I had."

After she left, Loring called American Airlines. "I'm

calling for Mrs. Joan Heller. She's misplaced her ticket; can you please remind us what flight she's on tonight, to LAX?"

"One moment, please. Okay. J. Heller? She's confirmed on flight 29, departing John F. Kennedy at 7:30 this evening."

"Oh, good. Thank you very much."

It's for real. He felt better, freer.

He turned Liz's report over in his mind: The cops. A Lieutenant Trezevant. In charge of the "case." Sounds heavy-duty. Still, they're not television cops. They're real cops, capable of foot-dragging, denial, defensiveness. They have their point of view, the victim and his friends another. And it's negotiated. Even a crime has its politics. It was a matter of how much pressure the people could put on the police, and for how long. The Kingsborough Beach psyche—a busy and social one—can only maintain indignation for a certain length of time. Even terror, especially indirect terror, can't hang in forever. Then life will go on. Heat will go off.

Telling himself all that, he felt even easier.

He got out of bed, would work for a while. Later that evening he'd call Lewis, make an appointment, organize the money.

Briana had just taken her first piano lesson, on the brand-new secondhand upright her father had bought for her.

Loring was in his study, at the word processor.

Katie, reading a magazine in the girls' bedroom, thought about going downstairs for some predinner Mallomars and milk, now that the "music" was over.

Briana carefully put her music book inside of the piano bench and went up to the bedroom. "Did you hear my scales?" she asked her sister.

"I heard better scales on a fish," Katie replied.

Briana looked puzzled, then hurt. "Then I'm not gonna show you what I found." She went to her dresser, opened the bottom drawer, removed something and, shielding it from her sister's view, began playing with it. After a minute or two it caught Katie's eye. It looked pretty.

"What's that?" Katie asked.

"Nothing for you."

"What *is* it!"

"A box."

"A box?" Katie got off the bed, went for a closer look. There was a beautiful carved picture on top. "It's neat!" She opened it and saw the second picture, within. With a sidelong glance at Briana, she quickly shut it. "Where did you get this?"

Briana felt no guilt. "In the basement. In Mommy's stuff."

"Mommy's stuff? It was right with Mommy's stuff?"

"Yes."

Katie had been involved, to some extent, in the packaging and storage of her mother's things, two years earlier. This wasn't anything of her mother's. This had *never* belonged to her mother. She opened the top cover again, shook the little box. Something deep inside of it moved, with a little rattling sound. She shook it again, then looked closely at the second cover. There was more to this box than met the eye. She put a fingernail between the second cover and the smooth inside wall. It moved. It could be raised. She raised it, revealing a lower chamber. In the chamber was a folded piece of printed paper. She took it out, unfolded it. It was the front page of a Yankee Stadium program, a baseball program, autographed by a half-dozen different hands.

She knew what it was.

And to whom it belonged.

It was Eddie Kilowitz's, his prize, his treasure of treasures. Not trusting his usual safekeeping places, he had kept it, since last summer, inside his mother's "secret box." And, since yesterday morning, had been bemoaning its apparent theft. By the burglar.

She went down to the basement. There, in one of her mother's cartons, she found a few more things her mother had never owned. Including a big pin, a bracelet and a ring. All with red jewels.

How did Eddie Kilowitz's program and all this other stuff get here?

* * *

At eight-thirty Loring dialed Lewis's phone number, the one at his home, wherever that was. As usual, he hated making the call.

Lewis answered after one ring. "Hello?"

Loring said, "Lewis, this is Mike Sunglasses."

"Of course, my friend. How are you?"

"Fine. I have some things to show you."

"What kind of things?"

"Ruby jewelry."

"I love rubied jewelry. Are the pieces fine?"

"The stones are Burmese, I think."

"Burmese, are they! You remembered about Burmese! I am a good teacher, am I not?"

"Good enough."

"Good enough," Lewis repeated. Mike Sunglasses was always so terse. "Describe, if you would, the pieces."

Loring did, complete with "light traps."

His description didn't seem to surprise Lewis. "How long have you had them?"

"A . . . few days."

"Then why not meet me for a nice lunch on Thursday, after which—"

"I don't go to 'lunch,' Lewis." *Lunch. He's trying to make a fucking social club out of this.*

Lewis realized that Mike resented the invitation. He had often wished Mike hadn't so obviously hated their association. Lewis disliked most of his clients, but he liked Mike, respected his sensibilities. He had always tried to make him feel comfortable and had even hoped to make a friend of this nice Jewish fellow with the naïve cloak-and-dagger ways. But Mike had maintained (out of fear, Lewis suspected) a distance between them. And so it would have to be. "All right, then, Mike, meet me at Farraday Estates, at one o'clock."

Cody's. Shit. "Why there?"

"That is where I will be," Lewis replied, simply.

"Okay. I'll be there."

They hung up. Loring leaned back in his chair, lit a cigarette. Thursday was the twenty-first. He would get a bank

196

check for the cash on Friday morning—at any bank that didn't know him—and deliver it to Carlin the same day. The final day. Talk about cutting it close.

He thought about what was the only business relationship he had, currently. After the Goldstein watches (on which, he'd come to understand, Lewis hadn't taken a cut), he hadn't seen Lewis until the Pincus candlestick holders. Lewis had been surprised by them, knew their value and history and from that point on had dealt personally with Loring, at the pawnshop. Which Loring preferred. Lewis was bad enough, on a personality level, unctuous and boring and halitosic, but he didn't have the strong air of criminality that Cody did. Cody scared him.

Then he remembered, for the first time with any hint of pleasure, that he actually did have another business relationship, a real one: *Gold Coast* magazine, the burglary article. Long overdue. Long untouched. He should finish it. He had never, in his career, defaulted on an assignment, no matter how small the money.

As he slid the disk into the drive, Katie and Briana came into his study, in pajamas, ready for bed. Briana kissed him good night. Then Katie did. She looked at him. "Good night, Daddy."

"Good night, sweetheart."

Her look seemed oddly sad, held for an extra moment, as though she was about to say more. But she didn't. She and Briana went to their room.

Loring started to boot up The Piss-ant Crime, but while the disk drive was whirring, he realized he had absolutely no interest in working on it. Instead, he went to the closet and took down the Hot Prowl box, which, at that point, held three nearly full disks.

He loaded the current one, to which he was writing about the Kilowitz aftermath.

Briana fell asleep within her usual few minutes, but Katie lay awake for a long time, her twelve-year-old mind still struggling to bring some adult-type thinking to what was bothering her. But whenever she tried to think the way she felt a grown-up would think, it never worked out right. So she fell back to the first, and painfully strange, feeling she'd gotten in the basement that afternoon: that her father was a stealer of things.

Could it be? He had always taught her that taking what belonged to someone else was wrong. She had once kept a book from the library so long that she was embarrassed to take it back. When the letters stopped coming in the mail she decided to keep it. Her father found it in her room and told her that keeping a library book was the same as stealing. He made her take it back and pay the charges out of her allowance. She felt better afterward.

But then she recalled another time, another thing that happened: her father telling her mother to keep the blouse that a department store had sent her by accident; that she needed the blouse more than Macy's did. They had laughed about it. And her mother kept the blouse. And had felt it was a good thing.

What was the difference between what she did and what they did? She wasn't sure, but felt it had to be a matter of "need." With big people, "need" made it okay to steal, okay to lie. Maybe there are two kinds of truth.

Her father's need to steal stuff . . . how much of that had to do with her? If you steal a necklace and a bracelet and a ring, does it have anything to do with tooth braces and a new bike and jeans and summer clothes?

Daddy? A *stealer* of things? Only if he really had to.

Wednesday, June 20 _____

L EUTENANT TREZEVANT CREATED a new case folder, labeled it *KBNB*, for Kingsborough Beach Nighttime Burglar. In it he consolidated the paper work of four cases: Pincus, Isaacs, Mushkin and Kilowitz. Each case had its squeal sheet, the form PD 313-152 Preliminary Complaint Report. In addition, the Pincus, Mushkin and Kilowitz cases each had a DD5, a Supplementary Complaint Report, which had been filed by the detectives who "followed up." The patrolmen each time had made the cursory reports that were common in such cases, and his detectives, a day later, had not really tried to add anything substantive, supposing (as they had had every reason to) that after a certain amount of jerking off, the cases would be consigned to a departmental oblivion. The sum total of all of this was that no evidence had ever been found, and, with the exception of the Kilowitz daughter's, the descriptions of the perpetrator were what Trezevant would call "imaginary."

But the meeting at Costello's office precluded oblivion. And since then, in fact, there had been a call from Inspector Rose of the Chief of Detectives' office. Kingsborough Beach had some juice, and it was flowing. Inspector Rose hadn't farted around: "Like it or not, Frank, you just caught the case, personally. Keep it alive and stop that cocksucker. I'll put it this way: *get* the cocksucker."

With nothing except "M/W/30–40." An unusual burglar description, especially the "W" part, but so what?

Costello had already given the sector—Charlie Sector—all

the increased patrol activity he could spare: its very own full-time RMP from 1600 to 0800. Two tours. It was the first RMP The Beach had ever had on that basis, and it got around the neighborhood often enough to be seen once or twice each night by anyone who cared to watch for it, so, for the time being, at least, the citizens should feel a little better.

Yesterday Trezevant had stayed at the station house until after midnight to catch and interview every one of the patrolmen and detectives whose names and shield numbers were on the reports, but, as expected, got little from their notes that wasn't already in the skinny folder. And this morning he'd gone into Kingsborough Beach and talked to the Pincuses, Mrs. Isaacs, Judge Mushkin and Mrs. Kilowitz, then went up and down Horning Street and around two of its corners to Baldwin and then Levon, talking to those people who happened to be home, twenty-one of them. After which he had phoned Mr. Isaacs and Mr. Kilowitz at their offices and spoken to them. And got little that wasn't already in the case folder.

So, while unwrapping the cold roast beef on rye that one of his men had left for him an hour earlier, Trezevant considered what they had:

1. Male, white, thirty to forty.

2. An Identikit composite from the Kilowitz girl's description that even she didn't recognize when it was done.

3. Perpetrator always seems to know what's best in the place and where they keep it, does very little or no ransacking.

4. No vehicle used.

Nobody, in fact, had ever seen or heard a vehicle. Nobody within blocks of any places of occurrence—a very quiet neighborhood of nervous Jewish people who hear their newspapers landing on their lawns at 3 A.M.; a car starting up after midnight would sound like Mount Vesuvius—recalled seeing or hearing a vehicle. Even in regard to the Kilowitz occurrence, when practically everybody in the area was at their front window seconds after the first shot was fired.

Number 4 seemed interesting to Trezevant, in the light of

number 3. He knew a lot of talented burglars. He knew good burglars who always used their own car, or van, because they felt safe, like bringing their home away from home. He knew other good burglars who worried about their license plates being made, so they used only stolen vehicles, one for every occasion. But he never knew any good burglars who wanted to walk for blocks through an exclusive-type residential neighborhood—a strange neighborhood—late at night carrying something they had just stolen.

Trezevant took a bite of the sandwich, poked inside the bag for a piece of pickle.

Unless it's not . . .

He found the pickle, looked at it disapprovingly. He hated new pickles.

Unless it's not a strange neighborhood.

Andy saw the key.

He was changing out of his suit, she was sitting on their bed, cleaning out one of her purses, the big, baskety "weekend" one. Out of it, among a small handful of old tissues and used-up lipsticks, Liz brought a key that was attached to a large white plastic tag. She instantly thrust it back into the purse, then turned a bit toward him, trying, peripherally, to judge whether he had noticed it or not. She apparently decided he hadn't. Casually she hung the purse back in her closet and went downstairs to get dinner.

Andy fished out the key and read the tag. It was from an East Hampton hotel to which he had never been. Impulsively he dialed the number and asked them if a Mr. Loring Neiman was registered.

They said he was not.

Andy then told the clerk he might be mistaken about the date by a full week; had Mr. Neiman, by any remote chance, been there *last* Wednesday?

The clerk checked for a moment and said, "Your thought is correct, sir. A Mr. and Mrs. Loring Neiman did stay here *last* Wednesday night."

He said nothing to Liz.

Later that night, as she slept upstairs, he sat out on their rear veranda, staring out into the moonlit yard, wondering how much of this was his fault; what hadn't he done that he should have? He had always been aware that OBs were commonly thought to either hate women, or love them too much. He did neither; he didn't hate women and certainly didn't love them too much. In fact, the only woman he had ever loved was Elizabeth. And she, as far as he had ever known, loved him and had always been faithful.

In spite of her effect on men, an effect of which she was unconscious. She always had attracted them, always would, for at least another twenty years of time and gravity. From their earliest days at Mass General—not only at the insanely bawdy intern-resident-nurse parties that would periodically arrive, in a ball of people, at the door of their tiny Revere Street apartment, but in the hospital corridors, cafeterias, lounges—he had watched men watching her or positioning themselves to watch her: her face when she talked, her body when she walked, sat down, crossed her legs, stood up. The sheen of her nylons or the tan of her bare leg. Her thighs against her skirt. Her behind. Sunlight or lamplight through the material of her blouse. Oh, the many times he had sent signals into countless roomsful of other men, signals that said he was aware but didn't care—he was still in charge!

And he had always been.

But now, this Loring Neiman.

It hurt.

Thursday, June 21 _____

LEWIS LOOKED AT the stuff. "This came from Brooklyn, last Sunday night. The name . . . Kilowitz. Am I correct, Mike?"

Loring adjusted his sunglasses, said nothing.

"Lovely things from Burma, as you said. It always disappoints me that people cry about their losses to the newspapers in terms of dollars and cents, never mentioning the beauty that has been snatched from their lives."

Loring hadn't considered the fact that the Kilowitz jewelry had been described in the newspapers. He felt oddly embarrassed, as though he'd been projecting an image of impoverished respectability all along that had just been blown. And that he was now, suddenly, just like them. The firm of Lewis, Cody & Mike Sunglasses.

"I don't know anything about that. I never read the newspapers," he said. "Can we do this . . . transaction, please? I have to be somewhere."

"Of course," Lewis said. He was seated at Cody's desk, bent to the three pieces of jewelry, his loupe in place.

Cody, staring at Loring, grinned. "Lucky you didn't get your ass shot off that night, right?"

Loring kept his eyes averted, nodded in a vague way.

Cody leaned in his chair to catch Loring's eye. "You try to jump that cunt?"

Loring didn't answer.

"Did you?"

Loring felt badgered, wanted away from him. Finally he let his eyes meet Cody's marbles. With an edge to his voice, he asked, *"'Jump the cunt'? What 'cunt'?"* He lifted his hat for a second to let some cool air under it.

"Kilowitz broad, the daughter on TV."

Lewis looked up from the jewelry and said, "Cody, leave Mike alone. This is a business meeting, not an American Legion smoker." To Loring, he said, "Our associate is a hopeless provincial."

Our associate.

Lewis took his time poring over the pieces. Loring tried to appear relaxed, leaned against a packing crate, took out a cigarette.

Lewis marveled. "Very fine. This large one is better than two and a half carats. The ring is spectacular, star ruby, cabochon, surrounded by faceted diamonds. The pavé bracelet is platinum, Van Cleef. Beautiful. The Kilowitz woman has taste."

The third time the name had been mentioned. Three steps closer to home. Loring's discomfort grew.

Finally the old man flipped the loupe up and turned to Loring. "Ten thousand."

Loring was shocked. Ten thousand was not enough. He had to have fifteen by the following day. "I expected—expect—twenty for this," he said.

"On what basis, Mike?" Lewis asked quietly. "How much do you feel these pieces are worth?"

Loring, of course, had no real idea. The news had said a hundred thousand. He shrugged. "Eighty, eighty-five."

Lewis smiled, shook his head. "Not quite, my friend. Let me be frank. I am excited by these things; they are good, and not so distinctive that they would have to be dismantled and sold stone by stone. My little network provides me with customers from all over the eastern seaboard, and some discerning woman of diminishing means in, say, Philadelphia, could wear these pieces to the ballet this very night just as they are now.

"But as to their value . . ." He stood up. "On the street

they are only worth around sixty thousand, and on my market perhaps only forty. Then, two commissions will have to be paid. One, naturally, to our good associate here"—he indicated Cody—"for routing, and the other to whichever colleague of mine, in whatever city of destination, resells them. Ultimately, the net price will settle to around thirty thousand." He stared at the ceiling for a moment, plucked at his beard. "For the pleasure I've already gotten from looking at them, as well as the danger you were apparently in on Sunday night, I will extend myself and offer you fifteen."

Loring still felt he was being lowballed, but he nodded. Lewis counted out the cash and handed it to him. He put it in his pocket.

Then Lewis said, "You won't be coming back to us anymore."

"Pardon?"

"We cannot do business together anymore, Mike. Or do you already know that?"

"I don't understand. What do you mean?"

"Someone asked me—for your own good—to stop dealing with you. And I shall respect his wish. This was our last transaction. Our swan song."

"Who asked you?"

"You have no idea?"

"No, I don't."

Lewis studied Loring's expression; it was one of true bewilderment. "Then I'm afraid it's not for me to tell you. Suffice it to say it was a mutual friend."

"You and I don't have any mutual friends, Lewis, and I haven't the faintest fucking idea what you're talking about!" *Suddenly it's a scene from a Charlie Chan movie. Why am I standing here having this surrealistic conversation with a guy who isn't credible in* any *context?* Loring's hand, in his pants pocket, had been massaging the wad of cash; now it felt clammy to his touch. "But whatever. It's been nice knowing you."

"I've enjoyed it. But before you go, Mike, I would appreciate a word of assurance from you. Dilettantes like you, if they are caught doing something wrong, sometimes tend to involve . . . the whole Western world."

My father: Kid, the only man you ever have to fear is the one who's afraid of you. "Well, let me tell you that you have nothing to worry about, Lewis, as far as that's concerned. I'm a very . . . discreet man and I'm under no suspicion and as a matter of fact—this was my last . . . time, anyway."

"Really? I tend to doubt that. In spite of your taciturnity, I've always gotten the feeling that you enjoy this work."

"Wrong, Lewis. Very wrong. Believe me, this is it. Anyway, take care, Lewis. And Cody. It's been a real pleasure."

He grinned more or less fraternally, turned and started for the front door, trying very hard to look like a really sweet guy ambling off into the sunset. As he opened the door, he felt a hand on his shoulder. Cody's.

"Well, Cody, so long—"

Cody plucked Loring's sunglasses off, then his hat, and peered hard at his face for a moment. "Wanna good look at you."

"Yes . . . but you don't have to ever worry about—"

Something the size of a railroad locomotive rammed into his stomach.

"Fuckin' well told," Cody said as he shoved Loring out into the street and slammed the door behind him.

Loring staggered like a drunk about twenty paces along the sidewalk, then reeled to a telephone pole which he held on to while he vomited; passersby hesitated, stepped wide around him as he vomited again.

Friday, June 22 _____

H E CONDUCTED SOME business at three different banks in
three different Brooklyn neighborhoods and got to the
law offices of Biolos & Biolos, foreclosure attorneys to the
Newgate Trust Company, at about two.

Carlin was surprised to see him. Loring handed him an
envelope containing three certified checks totaling thirty-five
thousand, eight hundred and sixty-three dollars and seventy-
seven cents and said, "I heard you found my papers."

While Loring sat on the edge of Carlin's desk, the young
attorney read the checks, added them up and then took a
folder from the bottom drawer of his desk. The folder was
labeled "NEIMAN—NTC—F." He carefully put the checks
into it and placed it in a basket on his desktop. "NEIMAN—
NTC—F" had come in from the cold.

Then he said, "I'm glad it worked out for you. Would you
care to wait for the paper work on this, or shall we mail it all
to you?"

"Mail it."

And that was that.

His home was still his home.

Carrying a tomato and lettuce sandwich on white toast and
a glass of beer, he went upstairs to his study. It was after
three, and he hadn't been able to keep food down since
breakfast the day before. The tomato and lettuce was in
consideration of the way his stomach felt. The beer was in
spite of it.

The girls were out, playing at Amy's house down the block.

Loring swiveled his chair around to face the Pincuses' house. A lot had gone down since that day in the middle of May. Four harrowing experiences, two repulsive confederates, two squeezed balls, countless buckshot whistling past his ears, one punch that flattened his stomach against his spine and a bird of pain sitting in his abdomen.

With his beer, he made a silent toast: *But I did it; nobody but me has been hurt; I got away with it.* Then he took a long cold draught and sat back in his chair.

And thought: *Now what?* He had a residue at that moment of about three thousand dollars, enough to cover regular living costs for another month. But there would be other discretionary expenses, such as three weeks at Kinderland this summer, the clothing to go with it, a transmission job on his car. He had paid much of what he owed on the word processor, but they were pressing him for more. Three thousand was not much of a cushion.

He booted up the current chapter, spent the next forty minutes roughing in the Carlin scene. Then

> I no longer have a fencing connection.
> That "mutual friend" Lewis referred to doesn't exist. I'm convinced of that. He's a careful man, and my hunch is that when Lewis heard about the gunplay he was worried that I was starting to fuck up my act, so he decided the prudent thing was to quit with me.
> I now also realize that Lewis insisted upon meeting at Cody's yesterday so that the marble-eyed cretin could "discourage" me from ever mentioning their names. And he did, he did.

The phone rang.

"Mr. Neiman?"

"Yes."

"This is Roger, the manager at Penny-Town." The voice had an acerbic edge. "You better get down here as soon as you can."

"Why?"

"There's a problem here . . . with your daughter. Kathleen?"

Loring stood up. "What do you mean a problem?"

"We caught her shoplifting."

In less than four minutes, Loring was at the store, in the Plum Beach Mall. He sailed down the center aisle to the small office in the rear, where an officious-looking man with a plastic badge that said "Manager" stood, waiting, in the doorway. Inside, Katie was seated on a chair, her face streaked by tears. Next to her stood a female clerk in a store smock. When Katie saw Loring, she ran to him and threw her arms around his waist, started to cry. Briana and their friend Amy stood sheepishly in a corner.

"What the hell is all this?" Loring asked the room, especially the manager. Then he bent to Katie. "What is this, Katie? What happened?"

While she tried to produce a voice, the man held a small package up and said, righteously, "She stole this off a shelf. This salesclerk saw her and—"

"Let me see that!" Loring snatched the item from the man's hand. It was a cheap salt and pepper shaker set, the glass kind with aluminum screw-off tops, packaged in plastic. The marked price was $1.98. He held it up with a shaking hand. "Are you trying to tell me *my* daughter *stole* this piece of shit?" He threw it into a corner. "You've got some goddamn nerve, browbeating a kid that age!"

"She *did* steal it! This lady saw her take it and try to stuff it into her—"

Loring pointed at him. "You shut your mouth or I'll stuff it right up your ass!"

The man paled.

The woman said, "You know, we could have called the cops on her, you know. Instead, we—"

"That's right," said the man. "We were nice enough not to call the cops. But I will now." He reached for the telephone.

Loring jerked him away from it by the collar. "No you won't and you're goddamn lucky you didn't because not only would my lawyers land on you and this shitting store like a bomb but I'd personally break your fucking head!"

Katie had stopped crying, was watching her father. Briana

and Amy exchanged excited smiles. The store manager retrieved the package from the floor. "Shoplifting is an offense," he said, in a nonthreatening voice. "It doesn't matter how old—"

"You want an offense, I'll give you an offense!" Loring grabbed the four-drawer metal file cabinet behind him, rocked it violently and then shoved it; it fell to the floor in the middle of the office with a crash. The entire store was shocked to silence.

"Come on, girls, let's go home."

Nobody spoke in the car. When they got to the house, Loring took Katie up to the study, sat her down.

Gently he said, "You want to tell me about that."

She nodded. "Yes, Daddy."

"Okay."

"I took it, like he said."

"Okay. You want to tell me why?"

"First, I took something else, this morning, from the supermarket. A box of golden toothpicks."

"You did?"

"Yes. I put it down the basement, in the box with Mommy's things."

"In the box with . . . I see. . . ."

Katie's face clouded again. Then she began to cry, softly. "Daddy, I know that *you* steal things."

His blood turned cold.

She went on. "I did it to help."

"Katie, sweetheart, let me tell you something . . . if you found anything in the basement that looks as though I stole it, I didn't."

"Then how did Eddie's mother's white box get there, and those red jewels?"

Dear God in heaven. "Those things? I found them, Katie, one night, in the street, and I called the police. They told me they were stolen by the burglar, you know, the burglar who's been robbing around here? They said that burglar stole them and they needed them for evidence and would I please hold on to it, secretly, while they tried to catch the guy."

"They did?" she asked. "You're helping the police?"

"Of course! Jesus, Katie, I wouldn't steal anything! People go to jail for that, and do you think I want to go to jail?"

She stared at him for a moment. Then she smiled, seemed to relax.

"Katie, can I ask you not to say anything about all this?"

Snuffling, she nodded.

"Good. Thank you. And, sweetheart?"

She looked at him.

"Did you tell Briana—or Amy—why you were . . . doing that?"

"No, Daddy. It's my and your secret."

He watched her as she washed her face and combed her hair. They would make spaghetti that night for dinner; if she started the water now, he'd be downstairs in a few minutes to help.

He sat down and stared at the screen for a while. Then he typed

I will have to do it one more time.

I need three or four months to finish this book, which means three or four months' worth of money; ten thousand, at least. And, without a fencing connection my career as a jewel and silver thief is over. This time it will have to be cash.

There must have been twenty thousand or more in Leo Goldstein's drawer that night. So much that he apparently never missed the thirty-six hundred I took. Maybe it's still there, and I should go for it.

Just this one more time.

Tomorrow Leo and Sandy are giving a barbecue to announce Norman Berger's decision to run for the Senate. Maybe while I'm there I can get back to Leo's bureau drawer.

This will be my last one. Absolutely. I'm corrupting my children.

I wonder how much of all this is compulsion?

Everything else seems dull in comparison.

This book gets better and better.

Just this one more time.

Saturday, June 23 _____

LORING'S GIRLS WERE at a movie matinee. He and Liz were
in his bed, where they had eaten a pound and a half of
cold boiled shrimp, peeling and popping them like peanuts.
Along with a split of champagne. She had brought the
champagne, took it out of her purse just as he was about to
open two bottles of beer. It was to commemorate a proposal
to him she planned to make.

But before what she considered to be the right moment,
they made a little love.

After which, seeping out, she once again brought up the
subject of his book.

He was more forthcoming than usual. He told her (a) it was
nonfiction and (b) it had a lot to do with his current life. "And
you're in it," he said. "You want to hear one of your parts?"

He cleared his throat and then recited: "She lay naked,
spread-eagled, on her stomach. Once again, she asked me
about my book. But I could not answer, because my tongue"
—he kissed the nape of her neck—"had begun its journey;
from the nape of her neck, it trekked the length of the plain of
her back"—He licked his way to the small of her back—
"grazed slowly down the valley between her buttocks . . ."
The rest of it was muffled: ". . . waded through the mysteri-
ous fen surrounding her labia and finally came to rest, to
bathe and feed and drink, at the sweet of her clitoris."

She allowed him there for a brief moment, but then drew
herself onto her side. Her face was impassive.

"You don't like my stuff?" he asked. "Well, I write it like it is. Nonfiction. And more or less true."

"Loring, Sunday night I called you, late, and your line was busy. I kept trying until almost three o'clock in the morning."

"You did."

"I did. And it was the second time that happened. Who the hell do you talk to at 3 A.M.? In the continental United States?"

"Nobody. I sometimes take the phone off the hook at night. I've gotten some . . . nutty calls lately."

"I see."

"I don't have any other women, Liz." He played with her hand, nervously.

"I'd almost welcome other women as a possibility. Where did you go on two other nights, when your daughters answered the phone at around nine-thirty or ten?"

He knit his brow. "I don't know. Which nights, specifically?"

"I don't remember which nights, specifically. But I think *you* do." She took her hand away, waited for a response. There was none. "Loring, are you involved in something you're ashamed of?"

He shook his head.

"Yes you are. And it's changed you."

"Changed? From what to what? From since when?"

"From since we met."

"That's only . . . what . . . five weeks ago, Liz. How do you know I've changed? Maybe this is the real me. . . ."

"No. The man I sat in a car with in front of my house that night and spent that fabulous day with at your friend's apartment and the couple of hours at Canarsie Park for which I caught shit from my husband was the real you: eager to talk to me, to open up. We'd only known each other for days, I grant you, but I knew who I was dealing with.

"Now, for the last few weeks—I can almost pinpoint the day, June first—I've gotten altogether different signals. There's something missing, something important, that I'm not getting. We can't go forward without it."

Please don't ask me, please don't, not so close to the end. . . .

She sat up. "Are you gambling? Or going to a . . . loan shark or something?"

Loan shark! Improved circumstances, secrecy! For a second he almost went with it. But he didn't. He said, "Oh, no. No."

He sensed her relief at that, wished he could share it.

"Then what is it?" She waited. "Loring, lately I've been thinking about . . . leaving Andy for you."

The words settled over him like dew on a thirsty flower. He took her hand again.

"But I want the whole person, or nothing. Are you hearing me?"

He said nothing.

"Are you *hearing* me?"

He said nothing.

"Go to hell, Loring." She got off the bed, picked her Bermudas up from the floor and began to get dressed.

Loring stared up at the ceiling for a long time, his heart thundering, trying to think clearly about whether and what to tell her and guessing at the risk, his mind avoiding, going to other things, to floating dust, to patterns of white and gray in the room, eventually noticing the phenomenon of sunlight striking the street and bouncing up through his window to project ghostlike pictures of passing automobiles onto his bedroom ceiling, wondering how he had gotten to age forty-two without ever having noticed that before.

Four, five silent minutes elapsed. He turned his head slowly toward her. She was fully dressed, standing a few feet from the bed, facing him; her eyes were waiting when his got there.

"Liz," he said softly, "I have something pretty fucking terrible to tell you."

And he told her.

Everything.

About his desperation, his anger, his fear.

About Leo Goldstein's watches and money.

About the Carlin bribe.

About the Pincuses' candlestick holders.

215

About Lynn Isaacs' jewelry.

As he recited his litany, his burden decreased and his voice became steadier. Liz listened intently, shaking her head a bit from time to time.

Judge Mushkin's silver pot.

Harriet Kilowitz's rubies.

Lewis.

Cody.

Katie, Penny-Town.

His book and his plans for it.

His guiltlessness.

When he was through, she seemed dazed.

"Say something, Liz."

With a half laugh, she said, "I don't know what to say. It's the most stunning story I've ever heard."

"Do you . . . hate me? Are you afraid of me now?"

"Neither. Neither. But if you ask me if it makes me love you more, I'd say no."

He got up and went to where she stood, put his arms around her. "But do you still love me the same?"

She rested her head against his shoulder. Quietly: "If you did all that because you were frightened and weak and unable to cope . . . the answer is yes, I do."

He felt her breath on his skin.

"Loring, I'm not going to say any of the obligatory things to you." Her voice caught. "Just one question: Is it over?"

He whispered, "Almost."

She looked up at him. "What?"

"There has to be one more. Just one more."

She walked home, through the locale of his story, the words still jangling in her head. At a certain point she remembered how his tone of remorse, when he'd begun talking, had gradually changed to one of excitement—as though he were describing a handball game he'd narrowly won. Images flew at her: her lover moving through the dark of people's homes, taking things that were theirs, looking into their privacies, sharing things they never intended to share.

Had all of that been an expedient—a drastic, foolish, dangerous expedient—or was it part of some aberration she might someday have to live with?

She recoiled.

There were at least a hundred and fifty people there, drinking and eating, fanning themselves in the sunless humidity of the late afternoon. Their attention was more or less on Leo Goldstein, Norman Berger and Norman's wife, Naomi, who were standing under the Victorian gazebo in the center of Leo's beautiful backyard.

Leo, wearing an oversized red, white and blue button that said BERGER U.S. SENATE, was speaking. ". . . and it's such a hot day, and it's almost six o'clock and you all ate so much barbecue you can hardly breathe"—the crowd laughed—"so we ain't going to keep you much longer."

Ellie Habib shrieked, "You can keep me as long as you want, Leeee-oh! George is out of town!" More laughter.

Leo put an arm around Norman Berger's shoulder. "The reason for this little party here today is no secret." He looked at Norman. "Ever try to keep a secret in the yenta capital of the world?" More laughter. "So we'll get to the point. The commercial." Norman leaned over and said something to Leo. Leo nodded, and said, "Our distinguished congressman just told me to be brief, so he could say a few words after." Leo grinned. "'A few words'? Since when did a Washington politician ever say just 'a few words'?" Norman smiled, hugged his wife. Leo continued. "Congressman Norman Henry Berger, our good friend, who represents us here in Kingsborough Beach so terrifically for the last three and a half years, is going to run for the Senate seat that's going to be vacated by that asshole incumbent." Laughter, and a lot of applause. "For the special primary he's been assured the support of the state Democratic organization, and now, today, we're going to ask for the most important support of all, the support of you, his neighbors here in Kingsborough Beach. Because this is his base, right? His power base. And this is where it's all going to start."

Loring was standing at the back of the crowd, close to the house, not really listening. The Blaugs were not there, and he wondered what Liz was doing at the moment, what she was thinking.

As Leo went on, Loring opened the door to the breakfast room and walked inside. Across the hallway, in the kitchen, the Goldsteins' part-time manservant, Fernando, was working with the caterer's people. Loring helped himself to a Perrier and lime, asked Fernando if he'd had a long day.

Fernando smiled. "You wanna believe it, Mr. Neiman. But in a hour I be home in my own place, layin' it back, you know?"

With his Perrier, Loring strolled through the living room. There were people all over the place, escapees from the heat and the bullshit outside.

Elias Shapp sat, with a drink, in the dark cool of the library. "Hiya, kid, long time no see. How ya doin'?"

"Fine, Elias." Their stock dialogue.

"You been visited by detectives yet?"

New material. "Detectives? No. Why?"

"They're all over the neighborhood, talkin' to people. The way they dress nowadays is a fuckin' disgrace."

"I, ah, haven't seen."

Shapp nodded. "You will, kid. Sooner or later, hah?" He stood up, gestured toward the yard. "They start the festivities?"

"Yes. Leo is introducing Norman."

"Then I gotta be there." Shapp left.

Stevie, the Goldsteins' son, came downstairs carrying a duffel bag. He told Loring he was on his way to Cape Cod, hoped to see him soon and dashed out the front door.

Loring wandered to the foot of the staircase, leaned casually on the banister, trying to determine if there were any other people upstairs. He realized there were: Sandy Goldstein and several other women, apparently, chatting in and around the master bedroom.

He would have to wait.

* * *

Liz and Andy Blaug had stayed home. Andy had some journals to read, and Liz, considering his current mood, had decided not to go to the Goldstein party without him. Instead, she made plans for later that evening, a few hours in the city with her girlfriend from Chicago. Real plans, this time.

Andy's reaction made her uneasy.

He said, "You saw her last Wednesday. Or so you told me."

She let the implication pass. "Yes, I did. But she's so lonely here. Really pathetic about New York. She needs help getting organized and I'm all she's got. Tonight I'm going to take her to dinner."

"Does she have a telephone yet?"

"Not yet."

Andy nodded. "Where did you go this afternoon?"

Holy shit. "Lydia Kramer, for a while, then I went to Kings Bay to look for some cruise things. In case we ever actually do take that trip."

Again, Andy just nodded, went back to his *American Journal of Obstetrics and Gynecology,* she to her magazine. They sat in the screened-in veranda at the back of their house silently, then, each apparently engrossed.

Her mind spun, once more, to Loring: her empathy with his motives (because she loved him), her horror at what he had done (also because she loved him), her repugnance at the simple generosity toward himself with which he seemed to view his acts (also because she loved him; very much).

A slight chill made her shudder. She glanced at Andy. Boring, humorless Andy, usually surly and often, of late, suspicious. But there was a comfort in his predictability. There were no moral dilemmas in the life he was giving her.

There was no way, Loring realized, that he could get to Leo's bureau drawer this afternoon; altogether too much traffic on the bedroom floor. So—Plan B—he went down to the finished basement.

The window he selected was at the back of the basement. Through it he could see Norman Berger, making his speech, Naomi, in her white cotton dress, standing at his side, smiling her pretty face off.

The window was a fairly new installation, of the metal casement type, and it locked, securely, from the inside. It had no open-close switch to the alarm system because it didn't need one; the only way anyone could breach the locked window from the outside was by breaking the glass, and that exigency was covered by a small round "bug"—a shock sensor—that was cemented to it. The wire that connected the bug into the system entered the device at an angle of about seven o'clock, the best angle.

Loring unlatched the window; it could then be pushed open from the outside very easily, and certainly without shocking the sensor. But just to make sure, he took a dime from his pocket and with it loosened the screw in the center of the bug; it enabled him to twist the top of the bug so that the wire pointed to eight o'clock. He tightened it there. That position, he knew, was much less sensitive, and the bug would then not react to anything short of a direct hammer blow.

He went back up to the top of the basement stairs, listened at the door for a moment, then opened it and reentered the main hallway of the house. Sandy's cocker greeted him there, with friendly curiosity. Loring patted the dog.

Through the front window, Andrew Blaug watched his wife's car pull out of their driveway onto Ramsgate Boulevard. She turned right, to Oulden Street, and he lost sight of her.

There was no question in his mind that she was going to meet Loring Neiman.

And it hurt.

Soon her car would be parked over on Knapp Street and she would be walking—running—back over the causeway to his house. Or he will meet her with his car and will drive her back to his house, she hiding on the floor in the backseat so that no one will see her. Into his driveway and up into his bedroom. His children asleep.

God damn Loring Neiman. God damn him.

Later, close to twelve-thirty, Liz had still not returned home. Dr. Blaug put on an old cardigan sweater, got into his car and drove the few blocks to Averly, where (at just about the moment his wife did get home from her evening in the city with her old girlfriend) he parked across the street and a few doors up from the Neiman house. Leaving the motor running, he turned off the headlights and waited.

Within three minutes he saw Loring, dressed in a running suit, emerge from his side door and go into his backyard. On a hunch, Andy put his car in reverse, backed slowly to the next driveway, Mrs. Libo's, just in time to see Loring cross it into her yard. A second or two later he saw another, tinier, figure cross Mrs. Libo's driveway, hurrying on short legs from beneath a long coat. Andy backed up another thirty feet, opposite the Estrins' driveway. Up at its end he saw Loring come through the hedges into that yard, followed, a beat later, by the tiny figure, which he now realized was Neiman's little girl, the twelve-year-old, in a bathrobe.

He watched their strange progress, driveway by driveway, until they reached that of the Goldstein house on the corner. There he saw Loring disappear behind the house as the girl hung back, apparently waiting.

Her heart in her mouth, Katie peeked from behind a stand of bushes and watched her father push open a basement window and let himself down into it, out of her sight.

She wondered what to do: Should she go back to her house, get back in her bed, wait for him? Or should she follow him in, see if he was really doing something he shouldn't? And get him out of there? And would he yell at her if she did?

A minute later she started after him again.

Andy was mystified. The Goldsteins had had a party that afternoon; could it still be on, almost 1 A.M.? There were no lights visible from within the house, nor any other cars around.

He decided to wait and see what else would transpire.

With his penlight, Loring went up the basement steps to the door, quietly opened it. Two yellow eyes, low to the floor, shone up at him: Sandy Goldstein's little dog, waiting, silent and wagging, for him to come through the door. Loring knelt to it, stroked its head. The dog, pleased to see him, rolled sublimely onto its back so Loring could stroke its stomach.

Katie put herself in through the same window. It was higher from the basement floor than she had expected; she fell, hit her head. For a minute she sat on the floor in the black room, her arms wrapped around her head, rocking to dilute the pain, holding back the cry.

Andy Blaug turned off the engine of his car.

The alarm system control panel in the front vestibule was visible from the basement door in the center hall. Loring could see that the red light was on and the amber light was out, which meant that the rug traps were armed. No surprise, but it would slow him down. The entire ground floor was carpeted wall-to-wall; he had no idea where the traps were located and so would have to negotiate the floors flat on his stomach. He got down, prone, arms and legs as wide as possible so as to distribute his weight, and started along the hall toward the staircase, slithering, an inch at a time.

The dog trailed after him, its tail going like sixty. It was an unusual physical attitude for a large human being, and a very intriguing one. The dog enjoyed it, began to lick Loring's face in appreciation. Loring pushed it away, gently and deliberately, but the dog went right back at it. This was a good new game. The man pushed, the dog came back, the man pushed, the dog came back, each time with a little more enthusiasm, a little friskier, a little wilder. Loring's stomach knotted; the fucking thing was going absolutely stupid with delight. It might start yapping at any second and wake up the family. Or one of its mindless bounces could kick off a rug trap and wake the whole neighborhood. He stroked the dog, trying to encourage it to lie down and relax.

That was when Katie opened the door to the center hall and looked into the house. It was not as dark as the basement had been, so her young eyes adjusted very quickly to the dim light; she saw her father, lying on the rug, playing with Muffie, the Goldsteins' dog. The dog spotted her, suddenly quit the game.

Loring realized Muffie was staring at something behind him. Reflexively he aimed his penlight in that direction, flicked it on.

He couldn't believe his eyes. Embarrassment almost transcended peril, until Katie took a step toward him.

"No," he whispered, hoarsely. "Katie get back get back don't walk on the rugs!"

Katie stopped, not knowing why. But she understood his order and certainly the predicament he was in. And the solution: with a remonstrative look at her father, she turned and went into the kitchen.

The dog's favorite place. Muffie was torn; should it go with the nice kid or stay and play with the nice man?

From the kitchen a faint, crushy sound. Then Katie reappeared, her arm extended, a doggie treat in her hand. She made a low, kissing sound.

Muffie went with the nice kid.

Katie took hold of its collar, led it into the kitchen.

Loring sank back to the rug, frustrated. Crime of the Absurd. Going upstairs was now out of the question. He must take Katie the hell out of there and go home. As he was about to backtrack, his eyes fell on the Belimbau pencil sketch, on the wall, twenty feet away. Something for him. To keep.

He crawled, as quickly as he safely could, to the framed drawing, and stood up; rug traps were never laid that close to a wall. He took it down and, with a fingernail, cut a long slice

in the paper on the back of the frame. Then he quickly peeled
it back and removed the drawing, which he rolled up and
stuck under his shirt, in the waistband of his running pants.

Katie reappeared in the kitchen door as Loring was bellying back up through the center hall.

He decided they would leave through the kitchen door.
Loring forgot about the alarm system with its fifteen-second
delay. . . .

Andy Blaug watched, fascinated, as Loring, carrying his
daughter, came down the Goldstein driveway, turned left on
the sidewalk and strode rapidly toward his own house. . . .

Richard Feld, who lived across the street from the Goldsteins, turned off the TV in his den and walked toward a front
window. He wanted to see what the weather was.

The Neimans were almost halfway home when the fifteen-
second delay ended and the Goldstein burglar alarm bells—
two large ones—suddenly ripped the night open.

Andy was shocked.

So was Richard Feld. He dropped to his knees at his front
window, peered out. He saw the Goldsteins' upstairs lights go
on, realized it was their burglar alarm. Worse, there was a
strange car standing in front of his own house: a dark Buick
Electra, with its lights out.

Frantically trying to start his car, Andy accidentally pulled
the keys out of the ignition, dropped them to the floor. He
groped, groped, found them and tried again. The car started
up and drove off.

But before it did, Feld clearly read its lighted license plate
number.

He called the police.

Loring and Katie got back in their house by the side door.
Without a word, she ran upstairs, went directly to her room

and got into bed. A moment later, Loring followed her up. He stood in her doorway, stared dumbly into her room.

Presently he heard her crying.

Quietly, so as not to awaken Briana, he said, "Please, Katie, let's talk. . . ."

"No," came her muffled, wet reply.

He stepped into the room.

"No, Daddy!" she said, almost a shout.

He backed to the doorway again, not knowing what to do: Persist, force the issue now? Wait until morning? Would she even talk then? Or ever again?

He heard a car race past the house, saw a quick flash of red and white through the white-curtained window. It came to a rubbery halt farther down, the Goldsteins' house. More police cars, with sirens, were on their way.

He went to his own room, thinking he would check the answering machine for a message from Liz. But then he remembered there was no longer an answering machine. Maybe no longer a Liz. He sat down on the edge of his bed, at a loss. The rolled-up Belimbau drawing was still in his waistband. He removed it and dropped it onto the floor, then got up and walked—wandered, really—into the study. He sat down at the word processor.

Katie. Katie. He remembered hours at her cribside, staring at the wondrous details of her face and fingers and feet, remembered thinking how someday certain men might come along who had been trained to believe that for the price of a marriage license they could buy the right to trash her life. He remembered thinking how any man who married her would be on probation for years and years and years, and if he ever fucked up, that yet-to-exist man, he would be finished, banished from her life. He remembered vowing to stay alive for enough years to kill anyone and everyone who ever moved into her life without enhancing it somehow.

Now he—her own father, protector, avenger—had, himself, trashed her life.

Suddenly his mouth opened wide and he retched a long, soundless scream and then cried in a strange soprano, the guilt coming like an abscess finally burst; he throbbed with an ache long past its time.

A welcome ache.

After a while, empty, he switched on the little tensor lamp that was affixed to the computer, and typed

Fantasy and reality collided tonight.

What hell have I put my daughter through?

Will she ever forgive me?

I brought her and her sister into the world at my own pleasure; they owe me nothing, I owe them everything.

What have I done to their lives?

What if I had been caught, all these weeks?

And sent away?

What would have become of them? The shame.

But now I swear to God it's over.

Goldstein tonight was the final chapter, and now it's over.

Tomorrow I start looking for a job, a regular job. Any kind of job. Even Sidney's.

As to this book, I suppose I could show it to Jamie now, and

But no. Involving Jamie Gelfmann so soon could be dangerous, for both of us. The four—*five*—burglaries are still too fresh to make Jamie an accessory. Much too early under the statute of limitations.

No, clearly no.

I'll finish it, as long as it takes, then lock the manuscript away and keep my fingers crossed until it is safe to submit it.

And, in the meantime, a job during the day, writing at night. Evenings of enforced writing are not quite beyond my spirit, yet.

The other day, I called Gold Coast, told her I was sorry, but prior commitments made it impossible for me to finish the burglary article. She sounded bitter, said they were counting on the piece and hung up on me.

Just before I balled up the printout and threw it away, I read through it for the last time. One line jumped out at me.

"More importantly, when did the forceful invasion of a person's home by anti-social people with felonious intentions become a 'PISS-ANT CRIME'?"

Anti-social people with felonious intentions. Am I anti-social people? And is it possible that I have burned out my immunity, tried my neighbors so, insulted our relationships to the point where, had they caught me, they would have destroyed me?

And did I slip from being a criminal strictly in the legal sense, to a sociological one

Katie came into the room.

She stood a few feet from him, and they looked at each other. Pallid face to pallid face. He was saddened by her troubled expression, the tiny furrow between her brows.

Is that how it starts?

"You didn't tell me the truth yesterday, Daddy."

"No. I felt the truth would hurt you."

"Daddy, how could you do this to your best friends? Don't you think they'd be disappointed in you if they knew?"

"Yes." His voice quavered. "The things I did are terrible." Second confession that day.

"Is it because of me and Briana needing things? I could walk dogs and do baby-sitting and give you the money."

"No, darling. It had nothing to do with you and Briana. It all came from my own weakness, as a person. I had a big, serious problem, one of my own making, and it made me angry at myself. And I thought that the way to handle it was to make other people pay for it. I was wrong."

She paused for a moment, then asked, "Are you going to do it anymore, Daddy?"

He shook his head, slowly and seriously. "Never."

"Can I trust you not to sneak into people's houses anymore?"

"Yes, sweetheart. You can."

Katie walked to him and climbed onto his lap, for the first time, he realized, in a couple of years. He held her for a long moment.

"I still love you, Daddy."

"I always love you, Katie. More than anything in my life."

She felt her cheek become wet with her father's tears. She

had never felt her father's tears before. She saw some once, when her mother died. But she never felt any before. It made her cry.

He tightened his arms about her.

After a moment she looked at him. "How will you get money, Dad?"

"Dad." What happened to "Daddy"? He smiled at her. "The old-fashioned way . . ."

Together they said, "EARRRRN it!" and laughed.

They went down to the kitchen and had some Mallomars and milk. She told him she now knew why they hadn't danced in a long time, many weeks, and asked him if they could go into the living room and put on a little Bing Crosby and would he dance with her. He said he'd be delighted, and, at two o'clock in the morning, by the light that shone in from the kitchen, Loring Neiman and his twelve-year-old daughter Kathleen did their lilting, peculiarly dignified lindy together. And sang along: "A mule is an *an*-imal with lonnng funny ears . . . kicks up at *ev*-'rything he hears. His back is braw-ny and his brain is weak . . ."

As they danced, a flash of fear: *What if it's not over? What if it somehow comes to rest on my doorstep, after all? But no, it won't. It's over. Over. Over over over over over*

"And though he's *slip*-pery he still gets caught . . ."

Loring got into bed. Rather than slotting himself, as usual, onto the left side, he spread himself wide in the cool center, a sure sign of a new expansiveness, an unaccustomed easiness. A freedom.

On the warm edges of sleep, he decided he would call Sidney Lieb in the morning and ask him if the job offer still held. *Tomorrow I rejoin the ranks of regularly conducted society, tomorrow.*

But the night was not yet over. The phone rang. Eyes closed, he groped for it, expecting it to be Liz.

"Hello?"

"Hiya, kid."

"Who is this?"

"Elias Shapp."

"Elias Shapp . . ." He looked at the clock radio; it glowed 4:10 A.M. "It's four in the morning. . . ."

"Right, kid." No hint of apology in his voice. "I want you to meet me tomorrow morning."

Loring sat up, suddenly, tingling with alarm. "Meet you?"

"Yeh. On the beach. Eight o'clock."

"What the hell for?"

"Be there. Have a nice night, kid."

Shapp hung up.

Sunday, June 24 _____

A LIGHT PREDAWN rain had cooled the weather. Loring put on a warm pair of pants and a sweater and set out for the beach, on foot.

Parked in the front of the Goldsteins' house was an unmarked police car. When Loring saw it his shock was small and dull; he had unconsciously expected it. He wondered, *Are detectives still there from last night or have they only just shown up? Did they or will they find anything?* He passed the house. *No, there's nothing to find. That car and the feeling I get from seeing it are the very last vestiges of a few yesterdays. When those detectives come out—baffled, still—and get back into that car and drive away, it will all be over and things like that will have nothing to do with me, ever again.* He walked a little more rapidly.

Farther along, crossing Ramsgate Boulevard, he looked, out of habit, toward the Blaug house, two and a half blocks east, but his gaze was stopped at the next corner by the sight of two RMPs at the curb, four patrolmen in conversation. More uniforms at one time than one was likely to see in The Beach. Loring did not know that Captain Costello had ordered another emergency system into effect that very morning: a "satellite" precinct—nothing more than a phone box at the corner of Barnsworth and Ramsgate—had been designated so that the change of shifts could be accomplished right there in the sector, rather than back at the station house. The point was to increase the police presence, make the Kingsborough Beachers feel safer. The two RMPs and the four cops were changing tours of duty; the eight-to-four was relieving the midnight-to-eight.

Shapp, wearing a white nylon jacket and a plaid cap, was seated on a bench facing the sea. A few feet from him his five-year-old granddaughter played on the sand with her pail and shovel.

Approaching from behind him, Loring said, in a neighborly manner, "Hi, Elias."

Without looking up at Loring, Shapp pointed to the birds feeding at the shoreline and growled, "Look, the little pishers make a living from the ocean but they never even get their feet wet. Water goes out, they're right behind it, water comes back, they're right ahead of it. Terrific." He turned to Loring. "How ya doin', kid. Long time no see. Sit down."

Loring sat down.

"Beach is nice right now, hah?"

"Yes," Loring replied, and looked studiously at the beach. It did have certain new aspects: millions of dime-sized craters left by the raindrops; no people, no boats in sight, the Gil Hodges Memorial Bridge, to the east, obscured by a mist; Riis Park, across the Rockaway Inlet, looking like a cut of alabaster in the weak sunlight. But the weather was chilly, unbeachlike, he had no socks on and his feet were cold.

Then Elias Shapp said, "Kid, I wanna talk to you about all the hell you been raisin' around here."

Loring swallowed. "What, actually, do you mean?"

"I mean that after Isaacs is hit I begin to get a little pissed. It's a nice neighborhood and I don't want it cocked up, hah? Now I want to know who's doin' it, so I start callin' people—fences—to see who's handlin' the Isaacs stuff. When I get to Lewis, he tells me he is, but he don't know the mechanic's name, only 'Mike.' So I says to him, when you know he's comin' in again, call me.

"Two days later he calls, says the same guy's bringin' in a sterling silver chocolate pot. Which I know is from the Mushkin job, hah?

"So, the time he expects the guy to show up, I wait across the street from Cody's place, watch the guy go in for a while and then go out. And picture my surprise, it's you." He looked at Loring.

Loring's throat dried; Shapp was the one who told Lewis not to work with him anymore! He'd just gotten two revelations for the price of one.

"Kid, I wanna keep the neighborhood peaceful. And you been shittin' where you eat. That's somethin' *I* never did."

Loring said, "Yes. Well."

"That's an answer, 'Yes, well'? Lemme tell you somethin', kid. In the old days they used to call me 'Voncie,' you know, for *vonce*—cockroach. I'm proud of it, it's a compliment, and I'll tell ya why. You know the cockroach is the world's oldest living creature? Survived billions of years. And that's me. I always survive. When thirty other guys took falls I survived."

He stopped.

Get to the point, Shapp. "Why are you telling me this, Elias?"

"Because you ain't the same kind of a survivor. You're a nice family guy. Nice kids. Had a nice wife. I hear you're a writer, I hear a good one. I ain't gonna ask you why you steal, I can figure that out, but I gotta tell ya you're on your way to losin' your membership. Take me: you think I fit in down here? Everybody likes me? Nobody cares what I was? Yeh, but no. It tickles them to be near me, like I'm a tiger without no teeth, but there's a space they'll never let me acrosst. I never feel a hundred percent right with straight people, never have and never will. And it hurts."

He nodded toward his granddaughter. "And when she finds out—and bet your balls someday she's gonna—she's never gonna think of her grandpa the same way again."

Loring's heart skipped; he thought of Katie.

"I say it hurts, kid, and I'm a hard guy. But you"—he tapped Loring's arm—"ain't so tough. And it's gonna hurt you worse. You should quit, kid, while you're ahead."

Loring's fear slipped away from him, completely; last night's summons was a benevolent one, he and his secret were actually safe with Voncie Shapp—the last living relic of the Golden Age of Jewish Crime—who had just become a sweet, paternalistic old man right before his eyes. He smiled at Shapp. His voice airy with relief, he said, "I appreciate your concern, Elias. I really do."

Shapp laughed. "I don't know if you're shittin' me."

"I'm not. I'm really moved by what you've said. And I *have* quit, Elias. I've already quit."

"Now you're really shittin' me. You hit Goldstein last night."

"That was it, the last one. I'm finished now. I've quit."

Shapp peered closely at him for a long moment. Then a grin began to crease his face. He took Loring's hand in both of his.

"I'm happy to hear that, kid, really happy. You're gonna quit." He squeezed Loring's hand. "Except you're not gonna quit for a couple more days."

Loring, misunderstanding Shapp's meaning, said, "Oh yes I am, Elias—"

"No, not for a couple more days. Lemme explain to you why: last night I handed Norman Berger fifty thousand for his 'campaign fund.' Cash. Small bills. In exchange, he makes me a couple promises.

"The thing is, now that I got his promises, I want my fifty grand back. You're gonna get it for me."

It took some time for Loring's brain to interpret what his ears had just heard, and during the process the ocean and the sky switched positions. "Just why the hell should I do that?" He stood up, feeling dizzy.

"First of all, kid, I can't talk lookin' up. Sit down."

Loring did.

"A couple good reasons. First of all, I give you a fourth—twelve thousand five hundred bucks—"

"I don't want it, Elias—"

"Call me Voncie. It's more businesslike."

"There's no way I'm doing it. No way."

Elias glanced at his granddaughter. "Tiffany Dawn, sweetheart, don't pick your nose." To Loring, he said, "And the other good reason is, if you do it, I don't blow the whistle on you and see you and your nice little family shamed, and who knows, you maybe in the slammer."

They stared into each other's eyes for a long time, Shapp's leonine silver head tilted slightly, a forthright smile on his lips.

"Shapp, why me?"

"I can trust you, you ain't gonna take the money and disappear because your type don't disappear." He was now observing his birds. "Also, there's the same reasons you done your last five jobs: you know the territory, you're pretty good at it and you need the dough. And if anythin' goes wrong you're a classy, connected guy; the cops can't squeeze your balls to hear you sing like they would if you was some dumb grunt from Jersey with a rap sheet out to here." The older man looked at Loring again and winked. "Not that you'd mention *my* name anyway and embarrass me"—he pointed to his granddaughter—"and my family . . . and Congressman Berger . . . because you know it's much better to maybe do a short time for a burglary than do a long time dead, hah?"

Loring began to massage the bridge of his nose, trying to recollect exactly how much despair he had felt, less than six weeks before, when his novel had been rejected and his house was about to be repossessed. He could not recollect.

Shapp rolled on: "The Bergers go outa town, tonight, for four days, the house empty. Mechanic like you, this job comes like on a silver platter—"

"Shapp, do you still owe a debt to society?"

Shapp stared at him.

"Pay it now. Leave me out of this and on behalf of everyone you ever robbed, cheated, extorted from, beat up or killed—I'll forgive you. Just leave me alone, please."

"I will, kid. After this. Think it over. You got"—he looked at his wristwatch—"five minutes."

Loring watched the little girl drop some mussel shells into her little shoe and push it across the sand like a boat; Briana had been pasting yarn koala bears onto her Kinderland moccasins when he left the house.

He considered his option: if he refused and Shapp fingered him as the burglar, he could simply deny it, and the police, the neighborhood, everyone might just believe him. Or they might not. But there was one person—besides Shapp—who would know the truth: Katie. At the moment, what she knew about him was probably still hazed over by her little-girl perception of it, still only slightly real, semitangible. But what if it suddenly exploded and riddled her world with indignant neighbors, overblown accusations, newspaper stories, television cameras, bragging cops, righteous district attorneys, wrathful judges? What would such a firestorm of experiences do to her and Briana and their relationship to their father?

He lit a cigarette. "Tell me about it. You filthy, fucking gangster."

Shapp was unfazed by the insult. "Like I said, kid, Normie and Naomi are goin' to Washington tonight and ain't comin' back till Wednesday, so you got three clear nights, your choice. They got a safe in the master bedroom closet, bolted to the floor. The cash is in it in brown paper."

"Safe? I don't know anything about safes. . . ."

"Can you read numbers? Here." Shapp handed him a slip of paper from his shirt pocket. "The combination."

Loring examined it.

"Cute, hah?"

"Cute."

"Feelin' better already, hah?"

"No, murderer. How can you be sure the money is still in the safe and will be for the next few days?"

"Where's he gonna put it, the bank? And Normie ain't the backyard-burying type."

Loring said, "You're asking me to put a lot of faith in tired, aging, stupid, forty-I.Q. Brownsville-hoodlum logic. What if it's just simply fucking *not* there? Are you going to believe me if I have to come back and tell you that?"

Shapp shook his head. "No."

"I didn't think so." Loring took a deep breath. "Do you know the best way in?" It occurred to him that this conversation was adding Conspiracy to his list.

236

"Yeh. There's this big terrace outside their bedroom, it's got French doors with a bullshit lock."

"The terrace is on the second floor. . . ."

"You'll get up there easy. There's a lot to grab on to on that side of the house. How you handle th' alarms is your department."

Loring contemplated that, calling on his own recollection of the Bergers' house. It seemed to fit. "And so when do I get my twelve-five?"

"Right after the job, when you come to my house. I drive you home."

"Okay." Loring stood. "So long, Cockroach."

Shapp's smile faded. "Voncie," he said.

"Voncie is too distinguished. To me, you're plain, fucking Cockroach." He walked off.

Shapp stared after him for a moment, then said, "See ya, kid."

By nine-thirty Lieutenant Trezevant had finished a large Sunday breakfast with his family. Carrying the *Newsday* sports section, he went out into the backyard and was about to flop onto a beach chair when he heard the phone ring.

"Frankie, it's Officer Mary Moska."

He went back inside and took it.

"Mary?"

"Yeh, Lieutenant. Sorry it took so long. On your license number, the DMV made it as registered to 'Five Towns Clinic: A Medical Corporation' in Cedarhurst. Nobody answered at the clinic until just now, a bookkeeper, and he said that vehicle is used personally by an Andrew Blaug, M.D., of three-four-four-one Ramsgate Boulevard, Brooklyn."

"No shit. A doctor's car. Is it stolen?"

"There's no report on it. But it's still early. Maybe it was and he doesn't know it yet."

"Mary, do you think the guy at the clinic has called Andrew Blaug, M.D., by now?"

"Who knows, but I doubt it. I advised him he must not or he could be charged with obstruction of justice."

"You did good, Mary." It usually worked, sometimes even with lawyers. "Okay, thanks." Trezevant hung up.

While changing into street clothes, he mulled over the Goldstein job. It was a funny one. At the house, three o'clock that morning, he had found the altered bug on a previously unlocked basement window. The guy who worked for them, interviewed at his Sheepshead Bay apartment, claimed he had checked those windows as late as Friday evening, knew them to be locked. Which made Trezevant think that the window might have been fucked with by a guest during the party. Then there were the dog biscuits in the kitchen; neither Leo Goldstein nor his wife had seen them there before they went to bed, and the dog couldn't have done it himself because they were kept on a high shelf in a closed pantry closet.

Most interesting, the only thing stolen was a drawing that Goldstein himself said wasn't worth a hell of a lot. Maybe the guy was interrupted by the dog (which didn't bark; did he know the guy?), fed him a biscuit, got cold feet about going upstairs and settled for the drawing, thinking it was valuable. Or maybe not.

All in all, though, Lieutenant Trezevant had come away with the net feeling that they were dealing with the same burglar. True, there was a car reported, and the use of a car didn't fit the previous M.O.s. And unless the car was stolen, an "Andrew Blaug, M.D.," didn't sound a hell of a lot like a burglary suspect. Could be, but he doubted it. Besides, the neighbor who reported seeing the car said it started up and drove away "almost a minute" after the alarm went off; given the fifteen-second delay on the door by which he exited, a good burglar in a car would have been blocks away by then.

No, he thought, Andrew Blaug, M.D., or whoever was driving his car, was not their burglar, but he smelled like a fucking good witness.

As Trezevant pulled onto the Southern State for the drive to Brooklyn, it occurred to him that the name Blaug sounded familiar.

* * *

Oh hell, yes! He recognized her the second she opened the door.

"Can I hel—" Liz recognized him, too, but without the thrill that he felt. "Oh. You're . . . Lieutenant . . ."

"Frank Trezevant. Nice to see you again, Mrs. Blaug, and I'm sorry to bother you like this on a Sunday morning."

Liz nodded; she had no idea why he was there. "Can I help you with something?" Remembering that she wasn't wearing much—just the famous shorts and halter—she stepped back a little, stood half behind the door.

"Dr. Blaug, he's your husband?"

"Yes?"

"Can I talk to him for a minute or two?"

She said she'd get him, asked Trezevant to come in.

He stood in the foyer and watched her walk up the stairs. Underneath her shorts he could see the band of her panties on the round of her ass.

Liz woke Andy, told him there was a detective to see him.

Andy blinked once or twice and got out of bed. "Tell him I'll be right down."

But she didn't. She waited, instead, for Andy to put on his bathrobe so they could go downstairs together.

When the two men sat down in the living room to talk, Liz stood in the doorway, her arms folded across her chest, hoping that, regardless of whatever this was all about, Loring Neiman was in no way involved. . . .

"Dr. Blaug, I'm investigating a burglary last night, on Averly Street." Andy appeared impassive. Trezevant glanced over at Liz, saw that she'd moved one of her hands up to her lips. "Did you know about the burglary?" Trezevant asked them both. "At Mr. and Mrs. Leo Goldstein's house?"

Liz, her face drawn tight, shook her head.

Andy said, "I don't think so."

"You don't think so?"

"No, I haven't heard about it. I just got up."

"You own the 1983 Buick that's parked in your driveway?"

"Not really. It's on permanent loan to me."

"It's loaned, okay. It was reported as being parked right

across the street from the house that got hit, at the time of the burglary." He paused again, looked at Andy for a response. Andy made none. "Dr. Blaug, were you using your car last night, around one A.M.?"

"Yes, I was."

"Good. I need to know why you were on Averly and Dale at that time."

"I'm not sure that's anyone's business."

Trezevant tried to smile. Oddly enough, it was interviewing unlikely, purely circumstantial suspects such as Blaug that put him, in all of his work, under the most stress. Knowing in his bones that the guy had nothing to do with whatever had come down yet having to come on in a suspicious, accusatorial way was always hard for him.

"Well, it is. It's police business . . . my business. There was a crime, you were in the vicinity." He shrugged. "I need to make sure you had nothing to do with it."

Andy said, "Can you and I . . . go out back, Officer?"

"Sure. Sure."

On the veranda, Andy said, "I was there last night but I didn't want to discuss it . . ." He nodded toward the house.

Trezevant nodded. *With a wife like that the guy's humping a neighbor!* He was delighted.

Andy went on. "I . . . My wife and I have been having a small problem, and last night I thought she had gone to have a, uh . . . a rendezvous . . . with someone. So I drove over to where I thought she might be—his house—and parked. To wait."

El switcherino, thought Trezevant. "Whose house?"

Andy shook his head, dismissively. "It turned out she wasn't there at all."

Trezevant waited for more, but Blaug apparently felt he was finished.

In a pig's ass he is. "I'm glad to hear that, but you're going to have to be more specific, Dr. Blaug: whose house did you think your wife was at?"

"Is that truly relevant, Officer?"

"Everything is truly relevant, in your position."

Andy didn't like the word "position." He said, "I thought she was at Loring Neiman's house," and watched Trezevant write the name in his notebook.

"Could you spell that?"

"L-o-r-i-n-g N-e-i-m-a-n."

"Who is he?"

"A man who lives on Averly Street, a few houses from the Goldsteins'."

"How many houses?"

Andy thought. "Five or six."

"Then how did your car wind up right across the street from the Goldsteins' when their alarm went off?"

"That's just where I happened to be."

"Yes, but *why?*"

Andy sighed heavily, then said, "Because while I was parked in front of Neiman's house, he came outside."

"You mean like for air? Garbage? What?"

"No. He went into his own backyard."

Trezevant pictured Averly Street; it was a one-way, north.

"So why did you *back* away from his house?"

"It was just a feeling, a hunch, you might say. I backed up a little and saw him cross the driveways from his own yard into the yard next door, and then the next and the next."

"He went from yard to yard? Why was he doing that?"

"I don't know why, but he was making his way . . . to the Goldsteins'."

"He went there?" Trezevant felt a warm sensation. "What time was that?"

Andy shrugged. "I think very near one o'clock."

"One A.M."

"Yes."

"How was Neiman moving? I mean, what was his manner, his physical attitude?"

"Surreptitious."

"Surreptitious. Then what did he do when he got to the Goldsteins'?"

"He went in."

"Through the front door?"

"No, I don't know how he went in, but he didn't use the front door. I lost sight of him when he got to their backyard."

"Mr. and Mrs. Goldstein told me they went to sleep at ten last night and slept right through until the security alarm went off. They didn't mention any visitors. What makes you think Neiman went inside if you only saw him disappear in the back?"

"Because twenty minutes later I saw him leave the house, through the side door, the driveway door."

Trezevant was excited. "How long before the alarm went off was that?"

"A very short time, maybe ten or fifteen seconds."

"And where did he go?"

"Toward his house, back in that direction."

"Was he carrying anything?"

"His daughter."

"Say *what*?"

"His daughter was with him. His twelve-year-old daughter, in her bathrobe. She had followed him there, through the backyards."

"Followed him. Surreptitiously, also?"

"Yes, in her own way. He didn't seem to know she was following along. But when he came out, he was carrying her in his arms."

"His daughter. All right. Was he walking fast?"

"Yes."

"How far did they get when the alarm went off?"

"Almost back to their own house."

"How did Neiman act when the alarm went off?"

"I didn't see. When the alarm went off I drove away, came home."

"Directly home?"

"Yes."

"You were nervous."

"Rather. I still am."

"I don't blame you."

"Am I getting a neighbor of mine in trouble?"

"Not necessarily." Trezevant put his notebook in his jacket

pocket. "Tell me more about Neiman. What is he, a business-man?"

"He's a writer."

"A writer. Married?"

"No."

"How old?"

Andy didn't know. "Around forty."

"How long has he lived here?"

"I don't know. Long, several years."

"Okay. By the way, what time did your wife come home?"

Andy wondered what that had to do with anything. He replied, "It happens she was home when I got here."

"Oh, that's good," said Trezevant.

Liz was not in sight when Andy walked the detective to the front door. Trezevant would have liked another look at her.

He gave Andy a card with his phone numbers on it and asked him to call if he remembered anything else of interest. The last thing he said was, "You realize that if you tell anyone else—even your wife—what you've told me, I could charge you with obstructing justice?"

Andy said he realized it and wouldn't say a thing.

Monday, June 25 ⎯⎯⎯⎯⎯

L ORING WAS REWRITING his notes on the Kilowitz break-in.
The phone rang.

"Loring Neiman, please."

"Speaking."

"Loring, my name is Frank Trezevant. I work for Cal
Costello, at the 65th Precinct. He says he met you once?"

"Costello? The captain? Yes, I remember."

"Yes, well, he says you told Lucy, his wife, you'd be willing
to take a look at some of her stories, and since I have to be in
your neighborhood, he asked me to do him a favor and drop
them off. Would that be okay?"

Loring remembered: the rabbi's dinner. "I, ah, sure."

The voice chuckled. "You sound like you're sorry you got
involved. But I'd be obliged. . . ."

"No, no problem."

"Thanks. It'll make me some points with my boss. I can be
there in fifteen minutes. Is that okay?"

"Yes, fine."

"Thanks."

When he heard the doorbell, Loring saved the file he was
writing to and turned off the word processor. Actually he
hadn't typed a word since the phone call; he'd spent the ten or
twelve minutes worrying about it. Frank Trezevant, who
"worked for Cal Costello," had to be a cop.

But the man whom Briana brought up to the study looked
more like a siding salesman: shy smile, apologetic air, neatly
combed blondish hair. He carried a manila envelope.

245

Loring, nonetheless tense, invited him into the room and offered him the chair.

Trezevant shook his head. "Thanks, but I don't have time to sit down." They both stood. He handed Loring the envelope. "Here's Lucy's stuff. Cal told me to thank you in advance. He wanted to call you, but between you and me I think he's a little embarrassed about bothering you like this." He touched his chest. "So that's why he's got flunkies, like me."

Loring peered inside the envelope. "I hope there aren't too many. What am I supposed to do after I read them?"

"Beats me." Trezevant held up his hands. "My involvement ends here. That's between you and Cal. I guess you give him a call, tell him what to tell Lucy."

It was apparent that Trezevant wasn't wearing a gun. Loring said, "You *work* for Costello?"

"Yes."

"In what capacity?"

Trezevant was looking at the things hanging on the walls. "Lowly, very lowly. I head up his detective squad."

Why is he making such an effort to shrink himself? "Then that makes you, what, a lieutenant, doesn't it?"

The detective smiled and nodded. "That's right. Eighteen years and they have to throw you something." He moved toward the door, ready to leave, but Loring's workroom seemed to intrigue him. The books, the photographs. General Westmoreland in a funny frame.

"Vietnam?" he asked.

"Yes," Loring replied.

"I missed it. Oh, you've got a computer. You write on that?"

Loring nodded.

"Fantastic. State of the art."

"The computer is. I can't always say the same for my product."

"Interesting. Imagine, working at home. That's got to be the greatest."

Loring began to relax. "It was my main motive for becoming a writer," he said.

Trezevant admired the prints on the wall.

"Those artists are all of a certain school," Loring explained. "They're called the 'Jewish impressionists.'"

"Really," Trezevant said. "I don't know much about art, but they're beautiful pictures."

"I don't know anything about art, either, but I've always been fascinated by the fact that, for centuries, Jews were prohibited, by their own religious beliefs, from depicting the human face. The image of God, you know? So there weren't many Jewish artists, except for those few who were willing to draw birds' heads on human bodies. Eventually, though, a body of good Jewish painters began to emerge, and these particular ones represent, to me at least, the best ever."

Trezevant looked from print to print, nodding respectfully. "Jewish impressionists, you say. Very fine work. Very interesting." He glanced at his watch. "I better go. It's been great meeting you, Loring. Cal said you were a nice guy." He extended his hand, for the first time.

Loring shook it. "Same here."

Downstairs, at the front door, Trezevant suddenly fished something out of his pocket. It was a tiny replica of a police shield with the letters *PBA* on it. "Here," he said, "give this to your daughter. If she ever wants to get close to a parade or something, tell her to wear this on her collar, and our guys'll do the rest."

"Thank you," Loring said.

"Cute kid. Is she your only one?"

"No, I have another daughter."

"How old?"

"Twelve."

"That's great. Kids are great."

Trezevant stopped at the public library (for the first time since high school) to see if they had any Jewish art books. They had several, one of which he took to a table and opened. The table of contents suggested that the impressionists would be dealt with in the chapter that started on page 208. He skimmed no further than page 210 when the name leaped at him: Adolfo Belimbau.

Was it something? Or just shit?

Later, at his desk in the squad room, every bit of paper on the case spread before him, he tried to reconcile the man he'd just met with the methods and manner of the KBNB's five jobs.

That night Loring typed

The visit from Lieut. Frank Trezevant this morning was interesting. I was scared shitless most of the time he was here, expecting him to suddenly snap handcuffs on me. But by the time he left I realized he was just what he seemed to be, a harried, not-too-bright man running an errand for his boss.

I wonder if I will feel nervous around cops for the rest of my life?

Lucy Costello's stories, by the way, are very bad.

Voncie Shapp called me early this morning to remind me (to warn me) that tomorrow night is my last clear night for the Bergers. I told him it was all under control.

I've decided to wear a ski mask.

Yes, Raddit, yes.

Tuesday, June 26 _____

COSTELLO AMAZED TREZEVANT. Yesterday, on the phone, the captain had whooped with joy when he'd heard they finally had a good suspect. But only until he heard who the suspect was. Then he got cold feet, afraid Trezevant was making a mistake, feeling that Loring Neiman was not the type and that Kingsborough Beach would feel resentment if such a solid, well-liked, respectable resident were needlessly humiliated. A resentment that would live forever in his, Costello's, folder.

He had also raised a question about the reliability of the eyewitness. Dr. Blaug, he said, was a strange little man who could very easily be lying out of jealousy because he thinks his wife is involved with Neiman. "And, if not, a good defense lawyer could paint him that way."

Costello had ended their conversation with an admonition: "This Neiman is not the kind of person you can roust."

That amused Trezevant. "Roust?" he had asked. "You mean like he was a Coney Island nigger?"

There'd been a beat of silence over the phone. Then Costello had said, "Don't you ever say that word again in my earshot, Lieutenant, or it's going to cost you a month!"

Trezevant smiled at the memory. The biggest tit-sucker in Brooklyn South, lecturing him.

He looked at his watch. The bank whose mail he'd seen in Neiman's room wouldn't be open for another forty-five minutes. But he expected a callback at any time now from the Defense Department in Washington.

10:00 A.M.

Katie was washing the breakfast things, thinking about eggs, wondering if they get hard and stick in your stomach the way they do on dishes. Briana and some of her friends were playing in the yard.

And Loring was in his study, trying to get rid of the headache he'd had since 5:30.

10:30 A.M.

Sergeant Scharlach listened to the question, thought for a second and said, "You ask me why would a guy like him burglarize his neighbors' houses?" He ticked reasons off on his fingers: "You got Money. You got Kicks. You got Sick in the Head. Who knows? He's a writer, maybe he's writing a book."

Trezevant looked over at Costello.

The captain said, "The man has a successful career, for crying out—"

"According to the operations manager of the only bank I know he deals with, Neiman not only hasn't got a pot to piss in, he owes the fucking world, has had liens up the ass this past year or so."

"Middle-class people often need money," Costello said. "But they don't usually steal. This is all crap."

"Right. It's all crap. And this is also crap: I heard back from our friend at the DOD, and he told me Neiman was an army cop in Vietnam, CID, and did enough black-bag jobs there to make the Guinness Book. And here's some more crap. . . ." Trezevant motioned to Scharlach to wheel the rolling blackboard up closer. Besides the Identikit drawing the Kilowitz girl had created (which, Costello had earlier pointed out, looked very little like Loring Neiman), the board had a blown-up street map of Kingsborough Beach taped to it. Six locations on the map had red circles drawn around them. Trezevant pointed to one. "Look, Cal, this is where Neiman lives, see . . . and these are the nighttime series houses. They're all in the west half of The Beach, and all within three blocks of Neiman's house. It's all crap, but don't you find it interesting?" He waited for a reaction, got none. "No. You don't find it interesting."

Sergeant Scharlach said, "Captain, the first job, the Pincus"—he tapped the map—"was right here, just over Neiman's back fence."

Costello shook his head. "Are you telling me you would try to get an indictment on this kind of evidence?"

"Who's talking about indictments?" Trezevant asked.

"Then what the hell *are* we talking about?"

"Cal, this kind of burglary is not something anyone seriously expects to prove. Especially not me. No, I need to catch him, doing it."

"That supposes he's going to *do* any more, Frank. What makes you think he will do any more? In Kingsborough Beach, anyway? Maybe the Goldstein alarm scared it all out of him."

"You're kidding," Trezevant said. "If the Kilowitz shotgun didn't scare him off, you think a fucking burglar alarm would? No, Cal, he's done five. We'd be nuts not to expect a sixth, especially since he didn't get much of anything from Goldstein. And I want to collar him doing the sixth. And I need your cooperation."

Costello leaned away. "Of course."

"I'm overwhelmed by your enthusiasm. But I'll take it as a yes. And for one thing, I need complete silence about this. A blackout. He must not know he's under suspicion."

"On that score, I wouldn't put too much faith in your Dr. Blaug."

Trezevant said, "I put the fear of God in him."

11:15 A.M.

She wasn't going to call him.

He called her.

"Hello, Liz. Is the jury still out?"

"Do you know the police were here Sunday morning?" She sounded on the edge of hysteria. "Asking Andy questions?"

251

"About what?"

There was a pause while she strengthened her voice. "About what happened at the Goldsteins'."

"Goldsteins'? Saturday night?"

"Yes."

"What does he have to do with it?"

"How do I know? That terrible detective I met at the meeting, he was here. Trezevant, Lieutenant Trezevant."

"Trezevant. Well, why . . . what did he talk to Andy about?"

"His car was seen there, I don't know how come, although it's right near your house. Andy could have been there checking up on you and me, I don't know, he won't tell me . . . and he won't tell me what the hell the police wanted."

"Can't you find out from him? Jesus, honey, you never had any trouble getting information out of *me*. Please."

She shrieked. "What am I, a goddamn *gun moll?*"

Loring was stunned. "I'm sorry, darling. I'm really sorry—"

"Loring, if you had leprosy, I could deal with it. But all I know now is that to continue seeing you would be throwing open my door to some kind of . . . lunacy, watching you self-destruct. . . ."

Loring couldn't respond. After a long moment of mutual silence, he heard her quietly hang up.

12:05 P.M.

"I need twenty-four-hour surveillance on him," Trezevant said.

Costello said, "That's . . . I'm not so sure it's a good idea."

"It's a good idea. I want four teams, my men and yours. Six different kinds of cars—sedans, vans, service trucks, all that shit—eighteen costumes and a forty-piece orchestra."

"No. I'm not going to fill Kingsborough Beach with cops. I

know these people, they ask for police protection, and when they get it, it makes them nervous. They'd wind up breaking my chops. I'll let you put one man undercover on Neiman's street at all times. Period."

Trezevant said, "Okay. But let me tell you something, Cal. You're thinking like *he's* thinking: that because he's some hot-shit respected writer his hot-shit friends will save him out of anything. But you want to know what I think? I think that when they find out what he is, they're going to decide he's a great big bag of poison." He stood up. "And, Cal, I also want you to know that when I do get Loring, I'm going to treat him as exactly the same kind of scumbag as your average nigger we drag in here. Sir."

1:30 P.M.

Loring looked at himself in the bathroom mirror and laughed; the ski mask—red and yellow, bought twelve years earlier at Grossinger's—did not have the menacing effect he'd expected but made him look rather like a comic book character.

2:15 P.M.

The phone rang in his basement workshop.

It was Judith Lieb.

"Hello gorgeous I hope you're not busy on the Fourth of July because we're having a big party and we want you to come and bring the girls. Will you come?"

Mindlessly he said, "It sounds nice, Judith. When is it?"

"Christmas you idiot!"

"Oh, right, you did say the Fourth. Sure, Judith, we'll come. Thanks."

"Good. So what's new with you and—"

"Judith, can we talk later? I'm kind of busy right now. . . ."

Wearing his cotton gloves, he sharpened the small hatchet

he'd bought. Afterward he looked for a nail with a large, flat head.

2:45 P.M.

In his desk he found the card Captain Costello had given him at the first Neighborhood Watch meeting. He called the number.

Costello seemed astounded to hear from him. Or very, very grateful.

"Mr. Neiman. It's nice to hear from you!"

"Thanks, Captain. I just wanted to tell you I've read your wife's stories, and they're very good. They need some work, but that's been said about every piece of fiction since Homer. On the whole, they show a lot of talent."

"Oh. She'll be delighted to hear that."

"I hope so. Tell her to keep on writing."

"I will, Mr. Neiman."

"That's it, Captain. I hope to see you soon."

"Same here, sir. And thank you. . . ."

3:10 P.M.

"I had enough already with police," said Miriam Pincus. "They came again, before, to look out my kitchen window."

"That's all? Just to look out your kitchen window?" asked Mrs. Miller.

"That's all. For two minutes. But you know they're always such big *shgutzim*, like Cossacks."

"What then, like certified accountants? My God, you had enough, already, with police."

"That's what I said."

3:15 P.M.

The minute Elliot Silverbach got back to his office he called Loring.

"Lor, I just had lunch with Simon Karr of Clover Books.

Turns out he's from Bensonhurst—his real name is Kossoff
—and he loves our idea for a Brooklyn book, and he wants
to talk about it. I want to set up a lunch. When's good for
you?"

4:00 P.M.

The air-conditioner service truck had been parked across
the street and a few doors down from his house since just
after noon. It occurred to Loring that the man who was sitting
in its open door, playing with condensors and wires, had been
doing so all that time.

4:50 P.M.

Jamie Gelfmann said, "Loring, when I find that I am
thinking about a book six weeks after rejecting it, it occurs to
me I may have been wrong."

"Wrong, Jamie?"

"I am referring to *Quarantine,* Loring. If you are willing to
have another go at it, I think I know a way it can be fixed."

The phone almost slipped from Loring's hand. "I . . . I'd
like to very much. . . ."

"Then can we have dinner tomorrow night? Open-ended. I
will stay in town. We can talk as long as we have to."

5:25 P.M.

He sat with the *Quarantine* manuscript in his lap. *What if I
call Shapp, tell him I won't do it? What would he do? He'd
blow my life away, that's what he would do.*

8:45 P.M.

The air-conditioning truck was gone. Near where it had
been parked there was now a small U-Haul truck. It didn't
appear to have anyone in its cab.

Loring and Katie and Briana had been playing Junior
Sentence Scrabble. As usual, he and Katie played their own

secret game, against each other, for blood, while dealing with Briana's non sequiturs and allowing her to make fantastic points with them until she was finally declared the winner. As usual.

When they had put the stuff back in the box, Katie asked, "Are you staying home tonight, Daddy?"

"Yup. Working."

"Good."

They all marched upstairs. The girls went to bed. Loring went into his bedroom and took his navy blue running suit and ski mask from the closet.

10:30 P.M.

Liz had been driving at her husband since dinner. Now, on their rear veranda, standing with his back to her, looking out over their yard, the damp breeze carrying away the smoke of his semi-weekly cigar, he finally said, "It was about the Neiman man."

But she'd already supposed that. "What about him, Andy?"

"Elizabeth, the police have warned me not to talk about this. I could get into trouble."

"*What* about him?"

He turned to her.

She thought he appeared to be in pain; whether it was from fear of police wrath or some remorse about betraying a neighbor, she didn't know.

"They suspect him of being the burglar."

"They told you that?"

"Lieutenant Trezevant told me that."

"How did he come to tell you that? What have you got to do with it?"

"I am a witness. I saw him leaving the Goldstein house right after the burglary there."

"And you told them so?"

"I had no choice, Liz. My car was seen there."

She stared at him. "You had to tell them you *saw* him?"

She stood up, shaking. "Was it *necessary* to tell them you *saw* him?"

"Yes. I could have been under . . . suspicion myself."

"Not goddamn likely."

Andy knew nothing beyond what he had just told her. That was apparent to her. There was nothing more for them to discuss. She started into the house.

"Liz . . ."

She stopped, waited for the question.

"You and Loring Neiman."

She didn't respond for many moments. Then, quietly, she said, "Yes."

11:40 P.M.

Loring put on his running suit, then stuffed the ski mask into one deep back pocket, put the small hatchet, a glass cutter and the nail in the other.

He went to the phone on the nightstand. Peering past the window shade, he could see the U-Haul, still parked across the street.

He dialed 911.

"Police emergency, how may we help you?"

"I'm reporting a burglary in progress."

"What address?"

"Twenty-nine thirty-three Timberlane Street, Kingsborough Beach."

"Are you—"

"Please hurry." He hung up.

Two minutes later he did it again.

"Police emergency help you?"

"There is a burglary in progress, right now, at Gerrold Street, in Kingsborough Beach."

"House number?"

"Uh, 2941 . . . they're in the house. Hurry." He hung up.

Soon he heard a police car on Bay Boulevard. It yipped past Averly Street, eastward toward Timberlane and/or Gerrold streets.

Then another one, same direction.

He picked up the phone, dialed 911 once again. This time he told the operator there was a police officer in trouble on the beach, attacked by youths. She asked for the location, and he told her it was out near Easterly Street.

A minute later, from his window, he saw the U-Haul suddenly come to life; it backed into the nearest driveway, turned around and headed down Averly, the wrong way on a one-way street. Toward the beach.

His suspicions of the truck and the air-conditioning van had been based on pure paranoia, so Loring was surprised to see the truck take off. Surprised and shocked. He knew that his first two calls would get all the available RMPs, and he had guessed that if the U-Haul was really police, it would be ordered to respond to the officer-in-trouble.

And he appeared to be right. Unless it was just an amazing coincidence. *Why would there be undercover police on my street? And if they were the police, where is it written that it has anything to do with me?* He recalled a movie he'd seen decades ago about a man who escaped from a Nazi concentration camp and was making his way through Germany looking over his shoulder all the time and almost giving himself away when he was stopped by a uniform who turned out to be a traffic cop with a ticket for overtime parking.

Whatever, he now had something extra to be nervous about.

He took his Hot Prowl disks out of their plastic box and hid them under a corner of the rug in his study, just as he did before every break-in. Then he peeked in at the girls. They were fast asleep. He would be back home, he felt, within forty minutes.

11:46 P.M.

Andy was finally asleep after having lain awake for a long time. Liz got out of their bed and went down to the kitchen to call Loring. Loring had to be told.

11:47 P.M.

Loring phoned the Bergers' house, let it ring about ten times, expecting no answer and getting none.

Just before he left his house, he took the phone receiver in his bedroom off the cradle.

11:48 P.M.

She tried again. The line was still busy. The significance of a busy line at his home at that hour was beginning to dawn on her.

She tried one more time.

It was still busy.

11:50 P.M.

Congressman Norman Berger and his wife Naomi arrived at LaGuardia Airport a full day ahead of their intended return.

They were in a happy, celebratory mood. Norman's meetings in Washington with the Speaker, the senior New York senator and several others had gone well; his Senate nomination was almost a fait accompli.

The couple headed for the taxicab area with their carry-ons. When you have an apartment in Georgetown you don't have to shlep a lot of luggage back and forth.

12:08 A.M.

The low quarter moon was obscured by clouds. It was going to rain.

Loring jogged north to Bay Boulevard, then south on Horning all the way to the beach. From there he doubled back to the Berger house, on Baldwin between Dale and Ramsgate. Three houses south of Elias Shapp's.

In the Berger driveway, he put on the ski mask and the cotton gloves.

Why, Officer? Because when I run I sweat and I feel more

comfortable with this on my face, instead of dripping like a pig. Speaking of which, have you ever done duty on Staten Island? I was just speaking with Carroll Costello, your commanding officer, this very day. About Lucy's stories. I'm Loring Neiman, the writer, I live three blocks over. Who's your partner in the car? John? Is that you, John, you old hot dog?

The house was a modified Victorian, with a graceful open porch in the front and on one side. They had bought it eight years before, when they moved from upstate to establish the residence requirements for Norman's run for the House of Representatives.

The houses on either side were quiet and dark, with just some nightlight showing.

He had known that the outside of the place would be brightly floodlit, but he also knew that the lamp units were all aimed just a little too high, leaving a generally dark area in the bushes at the base of the building. Loring went through the light and into the dark very quickly.

The telephone wire connected in just under the roof, at a rear corner of the house that was reachable from the second-floor terrace off the master bedroom. This was good.

He stepped up onto the brick barbecue oven; from it he reached up and curled his fingers onto the floor of the terrace. Using his deck shoes against the wooden siding of the house, he pulled himself up under the terrace railing and onto its asphalt floor.

One swipe with the hatchet cut the phone cable. It sprang loose and snaked down into the yard. If the alarm should go off during the course of things, there would be no automatic signal to the police or the Bergers' private security company.

He dropped the hatchet down into the yard. He'd have no further use for it.

On his knees, he tried the handle of the double french door. It was locked, as expected, but singly; the Bergers placed most of their reliance on the alarm system. With the

260

glass cutter he scored the pane nearest to the door handle, two lines across, one line down, forming a square with the wooden frame of the door. One short punch with his fist, and the glass snapped inward, but didn't fall. It was held in place by the wood and putty of the frame, like a little glass door in itself. He reached in through it and around it and unlatched the door. Then he tossed the glass cutter out into the yard.

Holding the nail he'd brought with him, he slowly pushed the door open, a millimeter at a time. The alarm switch was of the spring-loaded plastic protrusion type, set into the door-jamb. When the door opened to a certain extent, he was able to meet the protrusion with the nail and force it back into the socket whence it was trying to come. Then he quickly slid the point of the nail between the protrusion and the side of its socket, jamming it in place. The circuit remained unbroken.

He opened the door, entered the master bedroom.

Then can we have dinner tomorrow night? Open-ended.
. . . pushed the glass pane back in place and closed the door behind him.

12:23 A.M.

The cabdriver watched in the rearview mirror as Naomi pushed Norman back onto the seat and kissed him. Norman laughed nervously, conscious that the driver might be watching them, hoping he didn't know who they were.

"Honey, wait, hang on there, we'll be home in a few minutes. . . ."

"Mr. Senator. Oh God I love you, Norm, I love you so damn much."

12:24 A.M.

Trezevant was still awake, watching TV in bed, when he got the call from Leroy on the night duty team. Leroy told him there were two 10–31s and a 10–13 in Kingsborough Beach during the past hour, all false alarms.

"False alarms. That's weird."

"Yeh, Lieutenant. By the way, the 10–13 took Mandel for a couple of minutes."

"It did?" Trezevant sat up in bed. "Where is he now?"

"He's back in place, don't worry."

"'Back in place, don't worry,'" mimicked the lieutenant. "That fucking asshole had no business moving!"

"Aw, Lieutenant, an officer-in-trouble, come on, give him a break. He's supposed to sit on a plant like a turd while something like that's going down a couple of blocks away?"

"Yes!" Trezevant shouted, and slammed down the phone.

Three false alarms.

He decided to drive out there and cruise the area himself for a while.

12:25 A.M.

The room was pitch-dark. He turned on his penlight. On the wall ahead of him were a small closet, a dresser and the door to the hall. To his left was a large brass bed. To his right were the master bathroom and the walk-in closet.

He went into the closet. Under a lot of shoe boxes was the floor safe.

Then a car door slammed. Out in front of the house.

He listened: Small voices. High heels. A pause. A jingle. The metallic *shtuck* of key in lock. A click. A squeak. A slam. Big voices. In the house. Downstairs. Coming up the stairs.

The Bergers were home.

Loring hunkered down into the corner of the closet, quietly replaced the boxes he'd moved, closed the accordion door as far as it would easily close, pulled some of her clothes around him and sat tight.

"Ohhhh God it's good to be home!" Naomi's voice.

A lamp came on. Through the crack of the door Loring saw Norman walk into the room, shuffling through a small pile of mail. His suit was rain-spattered.

"Now you know what I go through forty damn weeks a year. There's no such thing as a short airplane trip." He tossed the mail on the dresser, stepped to his closet—the smaller one—and started taking off his tie.

Naomi kicked off her shoes and pulled her dress off over her head. The first garter belt Loring had seen since the girls in Cheap Charlie's in Saigon. Naomi put the dress on a chair, sat down on the edge of the bed and took her stockings off. Norman, in his boxer briefs, went into the bathroom. Loring heard the toilet seat clunk down.

"Greece," Norman said, from the bathroom.

She looked in his direction, made a funny face. "Stop it already, Norm."

"Greece. Better than a cruise down the Nile. Anyway, I don't know how comfortable I'd be in Egypt, Camp David—Shmamp David."

"We can't afford anywhere that far, that exotic." She stood up, naked, looked at herself in the full-length mirror on the door. Very black hair against milk-white skin.

Loring became conscious of the faint smell of perfume from her clothes in the closet.

She went into the bathroom. "I think that vodka drink went to your head, you know?"

Water running. Noises.

"Hey, knock it," Norman whined, "you're getting me all wet."

"You're all wet anyhow." She giggled. "Stop it. Horny beast."

"Water-shpritzing cunt. You're being bad."

A slap on a tush. Laughter. Gargling. Toilet flush.

Naomi came out of the bathroom, crawled onto the bed and lay down on top of the comforter.

"The fact is," Norman said, coming out of the bathroom, "we've got no money problem." He dropped his shorts on the floor and got onto the bed.

"How come?"

"Huh?"

"How come?"

He smiled knowingly. "Because. Believe in me."

"You're not talking about a junket? With fifty congressmen and their silly wives and their pimpled kids?"

"Noooo."

"The National Committee?"

"No, of course not."

"What then? What money?"

He turned to her and kissed her. "Shut up and suck on Mr. Poopie a bit."

12:45 A.M.

Trezevant slowed down from seventy-five miles an hour and pulled off the Belt Parkway at Knapp Street. He made the turn and drove across the causeway on Brigham Street into a very quiet Kingsborough Beach. He went straight down Castor, turned left on Dale Avenue and left again, five blocks later, onto Averly. There, parked across the street and three houses down from number 2906, was his U-Haul. He drove slowly past it.

Into his portable DVP, he said, "You awake, Snake Eyes?"

Inside the truck, Snake Eyes leaped in his seat. The loud signal on his own MX330 had splattered painfully; the transmission was from too close.

"What?" he said.

"This is Snake Leader." By this time, Trezevant's car was far enough up the block for normal reception. "You asshole."

"Oh, shit, you scared me. What's the matter? Where are you?"

"The Monte Carlo up ahead of you. What I want to know is why the hell you responded to that 10–13?"

"Oh, you heard, huh? What can I say? It was a, uh, conditioned reflex. You know. I was only gone a couple minutes."

"Shithead. What's happening here?"

"Nada. Not a move, not a peep. He's got to be asleep. Like I wish I was."

"Like you probably were." Trezevant turned the corner.

"Okay. I'll be around for a while. It looks good here but it doesn't smell good. Out."

" 'Kay."

12:50 A.M.

Naomi slipped out of bed and came to the closet. Loring, invisible in the corner, shielded by hanging garments, wondered how she could not hear the banging of his heart as she rummaged on a shelf about three feet above his head. She found what she wanted and, leaving the closet door open, took them back to bed with her.

They were two pairs of handcuffs.

The tableau lasted thirty-five minutes. When it was over, Norman, exhausted, his voice throaty, asked, "You be a good girl?"

"No, no," she replied. "I'm still bad, Norm. I should stay this way. . . ."

Which meant, Loring guessed, that she preferred to sleep the rest of the night with her hands manacled to the brass headboard.

"Okay." He made one attempt to reach the lamp on his wife's side of the bed, but couldn't make it. He fell asleep.

Trezevant slowly cruised Kingsborough Beach. The summer overnight parking restrictions had been in effect since the fifteenth, so there were only three or four vehicles parked on the streets. He ran radio checks on each and found them all to be duly registered to the addresses at which they were parked.

At one moment, on Ramsgate Boulevard, Trezevant saw the regular RMP coming from the opposite direction and beeped them as they went by, but the stupid bastards were talking and had never even looked his way. Costello's fucking patrolmen.

When he was sure the Bergers were asleep, Loring quietly removed the shoe boxes and bent to the safe.

His fingers were on the dial when he realized he had forgotten the combination.

But he *knew* the fucking combination. He *knew* it. *I've memorized it, read it and said it at least fifty times, sixty times. I know it I know it I know it.*

But he couldn't remember it.

Relax. Think. Think. Relax. Think.

But he'd forgotten the combination. Kicking his brain for the right numbers, he spun the dial through one imagined combination after another after another after another. . . .

With an elbow he knocked over a couple of Naomi's shoe boxes.

Across the room, Norman Berger sat up in bed, stared at the closet.

Loring looked out at him.

Norman saw the red and yellow head and shrieked like a woman.

Naomi woke up. She lifted her head and saw what Norman saw. She screamed, too.

"Stay right where you are," Norman shouted. He slid open the drawer of his nightstand and took out a nickel-plated revolver. "Naomi, call the police!" He pointed the gun at Loring. "Call the police, god damn it to hell!"

"I can't," Naomi said, rattling the handcuffs. "I can't!"

Berger got out of the bed. White-faced, he held the pistol straight out in front of him, legs apart, like the FBI men he once watched on the firing range at Quantico.

"Stand up, you."

Loring rose to his feet. His knees felt weak.

"Hold up your hands," Berger said, in a remarkably firm voice. Then, remembering Naomi's condition, he added, "Face the wall. That wall. Go over to it, stand facing it. . . ."

Loring obeyed, moved to the wall, midway between the dresser and the door.

Keeping the gun and one eye on the intruder, Berger threw the comforter over his wife. "Naomi, can you *believe* this? With that mask, that bizarre goddamn mask?"

"I don't want to see his face, Norm, don't make him take it off . . . just get the police, *please.*"

"I will, in one second. . . ." He crossed the room to the

closet and looked at the safe. It was exposed, the shoe boxes having been pushed aside. He stooped for a closer look and saw, with relief, that the safe was closed and the piece of black thread he'd stretched across it was undisturbed. He stood erect again. "How do I call the police?" he asked. "What is it, 'O' for Operator?"

"Just 9-1-1," Naomi said.

Loring—his hands high, his nose inches from the flocked wallpaper, a gun pointed at his back by an outraged person— still did not have any sense of having been captured. Rather, in his mind, he was frantically testing that phenomenal feeling of his recent adventures, that feeling that he could simply step out of the shadows—the role—rip off his mask, say, *Hello, it's me!*, explain a few things, have some coffee and go home. . . .

Not this time. This time it's gone too far, this time they'd destroy me.

Behind him, he heard the telephone receiver being lifted. Then the click-click-click of the disconnect button. "The phone is dead," Norman said, shock—and awe—in his voice. "He killed the phone, cut the wires!" The intruder now had another dimension. Norman was now officially afraid of him.

Naomi said, "Push the panic button!"

She referred to the device that was affixed to the wall close to her side of the headboard. Pressed, it would cause the alarm bells to go off.

"The panic button?" He was still not used to the recently installed system. Without taking his eyes off the intruder, he began shuffling slowly around the bed toward Naomi's side to get to the device. Suddenly his bare feet contacted his shorts, on the floor. The sensation startled him; he uttered a sound and looked down.

Loring heard the opportunity and went out through the bedroom door.

It took Berger a second to realize that the intruder was gone; he looked helplessly at the door, then at the panic button. He started for it, then suddenly reversed direction and moved hesitantly toward the door.

"Norm, don't go after him!" Naomi said.

God knew he didn't want to. He didn't want to get hurt, didn't want to shoot anyone. Not that he was a coward; he was a senatorial nominee. He remembered the crazy Kilowitz thing, the "shootout at the O.K. Corral," as the TV news people had called it. Even defensively based, a firearm incident would do him no good, especially with the Handgun Control people. Nor, it dawned on him, did he really want to capture the guy; the situation Naomi was in gave the whole episode an especially sour undertone.

He felt guilty about suffering this whole goddamn break-in.

Another few moments, he figured, and the guy will be well out of the house.

Downstairs, Loring quietly unlocked the dead-bolt, slipped off the brass security chain and opened the front door, expecting the alarm to go off. But it didn't. The Bergers hadn't reset it when they came in. He peered out: there was a man with a dog across the street. Without closing the door, Loring turned and went as quietly as he could down the carpeted center hall toward the rear of the house.

Norman Berger stepped carefully out of the bedroom, glanced toward the attic door at the end of the hallway, then went to the head of the stairway and looked down. The front door was slowly opening in the breeze. The sight cheered him. Still holding his gun, he went downstairs to the door and looked out in time to see Lester Espy entering his own side door with his dog. Norman glanced along his porch to either side. Nobody. The lawn, the bushes. Nobody. He was immensely relieved. He would check through the house to see if anything was missing (although the only thing that mattered was the money in the safe) and later, perhaps tomorrow, he'd call the police and report the intrusion. It would be handled routinely, without sound and fury. He'd make a nice, neat, maybe even slightly heroic statement. The resultant publicity would be controlled and the story that made the papers would redound to his credit. He leaned against the doorway, breathed deeply.

Upstairs, his wife had kicked the comforter off the bed and raised her legs up over her head. She had stretched her right one back and over to the wall beside the headboard, and was bumping the foot clumsily along the wall, trying to reach the panic button with it, hoping to hit it with her toe.

And she did.

Loring was on his way through Norman's billiards room toward the kitchen when the quadruple outdoor bells and two interior klaxons went off. The bells of hell.

The sound stunned Norman Berger. He stood dumbly in his open front door. Across the street, a light went on in the Espys' window. Then one in the window of the house next to it. Faces appeared at them. Norman staggered back into the house, ran upstairs to ask his wife how to turn the alarm off.

John the Hot Dog and his partner were sitting in their RMP car on Castor Street, two blocks away, eating the steamed pisser clams they'd picked up on Emmons Avenue. When the alarm went off, they looked at each other. John dropped the carton of clams out the window, hit the siren and they were rolling.

Lieutenant Trezevant had just turned onto Horning Street, his second time around The Beach, when he heard the alarm go off. It sounded to be back the way he'd just come, Baldwin Street. He turned his car around and headed for it, radioing Mandel as he went, telling him to go immediately into the Neiman house and see if the guy *was* home.

Through the windows of the billiards room, Loring saw lights go on in the house next door, faces at its windows. Same thing in the house beyond the back fence. In the semidark, he tried to discern exactly what was in the billiard room, whether there was someplace to hide. There were built-ins along one wall, with a long row of cabinets at the bottom. He opened a cabinet at random. It held nothing but a few tablecloths; he felt that he could fit himself into it, on one of the shelves. He got down, inserted himself into the cabinet and closed the door after him.

Elias Shapp was at home, three doors away, listlessly watching an old movie on television, but thinking about Loring Neiman. He had been surprised, earlier, to hear the Bergers come home, and wondered if Loring was in the place when they did. In fact, he wondered if he'd been there at all. And if he had been, where the hell was he now? He had been trying to call him at his home for almost an hour but got a continuous busy signal. Did that mean he was home? Shmoozing with some broad when he had a job to do? Shapp was getting very angry.

Then he heard the Bergers' alarm go off.

He went to his back door to wait.

Lieutenant Trezevant arrived in front of the Bergers' house at the same moment as the RMP. He wore his gold shield on the breast pocket of his sport shirt. The alarm was deafening. At the top of his lungs he ordered one of the patrolmen to cover the back of the house. He and the other, their guns drawn, ran up the steps and crossed the porch to the front door. It was unlocked. They opened it and entered the house.

Norman and Naomi had heard the cars pull up outside. Norman tossed his revolver back in the nightstand drawer, pulled a bathrobe from his closet and put it on.

"How do I turn off the goddamn alarm?"

"It's right in your closet on the side to the left, the metal box. Norm, please get these things off me . . . I'm going crazy. . . ."

Norman saw a little black plunger on the box, with the word "panic" next to it. "I push this?" He pushed it. The noise ended.

"Thank God," murmured Naomi.

Trezevant told the patrolman to search the downstairs floor, then he took the stairs to the second floor two at a time. When he barged into the bedroom, shouting, "Police!," Norman Berger was up on the bed, kneeling over his wife, trying to unlock one of the handcuffs with the key that was tied to it by a string.

Naomi, her head turned away, burst into tears of humiliation.

Norman looked at the detective. "I'm . . . Congressman Norman Berger . . . we had an intruder, a deviate. He did this to my wife. At gunpoint. Could you turn your back, please, Officer?"

As Trezevant averted his gaze, the radio strapped to his belt crackled to life. "Snake Leader, this is Snake Eyes."

"Come in," said Trezevant.

"Our man is not home." Mandel sounded sheepish.

"Say what?"

"He's not in his home. Just his two little kids. They said he wasn't even supposed to go out."

Trezevant thrilled. "Then he's got to be in the neighborhood."

The Bergers, wishing desperately to mind their own business, had no idea who "he" was.

Loring was afraid to remove the ski mask for even a minute, even though it chafed his face. His hair underneath it was matted with sweat. He opened the cabinet door an inch more, for air.

One of the patrolmen called up to the second floor. "Lieutenant? There's nobody down here or outside." He started up the stairs.

Lieutenant Trezevant stepped out into the hall and stopped him. To the radio, he said, "Snake Eyes, I'm sending Patrolman"—he looked at the cop's name tag—"Woodcock over to you. I want him to stay inside the house until I get there." To Patrolman Woodcock he said, "It's 2906 Averly Street. Go on foot. Run. Sergeant Mandel is in the U-Haul that you hung that parking ticket on. When you get there you need to knock on the back of the truck and inform him, then go inside the house and stay there. There's two little girls, make it look normal from the outside. Tell the kids something

271

to keep them from getting nervous. Read to them, anything. If the guy of the house shows up, his name is Loring Neiman. Arrest him."

"Go on foot, you said?"

"Yes, yes, yes," Trezevant said, irritably. "Get moving."

Woodcock nodded and left, muttering something about how hard it was raining outside.

John the Hot Dog appeared at the foot of the staircase, looked at the lieutenant for instructions. Trezevant told him to go outside and make sure nobody stuck his nose out into the street. "Tell them we've got an armed perpetrator loose and there might be some gunplay."

The detective went back into the bedroom. Berger was helping his wife into a dressing gown.

"Where are those handcuffs?" he asked.

Congressman Berger looked at him quizzically.

"I need to take them. They belonged to the intruder, right?"

"Right," said Berger. He pretended to think, poked a little among the bedclothes, then lifted a pillow and found them. He handed them to the lieutenant, who stuck them in his pocket.

Trezevant realized Berger was lying, he and his wife had been playing games with the handcuffs, but he didn't care. Anything that would complicate the case against Neiman was okay with him. He liked their bullshit story, so far, and wanted to give them a minute or two to get together on it.

To Berger, he said, "Congressman, why don't you take your wife downstairs and make yourselves comfortable with some coffee. I just need to make one call here and then I'll join you and take your statement. A good, detailed one."

Grateful, but also nervous, Norman shepherded Naomi out of the room.

On the phone, Trezevant told his night duty people to come out and back him up. An armed intruder had attempted burglary and tried to rape a congressman's wife.

* * *

Loring could hear the Bergers whispering in the den, which was almost directly across the center hall from the billiards room. He was cramped; his back was beginning to hurt.

After a minute or so, he heard another voice join them. It sounded like a cop. He knew that two cops had already left the house, and had felt there was a third one still upstairs. This new voice was probably him.

He began to consider the possibility of slipping out of there and exiting the house, maybe through the side door, hiding in the yard until it was safe to go.

Then, for some reason, he pictured himself talking to Voncie Shapp on a bench at the beach the next morning: Voncie is staring at the birds.

I'm awfully sorry, Voncie, but I fucked up, didn't get the money.

You didn't get the money.

No. You see, they came home unexpectedly.

They did, hah. Ain't that a shame.

Yes. And besides, I forgot the combination.

No shit? That's a even worse shame.

And then he pictured Voncie Shapp turning to look at him. *Loring suddenly remembered the combination.*

He slid himself out of the cabinet, crawled through the billiard room, out into the center hall, past the den in which the three were talking (with Naomi saying, "I don't mind telling you, Lieutenant, as the wife of a United States congressman, that you are behaving like a Gestapo . . .") and up the stairs to the master bedroom.

He went into the room, to the closet. The shoe boxes had been put back in place, on top of the safe. Loring pushed them aside and began turning the dial through the series of numbers.

The safe door unlocked.

Loring took out the only thing it contained, a smallish brown paper package, Scotch-taped. He ripped open one corner, put it to his nose and sniffed. It was money.

With the package tucked inside his running suit, he went

out on the terrace—it was raining heavily—and jumped down to the yard. He landed on his feet, but then slipped and fell flat on his face in what had become mud. There was a flash of lightning; by the time the thunder came he had gotten up and was over the cyclone fence and into the next yard.

Three backyards from the Bergers', Loring leaned against Elias Shapp's back door to get his breath. He took off the ski mask and wrung it out.

He couldn't hear them, but he knew that out in front there were people in nightclothes standing in their doorways and on their porches. They would be there as long as there was a police car at the Bergers' house. He wished he could join them, commiserate, and then drift home, like on the Kilowitz night. Or even just *see* them. He felt as though he'd been away for a while, in a strange town.

It was ten after two. Katie. He hoped she hadn't gotten up, checked to see if he was home. Had he closed his bedroom door before he left?

He rang Shapp's back door bell.

The Neiman house was now the police command post.

Trezevant sat on a living room chair with the DVP in his lap. From time to time he would speak into it or hear something from it. All in low tones.

Staring at him from the couch across the room were Loring Neiman's two little girls. They had been unwilling and sullen hostesses to strange men with guns on their belts and badges on their sport shirts and sweaters for the past half hour, and no matter what this "Frank" said, they refused to go back to bed until their father got home.

The house was lighted only by the small table lamp Loring had left on. From the outside the place looked normal. The street itself looked normal. There wasn't a cop in sight, although four of his detectives were deployed within spitting distance: Mandel, his U-Haul gone, lay on his stomach in a garden across the street; Scharlach was in Neiman's garage; there was a detective in the Pincus hydrangeas and another peering through a space in Mrs. Libo's rear fence. Their cars, all either personal or unmarked department ones, were parked far apart from one another on Averly, Bay and Dale. Trezevant had ordered the RMP to resume its normal patrol, not to do anything unusual and especially not to hang around Averly Street. If they did happen to see the white–male–forty–average build–wearing a dark running suit, they were to contact Lieutenant Trezevant before doing anything.

He also had his search and arrest warrants, signed twenty minutes ago by the judge who lived in Flatbush and always obliged the police when they woke him up in the middle of the night. And better, Trezevant also had his first piece of hard evidence: the Adolfo Belimbau drawing he'd found in the closet in Loring's study only five minutes ago.

The question in Trezevant's mind now: Exactly where is Neiman? Assuming he got out of the Bergers' when Berger thought he did, it had been over forty-five minutes. Neiman knew that his face had not been seen and identified, but he must know that his blue running suit and deck shoes *had* been; reason enough for him to keep a low profile, so he was probably making his way home by way of the backyards.

Lieutenant Trezevant waited.

Shapp looked at him inquiringly.
Loring patted the lump on his chest.
Shapp grinned. "Do they know it was you?"
"No. They never saw my face."
Shapp grinned. "See? You *are* a good mechanic. I was worried about ya. Tell me the story." He led Loring through the mud room, into the large kitchen.
"I don't tell stories for free." Loring drew the package out from under his shirt and set it on a butcher block table. He dripped rainwater on the floor.
Shapp tore open the paper. They were all fifty-dollar bills, a thousand of them. Two reams. One neat handful.
"Count off two hundred and fifty of those, kid, for yours." He opened the icemaker. "I bet you want a drink, hah?"
"No." Loring was counting out his share.
"No? Kid, it's your retirement party—"

"Shut up, Cockroach, I'm counting."

Shapp's jaw muscle twitched.

Loring held up his wad. "Okay, here's mine. You want to count it?"

"I already did, while you was. I'm good at that."

"That's because you understand money. Which is as it should be. It's your profession. You're a certified public gangster." Loring stepped to the sink, turned on the water, stuffed his twelve thousand five hundred dollars into the Waste King and flipped the switch. "To me, on the other hand, money is . . . I don't know . . . garbage."

He watched Shapp watching the end of the wad slowly disappear. The old man's expression was worth the expense.

Shapp finally said, "That was good, kid, real good. You got a lotta class."

"Good night, Cockroach."

Shapp said, "Deal was I drive you home. Let's go." He headed for the door that led down to the garage.

"I don't want you driving me home. I don't want to owe you anything. You owe me."

"You're a shmuck, you shouldn't be on the street tonight."

"My wife Arlene would have said that nothing attracts less attention in Brooklyn than one more depressed-looking Jew."

He went out through the front door. The doorways and porches were clear of people, the police cars were gone. He started north on Baldwin. Not at a jog or even a fast walk. He ambled in the rain. This was his neighborhood.

At the corner of Levon he saw a car almost a block away coming his way behind the sheets of rain. As it passed under a streetlamp, he saw the blue and white; it was a police car. He turned his back toward it, began to jog in place, like a runner warming down.

In car 1188, John the Hot Dog leaned forward for a better look. He said to his partner, "Guy on the corner, see him?"

"Yeh." The car moved a bit faster. As it got closer, John the Hot Dog said, "Kiss my petunia." The man at the corner was wearing a dark running suit.

The driver said, "Call the lieutenant."

"Not yet," said John the Hot Dog. "Not yet. Why shouldn't *we* make the collar? The glamour-boy detectives get all the fuckin' glory. . . ."

Loring heard the car bearing on him. But he was calm. He had done this shtick before. He would be natural, talk, kibitz. *Me? Hey, I'm Loring Neiman, the writer, I live on . . .*

Car 1188 came to a slow squealing stop forty or so feet from him, and he did not turn to look at it; a new, cold intuition of danger was rising along his spine. *Something is different, this night. Different than all the other nights. . . .*

It suddenly struck him: the Bergers had to have given a complete description of what he was wearing, down to the eyelets on his deck shoes. These cops must have it. *They'll take me back there. . . .*

John the Hot Dog and his partner got out of their car, guns pointed at Loring's back. *"Hands up motherfucker we blow your ass off!"*

Loring disappeared into someone's side garden.

The partner leaped the hedge and gave chase.

John the Hot Dog hit the key on the MX330. "Snake Leader . . . ?"

Katie and Briana looked at each other.

"Frank's" radio had suddenly crackled something they couldn't understand, and a second later he ran out the door. Briana's face lit up in a smile. But not Katie's. She had felt all along that her father would come home at any time, be dropped off outside from a friend's car or a neighbor's, home from something or someplace he had forgotten to mention. But now she wasn't so sure. Her first scare, when she was awakened after one o'clock by a strange man who asked if her father was home, and her second scare, when "Frank" came and told her he needed to wait for her father to come home to talk to him about something, were little scares compared to the one she was having now.

At the corner of Levon and Dale, John the Hot Dog—they knew him as Patrolman Severing—told the detectives that his

277

partner was in pursuit of the suspect and they had run "somewhere behind that house." It was in the block that ran from Dale Avenue to Ramsgate Boulevard, between Levon and Horning streets.

Trezevant knew they could hunt in the rain all night through twenty-four or more backyards; he decided instead to surround the block, one man on each street, and wait for Neiman to reappear. Sooner or later he had to. Until then there was no rush, no mortal danger to anyone.

He ordered Loftus to cover the Horning Street side, Scharlach to watch Levon Street, Mandel to stay on Dale Avenue and Patrolman Severing to go to Ramsgate Boulevard. He, Trezevant, restless, would keep driving around the block and stay visual with them all. He'd left one guy back at the Neiman house.

Adrenaline, quarts of it, had altered Loring's conception of time and relativity. From Spencer Lieb's tree house, in which he was huddled, Loring could see a *yahrzeit* candle burning on the sink counter in Judith Lieb's kitchen *(her parent or Sidney's?)*. Despite the solemn significance, it gave the kitchen a soft, warm, cheery glow. He wished he were within it, sitting and drinking hot coffee and talking and enjoying Judith's red hair and Sidney Lieb's face. Would they take him in, were he to knock and explain? The rain on the tree house roof sounded like a monsoon. Shit, it *was* a monsoon; it sounded like Victoria Falls. And he was Neiman of the Apes, up a tree. Lightning crashed, turning off for a second the glow from the kitchen as it made the outside world brighter than bright. He didn't want to move but couldn't stay. At any moment that incredibly agile young cop would be over the wall and in this very yard with him. *Him?* The cops weren't pursuing *him;* they didn't know who the fuck they were pursuing, except that it's a guy in a dark blue running suit. He could take off the running suit and the deck shoes and go home in his underwear. If he got picked up, it would only be for indecent exposure. He'd say he was kidnaped by muggers, stripped of his clothes, beaten up (his face and forearms were already scratched from somebody's holly bushes) and left for dead. If that didn't fly, the judge would send him to Bellevue for a day of observation and he'd be home tomorrow night, playing Scrabble with the girls and working on his book.

The Virshups' dog suddenly began to bark in the next yard; that fucking cop had probably just climbed into it.

Loring jumped from the tree house, loped to the edge of the Liebs' patio and pulled himself up onto the retaining wall. Two houses south was Ramsgate Boulevard. He would go to it, wait for the circling car to pass and make a run for the beach. They would never know he'd gotten off the block. He'd hole up in the bathhouse until dawn, when he would pull himself together and go jogging. Home. He'd worry about the rest—explaining to Katie and Briana—then.

By 2:48 Patrolman Severing's eyes were beginning to hurt in their sockets from the strain of peering through the rain-waved windows of his patrol car. Also, the rhythm of the windshield wipers was becoming soporific. So by the time he spotted him, the guy was already across the boulevard and running down the short leg of Horning Street that ended in the sand where the beach began. With every step he made a splash.

"Hey Snake Snake the guy is on the beach."

Trezevant and his five men covered every inch of the beach, from Castor to Easterly streets. From time to time the entire shorefront would light up like broad daylight, thunder would void the ocean's roar. Through the rainstorm and the spray from the pounding surf, they explored the rocks of each of the three jetties and kicked through every rise of sand. They searched the bathhouse. Neiman had disappeared.

When they stopped looking, more by silent agreement than direct order, his men, soaked to the skin and shivering, huddled together as far from the water's edge as they could get without being accused of leaving the beach, while the lieutenant stood several yards off by himself, a brooding, Napoleonic figure, and pondered the situation, wondering if maybe Congressman Berger had lied to him about more than his wife's handcuffs because maybe Loring Neiman did make some kind of big score, one that Berger preferred not to claim, and never had any intention of going home to his two little girls and has long since swum the ninety-foot channel to Manhattan Beach and is on his way through Brighton and Brooklyn and does not plan to stop until he gets to Rio de Janeiro.

The police walked off the beach.

Less than forty feet from where Trezevant last stood, Loring had been submerged in cold seawater, his lungs boiling with pain, pitching madly in the violent surf, clinging to a forest of kelp to keep from being thrown back onto the sand by the force of the incoming waves. The breakers would explode on the shore and then recede, leaving him in inches of water with seconds of time in which to gasp loudly for air, suck it in and hold it against his next submarine ordeal. In the ten or so minutes it had happened thirty times.

Finally his numbed fingers could no longer clutch the kelp; his shoulders and back and legs gave up struggling for stability against megatons of ocean water. He let go, allowed the sea to pull him in, dance him crazily one more time and then hurl him at thirty miles an hour back onto the hard wet sand.

He lay there on his stomach for a few minutes, trying to control his breathing and quell the pain in his chest. His face, neck and head stung in a million places, whipped to blood by the seaweed, even as it was saving him.

The rain had abated some and felt as warm as urine on his body, after the ocean water. He wondered, then, if six pairs of hands would soon grab him and haul him to his feet.

But they didn't. Loring raised his head and looked around. He was alone.

Presently—his watch said 3:43—he got up and walked from the beach. At Ramsgate Boulevard he turned east.

He rang the Blaugs' doorbell. Andy, in pajamas, his hair in his eyes, opened the door.

"Good morning, Andy. I've come calling on your wife." He stepped past the doctor, to the staircase. "She and I fool around, you know."

Andy blinked. "I know."

Loring went up the stairs.

She opened her eyes, saw him bent over her; there was no surprise in her expression at all, as though she'd been dreaming about him.

"I love you, Liz."

She nodded. In a voice husky with sleep, she said, "I like that stuff. Love, romance, magnolias, screwing. What else is new?"

"Well, let's see: I decided to quit stealing, get my high school diploma and work as a box boy at Waldbaum's. Also, my pimples are clearing up."

"Good boy. If you hear of anyone who needs a used gun moll, mention me. Good-bye, darling."

She meant it.

The rain had stopped and there was a faint pink wash at the edges of the eastern sky. He picked up the New York *Times* from his doorstep, took out his key and unlocked his door.

"You're under arrest."

"For anything special?"

"To me it is. I think burglary, possession of stolen property, attempted armed robbery, attempted rape at gunpoint is all pretty special . . ."

Katie and Briana watched as the detective lieutenant turned their father around and handcuffed him behind his back.

". . . but what the hell do I know, just a plain working stiff. Loring, I need to inform you that you have the right to remain silent if you give up the right to remain silent anything you say can and will be used against you in a court of law you have the right to have an attorney present during questioning if you cannot afford an attorney one will be appointed for you at no cost to you."

"Thank you."

"You're welcome." He patted Loring down. In one back

pocket he found the red and yellow ski mask, which he held up. "Good skiing around here in June, Loring?"

Loring shrugged. "Ask the man who owns it."

"The Bergers *alone* are going to get you three to five, you know that, don't you, Loring?"

"Would you mind if we had this conversation later?" He nodded toward the girls. "And what about them?"

"Detective Loftus is staying here to take care of all that. You've got a choice: either a relative or a friend or the juvenile authorities find—"

"My cousins, Mr. and Mrs. Monasch . . . may I call them?"

"No, Detective Loftus will call them."

"Their numbers are on the kitchen windowsill, home and office. Katie, you know where it is. . . ."

"Yes, Daddy."

"Make sure they get called. Call them now, in fact."

Just before he was taken out, he knelt down to the girls. "Don't worry, babies, everything's going to be all right." They hugged his head, he kissed them both. To Katie, he whispered, "I'm so sorry, sweetheart." His voice caught. "If they ask you anything, tell the truth."

Through her own tears she asked, "The real truth or the good truth?"

Wednesday, June 27 _____

H E WAS SEARCHED again, in the presence of the station house supervisor. Then the detectives propelled him, roughly, up a flight of metal-covered stairs and into the 65th squad room, where the handcuffs were removed so he could be fingerprinted. When that was done, someone indicated a phone on one of the desks, told him he could make three local calls. He made two; one for information—he couldn't recall Ted Krause's number—and the other to Ted Krause.

Then handcuffs were snapped onto his wrists again and he was pushed into a chair at a desk at which sat a female officer. She asked him his vital statistics, typed them onto the arrest report; Lieutenant Trezevant would provide the rest of the information.

After Loring was photographed, the lieutenant shoved him into the detention cage.

About the handcuffs, Loring asked, "Are these necessary?"

"Shut up, scumbag."

An hour later, Ted's partner, Seymour Kalish, came into the squad room, totally confused, not understanding whether Loring was really in trouble or playing a joke or researching a book.

Thirty seconds with Lieutenant Trezevant, and Kalish knew his client was in deep shit.

Trezevant told him Neiman was being booked for Criminal Trespass, of the Bergers' house, Attempted Armed Robbery, of the Bergers, and Unlawful Imprisonment, of Naomi Berger, with handcuffs to her bed. All of that, and Possession of Stolen Property, the Goldsteins' Adolfo Belimbau drawing.

"He's also a suspect in five burglaries, and you should know the investigation of those is going forward."

The lawyer, although dwelling on the image of Naomi handcuffed to the bed, was aghast to the point of nausea. He said, "My client denies everything and will not answer any questions. Now can I have some time with him alone, please?"

They were given a few private minutes in the cage.

They looked at each other. Kalish touched Loring's arm. "Loring, we're going downtown for a very horrible arraignment, in five minutes. Talk to me."

Loring said, "Handcuffs hurt. Did you know that, Seymour?"

Exhausted and wanting sleep, Loring never caught the name of the judge before whom he was arraigned, knew only that she listened to Trezevant, Kalish and an assistant district attorney. A clerk came to the bench and said to the judge, "No priors." The judge asked how Loring pleaded to the charges.

Kalish said, "Not guilty, your honor."

The judge then asked the district attorney if he planned to take this case to a grand jury, and he replied in the affirmative.

To Loring, she said, "Mr. Neiman, I'm inclined to release you in your own recognizance."

Kalish was pleasantly surprised and Trezevant was annoyed.

"Don't even think about going anywhere, Loring," the detective lieutenant said. "You and I need to see a lot of each other."

"Through me, Lieutenant," Kalish said. He was very small, came up to the detective's armpits. Arlene once said that Seymour Kalish was proof that a head could live without a body. "Through me."

* * *

Driving to Borough Park to pick up Katie and Briana, Kalish told Loring that the grand jury would hear only the district attorney's version of the case, and that of any witnesses he cared to invite, but neither Loring nor his lawyer would be present.

"It sounds like a fucking star chamber."

"In a sense," Kalish said. "If the grand jurors find there is no reasonable cause, they can refuse to indict. But if they do . . . then they do. Then the judge sets a date for the trial."

Loring, slumped deep in his seat, asked, "Will it be the same judge?"

"As today? Not necessarily," Kalish replied.

"Too bad." Loring liked this morning's judge; she was a loose-turning judge, an own-recognizance judge.

As they turned onto Loring's cousins' street, Seymour mentioned that neither he nor anyone else in the firm of Kalish & Krause have dealt very much with this sort of thing. "If you want to retain, well, more experienced counsel, I'd certainly understand. And even recommend someone."

Loring said, "I want you, Seymour. I'd never do business with a lawyer I couldn't beat up."

Seymour's little face smiled. "Thanks for the confidence, Loring. I'll do my best. And Ted and I have agreed, considering your finances, that it will be at no cost to you."

He brought his daughters home.

The house had been searched but not ransacked. The fine hand of Lieutenant Trezevant's men was most apparent in Loring's study, where his desk and file drawers and supplies closet had been gone through. They were left open, boxes of supplies opened and dumped on the floor. He lifted the corner of his carpeting, saw that his Hot Prowl files had not been disturbed. New York's "Son of Sam" law popped into his mind. It provided, if he remembered correctly, that the criminal might not profit before the victim; if he were convicted of anything, he would have to eliminate that part from his book. It didn't matter. He had no intention of doing any writing for the foreseeable future. If ever.

There was also no way he could keep his appointment with

Jamie Gelfmann that night. He couldn't even call him to tell him. Jamie would have to find out what had happened to him in the natural course of events.

Loring and the girls did a little straightening up, had sandwiches for lunch. Afterward Briana wanted to get out and bop around in her usual manner. Katie, who understood all too well that a certain grim process was beginning, took her little sister up to their room and advised her that Daddy was having a big problem and, until it was over, it was best that she didn't talk about it with her friends. In fact, she should probably hang pretty much around the house, with Katie and Daddy. Briana accepted it.

That night they watched TV.

Thursday, June 28 _____

KALISH CALLED WITH a little good news and a lot of bad. "They tried to indict you for the Goldstein burglary, Loring, but Dr. Blaug now seems unable—or unwilling—to identify you as the guy he saw that night, so the grand jury felt there was no prima facie evidence. So much for that one.

"Also, Berger has apparently *not* reported his fifty-thousand-dollar loss, although that's no surprise, right . . . ?"

Loring kept his heart still. "But . . . ? Go on, Seymour."

"But . . . I'm afraid they've seen fit to go along on the whole Berger enchilada—Criminal Trespass, Attempted Armed, Unlawful Imprisonment—and the Possession of Stolen Property."

"Jesus."

"Loring . . . they also added something."

"What?"

"Sexual Abuse. Of Naomi Berger."

"Sexual Abuse!"

"Yes. The police claim you . . . fooled around with her while she was manacled to the bed."

"The police claim it?"

"Obviously the Bergers have claimed it. Look, these things always sound a lot worse than they boil down to."

"To me," said Loring, "it sounds like a very exotic collection of major felonies and misdemeanors. One Captain Kidd would have been proud of. What . . . that is . . . what are the penalties for those things?"

Seymour hated to answer that one. He asked, "Legally possible? Or realistically?"

"Legally possible."

Quickly Kalish said, "For all those things a person could get twenty-eight years, but, Loring . . ."

Loring sat down.

". . . nobody ever gets it. Not even for murder. If, God forbid, a man were to be convicted on *all* of those charges, only a vindictive lunatic of a judge could possibly give him more than three to five years."

His kind use of the subjunctive did not escape Loring.

"What happens now, Seymour?"

"Tomorrow we go back to court to enter our plea on the new charge. I presu—"

"Will I be allowed to come home afterward?"

"Well, yes . . . I'm sure you will." He didn't sound it. "The judge will allow you to post bail."

"Unless he's the famous vindictive lunatic who gives more than three to five years. How much could bail be?"

"That I don't know. Their figures tend to run a little highish these days, but then again, he'll see you're not the type to run away."

"Not the type to run away." Shapp had said the same thing. "For an indicted felon, I inspire a lot of confidence."

Friday, June 29 _____

KINGS COUNTY SUPREME Court is at 360 Adams Street. Their route to it took them down Atlantic Avenue, past the Brooklyn House of Detention. It had a long line of women outside, waiting to get in, to visit. Mostly poor, mostly black and Spanish, but one or two, he glumly noted, who looked like Hadassah chapter chairpersons.

The judge, a new one, asked him how he wished to plead to the new charge.

Seymour Kalish answered for him. "Not guilty, your honor."

The judge conferred with his clerk for a moment, then set the trial date for September 10. He also put Loring's bail at $15,000, much less than the district attorney's office had sought.

Seymour Kalish asked Loring whether he had the resources to post it.

"I have the resources to maybe post a letter, Seymour."

Kalish nodded; he'd known that. He went to a pay phone. When he came back, he said, "I just talked to Ted. He said he'll be here soon with the money, and he told me to keep you out of detention until then or it's my ass." He smiled. "Exact words, I swear!"

Loring was beginning to realize the extent to which Ted Krause had been galvanized by the situation. And he was grateful.

Seymour slipped the clerk a little something, and they were permitted to wait for Ted in the back of the courtroom. It occurred to Loring that any system that allows an indicted gun-offense felon to sit around unattended before he's even posted bail really stinks.

They sat in silence, watching other arraignments, again mostly black and Spanish, but with an occasional Anglo juvenile.

Ted Krause finally showed up, waved as he walked past them to the cashier's window. He posted the bail, then came back to where they were sitting.

Loring looked at the little receipt, asked Ted to which bail bondsman he was indebted.

"My father-in-law," said Ted, with a smile.

Friday, September 7 _____

THREE DAYS BEFORE his trial, Loring told the owner of the small men's furnishings store on Pitkin Avenue that he had to quit his job, for reasons of health.

His boss of two months said he was not surprised. "I noticed you been very nervous lately. You should check it out with a doctor. But I'm gonna miss you. You been a good salesman, got terrific taste."

Loring was amused to hear that, because Arlene had once told him that his favorite tie looked like cirrhosis of the liver. He wondered what she would have thought of some of the pathology specimens he'd sold from that store.

Later, at home, barbecuing dinner for himself and the girls, Loring realized he would miss the job, the store, the other people in it. They had constituted his only adult society, because for the ten weeks since his arrest he had absented himself from Kingsborough Beach life, saw none of his neighbors. Katie, Briana and he stayed home every night, played games, did jigsaw puzzles and watched sitcoms. He was leery about taking them anywhere, even to the movies, afraid of running into people he knew. Once, early on a midweek evening, he had chanced going out, to Zellen's, for the baby lamb chops. Right after they sat down he saw Fred and Lynn Isaacs and Leo and Sandy Goldstein at another table. He avoided looking in their direction, told the girls they would be going somewhere else to eat. The three of them got up and slipped out. It was the only thing to do.

As to Liz, he had tried to call her only once, about a week after his arraignment, and was told by the housekeeper that Mrs. Blaug was not only *no en casa,* she was *no en estado.* Where, she was not allowed to say. Loring spoke to Justin, who was no help, either. His mother, apparently, had gone far away for he didn't know how long.

Loring knew he would never see her again.

He also knew he deserved it. She had done what she properly had to do, walked away from him. But had she also walked away from everyone else?

Katie's contact with her friends during the time had been minimal. While they were cleaning up after dinner, she got a phone call. Loring overheard part of it.

"I heard you tell Tracy you can't go to her party. Why not?"

"Because all the kids are going to ask me about you and it's none of their businesses."

They had avoided the issue for too long. "Katie, I must know how you feel, inside. Are you embarrassed? Afraid? Mad at me? What?"

She didn't take her eyes off the dish she was drying. Just shrugged.

He decided they would have to talk about it, and before that evening was over; it was the deepest and most gut-painful of all his anxieties.

"Been very nervous lately," his ex-boss had said of him. During the ten weeks, the possibility of more charges had almost driven Loring crazy. He imagined people rethinking their burglaries, deciding they had seen him, after all. And the police had worked the neighborhood, hard, in just that interest. Trezevant had gotten the department to buy Joanie Heller a round-trip ticket to New York, and, the afternoon she arrived, he had Loring picked up and brought to the station house. She had stared at him for several minutes, from various angles. She felt his arms, stood with her back close against him. Finally: "No. It's not the guy." To her, Loring was a middle-aged neighbor of her parents with wrinkles on his forehead who happened to have gotten himself into some really bizarre trouble. The man who had held her hostage for ten minutes was younger, stronger and much better-looking.

A week after that, Trezevant took Loring over to the Pincuses' and walked them all through the upstairs floor in accordance with Irving's recollection of his burglar's movements. Loring and the Pincuses exchanged not a word. Then Trezevant tried to get Irving to identify Loring as his burglar. Irving simply stared at the cop as though he were *meshuga* and walked away.

Loring had tacitly agreed to both of those things, but Kalish had been furious when he heard about them. He called the lieutenant and said, "Don't you dare hassle my client. If you have reasonable cause, there's a legal mechanism for that sort of thing."

Trezevant had said he agreed with him: two days later he put Loring through a zoo-like series of lineups at police headquarters, dozens of hysterical victims viewing hundreds of felony suspects and picking out those they thought they recognized. "The Scumbag Parade," Trezevant had called it. Frightening, to Loring, but less hideously embarrassing than being taken before his neighbors.

After the Scumbag Parade, Loring had forced himself to begin thinking post-trial, make the worst possible assumption and see if he could deal with it. Questions would pop into his mind, phrase themselves, full-blown. Questions like, "Did prison trusty-librarians and the like live in their own bookish little wing, or did they have to sleep among the general population?" And, "If I taught short-story writing could I ingratiate myself with the convict leaders by making them feel they had talent?"

His fear of jail was pernicious; it built to an obsession. For a couple of weeks he did exercises, thinking that if he were stronger he would be better able to repel homosexual advances. He even wished he could accelerate the loss of his hair; it would make him less attractive. It had become abundantly clear to him that armed robbers and sexual abusers don't get sent to tennis camp, and for some time after the hearing, his image of jail was based upon the view he had gotten of the Brooklyn House of Detention. Later, it became his motion picture memories of places like San Quentin and Alcatraz. After a while he remembered that when he was a kid, on a train going up the Hudson, they had passed Sing Sing, and he had become morbidly entranced by it, thinking how horrible a place it was to be locked up in, so near to the beauty of the river and the charm of a village, yet so far. That image became the official prospect.

The idea of prison soon made cancer seem like a sweet alternative. He almost envied Arlene her death in bed, saw himself stabbed in a shower.

Loring had thought of going for some crash psychotherapy, but as he really didn't believe in it for anyone over the age of twelve, the idea slipped away. Acute fear turned slowly to leaden depression.

In the middle of the evening, while they were watching a TV show, Briana fell asleep on the couch. He looked at Katie, expectantly. Finally she turned to him and said, "I guess I *am* a little mad at you." Then she added, "But I still love you."

"But I still love you." The way all kids love their fathers, regardless of what he is: they have to. It's their job. He's all they've got.

"I know you do."

"I'm only mad for now, Daddy, like when you get mad at me. I won't be, for always."

"Are there any questions you want to ask me?"

"Did you hurt anybody?"

"Yes, I did, in a way. Not on purpose. Besides taking what belonged to them, I put . . . fear into their lives, and I had no right to do that. I did hurt them, sweetheart."

She considered that. Then, "I guess you did. Well, I think you're brave for saying it, Daddy. At least you know the difference between right and wrong. Now all you have to do is the right thing, from now on."

He nodded.

She kissed him. "And you're brave for not crying."

* * *

Seymour Kalish did not know how to help Loring's psyche. He barely knew how to help him legally, his experience admittedly so slight in the arena he was about to enter. He had once defended an embezzler, but with expensive help from old classmates. Mainly, though, he had practiced the stock-in-trade of Kalish & Krause, general civil law. For the two months since the arrest he had dragged his imagination over the cobblestones for an approach to a reasonably sophisticated defense for Loring Neiman. He had no witnesses to place Loring anywhere that night. At one time, early on, he had considered going to Berger and threatening that unless he dropped the charges, they would tell all about the fifty thousand dollars and Shapp and so forth. But as a bluff it wouldn't work; it was deniable by Berger as well as an admission of guilt by Loring.

That day he'd had lunch with yet another criminal law specialist. He had suggested that inasmuch as Loring had never admitted to anything, maybe Seymour should try to bargain him into a guilty plea on one of the two misdemeanors, Criminal Trespass or Unlawful Imprisonment, settle for a year in the pen and a big fine. When Seymour rejected that idea, his friend said that Loring's clean personal image, then, was the only way to go. "If he's the gentleman you say he is, conduct a gentleman's defense. Don't cross-examine and don't deign to enter into any spitting contest with the D.A. In other words, don't do anything."

"Against the words and credibility of a United States congressman and a ranking officer of the New York City Police Department? Do nothing?"

The criminal lawyer had nodded. "And pray."

Sunday, September 9 _____

THAT NIGHT, WHILE he was trying to fall asleep, Katie came into his room.

"What's going to happen tomorrow, Daddy?"

He sat up, lit a cigarette. "They're going to say some things about me that are true, but a lot of other things that aren't."

"Will the judge believe them?"

"Maybe."

"Would he get mad at you and put you in jail?"

"Maybe. But if he does, you know, I've made up with Esther and Julie to"—the words caught—"take care of you and Briana until I come home."

"I know, Daddy. I already talked about it to Briana."

"Oh. Good. Thank you, sweetheart. Will you help her . . . get along?"

"Sure. I told her we might go to a different school."

"Would you mind that a lot, going to a different school?"

"No. I'd rather." She went back to her room.

She would rather. Move away. From the place she had lived most of her life.

He put out his cigarette. For the ten weeks since his arrest there had been no burglaries in Kingsborough Beach, and Loring knew that the residents must have debated to death the significance of this fact. But if any conclusions were reached, individually or as a group, he had no way of knowing what they were.

Just before he fell asleep, it seemed to him, after all, that he had worked unnecessarily hard to isolate himself from his neighbors; during that whole time not one of them had ever made even the slightest attempt to see or speak to him.

Monday, September 10 ____

KATIE CAME DOWN to the kitchen for breakfast wearing a good dress and her patent leather shoes.

"Where do you think *you're* going?"

"With you, Daddy. To the trial."

"The hell you are. You're staying home, with Esther, you know that."

"Briana is staying," Katie said, levelly. "I'm going to the trial."

He stared at her. If anyone had earned a ticket to Loring Neiman's trial, his daughter had.

Just outside of Part 37 was a bulletin board with several notices tacked to it. One of them, in bad hand lettering, said:

PEO. -VS- NEIMAN

Loring, holding Katie's hand, sadly regarded the sign, the naïve scrawl; he'd rehearsed for drama but had been cast in a kindergarten play.

Seymour Kalish stepped out of the elevator, spotted them. They embraced. To Seymour, Loring looked lousy, tired and drawn. "That's a good suit, Loring, very good. You look quite nice." Seymour looked around, bouncing nervously on the balls of his feet. Nearby, Assistant District Attorney Silverstein, the young man who would represent the People, was calmly sipping from a container of coffee. Kalish nodded to him, turned back to Loring, asked, "Why do these things always have to take place on such hot days?"

Loring shrugged. "Nobody else looks hot. Maybe we just think it's hot." He was peering through the little window in the door. The courtroom was already filled, and even by the backs of heads, he recognized most of them as Kingsborough Beachers. The entire audience of *Fiddler on the Roof*. He would enter the room as unobtrusively as possible, take his seat at the defense table and never look back.

He was surprised at the hubbub—the walking, whispering in ears, irrelevant laughter—that seemed to go on among the various officials of the court, even after the judge had taken her seat. The scene had no majesty.

Loring tried to figure out the judge: a woman of about forty, plump, with a working-mother look. Pleasant, intelligent. He hoped Justice Marion Z. Mitchell had gotten up that morning with an affinity for tired-looking middle-aged men in blue suits.

The jury was selected very quickly. Assistant District Attorney J. Daniel Silverstein exercised only one of his peremptory challenges, Seymour Kalish exercised none and in less than an hour and a half twelve ordinary people were empaneled.

"A good jury, don't you think?" Seymour whispered to Loring. "Working people, two Jews, two blacks. The ex-cop, I kind of like him, don't you, Loring? He has a humanity about him, and no great love for the force."

Loring nodded absently.

Justice Mitchell asked counsel if they were prepared to start without a recess. Both replied that they were.

Assistant District Attorney J. Daniel Silverstein rose to present his opening remarks.

Roaming the width of the room, the young man, perhaps twenty-eight, told the jury that the state would prove that the defendant, Loring Neiman, was the armed man who broke into the home of Congressman and Mrs. Norman Berger on the night of June 26 and committed four serious offenses. Because he was personally known to the victims, he had worn a ski mask over his face and head. The fact of their long relationship, the D.A. said, made the crimes all the more heinous, gave the defendant an advantage above and beyond all known bounds of human decency.

Loring listened intently; it was like watching scripted theater.

The D.A. didn't stop there. He segued to the five previous break-ins, ostensibly to acquaint the jury with Kingsborough Beach's recent history, but actually hinting that Loring was under police suspicion for those crimes.

Seymour jumped up and shouted an objection. Justice Mitchell sustained it, then said to the D.A., "You know that was improper. I don't want any more of this."

Chastened, but not very much, Silverstein wound up his opening statement by describing the physical exhibits that the state planned to enter. They were a ski mask, Loring's running suit and deck shoes, two pair of handcuffs and a drawing by the artist Belimbau.

It was Kalish's turn. He squeezed Loring's hand and stood up.

Seymour first described Loring to the court as a man of high repute, a respected writer and father of two, who had no doubts about his vindication and was suffering an affront to his dignity, more than fear. Then he outlined Loring's version of that night: Mr. Neiman had gone out late on the evening of June 26 to jog in the rain—a pastime that was his occasional wont—heard the alarm bells go off, headed for home, did not see the police car but heard the patrolman's challenge—in gutter language—thought he was the Beach burglar, or worse, and so panicked and ran—away from his house, so as not to lead them to his children—and hid on the beach.

"As the district attorney has already pointed out, Kingsborough Beachers, such as Mr. Neiman here, are very nervous, having been victimized so often recently."

In the meantime, Kalish told the jury, a squad of plain-clothes police, on the misdirected suspicions of a beset and fixated lieutenant of detectives, invaded Loring's house and terrorized his two young daughters.

As to the red and yellow ski mask found in his pocket, Kalish pointed out that while Loring was en route home he found it in the street and picked it up, feeling instinctively that something that unusual might be evidence in whatever crime had occurred that night.

"Just as you or I or any citizen might have done, Mr. Neiman took it home to hold for the police." He thanked the court and sat down, mopping his brow. To Loring, he whispered, "Good *gezucht?*"

Loring smiled weakly.

Congressman Norman H. Berger was the prosecution's first witness. He took the stand, pinstriped and congressional-looking.

As Berger was being sworn, Seymour Kalish, still flushed with the success of his objection, wondered about maybe making a motion for dismissal of all the gun-related charges, on the grounds that no such weapon would be introduced in evidence.

"What is your full name?" Assistant District Attorney Silverstein asked.

"Norman Henry Berger."

"Congressman Berger, could you please describe to the jury those events of the night of June 26 that occurred after you and your wife arrived home from Washington?"

Loring felt a tightening across his chest. *Please God, he swore to you, make him tell the truth.*

Norman's recitation was as spare as possible. He told them that he and Naomi had been getting ready for bed when a masked man, waving a gun . . .

Loring's heart sagged. Norman was sticking to the story he'd told the cops and the press on that night; his fear of embarrassment was stronger than his conscience.

. . . sprang from the closet. "I suppose he had been hiding in it for some time," Berger went on, in a rather easy manner. "He produced two pairs of handcuffs. . . ."

At a nudge from Seymour, Loring remembered to shake his head. Seymour had told him to do that, visibly, whenever a witness said anything terrible; the jury would notice it.

The prosecutor took the mask and handcuffs from a table in front of the bench. "Is this the mask, sir?"

"Yes."

"And these are the handcuffs?"

"Well, I believe so," replied Berger. "If those are the ones Lieutenant Trezevant took from my house, then they are the ones the man produced, in my judgment."

"Yes, good. Please go on, Congressman. He produced them, and then what?"

"He indicated to my wife to lie down on our bed. She did, and he handcuffed her to the headboard."

"'Indicated,' sir, because he did not speak, is that correct?"

"That is correct. He did not use his voice."

"Do you think because he was afraid you'd recognize it? Or what?"

"Possibly. I can't answer that for a—"

The judge interrupted. "Mr. Silverstein, your little 'Or what?' did not take the curse off your improper question." She looked at Kalish. "Mr. Defense Attorney, are you thinking about objecting on the grounds that the district attorney is leading the witness?"

Kalish looked surprised. "Yes, your honor, I am. I object."

"Sustained," said Justice Mitchell. To the reporter, she said, "Strike the district attorney's last question and the witness's response."

Silverstein continued. "What happened then, Mr. Berger? Did anything happen to your wife while he was handcuffing her?"

Berger nodded. "Well, while doing that, in certain ways he abused her."

"In what ways, sir, would you tell the jury?"

"Is it necessary for me to get graphic? It's my wife we're talking about. She's in the courtroom. I'm sure the jurors know what 'abuse' is."

Silverstein looked at the jurors. They were rapt; better to leave it to their imaginations. "You're quite right, sir. What happened next?"

Berger said the intruder indicated, by rubbing his fingers together, that he wanted some money. "I told him I had none; a congressman's salary was small. He then made signs that seemed to mean he might shoot me and . . . harm my wife. It was hard to tell exactly what he meant. It became a sort of stand-off, you might say. We stared at each other.

"Finally, I guess he got cold feet, because he suddenly dashed out the door. By the time I got downstairs, after him, he was gone."

"How much time transpired while the intruder was in your bedroom?"

"About fifteen minutes."

"Long enough for you to know"—the D.A. stepped to the evidence table—"if these are the clothes he was wearing?" He held up Loring's blue running suit with one hand and one of his deck shoes with the other.

"Yes. Those are definitely his clothes."

Kalish leaned to Loring. "If they try to parade you around to see if you walk like the intruder, don't do it. I'll object."

But they didn't. Instead, the D.A. thanked Norman Berger and turned to Kalish. "Your witness, Mr. Kalish."

Seymour said, "No questions."

Berger was excused from the stand. He took his seat next to Naomi. Neither of them looked at Loring.

"Lieutenant Frank J. Trezevant, Jr."

"You have been a police officer, a detective, for eighteen years?"

"A detective for ten."

In response to the D.A.'s questions, Trezevant told the jury that he had gone to the Bergers' house when their burglar alarm went off, found Mrs. Berger in the state described by the congressman. He said the congressman's account of it just now was exactly as he had heard it from the couple on that night.

Trezevant also testified that the defendant was not in his own home during the time of the Berger incident, described the sighting of the suspect in the street, the chase through backyards and the fruitless search of the beach.

"When I arrested him at his house, the defendant was wearing the clothing you showed Congressman Berger a few minutes ago, the things on the table.

"And when I searched him I found that ski mask in his pocket."

Assistant D.A. Silverstein asked him what he had found on the defendant's premises.

"That drawing." He pointed to the Belimbau on the evidence table. "Reported as stolen from the home of Mr. and Mrs. Goldstein."

Silverstein and Trezevant knew full well that the drawing could not be used to try to connect Loring to the Goldstein burglary: he was not on trial for that crime. But it did clearly put him in possession of a known piece of stolen property. There was nothing more he could ask the detective.

Kalish declined to cross-examine.

Oddly, Loring was disappointed when Trezevant stepped down. Even though everything he said was corroborative of Berger's lies, he had spoken only the truth, as he knew it.

The Assistant D.A. called Leo Goldstein to the stand, only to identify the Belimbau drawing as his property. Leo, seeming bored, did so.

Kalish said he had no questions right now for Mr. Goldstein, but reserved the right to recall him later. As Leo left the stand, he and Loring looked at each other—the merest glance—for the first time in two and a half months.

The prosecution rested its case.

Kalish said he needed the lunch hour to do some work, so Loring and Katie went to eat by themselves. The only restaurant around there that looked decent and reasonable was, of all places, the Stanhope Grill, the scene of his sub rosa meeting with Carlin. His first crime.

She ate her hamburger and fries, he sipped at his bloody Mary.

"You heard some awful stuff, sweetheart."

"I know. Mr. Berger lied about you. But don't worry Daddy, I can tell by that judge's face she knows when anybody lies. Except maybe Uncle Seymour." She took a bite of her burger. With a full mouth, she added, "He told me she's going to let *me* talk, did you know?"

After lunch, Kalish, with an apologetic look at Loring, called his first witness, Katie Neiman.

She took the stand, in the blue-flowered granny dress she had worn only once before, to a party. When she was sworn, the judge gently asked her if she understood her obligation to tell the truth. Katie nodded.

Seymour said to her, "Katie, I would like to ask you a question about the night the policemen"—he pointed to Trezevant, seated in the first row of spectators—"came to your house. Can you recall that night?"

She nodded.

"All right, then. Can you tell us how your father seemed to be, early that evening. By that I mean, did you get the feeling that he planned to go out?"

"No, Uncle Seymour, he told me he was staying home. To work."

"And if he had *planned* to go out, for any length of time, he would have arranged for a baby-sitter, is that true?"

"Yes."

"He was too responsible a father to knowingly leave you and your sister alone for a lengthy period, late at night?"

"Yes."

"And to your knowledge, Katie, did your dad make any attempt to hire a baby-sitter on that night?"

"No. Anyway, he would have told me and my sister if he was going out."

"Unless, he just decided, later on, suddenly, after working, to maybe take a walk for some fresh air?"

She nodded.

"Did your father ever just go out latish in an evening for a few minutes, to take a walk?"

She looked at her father. "Oh yes."

"Thank you, Katie. Unless the district attorney wants a word with you, you may go. . . ."

Silverstein said he did, and strode to the witness stand.

Loring turned to Seymour. "You bastard! Why did you let this happen?"

"Don't worry, Loring. She won't get hurt, I swear."

The D.A. said, "Katie, you love your father, don't you?"

"Yes."

"I'm sure he's a good parent. But sometimes even parents are unable to tell their children the whole truth about certain things. Things that would hurt or confuse them. Isn't that so?"

She thought for a second. "Sometimes not at that time, but always later, if I ask him. When I ask him something, that sometimes gets the show on the road."

While Silverstein was trying to decipher that, Katie looked up at Justice Mitchell and said, "Why can't you let my daddy just come home *now*? After this I don't think he'll ever go out at night again. He's very upset. If he gets put in jail it'll be like he's punished *twice*, and also me and my sister will be punished. I don't think that's fair."

Without the ceremony of being excused, she got off the chair and went back to her seat.

Loring smiled. The D.A. shook his head. Kalish looked at the jury and then, with an innocent shrug, at the judge.

She didn't see it. At that moment she was reading a note the bailiff had just handed her.

She looked up. "Will counsel please approach the bench?"

They did.

Justice Mitchell said, "Gentlemen, Mrs. Berger has just asked me if she might be permitted to take the stand. I'm inclined to let her do so."

"That's fine with me, Marion," the D.A. said.

But Kalish said, shaking his head, "Oh, your honor, the prosecution has already rested. This is my time. I can't quite see the fairness in a surprise witness at this moment."

"Just between us, Kalish," the judge said, "the way you operate, you haven't got a damn thing to lose."

He looked hurt.

"But with that aside, the fact is she says she wants to make a statement as an amicus curiae. Sworn, of course."

Kalish considered it. "Amicus curiae. Is she an expert on something?"

"Everyone is, on something. It couldn't hurt, Kalish. And if you don't like anything she says, or even her perfume, I'll strike her completely."

He nodded.

Naomi Berger was called to the stand and sworn.

"Since the night of the crime," she began, "my husband and I have had very little chance to recover from the shock of that horrible experience, between the pressures of his new senatorial nomination, and being questioned by police every fifteen minutes and his work in and out of Washington. We have not had time to do something very important." She looked at Loring. "The man who sits there is a friend of ours, a neighbor for many years. He is accused of all this. And, probably, rightfully so, I don't know for sure, I'm not a policeperson or even a lawyer. But listening to what's been said here today, and *knowing* the man it's been said about, I, at least, have suddenly realized certain things. And feel that I have to say them, you know, in the interests of justice.

"For one thing, I'm no longer sure the intruder had a gun. Oh, he might have—and in all the panic at the moment, we thought that he did—but *I* can't truthfully say that *I* actually saw one. In his hands.

"Also, I don't understand sign language and God knows I've never been good at charades, my husband always tells me, so I don't *know* if he asked for money. I don't *know* it.

"The main thing is, I'm a physically delicate person, and I was really knocked out that night from traveling. When I'm afraid, things are magnified in my head. Maybe I felt at the time that the man made an attempt to . . . bother me. But I tell you now, after a long, clear think about it, that he definitely did not."

The judge rapped her gavel to quiet the room.

Loring realized he had been sitting still, hadn't moved a muscle.

Naomi looked at the judge. "I think that's really all I wanted to say. May I be excused, your honor?"

"Not yet, Mrs. Berger," she said. "I believe defense counsel has a question."

He did. From the table, Kalish asked, "Mrs. Berger, without a gun to fend off your husband, how did the intruder manage to manacle you to the bed?"

Naomi stiffened. She looked at Norman. He looked at his lap, the same whiteness in his face Loring had seen on that night. There wasn't a rustle in the room.

Finally Naomi said, "The intruder didn't. We . . . I . . . am interested in psychology, I studied it at college, and my husband is, you know, involved with, ah, victims' rights legislation? Well, we did a, ah, sort of an experiment, about how victims of violence would, ah . . ."

"You're saying you did it yourselves, then, Mrs. Berger, and that is the point," the judge said. "*Why* you did it is of no interest to this court." She then complimented Mrs. Berger on her honesty and good citizenship and, banging the gavel again to quiet the spectators, excused her from the witness stand.

The steel bands around Loring's body snapped. He slumped in his chair.

Kalish had no intention of raising the question as to which of the Bergers had just committed perjury. Nor did Justice Mitchell see fit to prompt him in that direction.

Turning to look back into the courtroom for the first time, Loring watched Norman and Naomi hurry up the long aisle and out of the courtroom. He felt as much mortification for them at that moment as he had ever felt for himself.

Justice Mitchell looked at Seymour, expectantly.

He stood up. "Your honor, I move that the charges of

Attempted Armed Robbery, Unlawful Imprisonment and Sexual Abuse be dismissed."

"Motion granted."

He sat down, with a grin that filled his entire face, and squeezed Loring's arm so hard he left fingermarks. Under his breath, he sang, "You got a fucking he-ro for a lawwww-yer. I just knocked off twenty-five of those twenty-eight years."

Not enough not enough not enough! Loring thought Seymour was about to rest their case, was astonished to hear him call Jamie Gelfmann—he had no idea he was even in the courtroom—to the witness stand.

Jamie was sworn, stated his name and occupation and said he'd known Loring Neiman for eight years as a sensitive and dependable man who was firmly rooted in a serious work ethic. "It would be ludicrous to think of Loring Neiman as a thief." He also pointed out that Loring certainly would not have committed a robbery on the very day Jamie had phoned to tell him he wanted to publish his novel, *Quarantine.* "I am not an attorney, but I should think it muddles, somewhat, the question of a motive."

Then Elliot Silverbach appeared, told the jury about a certain publisher's interest in Loring's Brooklyn book idea, and then about the time he sent Loring a royalty check from which he had forgotten to deduct his commission, and how Loring had called it to his attention. "Not many writers would do that," Elliot observed.

Ted Krause, who was not one of the defense lawyers of record, testified next, as a friend. He said that in his opinion Loring had a rare quality found only in special people, namely, loyalty to friends and neighbors.

Seymour then called Judith Lieb to the stand. Looking like Kingsborough Beach on the hoof, she asserted to the court that as she had written the book on human nature, her belief that Loring Neiman was one of the most decent and responsible men she'd ever known could not be questioned.

Next came Sidney Lieb, who basically echoed what his wife had said, adding his feelings that Loring was like one of the family, a proud man who refused charity.

310

After thanking Sidney and excusing him, Seymour Kalish caught Leo Goldstein's eye, raised his eyebrows inquiringly. Leo, not to be outshone by Sidney Lieb, nodded, and Seymour called him as a defense witness. On the stand, Leo said that while he didn't figure Loring for a crook, nobody was completely honest and it was often a matter of who gets caught. Smiling, he said, "Half the guys in Kingsborough Beach belong in jail." He added that as far as "the Belimbau drawing bullshit is concerned, I think I once told Loring he could have it anytime he wanted. So maybe I gave it to him. Who remembers? Who cares?"

They were only the beginning. One by one, to the witness stand, came an amazing parade. Seymour Kalish, Loring realized, must have really worked the neighborhood, hard, for weeks. Sworn statements ran together in Loring's disbelieving ear: Fred Isaacs testifying that Loring was a nice middle-class man, "one of us," an ideal neighbor, a credit to the community; Lynn Isaacs telling the court that whatever else Loring might possibly be, he was the type she'd trust with her deepest secrets; Larry Kilowitz saying that the cops were stymied and were trying to pin it on the wrong guy and that his kid went with the Neiman kid, and if he wound up with Loring Neiman as an in-law someday, he'd be goddamn proud of it because he's a classy guy in a chickenshit neighborhood; Miriam Pincus saying she'd had five different neighbors behind her in fifty years and Loring was the nicest, with two lovely children he was raising all by himself like two little dolls, and besides, how could anyone who lives in the house right behind hers be accused of such terrible things?; Judge Mushkin saying that while he didn't know him as well as he would like to, he did know that if Loring ever did anything wrong, it would be out of dire necessity, because Loring was definitely not a sociopath; retired businessman Elias Shapp telling the court that Loring was the kind of man whose word was his bond. After Shapp, there were the Krupps, Mrs. Libo, the Koppels, the Habibs. . . .

At almost six o'clock, the judge finally refused to hear any more character witnesses. There had been twenty-two of them, the cream of The Beach, each in his or her own way suggesting that Loring Neiman was a desirable neighbor and an exemplary father.

And many of them believed it.

Loring never testified in his own behalf.

Kalish rested the defense.

After fifty-five minutes of deliberation, the jury returned. Justice Mitchell asked, "Have you reached a verdict?"

"We have, your honor. On the charge of Criminal Trespass we find the defendant not guilty.

"On the charge of Possession of Stolen Property, we find the defendant guilty."

Loring turned to Kalish; he didn't know how to feel. Kalish put a finger to his lips, pointed respectfully to Justice Mitchell.

She announced that she would waive the probation report and impose sentence immediately.

"Will the defendant please rise."

Seymour helped Loring to his feet.

"In the absence of any attempt on your part to refute or mitigate the charge of possessing stolen property, I must sentence you to sixty days in the county jail."

Through his numbness, he heard a gasp; his own or someone else's, he wasn't sure.

Then he heard the judge say, "But because the rightful owner seemed so unaffected by his loss and unconcerned with your possession of his property, I suspend the sentence."

There was applause in the courtroom. Loring, in a daze, found his arms filled with Katie; he hugged her, Seymour embraced them both.

On their way out, they passed Lieutenant Trezevant. The look on the detective's face said it all; he'd seen cases fall apart before, but never because of a conspiracy on the part of the victims.

Tuesday, October 9 _____

EPILOGUE

Loring sat down at his word processor and typed

> Over the last couple of weeks I have managed to personally call on and thank each of my neighbors for their kindness and decency to my family and me.
>
> During this time I accepted no social invitations.
>
> Many were extended.
>
> But, as Voncie so aptly said, there would always be "a space they'll never let me acrosst."
>
> In that light, I have quietly closed down our affairs here in Kingsborough Beach, and put our house up for sale. Tomorrow the girls and I move to Santa Barbara, California.
>
> Needless to say, there is no way I can bring myself to publish *Hot Prowl: The Diary of an Unlikely Burglar.* To do so would be to continue my betrayal of my neighbors and further affect my daughters.
>
> Maybe I'll write it someday as a piece of fiction, my second novel. In the meantime, I'm still working on my first, *Quarantine.*
>
> As to my daughters, Briana has never really understood any of this, and will recall it only as one very interesting night when a lot of strangers came to the house. Lucky baby.
>
> But Katie, poor Katie, will always know it for exactly what it was. And me for exactly what I was. Every time I look at her I realize I've lost a part of her, maybe forever, and it hurts, terribly.
>
> My only hope is that if the rest of her life is sweet enough she will find the grace to forgive her flawed father. But will she ever trust him?
>
> Liz Blaug called me from Reno to say that her divorce from Andy has become final. On Saturday she joins Katie, Briana and me in Santa Barbara.

Outstanding Bestsellers!